SIX WOMEN WEST

LOVE AND DANGER ON THE OREGON TRAIL

WANDA REED

Wanda Reed

Six Women West

I felt my hands tightening on the pitchfork. "You bastard! You don't touch me!" Overcome with rage, resentment, hurt, despair, hate, I plunged the pitchfork at him again....

Wanda Reed

**All rights reserved. -
Sedona Red Rock Publishing**

**ISBN-13: 978-0692372364
ISBN-10: 0692372369**

All rights reserved. No part of this publication may be reproduced, distributed, or transmitted in any form or by any means, including photocopying, scanning, recording, or other electronic or mechanical methods, without the prior written permission of the publisher, except in the case of brief quotations embodied in critical reviews and certain other noncommercial uses permitted by copyright law. For permission requests, send an email with description of reprint use to:

redrockwriters@gmail.com

Sedona Red Rock Publishing
2370 W. SR 89A - Suite 11 - #163
Sedona, AZ 86336

Six Women West

Printed in the United States of America

Wanda Reed

> **Comment [CJH]:** Adding a map of the Oregon Trail to the beginning would be a lovely addition and help keep things straight.

SIX WOMEN WEST

PART ONE

CHAPTER ONE

Manassas, Virginia - July 16, 1861

The air was hot and heavy, and the sweet aroma of ham frying mingled with the fragrance of the nearby azaleas. The morning was alive with the familiar sounds of chickens and horses. Pa and me had been up since midnight helping a mare who was having trouble birthing her foal. Now we admired her new gray foal, and Pa was thrilled—it was a stallion. We finished the morning chores, and I led the mares with their foals to the front pasture.

Today was my seventeenth birthday, but that didn't excuse me from work. We boarded twenty brood mares; there was always plenty to do. The hired man, Webster, had joined the Union Army. I had to fill in.

"Sure'n I can't believe we finally got our stallion," Pa said, the excitement in his voice matching the glow in his eyes as he stroked the foal's neck. "He'll be yours to train, Lassie. With any luck, he'll be a Derby winner. What'll you be namin' him?"

"Gee, Pa, I'll have to think about it," I said, not hiding the pleasure I felt. "He's Gray Lady's half-brother, so maybe I should call him Gray Thunder, or maybe Rollin' Thunder or Thunder Rolls. What do you think?"

"Well, that's a lot of thunder," he laughed. "I leave it up to you." He hung up the hayfork and patted my shoulder as we hooked open the barn door. He sniffed the air and inhaled deep. "I think your ma's got breakfast ready. Smells like she fixed your favorite."

"Yep, pancakes," I agreed. "I'll race you to the house."

"Last one there's a rotten egg," Pa shouted, bursting into a run. I passed him as I raced to the back porch with him right behind me. We burst into laughter while splashing water on each other as we washed for breakfast.

"Now stop that, Martha! You're a young lady now, and you need to act like one. My goodness—running across the yard with your skirt hiked up like that!"

"Ah, I'll never be a lady like you," I said as I walked to the breakfast table.

"Well, maybe not, but after two years at Miss Marbella's school, you'll be a lady and you'll be able to get a husband. That's important, young lady—a husband that can provide you with a beautiful home and social status in the community." She placed a plate of ham and pancakes in front of me and Pa. Smiling, she stuck a large candle in the pancakes. "Happy birthday, dear. We'll have your cake tonight."

"Can't believe you're seventeen, girl." Pa shook his head and chuckled. "Just when you're big enough to be of some help, you take off. Now who am I gonna get to help me around here? I'm in a fix with Webster gone, and you know I'll not find anyone who's as good with horses as you are." He took a big bite of pancake. "Sure'n, it's gonna be a long two years without you, Lassie."

I grinned. "I'll be back in time to train that foal. And truth to tell, I'd rather not be going. I'll miss you more than you'll miss me," I added. "As for all this talk about me being big enough, you know I've been big enough since I was ten. Hasn't Ma always said I should have been a boy cause I'm so big and ugly."

"Now, Martha, I never said you were ugly," Ma frowned at me. "Oh, I might have said it would be more fitting if you were small like me, but I never said you were ugly. Men like small women. I don't understand why you grew so muscular and tall."

"One beauty in the family is enough, darlin'," Pa told her. "Besides, the lassie is a grand lady. She has hair a queen would be proud to have and eyes as green as shamrocks. And she has your complexion, darlin'. Smooth as cream. Martha is a fine strapping girl who's got a good head on her shoulders," Pa announced. "Ain't nobody around knows horses better'n she does. She can outwork any man. Sure'n, it'll take a real man to husband my girl, not one of these silk-shirt dandies. There's more to bein' a woman than servin' tea."

I stared down at my plate not saying anything with the sweet pancakes turning to cotton in my mouth. I'd heard all this before—Ma finding fault with me while Pa tried to pass it over. Not that it mattered. I had long since accepted my size and the chance of marriage. If Ma had her way, she would pay a dowry to get me married. I'd been near six foot tall since I was fourteen—a full foot taller than Ma.

"I didn't raise my daughter to be a slave to some common man," Ma continued.

"You feel like a slave, Greta?" Pa looked at her with a hurt expression.

"No, Pat. You know I wasn't referring to you."

She leaned down and kissed him on his forehead, finger-combing his bushy red hair. In three more days I would leave to spend two long years with people I didn't know. I didn't look forward to going.

I dreaded the girls staring at me like I was a freak because I was tall. I had no real desire to learn to be a lady. The only gentleman I knew, I sure didn't want to marry. I knew Ma had her eye on that dandy who worked in Washington ever since he boarded his mare with us, but I also knew he was only looking for a roll in the hay. No thanks—no "woodscolts" for me.

Picking up the newspaper from the sideboard, I glanced at the war news. "They're still fighting," I said, fanning myself. Even though Ma had the doors and windows open catching what breeze there was, the heat was unbearable. "I thought everyone said the war wouldn't last long. It's already been six months. Why couldn't the slave owners just let the negro people go free? Why do we have to have a war? And what is states' rights?"

"It's all about money, Lassie," Pa said, shaking his head. "Those big plantation owners couldn't afford the life they live if they didn't have all that free help, plus the money crop the poor devils bring on the auction block." He lifted his cup and finished his coffee. "Of course, America's not the first to have slaves. Seems there's always been those who want to control others."

We were just finishing breakfast when the thunder of hooves announced the arrival of many horses. We got up from the table as one. Pa rushed across the parlor and stepped outside, but he motioned Ma and me to stay back. From the racket, I figured there was a goodly number of soldiers. Shivers ran down my back, and a feeling of dread came over me.

"Welcome to the Patterson Brood Mare Farm," I heard Pa say calmly, "I'm Pat Patterson. What can I do for you men?"

Wanda Reed

A man dressed in a gray shirt with stripes on his sleeve rode up near the porch. "I'm Major Becker. We're here to claim your horses in the name of the Confederacy," he announced.

"I don't have any stock for sale. I don't have any riding horses. What would you want with a bunch of mares that just gave birth? They're not fit to ride."

"I didn't ask if you wanted to sell," the major said, thrusting a paper at him. "This gives me the right to confiscate your stock. You can collect your money in Richmond. In case you haven't noticed, Mr. Patterson, there's a war. Different rules apply. We'll be taking the horses." There was a ring in the major's voice that said loud and clear he wasn't negotiating.

"Sergeant, get the mares now," he continued. "Leave the youngest ones," he ordered, turning away from Pa. "Couple of you men collect those mares in the paddock."

We hurried to the side window, pulled back the lace curtain, and watched in disbelief. Pa ran out, yelling and waving for them to stop. One of the men rode into him, knocking him to the ground.

Unable to control myself, I rushed out on the porch and screamed, "How dare you! Get off our farm! You robbers! Horse thieves! That's what you are! Thieves!"

"Let's take that filly, too," one of the soldiers shouted. Several men laughed. "She could be a lot of fun," another yelled. I ran to help Pa.

"Go back! Get inside, girl. Stay out of sight. I'm alright." Pa got to his feet, clenching his fists and staring at the major. "Control your men."

"He looked down at Pa straight in the eye. "Take your family and leave here, Patterson. This place will be a battleground by high noon."

He turned to his men and yelled, "Forward." With a rumble of hooves, they rode away. I helped

Six Women West

Pa up the steps, and he slumped against the porch railing.

"Pat, Pat, what are we going to do?" Ma moaned, lapsing into the German of her motherland, "Diebischen Wolf!"

I dashed into the kitchen, grabbed the brandy decanter, snatched a glass, and went running quickly back to Pa's side. Forcing the glass into his hand, I said. "Here, Papa. Drink this."

"How could they do this to us? What right do they have to take what we've worked so hard for?" Ma shouted, wiping tears off her face.

"What will I tell the owners? I couldn't stop them," Pa said, holding on to Ma and me.

"Pa, what did the major mean, this will be a battle field? Will they fight here?"

"Yeah, Lass. That's what they'll be doin'. Spillin' blood on our land. We best get packin'. The Major is a thief. He stole our horses for his own ill-gotten gains, but I believe he was tellin' us the truth about the fightin'. There are thousands of troops over across the river.

"Sure'n we've had the luck of the Irish all these years. Let's check the barn. The small dapple gray foal Pa had helped bring into the world only a short time ago now lay in a pool of blood, his head bashed.

"Mother-o-God!" groaned Pa.

My stomach wrenched as I retched up the ham and pancakes. Pa's lower lip quivered as he stooped down to lift the foal. He cursed and struggled under the weight of the dead body as he carried the little foal out behind the barn. "Them dirty bastards! He's dead before he lived." He shook his head slowly.

We finished in a few minutes. Carter's filly neighed, and I ran over to the stall and yelled to Pa, "The little filly is here, but the mare is gone." I didn't see Boots either. She was six months old. "They must have taken her," I said, referring to our

> **Comment [CJH]:** I added "en" to Diebisch making it Diebischen. Double check please as my German is very minimal.

chestnut filly. "That major said to leave the young 'uns, but it looks like they took everything that could walk."

"Yeah, they'll run the young foals to death, and the mares that haven't foaled will die from being run. It's a cursed shame what men will do for money. Check the stalls, Lass." Pa glanced around, dazed like. "Thank God the black is alive, but I don't know if we can save her. She's so young—with no mother for milk." He rubbed the foal's neck. "Wait—the nanny goat's still in milk. We'll bottle feed her with goat milk." I looked over as the barn cat carried one of her kittens out of the barn.

All twenty mares gone! All ten of them with foals under six months. The barn was empty and so silent that only the smell of horses and hay remained in the air.

I heard a soft snort and looked to see where it came from. I walked down the center of the barn. Yes, I heard another sound—the unmistakable clomp of a hoof against a wood floor. I opened the tack room door and saw Boots contentedly nosing the oat bag as if she hadn't a care in the world. I hugged her neck and said, "You hid real good, girl."

"Pa," I yelled, "I found Boots." I hurried to the front of the barn leading Boots. "She was trapped in the tack room."

"Put her in the stall next to the little black," Pa said.

"I fed Boots. That'll hold her for awhile. Pa, my mare, Blackie, is out in the far pasture with her yearling. I've got to go see if she's alright."

Pa was gathering up some of his tools laying them in the wagon. "Bring in the mules while you're out there. We'll need 'em to pull the wagon. If we're lucky, they didn't find them. If they did, we'll have to start walkin'."

I hiked my skirt and fairly flew the half-mile across the pasture to the creek. To my joy, Blackie

> **Comment [CJH]:** I changed this from, "I wonder if the old nanny goat has milk" because presumably they would know if she's in milk or not since she only would be if she had young kids or if they milked her every day.

> **Comment [CJH]:** Changed from the foal since it wasn't clear whether it was Boots or the little black foal. Is this what you meant?

and her filly were resting under the old weeping willow along with the two old mules. The tree's branches hid them behind a curtain of leaves. I stooped to enter their cool shaded haven, throwing my arms around Blackie's neck. I wept, shedding the tears I'd been holding back. It wasn't the first time I'd cried away my hurts into Blackie's mane. She had been my trusted friend since I was nine and she was nine. She knew all my fears all my secrets. "Why are we fighting? Why don't we just let the people of the South sccede if that's what they want?"

Feeling better for having voiced my frustration, I wiped my eyes. Taking a handful of mane, I jumped upon Blackie and touched my heels into her sides. We galloped into the yard with the gray filly and the mules right behind us. "Pa, I got'em. They were under the big willow."

"Good girl, Martha. By damn, we still got horses! Put them in the storm cellar'til we get ready to leave just in case those horse thieves return."

After putting the horses in the cellar I gathered Boots and then filled a bottle with milk to coax the foal to follow. "Come on, little Black. Follow me. Get your sugar tit. Come on, Sugar." I fed her and then gave the others some hay. They were calmer with my old mare, Blackie, filling in for their mother.

At the sound of gunfire we both looked off across the pasture toward the creek in the distance, the sound making the major's warning a reality. "I've got to get busy on the wagon," Pa said, "Got to get this wheel put on."

I entered the house. Ma was busy poking food in a burlap sack. There were tears running down her cheeks. "Ma, don't cry. We'll be alright," I told her, putting my arms around her.

Pa stuck his head in the back door. "Ma, where's that old canvas? I need it for the wagon."

"It's in the barn somewhere. Let me think," said Ma, wiping her hand on her apron. "Pa, that soldier said high noon. We can't be ready to leave by then, can we?"

"If we stop talkin' and keep packin', we can. You won't need to take everything—just enough to last a week. They'll be pushin' on by then. It's a bad time. We'll have to look out for ourselves. Ain't nobody gonna do it for us. War makes men do horrible things they wouldn't do otherwise." He paused and reached into the cupboard. "While I'm thinkin' on it, you best keep this with you." He handed me a small pistol. "A young woman needs protection. You saw how crude those soldiers acted. Next time I might not be there. When you see a bunch of soldiers, you get out of sight. If they start to lay hands on you, use that."

"Pa," Ma interrupted. "Too much, Pa. Too much for our girl to understand. You shouldn't say these things to an innocent girl." She placed her arms around Pa's waist and leaned into him.

"It's best Martha knows. The more she knows, the better able she'll be to protect herself." Pa started out the door. "I gotta' get busy on the wagon. Ma, did you recall where the canvas is?"

"On the top shelf in the tack room. I hope the mice haven't got it."

I tried to decide what to take. Where would we be staying? I shuddered at the thought of losing our farm. No matter how I tried, I couldn't picture living anywhere else. As far as I was concerned, the farm was a paradise, and I'd never been more than twenty miles from it. How could we leave? Would we ever return?

I could hear Ma mumbling in German and English at the same time. Seeing me, she went to English. "I'll pack the kitchen things," she said. "I mustn't forget to pack the Dutch oven." She held up her hand as if to stop me from going up the stairs. "First, you get the meat from the smokehouse and vegetables from the root cellar. Take them to your Pa so he can pack them in the wagon. And hurry, Martha. We must hurry."

I grabbed a bushel basket and hurried to finish the tasks so I could talk to Pa. Setting the basket down, I could see he was about finished with the wagon.

"Bring the rest of the stuff as soon as you get it ready. I'm gonna harness the mules. We need to get going. I've been hearing gunfire. They're getting closer. I already saw a wagon of folks moving out. Believe it was the Rodman's."

"I did what you said, Ma. Remember, Pa said just to pack enough for a week. We won't be able to take everything. He said to hurry." I ran up to my room to pack what things I would need. Glancing around, my gaze lingered on my bed. Pa had made it out of an old walnut tree. Ma and me had spent many an evening making the multicolored flower garden quilt. "Please God, don't let them ruin it," I whispered. In my head I heard Pa's voice say 'only what's necessary.' Opening my new valise, I packed the carved ivory hair combs and the silver locket necklace Pa had given me. I took my riding skirts, a yellow shirtwaist, stockings, and undergarments. On an impulse I grabbed my favorite blue Sunday dress and shoes, stuffed them into the valise, and quickly locked it. With one long last look I firmly shut the door. I started down the hall, then turned, ran back, and picked up my quilt. I would need it.

Leaving my valise in the hallway downstairs, I went up to my parents' room. I had to force myself to hurry. I got out Ma's large trunk and packed clothes and quilts along with Ma's hand mirror and Pa's favorite book, *Bloodlines of Horses*. I stood for a moment, staring at the tintype of my baby sister taken just a few weeks before she died. Elsa looked like those little blonde angels in books I had read.

All she needed was the halo. I carefully wrapped a pillowcase around it and tucked it in next to Pa's book. Next I tried to shove in the crocheted bedspread, but it just wouldn't fit. Finished, I pulled the trunk to the top of the stairs and carefully slid it down the carpeted steps and then pushed it to the front door next to my valise and the two burlap bags.

In the kitchen Ma placed her hands on her hips and stared at me. "I think I've packed what we'll need," she sighed. "I can't believe this is happening."

"I know, Ma. I can't believe it, either," I said, taking her hand as we moved to the parlor. Ma picked up Pa's pipe and the family Bible from the small table between the tall wingback chairs. "Put them in the trunk." She ran her fingers over the two small crystal figurines and silver candleholder on the mantle. With another deep sigh, she handed them to me. "Put these in too. I don't want to leave them. They're all I have left of my mother's things."

"Come, Martha, let's carry the trunk out." Between us, we carried the steamer trunk to the barn. Ma rested with Pa while I returned for my traveling valise and the bags from the kitchen.

"Martha," Ma said, "Fix last night's leftovers to take with us. Don't forget the cake."

"And hurry it up, Lassie. We'll need to be leavin,'" Pa reminded me. "Ma, see if you can help me tie this canvas on the wagon."

On impulse I went into Pa's office and opened his journal. I tore out the breeding records of the three young fillies, folded the papers, and stuck them in my pocket just in case. I hurried out to the springhouse and got the bowl of leftover chicken. Rushing back to the kitchen, I filled our picnic basket with the chicken, a loaf of fresh bread, a jar of honey and one of blackberry jelly. I was putting a second jar of peaches in the basket when the thunder of cannons broke the quiet. Jumping, I dropped the jar, sending peaches and glass flying across the floor. To add to the mess, the birthday cake Ma baked that morning tumbled off the cooling rack and splattered on the floor, and dishes fell out of the cupboards.

Ma ran into the kitchen screaming. She grabbed me and held tightly as cannon fire shook the house. Pa ran in, shouting, "Get to the cellar, Martha! Get to the storm cellar. Go! Go! Hurry!" He grabbed Ma's arm and began pulling her along. "Holy Mother of Jesus," he muttered. I followed with the basket. Inside the cellar Ma pleaded with Pa to stay with us.

"No! I'll get the wagon loaded. We got to get out of here as quick as we can. All hell's broke loose."

Ma sat sobbing as I watched through the open door. It sounded like the world was exploding as the cannons continued to roar, hitting the trees and splintering them as they fell. It seemed I could hear them moan in pain. The smell of gunpowder reeked in my nostrils, and the smoke from the guns darkened the sky. The terrified horses screamed, jumping at the sound of each cannon blast. It was all I could do to keep them from breaking through the fence Pa had erected to separate the stock.

Ma huddled in the corner, trembling and muttering in German. I was too busy calming the horses to help her. I prayed a cannon ball wouldn't hit the storm cellar. Instead, I watched as one hurtled through the roof of our house. It must have hit the stove, for the house burst into flames. Within minutes, it was a blazing inferno. I couldn't believe it.

"Mein Gott!" Ma screamed. I didn't realize she was standing behind me. She screamed again and tried to run out the door, but I pushed her back. Together, we watched in horror as flames and smoke filled the sky, blocking our view of the barn. We couldn't tell whether or not it had been hit. Ma sunk to the ground in a huddle, rocking and weeping. I knelt beside her, unable to hold back my own tears.

Another boom of a cannon, and Ma screamed and crawled toward the door. I grabbed on to her to keep her in the shelter.

It was near sundown when the cannons stopped firing and the sounds of battle ceased. We stepped out of the cellar and stood listening. There was nothing. Not a sound. Never was the sound of quiet so loud. No birds chirped. No frogs croaked.

"Pa! Patrick!" Ma yelled, running towards the barn. "Wo bist du? Where are you? Are you alright? Pat."

"Yes, yes, I'm fine. And you, darlin'? Are you alright, and you, Martha?"

"We're fine, Pa. Nobody hurt." I tried not to look at the small flames and smoldering ruins of our home.

"Oh Patrick, our house, our house, our beautiful house."

"Yes, Greta. Be grateful we weren't inside. We'd all be dead."

"But all my beautiful things," Ma sobbed.

I tried to change the subject. "Pa, is the wagon ready to load?"

"It's ready, but I couldn't load it. It was too dangerous. The mules were bad spooked, so I stayed put." He took my hand. "You can help me. We got to hurry." He glanced up at the house. "Sure'n it's good we got out what we needed."

"Yes, Pa," I agreed as we walked back to the wagon.

"Load the food in the front, then the trunk and bags in the middle. The foal will be in the back," Pa ordered. "I'll get the mules watered. They're pretty spooked," he said. "Randy is settling down, but Rowdy's still jumpy."

"Oh, Pat! Our house, our beautiful house. My china, my silver," Ma cried. "Can't we see if anythin's worth saving?"

"No, darlin'. There's nothing left. Not even time. We have to go now. It's terrible about losing your things, but they're just things, Greta. It's purely providence that it wasn't us in there too. Now stop cryin', darlin', and go get everythin' out of the smokehouse and springhouse. Get the basket of food. No use leaving anything. Martha, put some hay in the wagon for the foal." The goat began to push and chew at one of the burlap bags.

"Martha, the vegetables. Put them in the front. Tie Nanny to the back so she can't reach them. I'll get the mules and the other animals."

"Sorry, Pa, my mind is all confused."

"I know, girl. Everything will work out."

Ma returned with her arms full of things. I packed them as she handed them up to me. "Ma, hand me the spider cooker. Thanks, now give me your hand, and I'll help you up easy, Ma."

Pa brought the mules and hitched them to the wagon, shoving one last bag of grain under Ma's feet. He led the mules over toward the cellar. Pa carried Sugar into the wagon and tied the goat, Gray Lady, and Boots on the back. I climbed on Blackie. I thought we were ready to leave, but Pa stopped at the well.

"Martha, fill the water keg," he said with a wink as he dropped a rope ladder in the well and climbed down. When he came up, he held a leather poke. "Never did trust those banks."

I recognized the leather poke he'd used for keeping his gold coin. Pulling up the rope, he tossed it in the wagon, lifted the water keg onto the wagon, and climbed up next to Ma. Then he placed the rifle by his knee.

"Put this in the hidey hole," he said, handing the poke to Ma." Ma sat like stone. A tear rolled down her face as she stared at the thin column of smoke rising from the ashes. "Gott im Himmel," she whispered.

"Ma," Pa repeated sternly. "Put the poke away."

She slowly bent over, lifted a board, and shoved the leather bag inside the hollow underneath.

"Git up, Rowdy!" Pa yelled, flicking the reins. Rowdy kicked up his heels. "Git up, Randy!" The wagon lurched forward toward the main road and headed in a westerly direction toward Royal.

I stopped and looked back at our farm, saying goodbye to the only home I knew. The barn looked lonesome without the house. I knee'd the mare and caught up beside the wagon. "Pa, how far will we go?" I asked.

"Don't rightly know Lassie. Sure'n I've been too busy leavin' to think about where we're goin'."

"Do you think we can come back in a couple weeks?"

"Don't know, girl. Nothin' to come back to for now."

"Don't say that, Pat." Ma seemed to snap to life. "We rebuilt before. We can do it again. That's our home, and I plan to die there."

"We'll see, Greta, Nobody will be doin' any building 'til this damn fracas is over. And who knows when that'll be."

"Oh, Pat, why did this happen to us?" Ma leaned against him, tears running down her cheeks.

"Hell's bells, Greta, we're not the only ones struck down. We're luckier than most. We got each other and none of us hurt." He shrugged. "Right now I can't think very far ahead. We can plan later."

Glancing back, I watched hypnotized as the soldiers carried the wounded or the dead from our fields. My whole world had been destroyed in the span of one afternoon. I wondered if the terror in

Six Women West

my heart and the images in my mind of the battle
would remain forever.

CHAPTER TWO

On a clear, warm morning after seven weeks of traveling, we arrived in Charleston, West Virginia. Pa had us set up camp. There were trees, grass, and water. We had everything we needed at the grove of willows and cottonwoods near the Kanawha creek. We were grateful but still hoping to find a farm.

After two days of staying in camp, I walked to town to the general store. The store was empty except for the clerk.

"Good morning. Can I help you?" the young woman asked. She was little, blonde, and very pretty. The only distraction from her flawless complexion was a small scar on her right cheek. I guessed her to be a little older than me.

"Oh, I'm just looking. I needed a walk," I said.

"I haven't seen you before. You must be new in the area."

"Yes, we just arrived from Manassas. I'm Martha Patterson." I didn't know why, but I felt as if we were already friends.

"My name is Sara Dale. I recently moved here from Georgia. I'm pleased to meet you Martha."

"Say, it's time for my lunch. I'd love to have you join me," she said.

"I'd like that. Thank you."

Inside the eating house, we took a table by the window.

"Their special is usually good," Sara said, dusting the seat before she sat. "Today it's meatloaf with potatoes and gravy, probably carrots too."

"That sounds good."

"We'll have the special, Mabel," Sara called, and then turned to me. "So, are you planning on settling in Charleston?" she asked, looking at me as if she were really interested and not just being nice.

Six Women West

"Yes, if we can find a farm we like," I told her. Pa has been out looking, but they were too pricey. "I don't suppose you'd know of any we could look at."

"Matter of fact, I just happened to overhear some men talking about a farm twelve miles north of town on Old Hickory Road. It's held by the bank for an unpaid mortgage. No one has the money to buy it, and it's in pretty bad shape, but it's still a good piece of land."

"Thanks, Sara. I'll tell Pa."

The food came, and it was good. We talked about our lives as we became fast friends.

She picked up her gloves and bag as she stood. "Guess I'd best return to work, or I'll be late."

"Thank you, Sara. Next time, lunch is on me. I'll walk you back. Oh, and thanks for the information about the farm. I sure hope Pa will look at it."

We stopped in front of the store. "I think we'll come to the church service on Sunday. Will I see you there?"

"See you Sunday. I have to go. Good luck with the farm."

On the way back to camp I felt better than I had for weeks. I'd made a new friend and had information on a farm. Walking back to our camp, I picked some flowers to brighten our table.

Ma was napping under a willow tree when I returned to camp. Quietly, I busied myself getting things ready for dinner. I punched down the bread dough and shucked several ears of corn.

"Martha, is that you?" Ma called sleepily.

"Yeah, Ma. Go back to sleep." I used the afternoon to curry Blackie and hung my blue dress in the breeze to get the wrinkles out to wear to church in a few days.

Pa returned to camp about dusk. "Well Lassie, I located the farm. It was much too grand a place. To

> **Comment [CJH]:** I changed this from back taxes to mortgage since it was being held by the bank.

be sure it would have a hefty mortgage on it too," he said, sounding tired and discouraged. "We may have to move on."

"Wait, Papa. Sara, a girl I met in town, told me about a farm. She works at the general store. It sounds worth looking at. Could we look at it before we leave?"

"Oh? Did you get the location?"

"Yes. The bank owns it, and it's on Old Hickory Road, twelve miles north of town. She said it was run down but a good piece of land. It's small though—only about twenty acres."

"Well, that sounds mighty interesting. We'll all go look it over after breakfast tomorrow. If it's no good, we'll just move on." He patted me on the shoulder. "I'll go get washed up for supper."

The following morning Pa hitched the wagon, and Ma had bacon and pancakes ready. We ate in a hurry, anxious to get started. We broke camp quickly, and Pa drove out Old Hickory Road. I kept my fingers crossed all the way. I wasn't the only one full of hope. Even Ma was smiling happily. We located the farm, which looked as if it had been deserted a long time. It was in bad shape. The gate lay on the ground. I glanced at Ma. She wasn't smiling anymore. "Oh, Pat, not this place," she whispered, tears in her voice.

"Greta, Darlin', there ain't nothin' here that can't be fixed with wood and nails. It's the land you buy. The house you build. Let me look at the land. You women go on and look at the house and look at that stand of timber! Why, I could build you a new house out of that, and there's a whole field of hay ready for harvest."

Ma and me went on into the house, caught up a bit, I think, in Pa's enthusiasm. It was hard to stay that way once we got close to the place. Some of the shingles were missing off the roof, and all the windows were broken. The door sagged, and the step was loose. Ma shook her head. "Oh, Martha, do you really think we can make a home of this shack?"

"Sure, Ma," I said, stomping my feet to watch the homesteading varmints run. What we need is a cat for these mice. Bet there are a thousand of them."

"You know, Pa always said he could build a house, but it was you who made it a home. Whitewash and curtains will do wonders."

Ma smiled weakly, "Well, maybe, but you have to have something to start with."

In the front room were a couple of shelves next to a small fireplace. I wandered into the bedroom. "Come here, Ma. Look, there's a bed and a potbelly stove."

Ma looked over the bed and frowned. "Well, we'll have to drag out that filthy mattress. It's probably full of mice. The frame will be alright."

She pulled a pile of old clothing from the chair in the room. "Oh, my," she exclaimed. "It's a rocker. Let's move it to the front room to sit on for now."

I had to smile. We were both talking as if we had already taken the place. "Say, Ma, if we do decide to live here, where will I sleep?"

"We might have to make you a pull down cot in the front room. We carried the rocker to the empty living room and went into the kitchen, which consisted of one wall with three shelves and a window in the center. On that same wall there was a backdoor going to a small mudroom. There was a kitchen stove with an oven and a table with three chairs in the alcove. All were in dire need of cleaning and repairing.

"How wonderful, Martha. You can sleep there," Ma said, pointing to the alcove. "We can put the table in the center of the kitchen."

Pa walked in the door and looked around. "It'll do," he said. "The barn needs a lots fixin', but it'll work."

"Pat, there's a kitchen stove!" Ma exclaimed. "And a potbelly stove in the bedroom."

"To be sure, we can use them. I put the stock in the corral," he paused. "Had to prop up a couple posts is all." He put his arms around Ma and me. "This'll be our home for awhile, girls. I'll go in town come morning and take care of the papers."

We slept out under the wagon that night with plenty of soft hay close to the barn.

After breakfast Pa saddled Blackie and left for town. Ma started crying. "How awful to live in a wretched shack like this, Oh, I miss my beautiful home."

I lost my patience. "Ma, be grateful. This is an old house, but it's no shack. We got three rooms. It's better than living in the wagon and sleeping in the woods. Pa will fix it up real nice. Ma, it's a start. That bedroom is really large—and a stove to keep you warm this winter. Now come on, let's clean it up. I'm sure Papa will buy it." I grabbed what was left of a broom and started knocking down cobwebs. Ma joined in, and the dust fairly flew. I guess we both took out our frustration on that old house.

We dragged out the filthy mattress, and the mice scattered. Afterward we heated buckets of water and used the rags to scrub that old house from top to bottom. Next we used a scrub brush with lye soap for the floor. We boiled the rags again and again and then hung them to dry. "We'll make a rug out of them," Ma said. "Those old clothes came in handy."

"Ma, let's walk down by the creek and wash up. I feel like there are cobwebs all over me."

"Alright, we'll take a change of clothes and do it right. We can wash our hair with that honeysuckle soap. It will make our hair smell real good."

Six Women West

After a refreshing bath we had a meal of bread, cheese, and goat's milk. We rested only a short while and then spent a pleasant afternoon braiding a rug. "We'll put this in front of that old rocker," Ma said. "It will look nice. Did you notice how that rocker shined after I washed it and put wax on it?"

I was glad to see that her spirits had lifted. "Yes, Ma. That saddle soap does wonders." She seemed to have worked off her melancholia. "My hair is dry. You want to braid it?"

"Yes, we better get it done."

"Ma let's look in the barn and outbuilding after you finish."

"You go ahead dear. I'll stay here and read."

That was like Ma. Pa called her a house flower. Ma never set foot in the barn or field.

It was late afternoon when Pa returned. We met him on the porch. I didn't know about Ma, but I had my fingers crossed, and Pa didn't keep us in suspense. He was waving the deed as he rode up.

"It's ours. The deal is closed. The farm is ours. The bank said it had been empty a long time, and they were glad to sell it. Sure'n you'll be glad to hear, there's money left for some women things."

He laughed and handed Ma some coins. "Greta, you and Martha can buy what you need for the house. I left an order at the lumber mill. You can pick it up tomorrow. Don't forget the window panes."

I squealed with delight. An easy chair for Pa, ticking for a mattress with real cotton to stuff the mattress, and bright material for curtains. I ran out to the wagon and started unloading. We would sleep in our house tonight.

Early the next morning, Ma and me left for town. We wore our best dresses and high-button shoes. It felt nice to be dressed up for a change. Besides, I had a special reason for wanting to look good. Since we would be buying our piece goods at

> **Comment [CJH]:** This is pretty much the only instance of slang in Martha's narration. It's used consistently instead of __ and I. Just checking to make sure that is intentional. I think it's fine either way. It's throughout the manuscript.

the general store, I would have a chance to tell Sara we wouldn't have to move.

"Thanks Pa," I said, anxious to get going. "Don't work too hard."

The morning was bright and sunny. The road to town was dusty and well-traveled. Time passed quickly as we talked about what we were going to buy. "Martha, I think yellow-checkered curtains for the kitchen. What do you think? And maybe some yellow paint to trim the kitchen."

"That sounds lovely Ma."

"How 'bout an easy chair for Pa?" I asked. "He works so hard, he needs to rest in the evening."

Before we knew it, we were in town. The lumber mill was our first stop. "Load that wood so there's still room for a few pieces of furniture please," I told the man at the counter. "We have shopping to do at the general store, and we'll need room for a half a bale of cotton and maybe a chair. We'll be back in an hour or two to get the wagon. And Mister, do you know where we could get a cat?"

"I have several in the lumber yard. I'll get you one or two. They're young—maybe six months old. I'll put them in a crate on your wagon."

It was only three blocks to the main street and another couple to the general store. Ma, this is where Sara works. Remember, I told you about her?" I held the door open. "Do you suppose we could invite her for supper?"

"My land, Martha, I haven't even met the girl. We'll see."

As soon as I opened the door, Sara came over to us. "Martha, I didn't think I'd be seeing you before Sunday."

"We came in to buy some things," I explained, nudging Ma ahead of me. "This is my mother. Ma, this is Sara Dale. We got the farm, Sara." I grinned so wide, I thought my face would split. "Thank you so much for telling me about it."

"I'm happy to meet you, Mrs. Patterson. You bought the farm! That's wonderful. Now, how can I help you?"

CHAPTER THREE

An older man who was tall and skinny with a bald head came to stand beside Sara. "I'll take care of Mrs. Patterson's order, Sara. You visit with your friend."

"Oh, thank you, Mr. Weston. We won't be long." Sara took my hand. "Come with me. We'll look at the dress goods." She grinned. "By the way, you certainly don't look like a boy today. That yellow shirtwaist is most becoming with your dark hair."

"Thank you. I have to admit, it does feel good to dress up." Ma joined us and picked out piece goods for the curtains, mattress ticking, and other things.

I caught her eye, raised my eyebrows in Sara's direction, and mouthed the word "supper."

"We'd enjoy your company for supper, Sara," Ma said in answer to my unspoken plea. "Since you are more familiar with the town, perhaps you would recommend the best place to eat."

"Thank you, Mrs. Patterson. I'd be pleased to have supper with you and Martha. I hear the hotel dining room serves very good food."

"Thanks, Ma," I whispered.

I could meet you at the hotel around five thirty, Mrs. Patterson?"

"That will be just fine, Sara. Five thirty it is."

"Excuse me, ladies. I brought your wagon around." The man from the mill had approached while we were talking. "Your husband said something about windowpanes. Did he send the measurements?"

"Why, thank you, sir. I forgot," I said. "Here is the list."

"That's very kind of you," Ma said. "How much is the bill?"

Six Women West

"It's all taken care of. Mr. Patterson paid in advance. I'll deliver the panes to the stable if that's where you're leaving the wagon if that's alright."

"Yes. Thank you." Turning to Mr. Weston, she said, "Would you load my purchases?"

"Be glad to, ma'am," Mr. Weston said. "Joshua, how about some help loading this chair?"

"Sure, Mr. Weston."

"Your little friend looks more like me than you do, Martha," Ma said, adjusting her bonnet and primping.

I didn't reply, but it hurt me. I had always known, thanks to Ma, that I wasn't pretty, but did she have to point it out to my friend?

"I think you're very lucky to have Martha for your daughter, Mrs. Patterson," Sara said. "She's very beautiful with that thick chestnut hair and those incredible green eyes. She's quite striking. Tall women are so impressive. You must be very proud of her. You know what I hate most? When you're short and small, people treat you like you're a child."

"Oh, I am, my dear, I am," Ma flustered, reaching out and patting my shoulder out of duty. "Well, we must get going. See you at the hotel." She started toward the door. "Oh, Martha, drive me to the hotel first. I'll get us settled while you take the wagon to the livery. After supper, we will start for home.'

"Yes Ma. See you later, Sara." I paused and turned back. "Thanks."

The hotel dining room was very elegant with white tablecloths and waitresses wearing long white aprons. We had a wonderful dinner of baked chicken with dressing and bread pudding for dessert. It was my first experience eating in a fancy place. Everything went well. Ma liked Sara and talked to her a lot, practically ignoring me. It was after six when Mr. Weston came in. Ma invited him sit.

> **Comment [CJH]:** Fixed this confusion on 5-5-15

"No, I just came to escort Sara home. It's not safe for a young woman to be out alone this time of night," he said.

"I couldn't agree with you more," Ma said. "Sara's lucky to have an employer who looks out after her."

I just smiled as the thought ran through my mind. No point in telling Ma what Sara had said about the nice Mr. Weston who was always trying to touch her. I knew she would've liked another job, but there was no other except the saloon, and she couldn't make it on sewing alone. We said our goodbyes.

I fetched the wagon from the stable, and we started for home. Ma droned on and on about Sara being such a lady with her dainty stature and mannerly upbringing, a private tutor, on and on. I was tired of her comparing me with Sara and me coming up short. Didn't she know it hurt me, or didn't she care? I tried to keep my attention on the mules. This was one time I wished Rowdy would pass gas and offend her so she would stop talking. Sure, I wasn't the dainty girl Ma would have liked, but I'd bet Sara couldn't jump a five foot fence at a full gallop or deliver a foal when the mare was give out. I did the work of most men, but I'd never measure up to Ma's standards. I could live with that—I just wish she could.

Thank goodness for Pa, I thought. Unlike Ma, he made me feel like I was important, loved. Many times he'd told me he didn't know how he'd manage without me. I was glad when we came in sight of the farm, sure that now Ma would turn her attention to something besides Sara.

Pa yelled "You're late," from the front porch. "Did you have a good time in town? Did you get all the things you needed?"

"Yes, Pa, and we got you a chair," I said smiling, "and we had supper at the hotel."

"The hotel's fancy. I cleaned the stovepipes and patched the roof. I found some nails and a bucket of whitewash in the tool shed. You can see I put them to good use. Next summer I'll build a new kitchen with an indoor water pump."

"It really looks nice, Pa. You did well," Ma said, and I agreed.

"Did you remember the windowpanes?"

"We almost forgot, but Mr. Joshua reminded us. And he gave us two cats. I better let them loose in the barn."

"We got you an easy chair and a side table," Ma told him. "You bring them in, and I'll show you where to place them." When it was done, she told him to sit down and gave him the newspaper we brought from town. Settling in the chair, Pa sighed and got up and hugged Ma and said, "Thanks, Greta. C'mon Martha, we better finish unloadin' the wagon before I get too comfortable."

After unloading, we took the wagon to the barn. I let the cats go, and they seemed right at home.

"I'll get started on your bed right away, Martha," he told me as we stacked the lumber in the barn. I don't like you sleepin' on the floor." He grinned at me. "I gotta take care of my lassie."

"Thanks, Pa." He couldn't know how much his words meant to me after having listened to Ma for the past few hours. "I'll start sewing my mattress cover tomorrow morning."

"Let's scatter some corn for the chickens that have gone wild. Soon they'll be tame again, and then we'll have eggs and fried chicken."

"We were lucky to find this place, Pa. We can make it real nice. It's close enough to town that we can make it there and back in one day easily."

"There's a buckboard in the shed," Pa said, as we started back to the house. "It needs a wheel repaired. I'll have to wait to fix it. I put together a lean-to in the woods," he continued, "for the young fillies. After haying, I'll build a barn for them."

"I'll help, Pa," I promised. There's so much to do."

"Let's turn in for the night. You can sleep on that cotton bale."

The next afternoon, a man rode up. "Name's Abner. Need to see your Pa."

"Pa, there's a man to see you." I looked him over. He was tall and large-built with brown stringy hair. He wore coveralls, and he walked with a limp.

"Heard in town you bought the place. I figured you'd need help with the hay."

"Ah, well, you've made a fair guess," Pa agreed.

"Reason I'm not in the army is this short leg causes me to limp." He shrugged. "The army says they can't use a cripple."

"If you can do your work, you're not a cripple. You can sleep in the barn," he told him. "It will be just through hayin'. I'll pay you what's fair. You have a mule. You want to hire him out to work?"

"Yeah, he can work if you pay me."

"Put your bedroll in the barn and wash up. Ma serves breakfast at five." They shook hands.

The next morning the three of us started in right after breakfast. With me wearing Pa's bib overalls and my hair under a straw hat, no one would see me as a girl. Abner was a good worker, and we managed to fill the hayloft by the end of the day. Ma fixed a good supper, and Abner insisted on eating his in the barn. Pa and I didn't feel like doing anything but sleeping after the hard day's work.

The next few days were spent working hard from dawn 'til dusk. I thought to myself that Lady Sara wouldn't be of any help here except to help Ma with her cooking and canning.

I knew Ma loved me, but it was a trial to listen to her comparing me to herself after a long hot day of cutting hay. It was the little things she said that were the hardest to bear—about my size or my hair color, and my looks, although I didn't know what was wrong with me. What did she want? A blonde, angel-faced underfed house flower like herself who couldn't do anything but keep house and cook? Sure, like Elsa. She blamed me for my sister Elsa's death.

After we cleared the dinner table, Ma came up with her own revelation. "That Abner seems like a nice enough young man. He's not the husband I'd pick for you, but after all, a girl of your size and plainness, I suppose we have to face facts. Beggars can't be choosers, and God knows we don't have a rich dowry anymore to offer."

"Please, Ma. I'm not a beggar! Don't even think of marrying me off." I shuddered at the thought, "Just forget about a husband. I'd die first. I'll run away. I'd rather be an old maid."

"For God's sake, Greta, she's only seventeen. Quit worrying about getting her married. Would you like to ride over to the neighbor's farm and see if they'll sell us a milk cow?" Pa said, obviously wanting to talk to Ma alone. He handed me a gold coin. "I figure they might be willin' to sell one, since they have a herd."

"Sure Pa," I said, thankful for the chance to get away. I walked out to the barn to get Blackie. Abner was sitting outside. He got up and followed me inside.

"Can I help you, Missy?" he asked, grinning slyly, as his gaze rested on my bosom.

"No, thanks," I said, turning my back to him.

"Going somewhere? Maybe you'd like company?"

I ignored him and finished saddling Blackie, glad he'd be gone tomorrow. I took off at a fast trot for the back fence. For all her seventeen years, the mare could still jump a four-foot fence. The woods were beautiful even though they smelled strongly of rotting vegetation. I followed a path obviously used many times before. Late afternoon sunbeams filtered through the trees, creating a kind of spiritual effect. I felt some of the misery leave my soul. I stopped and sat there.

God, what is wrong with me? I asked silently. *Why did you make me six feet tall? Why aren't I little and blonde and blue-eyed like Ma wants? What happened to me? Am I a misfit? How do I find the answers, God?* I waited. There was no answer, so I rode on.

When I came out of the woods, I could see our neighbor's farmhouse about a field away. I rode on across the field and up to the house. An elderly couple was seated on the porch in rockers. "Good afternoon. I'm Martha Patterson, your new neighbor." The old man stood and held out his hand.

"Vell, it's mighty nice to meet you, young woman. Sit down, sit down and have a glass uv buttermilk wit us." He turned to the woman. "This is my vife, Lilia. My name is Harry. Harry Penrod." His smile lit up his face. "I bet you vonder where we're from? Yah? De vay we talk. Ve're from Sweden. I guess dat sounds funny to your ears."

I smiled and nodded, enjoying his unfamiliar accent. I walked up on the porch. Mrs. Penrod motioned me to a seat. "You sit. I bring you da glass uv buttermilk."

"Thank you," I said, thinking what a sweet couple they were. They were the pictures of what I imagined my grandparents to be. Mrs. Penrod was round and plump with white hair piled on top of her head. Cheeks of rosy pink showed off her bright blue eyes.

Mr. Penrod was tall, thin, and stoop-shouldered. He had the same full head of white hair as his wife. You could see they were very devoted to each other.

She brought back a large glass of cold buttermilk and a slice of cheese on fresh bread. Even though I had eaten a large lunch, I couldn't refuse buttermilk and cheese. It had been too long since I'd had any.

"Ve're glad you folks bought the farm," Mr. Penrod said. "Ve vere afraid da troops might camp dere."

"We're very happy with it, too," I said through a mouthful of bread and cheese. "My, this is the best buttermilk I've ever tasted. And cheese. Do you make it yourself?"

"Yah, I'm glad you like it," Mrs. Penrod smiled with pleasure. There was a lilt in the way she accentuated her words that made me smile.

"Well, Mr. Penrod, I better ask what I came for. We're in need of a milk cow, and we're hoping you'd sell us one."

"Don't have von for sale. Ya can take von uv da old girls. Dey still got plenty milk, but I try to trim de herd right now."

I started to protest, knowing Pa wouldn't take anything without paying for it, but the old man held up his hand. "Maybe, you Papa shoot a deer, he'll tink of me. I don't hunt no more. My eyes don't see so clear. So, Mother and me vould appreciate some venison once in awhile. Tink your Pa would agree to dat?"

"I think he'd be real agreeable, Mr. Penrod, and thank you." I held out my hand. We shook, and I looked at Mrs. Penrod. "Thank you. It was delicious."

"You come back, Miss Patterson. We like company." She handed me a large chunk of cheese wrapped in a cloth and a crock full of buttermilk. "Dis vill do you til you make some."

"It's near dark," Mr. Penrod said. "You start home now. Go slow wit the cow."

I could imagine how pleased Ma would be to have fresh milk and butter once again. Buttermilk, as I had decided to call her, walked very slowly. It was almost dark when I finally got back to the farm. Pa was sitting on the porch, smoking his pipe. I supposed Ma had already gone to bed.

He stood when I rode up. "Well, Martha, looks like you brought back what I sent you for." He stepped off the porch and looked at Buttermilk. "Looks like she's a good milker."

"Yes, Pa, she's pretty, ain't she? Mr. Penrod said she's fresh and been bred back. Just let me take this in the house," I said, showing him the cheese and crock of buttermilk. "They gave me this, Pa. They're the nicest people. They wouldn't take money for the cow."

"Whatta you mean? They wouldn't take money?"

"Mr. Penrod said he would really appreciate some venison when you go hunting. Says he doesn't hunt anymore. They're pretty old, Pa."

"Okay, take the cow to the barn. If Ma's still awake, I'll tell her about the cow."

I walked Buttermilk into the barn, tossed some fresh straw in a stall, and then turned to fetch her some hay. I heard a noise and thought it was Pa behind me. Instead it was Abner. "See our cow," I said, uncomfortable at his closeness.

"I've seen cows," he snapped, reaching out to grab me around the waist. "I'd rather see you, sweet thing."

"Stop it!" I yelled, pushing him away "Damn you! Stop it!"

"Aw, come on, give me a kiss," he begged, continuing to hold on to me.

I was ready to punch him when Pa yelled, "What the hell? Get your hands off her, you no account bastard!" Pa grabbed Abner by the shirt and pulled him away from me. "Get out of here now! Don't wait for daylight! Take your scrawny ass and get gone afore I give you a load of buckshot."

"Aw, Mr. Patterson, I didn't mean nuthin'," Abner whimpered, slinking away.

"Just get and don't be showin' your face around here again," Pa warned. I had never seen him so angry.

"Gee, Pa, I could have handled him," I said. "I was just getting ready to punch him."

"Yeah, girl, you could've for certain. You're a strong one." He grinned and patted my shoulder. "Never let no-accounts like Abner lay a hand on you. Fight like a hellcat. I mean, kick, punch, spit, and scratch anything. You can grab a stick or shovel—just get away."

"I will, Pa," I promised. "What made Abner act like that? He's not right."

"Well, he's kind of simple-minded, you understand," Pa stroked the cow to settle her in the new barn.

I led Blackie into the barn and removed her saddle. I gave her a rubdown and a bite of oats.

"Better go lower the milk into the well," he said, picking up a rope to tie to the bucket handle and lowering it to cool overnight. "I got to get a spring house built now we got a cow."

"Gosh, Pa, we can have butter and cream tomorrow."

We worked from dawn 'til dusk getting the place ready for winter. The days turned into weeks. Pa and me cut trees and built a stable next to the lean-to in the deep woods. We camouflaged them by planting young trees around them.

"We'll keep the fillies hid in case the army decides to confiscate again," he explained. "Martha, I want to go over to Mr. Garret's farm. He has a brace of mules for sale. He's selling out to go to Missouri and then on to Oregon. Sure wished I could talk your Ma into goin'. I sure would like to join him." He put his hand on my shoulder, "Spend the day with your Ma while I'm gone."

"Alright, Pa. Anyway, it's too cold to do much."

Wanda Reed

Pa left early, and I did the chores. Then Ma and me spent the day canning vegetables. In the afternoon we sewed new nightgowns for the winter.

Pa returned before dark with a pair of jenny mules. They were as black as coal. I met him in the yard.

"This here's Judy and Jenny. Judy has the white star," Pa said, leading them to the barn. He chuckled as he added, "Fine names for a pair of mules. Tell Ma I'll be in for supper after I take care of the stock."

We had chicken and dumplings simmering for supper. As I entered the house, I noticed again how Ma had made our house a home. She had sewed yellow-checked curtains for the kitchen and a matching table cover. She even made time to sew a curtain for the alcove. In the evenings we sat in front of the fireplace and worked on a braided rug for the parlor. Ma hardly laughed anymore. Pa and me never talked about it, but we knew Ma was never the same after the fire in Manassas. Her mind wandered, and she rambled about all her precious things that burned. She went through the motions of living, but the light was gone from her eyes. We had hoped the summer would bring her out of her melancholia, but harvest was over and there wasn't much change.

CHAPTER FOUR

Fall was apparent as the leaves turned to red and gold, but our life went on fairly ordinarily. We heard news of fighting all around. In early September a troop of soldiers rode onto our farm. The only difference was the uniforms were blue instead of gray.

Ma started crying. "They'll burn the house, Pa." she sobbed, wringing her hands.

"Now, don't get all bothered, Ma. Keep her here, Martha," he told me. "I'll see what they want." He walked out on the porch. I listened and watched from the front door.

"Sorry, sir," Pa said, "Sure'n the Rebels already took all we had back in Manassas. We got nothin' left except a twenty year old mare and the old cow."

"We're just here to water our horses and rest a spell. That's all. No need for you to get upset. We'd kind of hoped we'd be welcome," the lieutenant said, adding, "We're on our way to set up headquarters in Charleston."

There was relief in Pa's voice when he told them to help themselves to the water. Still, he stood stiffly with his hands in his pockets, obviously not quite trusting the officer's words. Ma held on to my arm as we walked out and joined Pa.

"Thank you for your hospitality. Sorry to have upset your missus, sir. Ma'am." He nodded to Pa, tipped his hat to Ma, and smiled at me. After that the lieutenant stopped by twice a week to water his horse. Every time he came by, he smiled at me and made a point of talking to me. My heart would race, and my stomach did flips. I looked into his deep blue eyes and wondered what it would be like to kiss him. I am sure he would've liked to court me. He seemed a real gentleman and handsome too, but because of the horses we had hidden, I knew I couldn't encourage him, so I started avoiding him.

Months went by, and the fighting continued. I didn't get into town often these days with soldiers everywhere. Pa had me carrying a gun when I went to town. I felt kind of silly, but I trusted his advice.

Winter came quick, and the nights grew colder. One morning while we were finishing up breakfast, there was a scratching at the front door.

"Those damn chickens," Pa grunted.

"I'll shoo them away," I offered, going to the door.

When I opened the door, instead of chickens there was a small dog. I reached down to touch him, and he licked my hand. He was covered with dirt and tangles and a tail going a mile a minute. "It's a dog, Pa—a puppy," I yelled. "Good boy," I said as I took him in my arms to hold him. I could feel his ribs. He was half-starved.

"Be careful, Martha. Don't let him bite you," Ma called. "I'll fix him something to eat."

"He's not going to bite—maybe kiss you silly."

A minute later she came and handed me a tin pan of leftovers. "Here, feed him this," she said, shaking her head.

"Does that mean I can keep him, Ma?" I asked, grinning as I sat the food down.

"If it's alright with Pa and nobody comes to claim him." She shook her head again. "That doesn't seem likely, as poorly as he looks."

"Well, boy, looks like you got a home, but I got chores to do. You can come with me if you want, but don't be chasing the chickens or Pa will get the shotgun after you." I felt kind of silly talking to a dog, but he seemed to understand.

Pa came out to check on the horses. "That mutt sure tags after you, don't he?" He said, chuckling, "A tag along."

"That's what I'll name him. Tag!" I reached down and patted the pup's head. "Come on, Tag. Time for you to have a bath."

The trees dropped the last of their leaves, and mornings were cold and overcast. The stock had gotten their winter coats, and Ma had brought out our long johns. One November morning after a light rain, we woke to ice on the ground. The trees coated in ice looked like frosted statues. I had to lower a bucket of rocks to break the ice in the well before I could draw water.

Tag took every step I did, apparently not concerned by the cold. Still, he seemed awful glad when we came inside. Since my room was the small alcove off the kitchen, the heat from the kitchen stove kept it warm. Pa had finished my bed, a shelf from wall to wall with shelves underneath for my personal things. He drove pegs in the wall to hang my dresses. Ma had made curtains around to give me privacy. Although it was nothing like my room in Manassas, it was my haven, and I enjoyed the time I spent there.

Despite the weather we attend church most Sundays. I looked forward to seeing Sara and doing a bit of socializing.

This Sunday after church, Sara came home with us for a visit. We changed into everyday clothes while Ma fixed us a picnic lunch. Taking a couple of warm blankets, we climbed up in the hayloft to eat and talk.

Tell me, Sara, do they bother you?" I asked, my mouth full of ham and bread.

"Who?" Sara did her best to look as if she didn't know who I was talking about.

"Oh, Sara, you know who—the soldiers, of course."

"They aren't bad. Most of them just want to be friendly and talk. Some folks have rented the officers rooms in their homes."

"I heard that some of the soldiers are courting the young ladies."

"Yes, I've seen several walking with the Union troops. I can't bring myself to be that friendly," Sara laughed. "The other day Lorrie Ann was sippin' sarsaparilla with a Yankee, and her ma came after her and pulled her home by the ear." We broke into a laugh.

"Come on, let's take a walk. I want to show you something."

I led the way through the woods to our stable. Tag followed on our heels. Sara was surprised, "Oh Martha, this gray one is so beautiful."

"I call her Gray Lady. She's mine. Pa gave her to me for my seventeenth birthday. Blackie is her mother. We call the Black filly Sugar because she was raised on a bucket. The Chestnut is called Boots for obvious reasons. Promise not to tell anyone about our horses." Tag bolted out the door running after some squirrel.

"I would never tell. You're hiding them from the army, aren't you?"

"Yes, when the Rebels raided our farm, they stole the mares, and these babies were all that was left."

"That's why you never gave the lieutenant a chance. You know, he ask me about you."

"Well, it just has to be this way for now."

We returned to the house and visited over tea with Ma. After tea Ma excused herself and went to bed.

"Your mother doesn't look well," Sara said, after Ma and Pa had gone to bed.

"I know. We're worried about her. She's not been the same since we left Manassas." Tag scratched at the door to be let in for the night. I let him in, and he curled up by the stove.

We stayed up and talked long into the night. After breakfast I hitched Blackie to the buckboard

Six Women West

to drive into town. "Here's a list of supplies to get and twenty eggs to sell to Mr. Weston," Ma said, "Be sure he gives you three cents each and apply it to the bill."

"Mrs. Patterson," Sara interrupted. "Eggs have been selling for twenty-five cents each. You should ask fifteen cents from Mr. Weston."

"Thank you, Sara, I will. Martha you heard that? Fifteen cent for an egg."

Pa walked out to the buckboard. "Martha, take my watch and time the drive into town and back." Then he placed a five-dollar coin in my hand and squeezed it tight. "Get a piece of goods for you for a new winter dress."

I smiled and hugged his neck. "Thanks, Pa. Thanks so much."

We drove off laughing, "Oh, Sara, at last a new dress." Tag ran beside the wagon.

As we drove into town, she warned me. "There's gossip around town that Abner was boasting that you're his girlfriend. You be careful, Martha. I heard he nearly killed a girl for not accepting his advances."

"People don't pay him any mind. They know he's simple-minded," I said.

"He's simple-minded, but he could be dangerous."

Arriving in town we pulled up in front of the store. Tag stopped at the water trough. "Come on, Martha. Have some lunch before you start back."

"Let me give Mr. Weston the eggs and the list to fill first." Afterward, Mrs. Weston served us cheese sandwiches and a cup of beef soup. Then we went downstairs to pick out the material for my dress. I glanced around for Tag, but he was off visiting around town.

I handled the material, deciding on lightweight wool. "Which do you like best, Sara? The green, blue, or brown?"

> **Comment [CJH]:** Even with the war, that seems terribly high—more than now.

"Definitely the green wool. It matches your eyes," Sara said. "That color of green will be just perfect. I'll trim the dress with black and buttons."

"Sara, I can't thank you enough. You're a wonderful friend. I'm so glad we met." I laughed. "It's almost worth the move to find such a good friend."

"Thank you, Martha. I feel the same way." We hugged.

"Here is the money for the material and sewing. I've got to start home. I'll see you in church next Sunday. Bye."

"After church, come for a fitting. Bye, Martha. Thank your folks for the nice time."

As I went out the door, I turned to wave goodbye and bumped into two soldiers who were passing.

"Excuse us, Miss," one said, lifting his hat.

"My fault," I mumbled and hurried past them.

"Now that's what I call a fine-looking woman," the same one remarked.

I walked faster and pretended I didn't hear. Tag was waiting under the wagon.

On the drive home, I reflected how happy I was with Sara spending the afternoon with me. It felt so good to have someone my age to talk to after so long—a friend, a real friend.

I smiled. That soldier called me a fine-looking woman. I wouldn't forget those words for awhile.

"I missed you, Lassie," Pa said, picking up a box of supplies. "How long did it take?"

"Close to two hours, Pa." I rested Blackie at the half way point for fifteen minutes. When he finished unloading, I drove the rig into the barn and unhitched Blackie, rubbing her down good. I threw a blanket over her and gave her a measure of grain and some hay. "You did good, old friend. Good night," I whispered. "You're still my best friend."

Six Women West

Later that night, in bed, I thought again of what the soldier had said: *That's what I call a fine looking woman.* I smiled. Maybe, just maybe I'm not so plain.

CHAPTER FIVE

We were well into the second year of our town being occupied by Union troops. I wasn't sure if they were a curse or a blessing, but there had been no raids near our farm.

Ma and Pa both took colds as the winter settled in. I did everything I could to keep our house warm, going so far as to tack quilts around their bedroom wall and stuffing the windows with old newspapers. Dr. Simon came by to check on them and told me they had pneumonia. He left a bottle of laudanum to help them sleep.

Pa called me to his bedside, "Lass, tie a rope from the house to the barn and one out to the stable in the woods. In case of a bad snow you won't get lost." His voice grew weak and trembling. "I'm sorry I can't help you."

"That's alright, Pa. I'll do that while I do the chores."

"Lassie, I'll be up and around in a week."

I knew he meant well, but I worried he would never be up again.

Tag started barking, and I looked outside. A family of negroes stood at the door. The old man said his name was Sam, and he asked if they work for some food and shelter.

"Yes," I said. Help had arrived and stayed for several days. They helped me with the chores, laundry, and mucking the barn. It felt good to have the chores caught up. Sam and I went hunting and brought back a young buck, and we all had a feast that night. He told me they would be leaving come morning, so I ask him to stay on as I fixed provision for their travel.

Sam grinned, the scar on his cheek gleaming white against his dark skin. "Yaz, Miss, I be pleased to. It be a sight better'n de souf. De soldier boys fum both sides come 'n take de stock and all the food." He shook his head sorrowfully. "Just a killin' and a burnin'. Dey din't leave us nuttin'."

During the next weeks more negroes came, two or three at a time, begging for food and a place to sleep. Most didn't understand why their masters told them to leave when they had nowhere to go. I couldn't turn them away. Some had rags wrapped around their feet. Sam used the deer hides Pa had tanned to make boot-tops on wooden shoes. The sick ones rested in the barn while others helped with chores. I was glad to help them, and truth to tell, I was glad for their company.

None of them stayed very long. "Headin' nowth," the black folks said, "We thank ya' fo' yo' kiness, Missy, but we has to keep movin' afore dey chains us up agin." Soon they were all gone except for Sam.

Ma was having trouble breathing. We kept a steam pot boiling. We could tell it wouldn't be long before she would pass away.

That day came, and Pa called me into the bedroom. "She's gone, Martha. Greta's gone. She went sometime in the night." She had slipped away peacefully just two days before her fifty-fourth birthday. Seeing her lying there, pale and old-looking, nearly tore my heart out. I rocked her gently in my arms as tears streamed down my face.

"She's at peace now, girl. She's with Elsa," Pa whispered, tears running down his cheeks. "She's not sufferin' any more. She's in the Lord's hands."

I carried Ma and laid her on my bed. After I changed the sheets on Pa's bed, I washed and prepared Ma for burial.

Hitching Blackie to the buckboard I hurried to town to buy wood for the casket and to hire a man for digging.

Mr. Weston said Abner was the only man available. I could go over to the saloon to ask him.

Looks like I'd have to hire Abner or a couple of Union soldiers. I couldn't do it alone, and Pa was still too sick.

"Oh goodness, not that varmint. I don't trust him a bit. Keep your little gun handy while Abner's there," Sara warned.

"I will keep it close. Now I got to push for home. I hope the weather holds."

Abner arrived late that afternoon, looking as grimy and disheveled as ever. "Well, Missy, knew you'd come 'round to needin' me," he smirked.

I decided to ignore his remarks and try to keep things businesslike. "I want you to unload the wood. Sam can start on the casket and you the digging."

"I want the grave on the hill overlooking the farm, near the tall sugar maples."

"Yassuh, ma'am," he snickered, tipping his sweat stained hat.

When the casket is finished, have Sam bring it in and put it in the parlor. While waiting, I finished preparing Ma's body. Sam knocked and said the casket was finished. We placed it on the two chairs, and Sam and I placed her in it for burial next morning.

I changed the sheets on my bed and washed up and then lay down for a long sleepless night. I was up long before daylight making coffee.

"Martha, is that you?" Pa called from the bedroom.

"Yes Pa." I went to him. He was lying on the bed. "They finished the casket. We'll do the service this morning," I said. Pa didn't seem to notice.

"Martha, hand me the deed for the farm. I want to sign it over to you."

"Pa, Pa were going to put Ma to rest. Don't you want to come?"

"My darlin's right here with me. Always will be," He patted his chest. "In my heart," he sighed.

It was a cold, lonely, funeral. I prayed all the words the minister spoke, believing that it was true that Ma was not in the ground, her spirit had left, and she was no longer in pain. *If that was really true,* I thought, *I could live with missing her. Amen.*

"You be waitin' please, Missy," Sam said. He went to the buckboard and came back with a large smooth stone. "The Missiz called me a few weeks back, said for me to make this heah, jus' in case." He placed the marker at the head of the grave. "I jus' put what she marked."

Tears filled my eyes as I knelt to read what Sam had chiseled into the stone: 'Greta Patterson - Wife and Mother.'

I said the Lord's Prayer, then to my surprise, Sam began to sing. "Swing low, sweet chariot. Comin' for to carry me home," he sang in a low, clear voice. When he finished, I hugged him tightly. "Thank you, Sam. Thank you," I whispered.

"Stop That!" Abner shouted. "Huggin a nigger—what's the matter with you, girl? You be sleepin' with him next!"

I paid him no mind and started back to the house.

"Well, Miss High-and-Mighty, yer gonna hafta get married iffen you wanna keep the farm. A woman can't own land, you know. So you might as well marry me." He leaned on the shovel, leering, and looked me up and down. "This place u'll be up for grabs." He spat on the ground, grinned, and showing his tobacco-stained teeth.

"That's not true. I don't believe you. You're just saying that, trying to scare me. I'd give up the farm before I'd marry you." I resumed walking back to the house. As I passed Abner, he grabbed me by the arm and pulled me to him. Tag growled and bared his teeth, snapping at Abner.

"Stop! Let go!" I jerked my arm away, and my blouse ripped at the shoulder. We struggled as he tried to force me to kiss him. I could feel his hot vile breath on my face as he rubbed against me. Remembering what Pa told me, I kicked him hard in the shins. He lost his footing and fell on the loose soil, dragging me down with him. Tag attacked him again, catching his pant leg. The front of my blouse tore away, showing my undergarment. I rolled to the side with a swift knee to his groin and scrambled to get to my feet. While he was still down, I grabbed the shovel held it up, shouting, "Get out! Now. Right now!"

Tag was barking loudly, trying to grab at Abner's leg. He was snapping, trying to get a good bite.

"Now Missy, just go easy," he groveled, watching the shovel, getting slowly to his feet.

"Get out!" I cried. I backed away, trying to cover my nakedness. "I don't need or want you here. Come on, Tag."

I cleaned up and ask Sam to sit with Pa while I ran an errand.

Sam said, "I'll watch fer you. What we goin' do about that Abner?"

"Maybe he won't come back. I'd rather do the work myself than ask him."

I rode as quickly as was safe across the snowy pasture toward the Penrod's farm. I found Mr. Penrod bringing his cows in to milk. Riding up, I asked, "Could we talk? I need some advice."

"Vhy sure ve can talk, Marta," he said, smiling. "Vhen I get cows to barn den ve talk as long as you need." Mr. Penrod's cows just kept walking to the barn.

"Thank you, Mr. Penrod. I won't be able to visit. I have to hurry cause Pa is alone and I need to get right back. Sir, is it true a woman can't be a landholder?"

"No, dats not true. Vhy do you ask, Marta?"

"When Pa dies, will they take the farm away from me?"

"Na' where you get dat ideal? It's yours 'til you ved. Den it's the husband's." He winked. "Very important you pick de good man for marry."

"Thank you, Mr. Penrod. That makes me feel a whole lot better."

"Glad to be of help, Marta." He stroked Blackie's nose. "If you 'tink you vant to sell your farm, I be interested. Give you fair price. You 'tink about it, hokay?"

I rode quickly back to the farm, put a blanket on the mare, and turned her out in the corral. Tag wagged his tail in greeting, and we headed for the house. Startled, I came to a quick stop. Tag's fur went up and he growled.

There was Abner sprawled on the steps of the porch. He tossed away the straw he was chewing on and asked, "Well, the old man tell you I was right? Ya ready to marry me now?"

"No. I told you to leave." I walked by, well out of his reach. "I'd marry a yank before you. Get off my porch. Get off my farm and stay off. You're not welcome here."

Abner walked over to his mule.

Sam walked up, "Missy, I can't do nothin' to hep you if dat Abner does sumpin' bad," he said. "Da white man hangs me."

"I understand, Sam. I can handle him. I'm sorry he was the only one to hire for help." I return to the house. I was so mentally and physically exhausted, I dropped off to sleep immediately.

Knocking on the front door and Tag's barking brought me out of my sound sleep. Startled and afraid it might be Abner, I brought Tag with me to answer the knock. I was relieved at the sight of a black man and woman along with three sickly-looking children shivering on the porch.

"Mornin', ma'am. Sorry to trouble you." An old black man with white hair and a toothless grin stared at me. "Miss, please can we work for vittles and stay 'til they be well? I'd do your chores."

My heart went out to them. "Of course you can. Go to the barn. Sam will show you where to sleep. Missus, bring the children in so they can get warm. I'll fix some porridge."

"God will bless you, ma'am. He surely will." They came inside and gathered shivering around the kitchen stove. I added wood and set a pot of water to boil.

"I'll get dressed," I said, as I stepped behind my curtain. "Watch the pot," I said to the woman.

"Yes, ma'am. Thanks you, ma'am. The Lord will bless you." The young woman smiled big as her head bobbed up and down. "Me an' my men folk do your work."

"That will be most helpful," I said truthfully, wondering when the Lord was going to start.

"They named me Homey," said the woman. "Ah done the cooking in da main house for the master. I can cook for you."

"It's nice to meet you, Homey. I'm glad you can cook. You can call me Martha."

"Miss Martha, the old man's my pappy, name of Nero and da three young 'uns. I jus' calls 'em Toby, Josh, an' Moses" She giggled. The boys nodded, grinning.

Pa called from is bed. "Lassie, who's there?"

"It's a family on their way north," I explained, coming in to stand beside his bed. "It's alright, Pa." I leaned down and kissed his forehead. He smelled of sickness. "I'll just get dressed, and then we'll get your breakfast alright?"

"Goin' north, you say? We're goin' to Oregon, aren't we, Martha?" My heart and hopes leaped. His voice sounded strong and sure. Maybe he was better today.

"Yes, Pa. Oregon." I dressed hurriedly. "Go ahead and fix biscuits with the porridge," I called to the Homey.

After a week, Nero and Homey felt like family. They were so helpful, and I felt rested.

"Homey, I'll get Pa ready for breakfast." Entering the room, I stared at Pa. He looked so pale. I went to him, and he had passed over. I laid my head on his chest crying "Homey," I cried out, "It's Papa. He's gone."

"He be wit' de Lord, Missy, No mo' pain an' misery. Your Pa, he's in a better place. Now I'll help you fix him for burial."

"I have to believe that, Homey. I have to. I picked up the shears from the night table and snipped off a lock of papa hair and placed it in the locket around my neck. Then I cut of a lock of my own hair and placed it in papa's nightshirt pocket. "Papa, I love you. I'll miss you. I will follow our dream."

"I tell the men folk?"

"Yes, please. Ask them to put him on the right side of my mother. The coffin's made. Have them fetch it on the buckboard." I hugged her. "I don't know what I'd do without you, Homey. You've been a real blessing."

Burying Pa was even harder than burying Ma. He and I had shared a closeness of the same dream. When Sam and Nero lowered the casket, it was all I could to keep from throwing myself into the grave. Homey walked me back to the house, comforting me while I mourned.

Later that day, I changed into my riding skirt and tucked the deed in my pocket. "I'll return shortly, Homey. I have business to take care of with my neighbors. I'll take Tag with me."

"I think he's off playin' with Toby, Josh, and Moses," Homey said. "Ya' want I should fetch him?"

"No, that's alright." I went to the barn and was getting ready to saddle Blackie when someone grabbed me from behind.

"Goin' somewhere, sweetie?"

Abner! "Let me go," I managed to say calmly, despite my panic. Where was Sam or Nero or the boys? Why hadn't they told me Abner was on the farm?

I struggled free and turned back to Blackie. "Just leave, Abner. There's nothing for you here."

"Don't be tellin' me what to do, bitch. Your Pa's dead, and you have to marry me. I'm gonna' make sure of it right now." He laughed and grabbed my arm, dragging me toward him and ripping my sleeve. "No man will want you. You won't be so high and mighty then when I'm through ridin' you."

I pulled to free myself and he slapped my face hard. "Damn you!" I yelled, and punched him with a hard right in the nose.

"Bitch!" he screamed and grabbed his face as blood streamed between his fingers. He staggered and then came at me. His fist glanced off my head. I brought my knee up and hit him in the groin. He moaned and doubled over. I pushed him to the ground, somehow grabbing a pitchfork. I shoved it hard against his chest, holding his eyes with a determined stare. "I told you to stay away from me."

"Come on. Let me up," he whined and held his hands out as if in surrender. "C'mon, Miss Patterson. I just want the farm. You can leave soon as we're married. I won't tell the blue bellies 'bout those horses you keep hidden."

"You won't tell anyone anything," I said, pressing harder on the pitchfork.

He kicked at me, cussing loudly, knocking the pitchfork out of my hand. "Ha," he grabbed my arm, pushing me off balance and ripping my blouse. "I'll come back an' show you a few things. I ain't done with you yet. I ain't rode a cow big as you. I'm gonna enjoy that." He laughed loudly, slapping me hard. I fell to the side.

My felt my hands tightened on the pitchfork. "You bastard! You don't touch me." Overcome with rage, resentment, hurt, despair, and hate, I plunged the pitchfork at him again, going deep in his chest. His eyes widened in surprise, and his mouth dropped open. His body twitched, and the front of his shirt turned red. Then he was still. Blood trickled out the corner of his mouth.

"Oh, my God, what have I done?" My breath came in short gasps.

Sam and Nero came up behind me. "You alright, Missy?" Sam asked. "We seed what happened."

Nero grinned. "Look like y'all kin take care o' yo'sef, ma'am."

"I didn't mean to kill him," I said, shaking, not entirely sure I was telling the truth.

"You did what needed doin'," Sam said. "He was a bad 'un. He needed killin'. Don't you worry, Missy. We'll take care of dis mess. You go on to de house. Nero, walk wit her. Hold on to her. She might faint."

"Pa, Pa," I whimpered. "I need you now." Nero pushed me through the door.

"Homey, we got bad trouble. Put her to bed. Fix her some tea."

"Oh, Homey," I blurted. "I killed him. I killed Abner." She gently pulled me inside. "Sam and Nero, dey'll take care of it." I grabbed her arm. "Oh, God, I don't want them to get in trouble because of me."

"Don' worry," said Homey. "Dey be knowin' what needs to be done." She gently pushed me into a chair. "You jus' sit. I fix some special tea."

I couldn't think straight, my head began to spin, my hands started to tremble, and my whole body began to shake. Homey took me by the arm and led me to the alcove. "You lay yo'sef down. De tea's almost done." She helped me to the bed and propped a pillow under my head. I lay shivering cold as she covered me with a quilt, feeling dazed and frightened.

In a few minutes she handed me a cup of hot tea. "Drink this. It'll warm you."

I sipped it, not really tasting it. "Drink it down," Homey urged, holding the cup to my mouth. She tucked another quilt around me.

When the cup was empty, she tucked the quilt around my shoulders and patted my face. "You rest now, Missy."

"Yes," I murmured. My tongue felt thick. Everything was clouded and fuzzy. "Rest, rest," my mind kept saying.

"I'm goin' to check on the boys," Homey said, her voice sounding as if came from far away. "Everythin' will be alright."

I felt tired, a heavy mind floating with a body that seemed to separate as I drifted off to a dreamless blackness.

CHAPTER SIX

I bolted upright in bed. The vision of Abner's body with a pitchfork sticking in his chest was so real. Was it a dream or real? How long had I been asleep? Where was Homey? I jumped out of bed and stumbled, falling to my knees on the rug as Tag jumped. I pulled myself back up, not trusting my legs, a bit lightheaded. What happened? Abner! "Oh, Lord, what have I done?" I've been asleep. The tea? What was in that tea? What time is it?

"Homey," I called, but there was no answer. Tag looked up at me and thumped his tail as if to reassure me he hadn't left. I patted his head. "Good boy. You have to go out?" I got up carefully, still not trusting my legs and using the chairs to balance. Making my way to the door, I let Tag out. There was no one in sight so I called. "Sam? Nero? Homey?" I screamed. No answer. My mind cleared. I knew it wasn't a dream and I truly had killed Abner.

Where could they be? Had they run away, fearing they'd be blamed for Abner's death? I certainly couldn't fault them if they had.

My legs had steadied, and my head cleared. Gathering my courage, I headed for the barn, scared to death of facing Abner's body. The pitchfork! Was it still in his body? Did I pull it out? I couldn't remember. What would I do with the body? Bury it, burn it. I couldn't report I killed him. I had to go to Oregon. Nothing was going to stop me. I'd get rid of the body somehow—maybe bury it in the woods or hide it in the wagon. I'd sell the farm to Mr. Penrod and head for Missouri. According to the newspaper article, that's where you signed up for the wagon train, which left in the spring. There's time. If nothing goes wrong, I can make it.

Bracing myself, I entered the barn. There was no sign of a struggle or blood. No dead body. Staring at the sight, I relived the whole scene, my eyes riveted to the spot where Abner died. Sam's words came back. "We take care o' everthin', Missy. Don' worries none." I let loose the breath I didn't even realize I'd been holding. Now Sam and Nero were gone. Homey and the boys all were gone. Where was the body?

"God bless you," I said, praying He would. Looking around, there wasn't a sign of evidence of Abner or the negroes. The stalls where they lived were spread with fresh hay. There was nothing to show they'd lived here for six weeks. Abner and his mule were gone. Remember, can't tell a soul. "Don't worry," I whispered, recalling Homey's words.

Tag sniffed where the body had lain. "No, Tag. Come here, boy," I called, when he began scratching at the straw.

"Let's go see Mr. Penrod. We've got things to do." Checking the corral, all the stock was out to pasture except Blackie. I tossed her some hay and then went to feed the horses in the stable.

In the house I decided it was too late in the day to visit Penrods. Instead, I went to the chicken house and gathered some eggs, stopped at the smokehouse and got a piece of ham, and then peeled some potatoes for my supper later. I filled the kettle to heat for a bath. My mind was buzzing like a beehive at swarming time. I felt I had no choice but to leave or take the chance of being arrested for murder. No one would understand the about the blackmail. Besides, I was looking forward to heading west away from the war, memories of the farm, and everything I could do nothing about.

While waiting for the water to get hot, I went into my parents' room and dragged the large leather trunk to the kitchen. Opening it and reaching for Pa's book on bloodlines, I pulled out the article on

Oregon: "One hundred sixty acres of land for each man and woman in Oregon for homesteading." I sighed. Plenty of room for a horse farm.

I removed everything from the trunk and began to gather the things I would take. I sat on the floor, placing my flower-garden quilt on the bottom, then Pa's crooked brown pipe, the family Bible, the figurines from Germany, and added a few things for housekeeping. I picked up Pa's book on bloodlines and reread the filly's birth record I had torn from the journal of breeding records. They would be the start of my horse ranch with the finest horses out of Virginia. A bolt of excitement surged through me coupled with a sense of sadness that Pa wouldn't be there to share the adventure. Taking the quilt off my parents' bed, I put it on top. The trunk was only half full. I added my dress boots and my three good dresses and the hat that Sara made me.

Tag walked around and whined. I laughed as he danced around, pawing me while kissing my face. "Better check the water," I said. In the kitchen I poked another stick of wood in the stove and added a bucket of water to heat. *Later I'll bathe*, I decided.

I could almost hear the guns firing as I set out the two boxes and then gathered up the Dutch ovens, a skillet, spoons, forks, metal plates, and the spider cooker. It was like reliving the day we'd left Manassas. I shivered and put it out of my mind. I didn't have time to worry about the past. In the smaller trunk, I packed my personal things. I sat it all by the front door to load. "Well Tag, let's have some supper, How about potatoes and eggs?"

It was well after ten before I took my bath. I washed my hair and brushed it by the fire 'til it was near dry. I put it in a loose braid and then went to bed. I woke up several times with horrible nightmares and was up long before daylight.

At daybreak, Tag following at my heels. I went and fed the horses and then checked out the wagon and tack. I finished the chores, saddled Blackie, and rushed off to the Penrod's with the deed to the farm in my pocket. Before yesterday I would have enjoyed the ride, but now all I wanted was to sell the farm and be on my way.

As I approached the Penrod's place, I could see Lilia sitting in a rocking chair on her porch.

"Morning, Marta."

"Good morning, ma'am. I need to talk to the mister. Aren't you cold out here?"

"No, I haf my lap quilt. Get down and visit awhile if you haf time. I get you a cup uff hot tea." She laid her mending down and stood.

Dismounting, I tied Blackie to the hitching post and told Tag to sit. "Thank you. How's your leg?" The last time I was over, she had taken a bad fall.

"Oh, I've been up and about for a week now. Yust a bad bruise, tank Gott. I thought I broke it." She pointed towards the barn. "Here comes Harry now. I make tea." She went into the house.

"Hello, Mr. Penrod."

"Hello, Marta," he greeted, coming up on the porch. "How are your Papa dese days? Last time you come, he was feeling poorly."

"Pa died early yesterday. We buried him right away." I sat twisting my gloves in knots. "Mr. Penrod, I'm ready to sell the farm. The deed's all signed. Do you still want it?" I stood and walked nervously across the porch.

"Yah, I still vant it." He reached out and patted my shoulder. "I'm sorry about your Papa. He was good man."

"Vhat is dis?" Missus Penrod asked, coming out of the house. "You papa died? Oh, you poor ting. You come live wit' us, hokay?" She bustled over and put her arms about me. "We need a sweet girl around dis place. You come, hokay?"

It was hard to keep from crying. "That is very kind of you, but I need to make a life for myself," I said. "I promised Pa."

"Ve go inside, yah? Ve talk." The old man took my arm and led me inside. "Ve eat."

The house was warm and cozy. "You sit," Lilia put her arm around me, urging me into a chair at the kitchen table. "You eat. Make you feel better."

The aroma of potato soup made me realize I hadn't eaten breakfast this morning. I started, "About the farm...."

"Ve eat first. Den we talk business," Mr. Penrod said, waving his forefinger at me.

When his wife placed a large bowl of hot soup in front of me, I decided he was right. "Mmm, this is good," I said, smiling at Lilia.

"Yah," she nodded in agreement. "Bread from the oven I make awhile ago. I giv de dog some scraps. He eat 'em up quick."

"It's all delicious. Thank you. It's just what I needed."

After we had eaten, the old man said, "Now ve talk. Vhat are your plans, Marta? You leaf Charleston?"

"Yes sir. I plan on going to Missouri. I want to keep the wagon, the four mules." I paused.

He interjected, "De three fillies."

"I didn't know you knew. Yes, we been hiding our fillies in the shed under the big trees."

"I know," he nodded. "And I know why. Is de var."

"Yes sir. We didn't want the soldiers to confiscate them like they did our other horses."

"Now, Marta, you're just a girl all alone. You're not afraid?" He looked surprised and impressed.

"Sure, I'm afraid." I wasn't about to confess my greatest fear of being hanged for murder was more powerful than the fear of what I might encounter on the way to Oregon. "But, I know I can do it. My parents taught me how to work, how to do for myself. I can do it. I want to."

"You're a brave girl, Marta. Vhat can ve do to help?"

"Well, besides buying the farm, would you be kind as to take Blackie, my mare?" Tears welled up and I swallowed hard. The thought of leaving her behind was very difficult. "She's too old to make such a long hard trip," I continued. "I couldn't stand to see her go down on the trail. She is nineteen. She may be able to carry one or two more foals if it is right away. And she's a wonderful buggy horse."

"Yah, sure, I take good care uff her but no foals. He stood and so did I. "You vant I should gif you da money now?"

"Yes, I'll be leaving right away. I have the deed right here." I pulled it out of my pocket and handed it to him. He looked it over and said, "I get da money. Is it still amount vee talk about?"

"Yes."

He left the room and was back in a minute with a bag of coins. "Gold coins, Marta. You vant to count?" He started to untie the bag.

"No, Mr. Penrod. Your word is good with me. Thank you. You've been a good neighbor and a good friend. I'll miss you both."

Lilia handed me a poke. "It's a jar of soup with some cheese and bread for your dinner and a hambone for you dog." She wrapped her ample arms around me and hugged me tight while she patted my back. "Take care, dear, and remember, ting's don't work out, you come here."

Mr. Penrod walked out with me. "Make sure you hide the money. Many desperate people aroun dese days, and desperate people do bad tings. Send us verd from Oregon."

Amen to that, I thought. I was one of them. I mounted Blackie and called to Tag. I waved goodbye and I headed for home.

CHAPTER SEVEN

"C'mon, Tag. We'll go say our goodbyes to Ma and Pa."

I knelt down between the fresh mounds of dirt, Tag beside me. Never had I felt so alone. The two people who been there for me all my life were gone. I couldn't stop the tears. "Oh, Papa, I've really messed up. I killed that damn Abner. He attacked and I fought back. Said he would compromise me and tell the soldiers about the horses. I couldn't let that happen, could I? Did I do right? Do you forgive me?"

Suddenly, I felt a warm glow surround me. It was as if he was standing right next to me, his hand on my shoulder. "Papa, ask God to forgive me." A feeling of relief spread over me. They weren't in this cold, hard ground. It was like the preachers said. Their spirits were still alive. I stopped crying.

"Pa, I've sold the farm to Mr. Penrod. He gave me a good price for it. I'm leaving in the morning for Missouri. Going to join the wagon train heading for Oregon. I'm gonna claim the homestead land and build our farm." I smiled. "And, Ma, maybe there'll be someone in Oregon who would like a tall, plain woman. I know you're happy being with Elsa. I never made you proud like Elsa, but I'm cut from a different bolt of cloth, like Pa. I hope you know how much I love and miss you both. I'll say good bye for now."

At dusk I walked to the hidden stable. Pa had hidden his cache of gold coins in a hollow cornerstone. I reached in and felt the soft leather bag, pulled it out, and tied it around my waist under my skirt.

I led the three fillies to the barn and stabled them next to Blackie. I filled their hay bins and chained the barn door. I tossed some hay to the mules in the corral. It would be a long day tomorrow.

Calling Tag indoors, I barred the door and shared the bread and soup Lilia had given me and then gave Tag his bone. Adding the fresh milk and boiled eggs, it was a feast.

Sleep evaded me as the questions filled my mind. The risk! The danger! Maybe I should consider buying a ride on someone else's wagon. When I reach Oregon, would I be able to manage by myself? Homesteading one hundred and sixty acres would be no easy task. Would they even allow a woman alone on a wagon train? Could I get my fillies to Independence? Could I avoid the soldiers? I would just have to find a way. I couldn't let our dream die. With visions of young foals racing across green pastures with white fences, I fell into an exhausted sleep.

Sometime after midnight, Tag's barking woke me. I jumped out of bed and grabbed the rifle. Going to the window, I pulled back the curtains. Several men on horseback milled around the yard. In the darkness I couldn't tell who they were. One stepped up on the porch. Terror-stricken I shouted, "Stop right there."

"Whoa, hold it, ma'am. Miss Patterson, is that you? We mean you no harm. We were asked to check on you. Miss Sara told us you were alone out here. She is worried that Abner fellow might be bothering you. Said he hadn't come back to town. Has he been here?"

I peered out the window just as the clouds parted, allowing the moonlight to shine on the men. Union soldiers, and none other than the handsome Lieutenant Washburn.

"He left over a week ago." I put down the rifle. "Thank you for coming. I'm fine."

"That's mighty good to hear. Sorry for the lateness of the hour. We couldn't get away any sooner."

"Yes, I understand. I'm sorry, but I'm not opening the door for anyone. I hope you understand."

"Yes, ma'am, that's the right thing to do. Keep your door locked. I'll ride out in a few days to see how you are. Would you like me to check the barn? Make sure everythin's alright there?"

Oh no, the fillies! Why did I bring them out of the hiding place?

"No, no need to do that. I have it all locked up." I hoped my voice didn't betray my panic.

"Well, we'll be going then. You take care, you hear? Remember I'll come call in a few days."

"Yes, thanks again," I called out. "Just leave please," I whispered. They rode away and I crawled back in bed. Balling up in a fetal position, I shook with fear, thinking of what might have happened. What if they had come earlier? What if they'd come while Abner's dead body was still here? Or when I was bringing the fillies in? Unable to sleep, I got up and paced the floor.

"Stop it, Martha. You're getting all worked up for nothing." My voice sounded loud in the quiet room. "They didn't find Abner. How could they find him? You don't even know where he is. They didn't find the fillies. So just calm down and go to sleep."

"You're right," I said to myself. I stoked up the fire. Then with my gun by my side, I lay on my bed. A short time later, I fell asleep. Abner's face swam before me. He was grinning as if to say I hadn't seen the last of him. Before dawn I woke drenched in sweat. How long would this go on haunting me? Would it ever stop? Would I always have that devil with his pitchfork prodding me?

Six Women West

    Shivering, I got up and splashed cold water on my face. I stoked up the fire and put on a pot of coffee, mixed a double batch of biscuits, and put them in the oven. I was wide awake now. I washed up while the coffee made and dressed in warm clothes. In the gray light of dawn I went to the chicken house and gathered over a dozen eggs, propping the door open. After a breakfast of biscuits, eggs, cheese, and plenty of coffee, I made ready to leave. I packed the remaining eggs and six potatoes for later. I took a trip to the smokehouse and gathered the last two hams, putting all of it into the food box. It was cold outside with frost as white as snow. I warmed myself at the house while putting the last minute things in the trunk. Checking the house, I doused the fire with water and headed for the barn where I loaded my saddles and tack, grain, water keg, and tools. I filled the rear of the wagon with armloads of hay.

    With my arms around Blackie, I said goodbye to her. She was more than my horse—she was my friend. She seemed to know I was saying goodbye. I swear there were tears in her eyes, but then maybe I was just seeing a reflection of my own. I turned her out with the cows. Mr. Penrod would be over to take them to his farm.

    In the yard, I hitched Rowdy and Randy to the wagon and tied the other two mules with the three fillies on the back. Tag danced around, obviously anxious to get going. I took the wagon up to the porch and loaded the trunks and food. Taking one last look at the place I'd called home for the past two years, I took a deep breath and walked out, closing the door and my past firmly behind me. It was February 1864.

    "Come on, Tag. Lead the way," I called, and Tag ran out in front of the wagon. I put fifty dollars in my pocket and half my poke of coins in the secret place. The other half I put in the hollow shotgun stock. Then I put the rifle under the seat and the shotgun next to my knee.

Pa had taught me well. I had no difficulty driving the wagon. It was midmorning when I stopped on the outskirts of town near a grove of willow trees. I needed to get supplies and say goodbye to Sara. I would miss her. She was the first friend I ever had.

Making sure the horses and mules were well hidden, I left an armload of hay for them to munch on while I drove on into town. At the store, Sara waved to me from behind the counter where she was waiting on a lady. "Good morning, Martha. I'll be with you in a moment."

"Good morning, Sara. Take your time. I'll just look around."

She finished and walked over to me and put her arms around me. "I'm so sorry about your folks. What will you do now?"

"Thank you. I'll miss them, but I know they're better off. They both suffered."

She put her arms around my waist, "Will you be moving into town?" she asked, stepping back. "Maybe you could find a job somewhere. Maybe we could share a small house. You can't take care of that big place by yourself."

"Sara, remember the covered wagon we followed into town awhile back?"

"Yes I remember. Why, Martha?"

"I've sold the farm, Sara. I'm leaving Charleston. I'm on my way to Missouri. I just stopped to say goodbye and get supplies."

Sara's expression changed and became serious. "Martha, may I go with you? I know I don't look like I can do much, but I could do the sewing and tend the animals and cook some." She grabbed my hand and looked up at me pleadingly. "I have a brother in Independence I can stay with. This is my chance. I really need to get away from here." She grimaced, glancing towards the backroom. "Things are getting worse around here. Just two nights ago, someone tried the door of my bedroom."

"Sara, you can't guess how happy you just made me." I squeezed her hand. "It will be a hard trip. We won't be sleeping in feather beds." I stared down at her. She looked too fragile for such an adventure, but there was a determined look in her eyes that made me believe she could do it. "Are you sure this is what you want. Do you want to take some time and think about it?"

"I just did. I'll be ready in half hour after I finish your order."

"Alright. Just bring what you absolutely need. We don't have a lot of room." I reached in my pocket and brought out the list I'd prepared. "Let's see—slab of bacon, flour, canned peaches, canned beans, tomatoes. I'll need a wagon canvas, a forty-five Colt revolver with holster, and two boxes of ammunition."

"My goodness! It sounds as if you're expecting trouble."

"Well, Pa always told me to be prepared for anything."

Mr. Weston walked out of the back room. "Good morning, Miss Patterson. Is Sara finding what you need?"

"You can probably help her better than I, Mr. Weston," Sara said, smiling sweetly. "I need to speak with Mrs. Weston." She wiggled her fingers at me and mouthed the words, "I'll hurry."

I repeated my order to Weston. He looked surprised. "I didn't realize your pa had gotten well. I heard he was near dyin'."

"He did die," I said. "These are for my use."

Now he looked even more surprised. "You expectin' trouble?"

"Possibly." I didn't see any point in telling him my plans. His wife would do that after Sara talked to her.

Picking up the food supplies with no offer of help from him, I left the store. I laid the canvas in the wagon bed and stored the gun and ammunition under the seat. I poked my head back in the door and asked him to tell Sara I'd be back shortly. Next, I went next door and bought a skinning knife.

Sara had loaded her belongings, and she looked every bit the lady, complete with parasol and kid gloves. "Come on," I said, climbing up on the seat. "We have to stop at the stable. Randy has a loose shoe. I want Thomas to help me put on the canvas. Some things I just can't do," I shrugged. "Any problems with the Mrs. Weston about leaving?"

"No, not really. She thanked me and wished me luck. I think Mrs. Weston is glad I'm leaving. I have the feeling she knows her husband is on the prowl." Sara shook her head. She patted Tag who was sitting on the floor with his paw on her lap. "Don't know why she puts up with him."

"Maybe she doesn't think she has a choice. Like most women."

"That's true. Not many ways for a woman to earn a living."

When we pulled up at the stable, there was a young boy hanging over the fence brushing a spotted mule. "Is Thomas here?" I asked, getting down.

"Not yet. I'm waitin' for him."

He was as tall as me and about the same size. He had a nice smile, green eyes, and a face full of freckles. I looked at the stable door. A sign said, "Back in ten minutes."

I unhitched Randy from the harness. "Been waiting long?" I asked.

"Not long. Name's Beck. That's a nice wagon. Where you goin'?" he added, smiling at Sara.

"Thank you. I hope it's sturdy enough to get me there." I grinned.

"Mind if I ask where?" He stuck his hands in his pockets and stared up at me.

"Well, don't be repeating it, but first to Missouri and then on west."

"West how far?" He walked over and began to pet Tag, who wagged his tail furiously. "I've been wantin' to go west. Any chance I could ride along? I can carry my own weight, and I'm sure I could be of some help to you." He grinned. "Safety in numbers, my Paw always told me."

"I don't know. Do you know how to drive a team?"

"Ain't done any, but I can learn."

Having a man along would be good, I decided, especially one as likeable as this one. He wasn't too clean, but he seemed kind. "What do you think, Sara? Shall we let him ride along?"

"You're the boss, Martha," Sara answered, smiling.

"Alright, we can try it. You pay your own way and make your own camp at night. If you think for one minute you can take advantage of us, you'll get a taste of my shotgun."

"Well, I cain't lie to you. I'll please you to know I ain't a boy." The person called Beck pulled off her hat, revealing a head of short curly red hair. Smiling, she pushed out her chest against the sloppy shirt. She was a girl. That was now obvious.

Sara gasped, and I know my mouth dropped open.

"I started pretending to be a boy a long time ago," she said. "I found out the hard way men will try to take advantage of females. You'll learn, too, if you haven't already."

"Beck, we'll try traveling together and see how it works."

"You waitin' on me?" Thomas walked up.

"Yep," I said, going along with Beck's disguise. "He was here first."

"I need three pounds of grain," Beck said.

"If you want, you can put your grain in the wagon," I said, turning to Beck.

"Thanks. Then I'll get a full sack if that's alright."

"Sure. Thomas, I need this mule's shoe fixed, two sacks of grain, and help putting a canvas on this wagon. Could you do that?"

"Sure, I'll check both their shoes. Looks like you're set to go somewhere. You in a hurry?"

"Yes, in a way. I'd like to leave as soon as possible."

"Where you goin'?"

Glancing quickly at Sara and Beck, I lied. "I'm going to visit family over in Virginia."

"No. Damn!" he exclaimed. "Sorry, I was thinking about calling on you. Well, really to ask if I could come courting."

I smiled. "Guess it is kind of surprising. Maybe when I return."

"I'll get busy right away, Miss Patterson."

"Thank you, Thomas. We'll go eat." I turned to Beck. "Hungry?" She nodded. "Come on, Sara. Let's go eat. You stay, Tag. I'll bring you back something."

"Does this mean I can ride with you?" Beck asked, pulling her hat back on.

"Yes, Beck, all the way to Missouri. We'll be happy to have you, won't we, Sara?"

Sara nodded.

"Call me Becky," the girl said, walking beside me.

"Becky. How old are you, Becky? Not that it matters. I just wondered how long it took you to get so smart." I grinned and winked at Sara.

"Seventeen, I think. But, people think I'm older because I'm so big. You know?" She looked at me as though I were a kindred spirit. "That blacksmith wants to court you."

"Yes, him and three others so far since my folks die. I owned a farm. Land grabbers! They don't want me. It's the farm they want."

At the eating house, we each had a big dinner. Sara talked a bit about her brother in Missouri, but Becky didn't have much to say. My own thoughts were occupied with how I was going to manage. Talking about it was one thing. Doing it was sure to be something else, especially when there were others depending on me.

When we finished eating, I asked Mabel to make up a poke of dog food for Tag. We returned to the stable. I was happy to see that Thomas had the canvas on the wagon. He handed me a bucket full of grease. "Here, Martha. Make sure you grease the wheels every morning. I nailed the shoe on that mule. It's fine now. You're all set. I'll put a new set on them when you get back."

I paid him while keeping my eye on Becky trying to lead Rowdy to the wagon. Rowdy was balking with a few kicks thrown in. I never could figure out why Rowdy was so ornery and Randy so gentle. I pitched in and urged the mules in line. Sara sat on the springboard and called encouragement. Within a quarter hour we were on our way.

Out of town by the Willow Grove we stopped to pick up the fillies I had tethered in the bush. Becky was surprised to see such fine horses. "Can't believe the army didn't confiscate them," she said, stroking the black's neck.

"They probably would if they knew I had them," I replied. "That's why we have to be extra careful and avoid any troops." No point in telling either woman that I had more than one reason to stay clear of the authorities.

Wanda Reed

CHAPTER EIGHT

It was a warm lazy afternoon in early March. We'd been on the road almost two weeks and, as near as I could figure, we'd covered a little over one hundred miles. I calculated we had two and a half months to reach Missouri. I wasn't sure when the wagon train was set to leave for Oregon, but according to that article, it always left in May or June.

> **Comment [CJH]:** IMPORTANT: According to mulemuseum.org, mules in wagon trains could travel 30 miles per day. Therefore, they should have covered far more than 100 miles in 2 weeks. The distance from West VA to Independence is about 850 miles, so that would be just 4-1/2 weeks, assuming they rested on Sunday which would have been generally the custom then as Sunday traveling was considered a sin, at least by some.. This changes quite a few things, including possibly the starting time in order to keep it tight to the wagon train in Independence. See related notes below.

The mules plodded slowly on the dirt road, kicking up dust. The dogwood trees were full of green buds, and wild azaleas bloomed on the roadside. There were signs of new life everywhere. The white-throated sparrow whistled old Sam Peabody-Peabody from the trees, letting everyone know spring was on its way. It was one of those days that made you glad you were alive.

Becky rode up alongside. "I'm off to scare us up some dinner," she said. "Tag, you stay here." He'd gotten in the habit of following her since I was confined to driving the wagon.

"Good, we could use some fresh meat," I told her. Becky was good at bringing in game. I still laughed about thinking she was a boy. "What do you say to fresh meat?" I asked, turning to Sara, who was busy mending one of my skirts.

"I say it better be skinned and ready for the fire. I can cook it, but I don't fancy cleaning game."

Early on, it was worked out that Sara did the cooking while Becky did our hunting and I drove. We all shared the chores of setting up camp.

"Martha, if I have to hem this again, it's going to be up to your knees. How do you get it in such a fix, anyway?" Sara held up what was left of my riding skirt, a disgusted look on her face. "We're going to have to purchase some goods to make you another skirt, and I need some kid gloves. Every pair I own is stained beyond cleaning."

"Oh, it gets caught on things. I've been noticing Becky's britches. I think I'd like to have a pair. What you need is a pair of leather gloves."

"Well, I suppose it would be better. Not very ladylike, though."

"Maybe so, but being ladylike has never been high on my list of things to be." I laughed and jiggled the reins, urging the plodding mules to a faster pace.

Less than two hours later, Becky was back with two rabbits hanging from her saddle horn.

Sara took one look and shouted, "Becky, you clean those before you bring them to me."

"Okay. Boy, you're sure squeamish. They're just dead rabbits. Well, here take the cabbage anyway."

"Where you get this cabbage?"

"I took it away from the rabbits," Becky laughed.

"If you want your supper, there better not be any innards or hides on them!"

About an hour before dark, we pulled off the road into a stand of trees. Becky cleaned the rabbits to Sara's satisfaction, and we had roast rabbit and boiled cabbage for dinner.

As we sat around the campfire enjoying the meal, I asked, "Sara, could you make a map of our travels so far, and then add to it as we go along?"

"I think so. I'm already keeping a journal."

"Soft deer hide makes a good map," Becky said. "I have one you can use."

"Thanks, Becky," I said.

Becky brought out a soft tan deer hide, and by the firelight we marked out a map of where we had traveled already and where we'd be going in the next few days.

"Good," I said, "Now we'll have a record of our trip."

"How far is it to Missouri?" Becky asked.

"I don't know. We can ask in the next town," I answered.

"When I get another hide, I'll make us a camp chair."

"You can do something like that? I'll wait and see it first." I teased.

"You just hide and watch," she laughed.

Three days later around noon, Becky came galloping back to the wagon with Tag in the lead, all excited. "Martha, there's a town up ahead. Best I could make out, it's called Brayville. It's just three miles. "You want to stop there?"

"Sure," I replied. "We need supplies and grain for the stock."

"We're almost out of coffee and flour," Sara chimed in. "I hope the store carries fresh milk. I better make out a list."

"When we get closer, take the fillies and circle the town and hide them on the far end, Becky," I said. "Hide them good. You know how important they are. Then meet us back at the mercantile."

"Right." About half a mile out she untied the fillies and rode off with them.

The town was like so many others with one main street with a stage office at one end and a blacksmith at the other. The population was scarce with most men off in the war. There were several small shops with two saloons across the street. I stopped at the mercantile store, taking time to brush the dust off my skirt before I went in.

Sara stayed in the wagon until she was looking presentable.

Becky came in. "All taken care of," she whispered.

"Good. What do you think?" I asked, holding up a pair of britches. "I'm tired of fighting these damn long skirts. They're always getting in the way. The hems are starting to look like picket fences."

"I think you're making a wise decision," Becky declared. "I sure do like mine." She patted her buttocks. "I can save you enough deer hides for a pair of buckskins."

"That would be great. Thanks, Becky."

As I rummaged through the selection on the table, wondering what size I should get, a buxom woman with yellow-gold hair wearing a large black hat with pink feathers shoved in front of us. She knocked Becky off balance, making her bump the lady's negro maid, which caused her to drop the packages she was carrying. The woman turned and slapped her maid across the face. "You stupid darkie! Pick those up and wait outside!"

"No need for that," I said, "there's room for everybody." The large, painted woman glared at me. "Don't interfere."

Becky knelt down and helped the trembling maid pick up the packages. I walked out on the boardwalk to cool off and wait until she finished her shopping. I knew if I stayed inside, I'd probably cause trouble.

Becky and the young woman walked out together. "You okay, miss?" I asked, looking into the eyes of a honey-colored woman with short-cropped hair.

"Yessum," she answered, setting the packages down and rubbing her cheek.

Raising her eyes to look at Sara who was just stepping down from the wagon, she asked, "Where y'all going?"

"To Missouri," Sara replied.

"Is that north?"

"Well, it's a free state," Sara volunteered. She glanced at me, raising her eyebrows. I nodded. "We'll be camped tonight on the edge of town in case someone might be looking for us," she added.

Wanda Reed

"Ah'm called Bessie." She smiled slightly and picked up the packages. "Y'all might look for me come dark."

The large woman came out and snapped, "Come along, Bessie. Hurry up! You have work to do." They stepped off the boardwalk and crossed the street toward the saloon.

"It was nice meeting you, Bessie," I called, knowing it would aggravate her owner.

"I wonder if she'll join us," Becky asked.

"We'll see tonight. Now let's get our supplies."

Back inside, the sales clerk came over to us. "I'm sorry about the fuss. That woman is new at the local brothel. Gives me nothing but trouble," he shrugged. "My name is Alfred."

Sara handed him the list she'd prepared. Then she browsed through the gloves near the counter. Becky and I went through the stack of britches, searching for a pair that would fit me. We finally found two pairs we thought would fit. I went in the back room to try them on. They fit. I'd never had my backside displayed in such a fashion before.

"How come they look different on you? Shucks, you don't look nuthin' like a boy," Becky exclaimed, shaking her head. I'm straight on both sides, and you're round in the back."

"I don't know. That's the way I am."

"I'm ready," Sara said, pointing to the supplies piled on the counter. "All you need to do is pay the man."

"Add these two pairs of trousers and two shirts. Sara did you get gloves? Do you need anything Becky?"

"Maybe some peppermint sticks."

"Alfred, any ideal how far it is to Independence, Missouri?"

"I'd say five to seven hundred miles. Can I help you with this, ladies?" Alfred asked.

> **Comment [CJH]:** See note above and consider if needs changing about the rate of travel.

Handing him a gold coin I said, "Thanks, we can manage."

"Here's your change. Come again."

Once loaded, we drove to the far edge of town, stopping at the blacksmith's for grain. There was a stand of cottonwoods near the creek where we set up camp. Becky disappeared and brought back the mares. Grass was plentiful, so the stock would have good graze.

Sara fixed steak and baked beans for supper. We shared a can of peaches.

"Martha, can we drive all those miles? Will we be okay all alone?"

"Sara, we can make it. We have each other. If the going gets too rough, we can hire a man."

After dinner Sara asked if anyone wanted a bath. I was the only taker. I knew she wanted Becky to bathe. We walked down the creek for a bath near the stand of cottonwoods. "Do you think Bessie will come or not?"

"Well, Sara, I hope so. She sure needs to get away from that woman. I wonder if she's a runaway or has free papers."

"Yes, that would be a problem, but one that could be solved," said Sara.

I didn't quite understand what she meant, but I was freezing and decided to ask later. "Let's hurry. This water is ice cold. Maybe Becky's right 'bout not taking a bath," I said. It was dark when Sara and I returned, cold but clean. I stoked up the campfire, not only for added warmth but for extra light in case Bessie tried to locate us.

The stars were out when Tag started growling. "What is it, boy?" I whispered, reaching for my rifle.

"Hallo in the camp."

"Come on in," I called with relief. We stood up, waiting for her to join us.

"Welcome, Bessie," Sara said.

"Ah had to wait 'til Miss Rosie was busy bathin'," Bessie explained in a trembling, breathless voice.

"Well, we're glad you could make it. I take it you're here because you want to join us on our trip to Missouri," I said.

" Y'all truly goin' nowth? I need to know right away, cus nobody knows ahz gone and if ah cain't go, ah got to get right back afore ahz missed. You see."

"Yes, I understand. We've been waiting for you. You're welcome to join us," I assured her.

"Ah surely do need to get away. Can ah buy a ride with y'all? Ah can cook and wash for you. Ah got a bit of money to pay my way." The poor girl was obviously scared witless.

"Yes, Bessie, you're welcome to come with us. We'll leave in the morning, about dawn. Did you bring your belongings?"

"Yessum. Thank you, ma'am." She turned, walked back into the darkness, picked up her carpetbag and blanket, and rejoined us at the fire. She sat on a log and breathed deeply. "Ah's scared. Ah want y'all to know Ah's a free woman. Ah bought my freedom. She got no right to keep me, that Miss Rosie O'Day. She got no right to slap me." She rubbed her cheek. "She got no right to make me work. No, sir. Ah don't want to be a ho' no mo'. Now, ah'ma goin' nowth far as ah can."

"Don't worry, Bessie. Try and relax. No one here will hurt you," Sara said.

"Let's all get some rest now. We have an early start tomorrow. We'll talk about chores and stuff later." I breathed a sigh of relief to hear she was free. I certainly didn't need any extra trouble from the law. I gave it some thought and decide to pull out early anyway.

We broke camp two hours earlier than we'd originally planned in case somebody might come looking for Bessie. Even though she was a freed slave, at least according to her, we might still have trouble for sheltering her.

I urged the mules into a faster pace than they were used to, trying to cover as many miles as quickly as possible, driving one team 'til noon and then switching to the other team. Much earlier, Sara had expressed a desire to learn to drive the team. I had decided to let her with Judy and Jenny in harness. "You sit here with Sara, Bessie. Give her a hand if she needs it, okay? I'm going to check the back trail. Make sure we're not being followed by old yellow hair."

"Yessum, Miss. Ah's sorry. Ah don't know nuthin' bout drivin' no wagon."

I laughed, "It's okay, Bessie. I think Sara will do just fine." I waved and rode off on Gray Lady. It felt good to be out of the wagon and on a horse. I was glad Bessie had decided to come with us. In fact, I was glad Becky and Sara had joined up with me too. I grinned. *Funny,* I thought, *how things work out. Not only was I on my way to Missouri with my horses, but I had found three fine companions as well.*

I felt closer to Becky because she seemed more like me. Sara was my first friend. She seemed so much a lady and obviously was not used to hard work. She had changed since we had been on the trail, though. She no longer wore white kid gloves or carried a parasol, her high-heeled boots had been exchanged for flat-heeled walking boots, and now she wore her hair tied back instead of in ringlets and curls. Becky, on the other hand, had had a much harder life. She was our hunter—not only for meat but fresh vegetables she'd help herself to from nearby gardens. She was free like the wind. I was sure she could wake up tomorrow and move on without looking back. I couldn't imagine being that complete unattached.

The scenery changed as spring came to life. There were crocus blooms shooting up everywhere, and the dogwood's buds were opening. It was cold of a morning but warm in the afternoon, which was good weather for traveling. For the past few weeks we had moved along without any problems. I felt we were making good time but still had a great many miles to cover before we reached Independence.

Often now I got off the wagon while Sara drove, and I enjoyed the time on horseback. Sara was doing well at driving the wagon. Today she was using Rowdy and Randy. Bessie sat beside her. Becky was just ahead of us. I was riding close by just in case Rowdy acted up. I was feeling pretty satisfied when old Rowdy came to a bucking stop. Sara flicked the reins and yelled at him, but he wouldn't budge.

"What's wrong with him, Martha?" Sara asked.

"Damn it! Now what?" I moved up close to Rowdy. "What is it, old fella? You're bein' a stubborn jackass."

I checked his hoof, and the shoe was loose. I shook my head. "Just what we needed."

I dismounted and went to unhitch him. He began to throw his head and kick. "Whoa, you damn mule," I cussed.

Becky came trottin' back and jumped off her mule. "Watch him! He'll bite you!" she yelled.

"Don't I know it?" I said. He was tossing his head, kicking and jumping, which upset Randy, and Tag's barking added to the uproar.

I was trying to get Rowdy to stand. Becky grabbed hold of his bridle. "Stand still, you son of dog-eared cur!" she muttered.

We were having a free for all when a buckboard pulled up beside us. "Howdy. Need a hand with those mules?"

I turned my head to see who was talking, and Rowdy swerved, hitting me with his shoulder. He knocked me to the ground. As I rolled away to keep from being stepped on, Becky slugged him, and yelling cuss words I'd never heard before.

"Let me," the woman in the buckboard said, jumping down. She walked up to his head and began talking to him in a low voice. "Whoa, big boy, settle down. I'll help you."

Becky and I watched in amazement as that ornery old mule settled right down. She adjusted his headgear, scratched his ears, and talked to him like he was a little baby. "You aren't hurt, are you?" she asked in a caring voice.

"No, I'm fine," I said, getting up and brushing myself off. Then I realized she meant Rowdy. Becky looked at me and grinned. I shrugged my shoulders. "Thanks for your help, ma'am. While he's settled down, let's take his rig off. I'm Martha Patterson. This is Becky, Sara, and Bessie in the wagon. That ornery mule you met is Rowdy. He bites, kicks, shoves, pin you to the walls, stomps your feet, and anything else he can come up with, including slapping your face with his tail."

"Sounds like a real smart mule. I'm Hattie Brown. Pleased to meet you all." We shook hands. I wasn't sure who had the most calluses. "Your mule's got a loose shoe," she said, lifting his foot. Hand me a nail puller. Whoever put this shoe on did a poor job."

"Watch him. He bites," I warned. Rowdy leaned against her, gentle as a kitten just to prove me wrong.

"I have an understanding with mules. They don't hurt me, and I don't hurt them." She laughed. "I really do have a soft spot for mules."

"Since we have to change teams, how 'bout we break for lunch?" I asked, looking up at Sara and Bessie.

They nodded in agreement.

"Good idea," Becky said. "I sure am hungry."

> **Comment [CJH]:** We never learn why Hattie was here instead of in Oregon. What had she left home for? See note below.

"Would you please join us?" I smiled at Hattie, thinking she seemed quite a bit older than us. Her skin was sun-browned, but she had nice teeth and a warm smile. The twinkle in her brown eyes made me think of Pa.

"I'll unhitch Randy and tether the animals over here by the trees," Becky said.

"Good. We'll have to leave the wagon on the road while we have lunch," I said. "Don't suppose it will be in the way."

"I believe you're right," Hattie said. "You're the only travelers I've seen in days," she said, leading her horse off the road. "I'll just put this rig over by your horses." She smiled, walking back to our wagon. "Lunch sounds real invitin'. It's been awhile since I had company. Besides, I'd be interested to find out what you girls are doing out here without men folks."

CHAPTER NINE

I gathered firewood, Becky and Sara spread a blanket, and Bessie got the food basket and made the coffee. Hattie walked over from her buckboard with a hunk of cheese. We all found a comfortable spot to relax for lunch.

"If you don't mind me asking, where are you girls going?" Hattie asked.

I had just taken a large bite and couldn't answer right away.

"And why aren't you using your full team?" She continued. "You'd make better time."

I swallowed and explained, "We're going to Independence, Missouri, to join a wagon train to Oregon. The reason I'm not using a four-up is because I don't have rigging for them, and the fact is I've never driven a four-up."

"Hell, woman, you say you're going to Oregon? I'm heading home myself. I have a ranch there. You're going to need to learn a lot to get there alive. Glory be, I know more about mules than any man alive. Let me join up with you, and I'll do the driving." She snorted. "And I'll teach you about the trail, teach you how to load and supply your wagon, and tend to the mules. I'll pay my way. What do you think?"

"Well, it sounds good to me," I said. "You girls want to talk about this in private?" I looked at each of them as they shook their heads no.

"As far as I'm concerned, I'd much rather have a woman than a man," Sara offered. "And with her traveling with us, you can take your wagon to Oregon."

"Yes'um. Y'all have a man and he'll be wantin' to...unh unh." Bessie murmured. "Y'all know what I mean."

Wanda Reed

Becky laughed. "She's right, Martha. I vote for Hattie."

"So, it's agreed." I held out my hand. "Welcome aboard, Hattie."

"Thank you. You won't be sorry. I can be a big help. I'll go all the way to Oregon with you. I've got a ranch and a son there, and I been wantin' to get back. Oh yes, and any time you want me to leave, just say the word and I'll leave."

> **Comment [CJH]:** This would be a good place for Hattie to explain why she is in the East.

"All the way to Oregon! I'd be real pleased to have you, Hattie," I said. I paused and remembered what Homey had said: 'The Lord will surely bless you,' and now He surely has with all these new friends.

She looked at each of us, as if to take our measure. Finishing her coffee, she looked at me and gave me a level stare and asked, "How much do you know about travelin' to Oregon or even to Independence?"

"Just what I read in the paper," I said. "The meeting place is Independence, and the wagons leave in May or June."

"I'll tell you, it's a big challenge to undertake. Do you know it's over five hundred miles to Missouri?"

"That's what a storekeeper in Brayville said—between five and seven hundred miles!" Becky said, reaching for another piece of cheese.

"Right! You have to go across Kentucky, parts of Illinois, and all of Missouri. You got to be in Independence by the first of May or June at the latest to get on a wagon train. We will try for May. You should be there a week or two before to get your wagon in shape and get supplies." She paused and took a deep breath and then continued, "Oregon's another two thousand miles."

"Mercy me, I don't even want to think about that yet," I sighed. "Just getting to Independence is all I can manage right now." I shook my head. "And there's the war and thieves. I got to take my fillies to Oregon."

"You're right to be concerned about your fillies. The South is hurting bad, real bad, running out of supplies. Those Rebs see you young women, they'd take your wagon, mules, horses, and no telling what they would do to you girls."

Hattie picked up the coffeepot and refilled her enamel coffee cup.

"They won't take anything of mine without getting a load of buckshot. How long does it take to get to Oregon? And how soon will my fillies are out of danger?" I asked.

"Well from Independence, it's about five months to Oregon if everything goes well. The fillies…" she frowned. "There are border ruffians in Kansas and Missouri, but once you reach Independence, they should be pretty safe. But, of course, there are the Indians once you head for Oregon."

"Indians?" Bessie's eyes opened wide.

Sara asked. "Oh, Martha, are you certain you want to continue on to Oregon? It sounds so perilous."

"Yes, Sara, I'm sure. I'm not afraid." I smiled at Hattie. "Besides, I'll have Hattie, and she's not afraid of anything, are you, Hattie?"

"Yes, I am afraid, but that's not going to stop me from living my life." She looked at us and said, "Any of you girls goin' to Oregon with her?"

"I'm going to Missouri," said Sara. "I have a brother there. The South holds nothing for me. It's all gone dead and burned to ashes."

"Ah wanna be free," Bessie volunteered. "Ah jes wanna go anywhere away from the Souf, soz I stays free. Maybe that Independence place, Ah be free. Ah can stay there near Sara."

"Don't matter where I go," Becky stated firmly. "I got nobody nowhere, so I'll stick with Martha and go to Oregon."

"So that will be three of us going all the way. Well, you could do a lot worse than Oregon," Hattie said, "but you have to be real certain if you do decide on Oregon. Be prepared for a long hard pull that will make the one to Independence seem like a piece of sweet potato pie. It takes hard work, determination, and luck. Think hard about it between here and Independence."

"Hattie, since you been over the trail, tell us what its like," I said picking up a water bucket from the horses and carrying it back to the wagon to break camp.

"Well, before my husband died, we ran a freight line from Independence to Fort Bridger. That's in the southwest corner of Wyoming territory. It was long, dirty, hot, freezin' back-hard work ever mile of the way." She shook her head and added, "It's none of my business, and it ain't polite, but how is this outfit fixed for money?"

I met Hattie's eyes and replied, "We have enough. We share expenses." I recalled Pa's advice. Rule number one: Never tell a stranger the size of your poke.

"Now look, ladies, if we're going to be partners, we have to trust each other." Hattie looked at each of us. "I have enough in my poke to take us all to Oregon. If you girls are broke, say so." After a quiet pause she said, "How about a little trust?"

"You're right, Hattie," I agreed, holding out my hand to meet hers to shake. "We each have enough to pay our share. We put an equal amount in a jar and use it for supplies." I smiled as we shook hands. "We're just a little shy about talkin' money. We don't aim to get robbed."

"You're smart there. It's not a thing you tell just anyone."

"Ain't nobody gonna rob us," Becky said. "The last fella' that tried it got my pig sticker in his gut. If you two are done jawin', could we get going?"

"Yes, Becky, we're through. Load up, and let's get going," I agreed.

"Hattie, could you learn us what to do?" Becky grabbed a slice of cheese and two biscuits from the food basket before Sara could put it away.

"Probably," Hattie said. "I think we can make it from the spunk of this outfit." She climbed into her wagon. "Starting to mist up. Let's get along. We'll talk more tonight in camp. Hey, Becky, would you ride with me? We can talk, and you can drive."

"Sure, be glad to. First I have to help Martha hitch up." She threw one biscuit to Tag, who had been waiting patiently for scraps.

"It sure does smell like rain," Sara remarked, sniffing the air.

"Let's stop at Hillsdale up ahead for the night and get the mules reshod before they all go lame," Hattie suggested. "They all need a heavy shoe."

"That's right, Hattie, Hillsdale's right outside Louisville. That bein' a racehorse town, we'd never get through with our horses. We will have to go in a back way and keep the horses hid. They'd be confiscated so fast, we wouldn't know what hit us." I shuddered to think of losing my fillies. As we hitched the mules to the wagon, Sara climbed inside. Bessie was just coming out of the woods.

I climbed into the wagon, taking up the reins and giving Bessie a hand up beside me. There was a light mist of rain, just enough to settle the dust and clean the air.

It was mid-afternoon when we arrived in Hillsdale. We skirted the main street, went down the back road through the alley behind the outhouses, and went out the far end of town. We stopped the wagon near the woods in back of the blacksmith's shed and quickly moved the fillies back into a grove of trees.

I walked with Hattie to the blacksmith's shop. "Mister," she said, "Could I get you to shoe these four mules with freight-hauling shoes."

"Ma'am, let me check their hooves and frogs. I'll get right to it. How do you call this one?"

"That's Rowdy. He's temperamental."

"Mean, you say," the man replied. "Ma'am, he needs a special shoe with a cross bar to build up the left inside of his hoof. With this shoe, he'll be able to walk better. I can have it done midmorning tomorrow. I have to check them all. That will be cash when you pick them up."

"That'll be fine," I answered.

While Sara and Bessie set up camp, Hattie and me unloaded her buckboard and drove to the livery. I listen while she bartered with the owner and finally got one riding horse, harness for the mules, and a bit of coin. We returned to camp hoping they had made coffee. The coffee was good and hot.

"Well, guess you gals are stuck with me now," she said, grinning. "I got no place else to rest my weary bones." We all laughed and Sara said, "I hope you don't snore."

Becky went to the livery and bought a bale of hay for the stock. Hattie checked the wagon and found several things to fix. We unloaded everything, got some boards from the blacksmith, and patched the floorboards and sideboards. We greased the wheels, and she insisted we brush the wood with tar-pitch to make it waterproof.

"I believe in teachin' by doin'," she explained, as we all worked with her. "This here wagon's gonna be our home all the way to Oregon. We best make damn sure it's in as good a shape as we can make it. It's a wonder you girls didn't break a leg with some of those rotten boards."

"Can you use these for somethin'?" Becky asked, pointing to the bundle of hides tied to the side of the wagon.

Hattie undid them, looked them over, and nodded. "Yeah, we can stretch them over the floor and the seat of the wagon. Peg 'em down so's they don't slide around." She chuckled. "They'll keep the splinters outta your bottom sides."

"Now, why didn't we think of that?" Sara asked, raising her eyebrows.

"Well, that's what you got me for," Hattie retorted, reaching for a cup of the coffee Bessie had just made. "Good coffee."

"Thanks. Guess ah's good for sumpin," she grinned.

I laughed "Bessie ,you're our cook. We couldn't make it without you. You know an outfit travels on its belly."

"Speaking of that, I finished mending your skirt, Bessie," Sara said.

"I'm sure Hattie has more to teach us." I wondered what my contribution was, other than the desire and the wagon to go west.

"You're right," Hattie said. "We gotta go over this used harness with saddle soap so it's waterproof. We gotta keep the equipment in top shape," she said. "I've been a muleskinner for many years and found the equipment is what counts." She paused and took a deep breath. "Since I'm the only one who can drive a four-up, I'll do the drivin'." She frowned. "But you're all gonna have to learn to drive. You never know when you'll need to."

"You are an answer to a prayer, Hattie. I love you already." I put my arm around her waist. "We'll

Wanda Reed

trade off driving if you'll teach me how to keep the doggone lines straight."

"It's not hard. You can do it. A four-up is no problem. We'll need a six-up most of the time." she said. "It just takes a little practice. You'll all learn or walk or ride a horse. When the wagon gets loaded, we won't want the extra weight of riders."

"I say we head out for town now. What do you all think?" I asked.

"Good idea," Sara said. "I'll get my bonnet."

"Oh, you and that bonnet," Becky teased, pulling her slouchy hat over her red hair.

"Well, I have to protect my skin, you know?"

" Y'all need mah skin, Missy," Bessie laughed. "I sho' don't has to worry 'bout burnin'. I jes' use my hat to keep that big old sun outta my eyes."

At the general store, Sara and Bessie picked out food supplies.

"Don't forget the cotton cloth. Get a whole bolt," I reminded them. Everyone was piling things on the counter. Sara pick out a McGuffey reader, slates, and chalk for teaching Becky and Bessie to read and write. Bessie bought two dresses and some personal things for herself as she only had what she was wearing.

I steered Becky toward the ready-made clothes and told her to choose two outfits. I had already bought soap and a towel to give her, hoping she would use them and not be offended. I didn't want to say so, but she smelled bad.

"I don't need any clothes right now but maybe for later. I'll take the green shirt and the brown one and two pair trousers."

I picked two blue shirts, two pairs of trousers, and a dozen pairs of wool socks. When I went to pay, Becky stopped me. "I can pay for mine," she said, pulling me back to an area of the store where no one else was. She took out a large gold poke and took out a nugget the size of a jaw tooth. "Don't tell

> **Comment [CJH]:** I just checked, and jeans were invented in 1873, so I'm changing it to trousers per some research. Also, while ready-made underwear and jackets were available for men by this time, I can't find evidence that pants were available ready-made other than uniforms, which started during the Civil War. This comes up several times. I'm not sure if it's worth changing for accuracy or not. Your call.

anyone I have this," she whispered, clutching the poke.

"I'll pay this time," I whispered back. "Later we'll take a couple small ones and swap them for coin. It's not safe to show that. Put it away."

The others were busy. Sara and Bessie were looking at bonnets, Hattie was trying on boots, and Becky and I walked to the bank to exchange three gold nuggets. The teller peered over his spectacles, "Where'd you girls get these?"

I looked at Becky and winked. "They're gratuity from a couple of old miners we met," I smiled sweetly. The teller turned red and shut up. We walked away laughing.

It was late afternoon when we returned to the campsite loaded down with packages. Dropping them to the ground, we slumped down beside them.

"Ah'll make us sumpin' ta eat," Bessie said.

"Not tonight, Bessie. I have a better idea." I got up and started rummaging through the packages. "Let's all go to the creek and wash up, put on our new duds, and go out for dinner. I noticed a nice looking inn near the bank."

"Don't you think we should reload the wagon first?" Hattie asked. "The tar-pitch has dried, and it will be after dark when we get back. It won't take us long if we work together."

There was a collective sigh from the rest of us. "She's right, girls," I said. "C'mon, let's do it. Becky grabbed a trunk." We were loaded in record time, following Hattie's directions to equalize the weight and make it workable for the girls to fix food.

"If you have valuables, there's a couple of hiding places on the wagon. I'll show you where they are," I said. "Just put your treasure in a poke and mark it."

"It must be well hidden for me not to have found it while putting on the tar-pitch," said Hattie.

"Here is mine," said Becky. "Now I got coins, I won't have to tote my gold. Sara, will you write my name on my poke?"

"Certainly, Becky," Sara smiled. "It won't be long until you'll be writing your name yourself."

"Okay, let's head for the creek. I'm ready for a bath, "How about you, Becky?" I called out.

"Naw, I don't think I will. Too much bathin' ain't good for the skin."

I looked at Sara and raised my eyebrows then winked.

"Well, why don't you come with us and be our lookout?" Sara said, winking at me.

"Yeah, we don't want no man sneakin' up on us," Hattie chimed in.

"Does y'all want me ta come?" Bessie asked.

"Of course, Bessie. That black don't wash off," I said, grinning so she'd know I was just teasing.

We grabbed up towels and soap and headed for the creek, which was just a short ways through the woods. Tag ran ahead, barking at us to hurry.

"Last one in's a cow's tail," I yelled. Tag jumped around barking and then ran into the creek.

Becky watching as the rest of us stripped off our clothes and jumped in the clear, cold water.

"Damn!" Hattie complained. "You could freeze your fanny off."

"Don't you want to join us, Becky?" Sara asked.

"Naw, too much water rots the skin." She stepped back further from the creek. She picked up a stick and threw it. Tag jumped in the water after it. "I'll just play with Tag."

"I think she'd really enjoy it once she got in, don't you?" I said, moving towards the bank.

"Yes, I think she would," Sara agreed. I looked at her. She nodded. I glanced over at Hattie and Bessie. They nodded.

"Are y'all gettin' out already?" Bessie asked.

"Gotta go pee," I said.

"Me, too." Sara climbed up on the bank.

"Wait, I'll go with you," Hattie said.

"Y'all ain't gonna leave me here by myse'f?" Bessie protested.

"Oh, come on then." I held out my hand and pulled her up on the bank.

The four of us circled Becky, who seemed unaware of our motives.

"Now!" I yelled. Before she could get away, we grabbed her. Sara, Bessie, Hattie, and me together half-dragged her and half-carried her to the edge of the creek. "Let me go," she yelled, twisting her body back and forth, trying to escape. "Damn you! Let me go! I don't need no bath!"

"Oh, yes you do," we said. "One, two, three, heave!"

She landed in the creek with a big splash and a torrent of dirty words. Laughing, we all jumped in after her, forming a circle so she couldn't get out.

"You take those clothes off, Becky. Then we can really give you a good scrubbin'," Hattie said. "You smell worse than a dead skunk," reaching under the water to pull off Becky's boots. She got hold of one and gave it a good tug, which caused Becky to fall back in the water. She came up sputtering.

Becky began to laugh. "Okay, y'all win. I ain't gonna fight."

"Washin' washin' in the River Jordan, washin' all my sins away," Bessie sang out in a loud voice. We all joined in and danced in the water as if we had lost our senses.

"Shit," Becky groaned. "What am I gonna wear back? My clothes and boots are wet."

"Don't worry about it," I said. "I brought you clothes and some leather slippers. And maybe we should check your boots. You may need a new pair."

"Anyway those are good boots. I took them off that man I stuck. He didn't need them no more. You mean you planned this?" She splashed water at me, but she didn't sound angry.

"Well, Becky, you gave us no choice," I grinned. "You smelled like you rolled on a dead polecat. I can't imagine what it would have been like by the time we reached Oregon."

"Can I get out now? My skin's startin' to shrink."

"We better get out. We're starting to look like dried prunes," I agreed.

"I'm starvin', "Hattie said, climbing out. She held out a hand for the rest of us.

"Looks like you was right—that black don't wash off. That's good. Ah kinda like that color," Bessie grinned. "Don't know what color ah be iffen it did."

"Do you think the town of Hillsdale is ready for some fine-looking fillies? And I don't mean horses," I stuttered, my teeth chattering with the cold.

"I don't know, but I'm havin' somethin' hot and a whole lot of it," Becky stated, drying herself vigorously.

"I'll race you all back to the wagon," I challenged, pulling on my clothes. I paused, looking at my new friends. "This has been the most fun I've had in a long while," I said.

"I'm sho' glad I got these new clothes," Bessie expressed.

"Well, we're clean," Hattie said, pulling on her leather vest.

"These here clothes fit good," Becky said. She smoothed the new britches over her narrow hips.

Well ladies, let's head for the inn and show 'em what ladies we are."

Hillsdale wasn't impressed with us. We were refused service at the inn unless Bessie ate in the kitchen. After a discussion between Hattie and the owner, realizing the amount of cash we would spend, he agreed to let Bessie eat at the table. We were his only customers. We weren't impressed with the Hillsdale inn either. The food was skimpy, and the service left a lot to be desired. When our food finally arrived, we had to order two more plates of meat and potatoes to have a complete meal. I was glad Becky had left her rifle in the wagon because she really got riled.

"Who do they think they are, anyways? Good enough to work for 'em but not good enough to eat with. And they charge high prices for half a damn meal. That's a miserable place."

"You're right, Becky."

"Why, for a nickel I'd bust that place up good."

"You don't go busting up anything," Hattie roared.

"Amen," Bessie said softly.

Wanda Reed

CHAPTER TEN

Tag's agitated barking woke us before dawn.

"What is it, Tag?" I whispered.

"There's somethin' goin' over at the blacksmith's," Becky said, crawling up beside me with her rifle in hand.

"Sounds like some fellow's yelling," Hattie offered from her bedroll. "Best keep out of it."

"I don't go for no man mistreatin' a woman," Becky growled, as she stood taking a few steps closer to the blacksmith's.

Curious, I followed, holding Tag's collar. Hattie was right. A woman and a man were arguing loudly. I watched as he pulled her roughly from her horse and slapped her across the face. "No, Harvey." She cried out and held her hands up defensively.

"Think you can run out on me? You can't do nothin' without me finding out," he shouted. "You owe me, and you don't go nowhere 'til I'm paid."

We stared in horror as he knocked her down and dragged her by the legs towards his horse, causing her bottom to bounce on the gravel.

"You dirty bastard, Harvey! Let me go. I don't owe you nothin'," she yelled, crying out with each bump.

"Stay put," Hattie said. She had come up behind us. "Don't get involved. You'll get yourselves killed."

"But, Hattie, we should do something to help her," I protested.

"It's none of our business. She's either his woman or his wife. It's up to him how he treats her."

We stayed silent in our hiding place as he grabbed her arm and yanked her to her feet. She was sobbing and cursing at the same time. Neither one seemed to know we were watching.

Comment [CJH]: This seems out of character for Hattie.

Six Women West

"You see why I dress like a boy," Becky whispered. "No son of a bitch is goin' t'do that to me. Or use me or sell me. Men are all bastards."

"There is nothing we can do. Girls, I don't like it, but maybe she'll get away one of these days." Hattie stated firmly, "So, let's get busy and get the coffee started and breakfast cooked and get out of this God-forsaken town."

"That po' gal," Bessie said. "Ah sho' does feel sorry fo' her. Ah know what she goin' through. He be sellin' her body."

"Yes," Sara agreed. "So do I, but Martha's right. You make the coffee. I'll make mix the biscuits," she said softly.

As we walked away, I glanced back over my shoulder. The man was shoving the woman down the road, holding her arm behind her. She was sobbing, but no longer struggling. Apparently, she had given up the fight. I wondered what would happen to her.

"Come on, Becky, we'll pick up some firewood," I said, trying to get my mind off that woman.

"Martha, we need a big breakfast after that skimpy dinner," said Becky. "My belly's been complainin' all night. I'll go shopping for some meat."

"Good idea. Maybe you can get enough for a few days." I gathered some wood for Bessie and Sara to start fixing breakfast.

"Coffee be ready right quick," Bessie offered.

Becky rode up, handing Bessie a large piece of pork she said the storekeeper had just butchered.

Hattie was busy greasing the wheels on the wagon. I walked over to help.

"Martha," she said, "I'd like to leave as soon as the mules are ready. We'll walk over and pick up the ones that are done after breakfast. We have a long way to go. I'd like to get the wagon finished."

"But, we're goanna eat first, right?" Becky asked, filling her plate with fried potatoes and fried pork chops. She grabbed a couple of biscuits and sat down on a log to eat it.

The rest of us laughed and joined her for breakfast.

Hattie brought three mules back and said it'd be another hour for Rowdy. He broke Rowdy's shoe.

I curried and brushed my horses and the mules that were finished. Hattie cleaned tack, passing the time while we waited. Sara used the time to teach Bessie and Becky their lessons.

It was toward noon when Rowdy was finished. Hattie was paying the blacksmith. "These should get you to Missouri without any trouble," he said, adding, "Sure you gals can handle the trip without a man to come along?"

"We're sure," she answered. Hattie brought Rowdy back to the wagon. Who's the lead mule of this team Martha?"

"Randy, I guess. He's the steady one. He's the one Pa used." As we started placing them in order, Rowdy put up his usual fuss of bucking, shying, braying, and generally being a pain in the butt.

"Let's try putting Rowdy in the lead. He's unhappy over something," Hattie suggested, holding his head and talking to him while moving him over to the left side of the wagon. He settled down and allowed us to put him in harness without a fuss.

Hattie laughed. "A full four-up. Now that's more like it. Rowdy wants to be the boss mule." Tying the extra horses on back, we were ready to head out. Hattie, Sara, and Bessie rode in the wagon while Becky and me rode horseback.

Hattie called "Yo, Rowdy!" cracking her whip over his head. Yo! Rowdy boy, show me your stuff." We moved at a lively pace, covering twelve miles by late afternoon. Along the way, we could see ruins, evidence of the war. There were burned homes and

Six Women West

trampled fields of crops. Wooden crosses dotted the countryside, testimonials to fallen soldiers. Toward evening, Becky scouted ahead and found an abandoned farm. The house was deserted, and there were several graves near by. "A house to sleep in," said Sara. What a great find. Too bad we can't stay awhile."

"No Sara. No one is to go near that house. Hear me? No one go near that house," warned Hattie, knowing well what would be found in the house. "We'll sleep in the barn with the stock. We don't want nobody stealing them." The barn was filled with plenty of hay, which would be handy for sleeping and for feeding the stock. "A good place to spend the night," Hattie said.

Together we unhitched the mules and turned them and the horses into the corral and tossed them several armloads of hay. Near dark, we put the horses in the barn for safety's sake.

I looked around and Sara was missing. *Oh, no*, I thought, and I ran to the house. She was walking around staring.

"Oh, it's a terrible mess. Look, everything has been torn up or broke," she cried. "How could they do that to someone's home? There's blood all over. People have been killed in here."

"Come on, Sara. Hattie said not to come in here. Let's go to the barn. You have to learn this is war, not games. There might have been dead bodies. Or a hiding deserter."

We returned to the barn, and Hattie stared at Sara and said, "Little lady, did you find what you wanted to know?"

Sara broke down in tears.

Bessie made a pot of ham and beans for supper and brought out the sourdough bread. We sat around the campfire awhile, discussing tomorrow's plans, and then turned in early. It had been a long day with many more to follow if we were to reach Missouri in time to join up with a train.

We were up at the crack of dawn. The air was clear and crisp with a heavy frost. We broke ice on the water buckets, and the horses blew silvery puffs of breath in the cold air. We threw the stock more hay. Hattie dug out a cotton sack, and we filled it with hay to take and put several armfuls more in the wagon. It looked like it would be a nice day. After a breakfast of ham, biscuits, and coffee we made ready to pull out.

"Come on, Martha," Hattie said. "Today you learn to drive a four-up. Bessie, you ride my horse."

"Okay," I said, climbing up on the wagon. She handed me the lines.

"Just hold them steady. Keep a light touch," urged Hattie. See how gentle Rowdy is now he's where he belongs? He has to be lead mule."

"Hey, this isn't so hard," I said, as we moved at a fast clip down a straight narrow road. "Not much difference than just a pair."

"Yeah, well, let's see how you do when you hit some curves or mountain stretches," Hattie grinned. "These mules might decide they don't wanna go. That's when you find out how good a driver you are."

"No," I corrected, laughing. "That's when I give them back to you."

Martha, that's a good day. We covered about seventeen miles with daylight left," said Hattie.

"I am tired, but I feel pretty good about what I'd accomplished."

Becky said, "I'm going to ride ahead to find a campsite." Tag ran close by.

"Hopefully, she'll find somewhere to make camp in the next hour," I said.

"Good. I'm tired and I know you must be, Martha," Sara said, "Riding that horse 'til noon liked to have killed me. How do you do it, Hattie?"

"Got used to it," she replied. "You won't hold your muscles so tight after awhile."

"We get to camp, ah can fix you some special tea. It makes you feel real easy," Bessie volunteered. "Ah'm goin' to have some after ridin' that horse. I may just sit my fanny in the creek—if there is a creek."

"I'll pass on that special tea. I had some special tea once," I said. "You and Sara need to get used to riding. Sometimes you won't be able to be in the wagon."

"What you going to do, Bessie? Stay in Independence or go on west?" asked Hattie, changing the subject. "You know that Missouri is a border state. They still take back slaves if they catch them."

"Ah don't rightly know. I kin stay with Miss Martha if she'll have me. Ah reckoned ah'll clean or cook fo her, ah spoze. Don't take much fo' me. Jes soze ah don't hafta sell my body no mo."

"Here, Hattie, I gotta make a trip to the brush," I interrupted, handing her the lines.

"Okay, that's enough for today anyway. Go catch Becky. Maybe you two can scare up a rabbit for dinner. Oh, by the way, you done real good," said Hattie.

"Thanks. See you later." I crawled out the back of the wagon and mounted Gray Lady.

"Hey, Martha," yelled Becky, riding up to the wagon. "Where you goin'?"

"I'm going to the brush and then huntin'. You wanna come?" I yelled back. "You find a place to camp?"

"Yeah, I'll tell you about it when you finish answerin' nature's call."

Hattie had stopped to give the mules a breather when I returned, and Becky said, "I left a chunk of wood in the road. Go to the left."

We set up a watch on a small meadow. Soon three deer wandered in. Becky shot a four-point buck. We dragged it close to a tree, looped the back legs with a rope, and hoisted it up on a limb to dress it out. Becky sliced the head open and took out the brains, rolled them in a piece of leather, and put them in her pack.

"You're not planning on us eating them, are you?" I asked, shuddering at the thought.

"Hell, no," Becky laughed. "These are for curin' the hide."

"Curing the hide?" I felt stupid asking, but I didn't remember Pa doing anything like that.

"Yeah, it's how the Indians do it. They mix the brains with ashes and then smear it on the hide." Together, we tied the carcass on Becky's mule. "You never cease to amaze me, Rebecca O'Brien," I said sincerely. "Let's get it to camp."

Camp was set up, and the coffee had been made. "We brought supper," I said, as we rode into camp.

"Great," Hattie said, helping us unload the deer. "Better get this up out of the way of Tag and other varmints."

"Who you callin' a varmint?" I asked, laughing and hugging Tag, who was jumping and barking. I didn't know if his joy was because of the deer or me. I believe it was the deer.

Hattie, Becky, and me managed to get the deer strung up in a nearby tree. Becky whacked off the antlers, and then the entire head she threw to Tag. He tackled it and dragged it off to the brush with his tail wagging.

We skinned it out and sawed off the hindquarter, and Bessie with Sara's help took the hindquarter, forced a rod through the meat, and placed it over the fire. "It'll be awhile 'afore it's ready," Bessie told us. I guess we better cut up some smaller chunks for supper."

"Good idea if we want to eat tonight," Hattie scolded.

"That's okay," Becky said. "I want to show you how to work this hide so it's soft. Like the Indians do it." She made a frame out of some dry branches and tied the skin to the frame. We watched, making faces, as she mixed up the brains with ashes and smeared it on the hide, working it in. Afterwards she scraped it off. "It has to be done again," she said, again smearing the brain mixture on the hide. She sighed. "When I'm finished, it'll be real soft, and Sara can make a shirt."

I marveled at Becky's skill and watched closely as she worked. "Would you teach me to cure hides?" I asked.

"Sure, you can do the next scraping."

"We've got meat to cut and jerk and smoke the rest," Hattie said. "Come on you two, help me fix up a smoke tent, and by the time we leave in the morning, it'll be dried. It'll be dark before that chunk of meat you're trying to cook is ready. I think you better cut it into two pieces."

During the following week Hattie taught each of us drive. Sara and Bessie did their best. My size and Becky's were of benefit to us.

"There's nothin' to it," Hattie said, "and you need to learn in case one of us ain't around. You two are doing a pretty fair job."

Using four mules we moved at a good pace, making fifteen to twenty miles a day—a big difference—and our wagon wasn't loaded heavy.

One late afternoon, Becky was off hunting and I was riding behind the wagon when a rider overtook us, slowing down to ride beside me. I recognized the woman from the fracas at the stable.

"Would you mind if I rode with you a ways?" she asked, sounding very tired.

"Fine!" I glanced at her, noticing the old bruises on her face. "Think he'll follow you?"

She reached up and touched her cheek. "What do you mean?"

"My friends and I were camped behind the blacksmith's back in Hillsdale. We overheard the fight." I looked away, still feeling ashamed at not coming to her aid.

"I hope he doesn't." She lowered her eyes, looking embarrassed. "I've run as far as I'm going to," she sighed deeply. "I don't owe him anything, and he doesn't own me."

"Glad you got away. How'd you do it? I mean get away?" I ventured to ask.

"I used a little sex and a lot of sleepin' powders," she snickered. "If he follows, I'll shoot the bastard. He's not going to make me whore for him or use me for a punching bag ever again," she declared bitterly. I hope he's dead.

"Well, I can't say I blame you, but I hope you don't have to shoot him," I said, thinking of Abner. "My name is Martha. What's yours?"

"Charlotte Taylor. Friends call me Charlie."

"Glad to meet you, Charlie," I said, "Where you headed?"

"I don't know. I've just been running. I haven't stopped long enough to make plans. The only time I stopped was to go into town for some beef jerky. Been living on it for a week now."

"Well, this wagon's headed for Oregon by way of Missouri. You can ride along."

"Thanks. I really appreciate the offer. I'd be real pleased to ride with you for awhile. I don't want to bring no trouble on you."

"If there's trouble, we can handle it. You'll fit right in. Come on," I nudged Gray Lady. "You can put your bag in the wagon." We rode up to the tailgate and threw in the bag.

"To the front," Hattie yelled.

"Better see what she wants," I said, urging Lady forward. "Come on. She's our wagon boss."

We rode up closer to the wagon. "Yes, Hattie. What d'ya need?" I asked.

"If memory serves me right, there's a creek over yonder." She pointed to the left side of the road. "Ride over there and look for a place to camp for the night. I'd like to set up camp afore too long."

"Okay, Hattie." I turned to Charlie. "This is Charlie. She's going to ride with us for awhile. This is Hattie. Like I said, she's our wagon boss."

"Hi, Charlie, glad your here," Hattie responded. She grinned at me. "When did I get promoted?"

Charlie and I rode ahead and scouted a campsite about a quarter mile off the road. We were gone about twenty minutes. Returning to the wagon, we met Becky.

There's a small creek where we're going to camp tonight." I nodded toward Charlie. "This is Charlie. She's joining us."

"Aren't you the gal from the smithies?" Becky asked, not showing any tact. She stuck out her hand. "I'm Becky. Glad to see you got away from that bastard." She grinned. "I was all set to put a bullet in him, but they wouldn't let me."

"Follow us," I interrupted. "We'll clear the trail for the wagon. There's a lot of underbrush. The trail hasn't been used in awhile. If that wagon gets stuck, we'll never get to Missouri." With the three horses we tromped the high weeds and pulled the downed trees off to the side. It wasn't smooth, but we would be able to get the wagon through.

Becky and I rode back to the wagon to give Sara and Bessie a ride. The road was rough and full of ruts. Hattie was braced securely, grasping the reins tightly. I was glad she was doing the driving. I had an idea this was one of the times she'd cautioned us about.

The campsite was about a quarter mile in from the road. There was plenty of grass for the stock, water for washing, and trees for shelter and privacy.

Hattie brought the wagon to a halt. Joining together, we stripped the rig off the mules. We turned them out to graze. They wouldn't go far. They were tired, the grass was belly-deep, and the water was cool and fresh. Tag was off and running to catch anything he could.

I introduced Charlie to Sara and Bessie who, always the ladies, made no mention of when we had first seen her.

"Can we stay here a couple of days?" Sara asked. "We've got washing to do, and I think we all could use some rest."

"What do you think, Hattie? After all, you're the wagon boss."

"I think we stay today and tomorrow. There are things we need to talk about." She paused. "It's a long ways to Oregon, and there's a lot you need to learn to get there alive."

"Sounds good to me," Charlie said. "I know I'm just a newcomer, but I'm dog tired and my horse is all wore' out. I've been riding hard, and he needs a rest."

"I think we all agreed," I said. "Here we stay."

"I got to tend to my horse," Charlie said.

She was obviously tired, but she gave her horse a good rubdown. When I gave our horses grain, I scooped her out a large measure for hers. Pa had often said a man who took care of his horse was a good man, and I respected her for that. I guessed that applied to a woman as well.

Bessie had built a fire, and the smell of coffee soon filled the air. We each took a tin cup, thanking Bessie for the coffee.

Charlie said, "I thought I'd try a hand at fishing. That's a nice-looking creek. Think there's fish in it?"

"You could try," Sara said. "We've got a pole and a line in the wagon. Nothing fancy, but it works."

"I'll go with you, Charlie," Hattie said. "Maybe I'll soak my feet, too."

Becky grabbed my shotgun, called to Tag, and the two of them took off for the woods, leaving Sara, Bessie, and me in camp.

When the three women were out of sight, Sara turned to me. "Charlie is the girl we saw at the blacksmiths, isn't she?"

"Yes. She told me she's running away from that fellow." I poked at the fire. "I didn't ask questions. I reckon she'll tell us when she's ready."

"Let's hurry and get this washing done so we can rest," Sara said.

About an hour later, Becky showed up. "Not only did I have to get the duck," she said, "but I had to shoot Tag his dinner too." Smiling broadly, Tag returned with a rabbit dangled from his mouth.

Charlie and Hattie walked up a few minutes later, proudly displaying a string of trout.

After a supper of fish and fowl, we settled around the campfire, relaxing and talking.

"Now would be a good time for that talkin' you mentioned, Hattie," I said.

"Right." Hattie nodded. "I believe you'll all agree you need help with the basics of wagon travel."

We nodded in agreement. "We look to you, Hattie, for advice and direction." I looked at her. "I meant it when I called you the wagon boss. Someone has to lead, and you're most qualified. Tell us what to do."

"We need to figure what each one can do best. If we work out a routine, setting up camp and doin' chores, we'll get it done faster.'

"That makes sense," I said, and everyone nodded in agreement.

"When the wagon boss yells roll'em, you better be ready. If you ain't, on the trail other wagons go around, and you wind up last. You'll be eatin' dirt and dust at the end of the line, tryin' to catch up." She frowned and shook her head. "We're too slow gettin' started of a mornin'. It should take thirty minutes at the most. I know we been makin' good time, but the road is a lot smoother than the trail. There's hardly a morning that we have broke camp before seven-thirty. We should be on the road by six."

Hattie sat down on a log, picked up a stick, and pushed the hot coals around in the fire. She looked at each of us to see our reaction. Hattie talked and we listened to what would be expected of us on the trail and whose job was whose. "From what I've seen, Bessie and Sara do a good job of keeping things in order inside the wagon." She chuckled. "Once they get them in the wagon, that is. This morning I saw Sara trying to bridle Jenny and wasn't sure who was going to wear the bridle."

There were several snickers. "I'll do most of the drivin'. Martha can relieve me, and we'll be in charge of the stock. Becky can hunt. Charlie, what can you do?"

"I can hunt, set a bone, or stitch up a cut. I studied with a doctor back home. I need to gather a doctoring bag, though. I sort of left mine behind."

"Okay, you help Becky." She grinned. "It's a relief knowing we have someone around that can fix us up if we get hurt. Real glad you're with us, Charlie."

"Loadin' and unloadin' the wagon will be mainly up to Sara and Bessie. We'll help on the heavy stuff. The things we don't need unloaded in the front and cooking gear in the rear. Okay?"

"Okay," we echoed in unison.

"Come mornin' we'll practice hookin' up, loadin' up, and breakin' camp 'til we can do it in our sleep. Okay?" There were nods of agreement. "The goal is to have it done in thirty minutes."

Six Women West

Laying a chunk of wood on the fire, I said "I've been thinking about men. They can be a danger. We're going into some rough country. There will be soldiers, deserters, outlaws. Some don't care what they do to get what they want, and we have a lot of stock and money besides our being women." That was a long speech for me, but memories of Abner and the soldiers who had stolen our horses were always in the back of my mind.

"Martha why can't we do what I did and dress like men? It worked for me," Becky suggested.

"Good idea, Becky," I agreed. I had already bought trousers for myself, but I hadn't started wearing them because I felt too self-conscious. "Course, we'll have to figure out how to get rid of our bosoms and derris-airs."

> **Comment [CJH]:** I added this sentence to explain the fact that Martha had already bought the trousers in light of this discussion.

"Don't know about your bottoms, but a binder will take care of your bosoms," Becky chuckled. "Speakin' for myself, I don't have much of either."

"If we wear baggy britches and loose shirts, put our hair under our hats, and don't get too close, I think we could get away with it," Hattie said.

"I don't know about Bessie, but I'm not planning on wearing any britches," said Sara. "I don't even have any."

"Sara," Hattie said, "Had you rather be raped and murdered or wear britches to fool some ruffian?"

"I'm sorry Hattie, but I'm a lady."

"And I'm hoping you'll live to be an old one."

Sara didn't answer, but she wasn't real happy. I could see the tight line about her mouth. She was angry. I knew I hadn't heard the last of the britches.

"Becky and I have extra trousers you two can wear 'til you get some. We'll let Hattie do the talking if we meet any men. We'll hang back until we're sure they're okay," I said.

"That might work," Hattie agreed, adding, "but keep your eyes open and your guns handy. There's a lot of border trash and deserters along this road. Speaking of guns, how many do we have, and who knows how to use them?"

Becky spoke up first. "I got two, and I can use 'em good."

"Becky's got two, a rifle and handgun," mumbled Hattie.

"I got a Colt and rifle," Charlie said. "I'm a fair shot."

"I have a handgun, a rifle, and shotgun. I usually hit what I aim at," I offered.

Bessie sat weaving a straw hat from the reeds she had pulled from along the creek. "No, ma'am, I never shot a gun, but I can learn, and I surely can cook what y'all kill."

"I don't have a gun. I've never shot one," Sara shrugged, "but there have been times I wished I could have. I'm willing to learn."

"I've got a shotgun and a Walker handgun. I can handle both," Hattie said. She held up her hand, counting on her fingers. "Let's see. That gives us three rifles, four handguns, and two shotguns. We could use another rifle or two before we get to Independence. Here I am talkin' like we're all goin' to Oregon."

"You make it sound like we're going to war," Sara said, frowning.

"Sorry, Sara, but it's best to be on the ready. We have to feed ourselves, and there's Indians and ruffians aplenty. We got to be able to defend ourselves. Just remember if you're ever attacked, everything is a weapon—a stick of wood, a frying pan, a pot of hot water, hatpin, and you can think of more."

"I suppose you're right," Sara agreed.

"Sometime in your life if someone tries to hurt you, you might need to have a weapon," I said. You don't have to learn to handle a gun.

"No, I will do it all. It will be good to learn," said Sara. "I just feel you're overrating the danger. The trail's been open for years."

"Maybe tomorrow we could teach those that can't shoot to shoot," suggested Charlie. I got here the hard way, and I'll never be without the means to protect myself. Sara, you saw what was done to me in that alley. Do you believe if I had a weapon I would have killed him?"

"Charlie, we all saw what happened. It's a lesson for all of us," said Hattie. "Now ladies we'll have to show the wagon master we can take care of ourselves so we won't be a burden. We can't disguise ourselves as men forever, and right off when he sees women, he's gonna say no. It's up to us to convince him we can shoulder our load."

I looked at Tag stretched out close to the fire and then into the flame. *A pitchfork is a good weapon, too*, I whispered to myself. "Yes, we got to get on that wagon train."

As I glanced at each of my companions, I felt a tugging at my heart. In the short time we had been together, we had become like family. We didn't know each other all that well yet, but I was sure that by the time we reached Missouri, we would. Each of us had our reasons for going west. Would we make it to Oregon? Heck, would we make it to Missouri? Becky punched my shoulder and brought me out of my reverie.

"Hey, are we gonna do any shootin'?"

"Why don't we wait 'til morning? I'd rather take a bath. Anyone else? This may be the last chance we have for awhile." I stretched, thinking how good the water would feel even if it was cold.

"I can't put it off any longer. Bessie, would you help me wash and braid my hair?" I asked.

Wanda Reed

"Uh huh." Bessie nodded emphatically. "I been waitin' for you to take it down."

I unwound my hair, letting the braid fall to my ankle. The girls stared.

"Holy shit, Martha, how long you been growin' that mane?" Becky exclaimed.

"Since I was born," I said, adding, "See why I keep it braided?"

"That much hair is a lot of trouble," Sara said. "Why do you keep it so long?"

"Ma never allowed it to be cut. She said a bountiful head of hair was a woman's crowning glory. I haven't been able to wash it by myself for years—not real well, anyway."

"Now is a good time to cut about half of that hair off. There'll be a shortage of water on the trail, and there's always a good chance of lice," Hattie reminded us.

"You're right." I sighed. I wasn't happy about the idea of losing my 'crowning glory,' but I saw the sense in what Hattie said. I looked around the group. "Okay, who can cut hair?"

Comment [CJH]: I added a sentence here to show that she wasn't cutting it without thought.

"Ah done cut a lots a hair workin' in da whore house. The girls tole me ah was real good at it," Bessie said, grinning widely, her teeth showing white against her dark skin. "Ah didn't bring my scissors though."

"Here, use my knife," laughed Charlie.

"Dat'll do," Bessie said. "How much you want cut off?"

"Oh, no, I can't believe I'm doing this." I held my head in my hands. "Ma will turn over in her grave."

"She'd understand," Sara said, looking sympathetic.

"I guess. I hope." I shrugged and closed my eyes. "Go ahead, Bessie. Make it short. Right below the shoulders, just likes Charlie's."

"Good for you, Martha," Hattie said. "You won't be sorry. Besides, it'll always grow back when you get to Oregon."

"Ah'll cut it off about here," Bessie said, taking hold of my braid. "Then, you best wash it before I give it the fine cut."

I closed my eyes and held my breath while she tied it with a piece of rawhide and chopped off the braid.

"Okay, now we'll get it washed so it'll be wet to cut."

"Real pretty," the girls said. I smiled. That was nice to hear. Maybe short hair wouldn't be so bad after all. Before returning to camp, I took the long braid and buried it on the bank of the creek.

Back at camp, we spread our bedrolls near the fire to talk. To my surprise we all agreed to go to Oregon except for Sara who would stay in Independence. We would continue west in my wagon. We would divide the cost, but no one would be left behind for lack of money. Hattie thought fifty dollars from each of us would take care of food and repairs along with the money left from the jar for a total of three hundred sixty four dollars.

"We'll need more, a'course, when we set out for Oregon," Hattie said. "We'll need food supplies, ammunition and two to four extra mules. It takes near a thousand dollars for a large family to make the trip. That includes wagons and mules."

"Will the mules we got make it to Oregon?" I asked.

"Well, if they all stay healthy and don't break a leg, then maybe, just maybe they could." She shook her head. "But, we can't take a chance. Even mules need a day of rest. One set can't work seven days a week pullin' a loaded wagon. That's why we need the extra team."

Soon the talk turned to hopes and dreams. We were still talking and laughing when the stars came out. Hattie rose up from her bedroll. "As wagon boss, I say it's time to go to sleep. We got a big mornin' ahead of us. You gals gotta be in good shape."

Tag got up, shook, sniffed the air, and moved to the foot of Becky's bedroll.

"Yes, Boss," we giggled in unison.

It was still pitch dark when Hattie woke us up bangin' on a pot with a spoon. "Wake up! We roll in thirty minutes," she yelled.

We scrambled out of our bedrolls, reaching for our boots. We slept in our clothes, so that saved us time.

Becky, Charlie, Hattie, and I took off to round up the stock. We rode them back to camp, and me and Charlie saddled four horses while Hattie and Becky hitched up four mules. It was just breaking day.

Bessie and Sara pretended to cooked bacon and biscuits and make coffee. Then the bedrolls and cooking gear were stowed in the wagon. A full fifty five minutes had passed before we were ready to roll!

Hattie shook her head. "Gotta do better than this. Let's try it again. Start over. End of the day. Let's set up camp."

"Good, do we get to eat first?" Becky asked, rubbing her stomach.

"Yeah, after you make camp. Load it the same way each time." Now we did the full exercise in reverse.

After breakfast, Hattie stood up and said, "Okay, gals, now let's get to movin'. Morning again. Break camp," she ordered, sounding very much like a wagon master.

We jumped to our feet and began all over again. We loaded and unloaded the damn wagon six times. I was sure we could do it in our sleep. I think even the hard-headed mules knew their place in line. The horses were acting spooked after so many times having their saddles taken off and on.

"If we can do it in thirty minutes twice in a row, you can take a rest," Hattie said. It took us a couple more times before we met the timeframe. By then it was after noon and time to eat again.

After we finished eating, Hattie said, "Okay. Now for that target practice. Let's see how you shoot. Becky, show Sara how to hold a shotgun."

"Sure. Here, Sara," Becky said, placing her shotgun in Sara's hand. "Hold it real snug up against your side. Like this." She tucked the gun in the pocket of Sara's side.

"How do I aim?" asked Sara. The shotgun looked huge in her hands.

"You don't. Just point and pull the trigger. You'll hit anything or everything in a fifteen foot spread."

Sara fired and immediately fell to the ground with a thud, dropping the gun. "Oof!" she exclaimed, rubbing her rump. "What happened?"

"That's called the kick," Becky laughed. "The power that forces the shot out forces the gun to recoil. You okay?"

"Yes. Why didn't you tell me it would kick? Let me try that again. You tricked me and made me look foolish."

"No, let Bessie try it first." She handed the gun to Bessie, who held it like she would hold a dead chicken. "I can see we got our work cut out for us," Hattie said, smiling and shaking her head. She positioned the gun against Bessie's side. "Now, Bessie, you know there's a kick, so be ready for it. Put your finger right here," she added, placing Bessie's finger on the trigger. Bessie's eyes were as big as dollars, and she didn't look at all happy with what was expected of her. She closed her eyes and squeezed the trigger. Boom! Bessie screeched, and the gun went flying through the air.

"Lawd save me," she moaned, rocking back and forth. "Ah ain't nevah gonna be able to do dat, Miss Hattie."

Becky was rolling on the ground, laughing like crazy. The rest of us tried not to laugh. Hattie just frowned.

"Maybe Sara and Bessie should stick to rifles or handguns. They don't kick so bad or make as much racket," Hattie said. "Charlie, it'll be your job to teach them. I want them to hit a tree."

"Okay. I'll do my best," she agreed, grinning. "That's quite a job you assigned me."

"Becky, Martha, let's pull the wheel hubs," said Hattie. "They got to be packed with grease."

"Don't we get to shoot?" asked Becky.

"Yes, you do Becky—when you get done pullin' the wheel hubs. Go out and shoot dinner," Hattie said very seriously and then laughed.

We made ready to move out at dawn. Rested and confident, we moved like a team and managed to get everything done in record time. Pleased with our success, we set off down the road, smiling and singing Stephen Foster's "Camptown Races."

The next few days flew by, making us feel relaxed and confident. Hattie was driving with Bessie and Sara sitting next to her. Me and Charlie were on the far side of the wagon. She was explaining the seedier side of life to me. We were moving slower than usual because of the hilly road. As we rounded a curve, two young boys rode out on mules. Hattie had her shotgun aimed at them as they passed. She called to us, and we approached the wagon. Needless to say she peeled our hides off with her tongue at our lack of awareness of what was coming down the road.

Hattie's instructions improved our abilities to her satisfaction for the job of outrider. I learned the finer points of driving. While driving the wagon, time passed slowly. I listen while she painted

Six Women West

pictures of Oregon—the cool rivers and tall fir and cedar trees and the wide green Willamette Valley where her son Colton ran their ranch. It sounded like heaven on earth. She assured me I would be able to find land near her.

> **Comment [CJH]:** This is never mentioned again. Just once later on would be good.

We discussed the problems of joining a wagon train to Oregon. Could we convince the wagon boss that we could take care of ourselves and not be a burden to anyone without any men? How could we convince him that we could take care of ourselves?

"Well," I said "if the wagon master won't let us join the train to go west, we'll have to go by ourselves, and we'll just follow behind them."

"Martha, hold the lines a bit tighter so the mules know your still in charge. That's right. He ought to see the humor in that," she laughed, then got serious "Strange ain't it? I can drive a six- or four-up better than most men, but it's being one that matters?"

"I know. It's not fair. I could run my farm and raise horses as good as a man, but I couldn't fight off the land grabbers. From the day my mother died, the men started moving in to take over my farm. It's wrong, and some day we'll live to see it changed. Everyone should be able to own land or live alone without fear."

"Out in Oregon, women run their own places. I'm working on a plan," Hattie said. "If I can get a chance to pull it off, just maybe…."

I glance at Bessie riding Gray Lady. "I better trade places with Bessie before she gets bounced off that horse. That girl ain't never gonna learn to ride. Maybe we ought to get her a mule, or she'll wind up walking to Oregon." Stopping the wagon, I waved to Bessie. "You ride in the wagon awhile, and I'll ride the horse."

"Thank ya, Miss Martha. Dat horse sho do bounce."

"I'll start riding lessons for you at night after supper. Maybe that will help."

121

"Martha, you and Charlie ride up ahead and find a campsite for the night," called Hattie. "Try to find water. The water barrel's empty."

Charlie and I rode nearly a mile before we found a good place to camp. "How about this, Charlie? There's plenty of grass and water."

"Good shelter with the trees and lots of deadfall for wood," Charlie stated.

We returned to the others.

"Hattie, the campsite is near a mile down the road on the left. Turn at the tree where the lightning struck. We're going to try to get a rabbit for dinner." We were gone over an hour and came back empty-handed, but Becky came in with a wild turkey.

We woke to the rolls of thunder, and dark skies split with flashes of lightning. An especially great thunderclap crashed with a flash of lightning followed quickly by a deluge of rain. It sounded like the world exploding. None of us had rain gear except Hattie. It rained for hours, and we were soaked. The rains stopped by morning, and we washed our muddy clothes and cleaned out the wagon. It was a good thing we didn't have much in the wagon because with six of us we were limited to one carpet bag each and the trunk for storage. The rest was food, tools, and cooking supplies. We left just a little before noon. We had spent two days huddled together in that wagon, and that was lost time.

We voted unanimously to buy a large tent in the next town so we could all lie down to sleep at once with rain gear for everyone.

We arrived at the town called Riverbank. The folks on the street turned and stared at our outfit. I was sure they didn't know if we were men or women. There were many raiders from both sides of the war, so they couldn't be sure of us, and we looked rough carrying guns and rifles.

We pulled to a halt at the mercantile. "Martha, you and Sara go in and do the buyin'," Hattie said. "We'll take turns going in three at a time so someone's always with the wagon. I'll go check on a mule for Bessie."

"Okay, Hattie." As usual Sara had her list.

"I'll pick up some medical supplies if there are any," Charlie said.

Inside the store I looked around. There were goods, but some of the shelves were bare. "Mister," I asked, "would you have a large tent?"

"Why yes, I happen to have one. Its big, 8 by 10 feet, and it's used. It'll cost twenty five dollars."

"I'll look at it," I replied. We walked back into the storeroom, and it was a good tent. "It looks good. Would you take twenty for it?"

"Since you're buying a lot of supplies, I'll let you have it for that," he agreed.

We laid in a goodly amount of supplies. Hattie returned with a mule for Bessie, a small jenny only about thirteen hands, grey-colored, and real gentle, and with her riding lessons the two of them were perfect. Now we could avoid towns so as not to draw attention to ourselves. The town folks must have been terrified of us. Our whole outfit was dirty, and we still had another week or more on the trail before we reached Independence, Missouri. We would be glad to get there. I would be glad to get a bath and take off this binder and not have to worry if someone knew I was a woman.

PART TWO

CHAPTER ELEVEN

We did it! Independence, May 5, 1864

Hattie pulled up at a small creek. I rode up beside the wagon. "Why are we stopping?" I asked.

"I thought we'd wash the dust off before we go into town," said Hattie. "We're only about three miles out of Independence."

"You bet we would," said Sara. "My brother wouldn't know me in these trousers with all this dust."

"You got thirty minutes to do what you can before we roll. We got to find the wagon camp before dark," explained Hattie.

Getting undressed and bathed and dressed again in thirty minutes took some doing. Charlie, Becky, Hattie, and I put on clean shirts. Sara and Bessie put on dresses.

"Don't forget your bonnets, ladies," I called in a teasing tone.

It was near two in the afternoon when we approached the edge of Independence. Compared to the towns we'd been in before, this was huge. The street were doublewide around the town square and crowded with wagons with kids yelling out the back and hanging on the sides. People in various styles of dress, from buckskins to organdy, were making their way over the wooden walkways and across the dusty streets.

"Well, girls, here we are—the jumpin' off place." Hattie shook her head. "I wasn't too sure in the beginnin', but you girls proved up, and here we are. Now we just got to convince the wagon boss we can make it to Oregon."

I couldn't stop looking around. So big and so many buildings! I'd never been in a town this big before. It was so noisy with the sound of laughter and swearing mixed together. It was all Hattie could do to keep our mules under control. Tag had positioned himself between my horse and Becky's mule for safety.

Hattie pulled the wagon to a stop in front of the general store. Tag darted under the wagon and hunkered down. Hattie seemed unaffected by the hullabaloo. I supposed she had seen it all before. In the small towns, all heads had turned to stare at us. Here, we were just another wagon of greenhorns going west.

"I'll let you off, Sara. You go find your brother. We'll wait. You bring him back here. I want to talk to him."

"Thanks, Hattie. Martha, I'm so scared. Will you come with me?"

"Sure." I dismounted and helped her down from the wagon. "You look real nice, Sara," I said, thinking how Ma would approve of Sara's blue dress and matching bonnet. I knew I must look like a farm hand compared to her.

"Thank you," she said, sounding nervous. "I think his shop is here on the main street. So far I've seen three. It's a leather and saddle shop. I hope he's still here."

We stopped at the first leather shop we came to. Looking like a scared little girl, Sara took a deep breath and pushed open the door.

"Wait a minute," I said. Taking her arm, I pulled her back. "You know if you don't want to stay here, you can come with us."

"Oh, Martha, I don't know. I've come this far with the idea of staying with Jeffery. But, thank you. Thank you."

"Alright, but if you change your mind...."

I followed her into the store where an older man with gray hair sat behind a counter working on a boot. I glanced around, and there was a fine selection of saddles, boots, and a few leather chairs.

"Afternoon, ladies," he said politely. "What can I do for you?"

"Good afternoon, sir. I'm looking for my brother, Jeffery Rite. I know he has a leather shop on the main street, but I don't know which one."

"Yes, this is the right place, only Jeffery Rite doesn't own it any more. He joined the army, and his missus sold it to me."

"She sold it? Would you know where she lives?"

""Nope, she sold it one day and took the stage north the next day."

"Thank you," Sara whispered. "Oh, Martha, what will I do now?" she moaned, as we walked out of the shop.

Turning, I looked at her. Her face was pale, and she appeared to be on the verge of panic. "You can go with us to Oregon," I said. "I'm sure they need a boarding house or a schoolteacher."

"But, Martha, I don't have enough money to go to Oregon. Right now I only have…"

"Don't worry, Sara," I interrupted. "We said no one would be left behind, but the truth is, I'm glad it worked out this way. You're my friend. I'd miss you something awful. Now smile. You're going to Oregon. I'll pay your share, and no one needs to know."

As we made our way back to the wagon, Sara confessed she was kind of glad too. "You're the best friend I've ever had, Martha. I know I would have missed you—all of you." She hesitated. "Do you think the girls will mind that I'm coming?"

"Heavens, no!" I exclaimed. "They'll be as happy as I am." I leaned down and hugged her tightly.

"You find him?" Hattie called as we walked up.

"He joined the army. Sara's coming with us," I said, smiling.

"Yea!" Becky yelled, and Charlie grinned.

"That be right nice, Miss Sara," Bessie said. "Ah was wonderin' how ah'd feed dis bunch witout you heppin' me."

"This is good, Sara," Hattie agreed. "We need you to help us remember we're still ladies." She held out her hand. "Now climb up here, and let's go find the wagon camp." She helped Sara up and then yelled to a fellow passing by, "Hey, Mister! You there, Mister! You know where the wagon camp is?"

"Sure do, ma'am," he replied, raising his eyebrows. "There's a camp north of town and one south. I hear the one by the river is best. That's the one south. You gals gonna' need to hire a man for the drivin'?" He grinned, and a spew of tobacco juice hit the ground.

"No, thanks. We're doin' just fine," Hattie answered.

"Are you gonna be doin' business at the campground?" He winked and hitched up his trousers.

Hattie snapped, "Why, you sorry son of a jackass. We ain't sportin' women." She flicked the reins, causing the mules to jump ahead.

I mounted Gray Lady, turned, and stared him right in the eye. "Mister, you could get yourself shot talking to our ma that way." Becky, Charlie, and I rode off following the wagon with Tag running along with us. Shops were everywhere. I counted three mercantile stores, a couple of wagon repair sheds, several barns filled with oxen and mules for sale, and a canvas shop. I spotted a prairie schooner with a sale sign—very costly. I'd thought of buying a larger wagon, but the price was not what I had hoped. We would have to make do with the wagon we had.

The wagons thinned as we drew closer to the river. Amidst a large grove of oaks were twelve wagons of different sizes and types. Children ran all over the grove around the wagons, laughing and yelling. Their mothers called to them, warning them of unseen dangers. Men were busy repairing their wagons, mending harness, or tending stock.

Hattie pulled to an empty space next to a small wagon with a negro man shoeing a mule beside it. "This spot taken?" she asked.

"No ma'am." The tall man grinned, staring at us with a curious expression. "Where's yo men folk?"

"No men," Hattie said sternly. "Where's your wagon boss?"

"Lessee, he done went to town 'bout a hour ago. Said he'd be back 'bout four to see iffin mo' wagons was in."

Me, Charlie, and Becky climbed down from our horses and stretched. Our new neighbor, Abel, helped Sara down from the wagon. He reached up to help Bessie as she stepped out of the back, and his eyes lit up.

"Law ha' mercy," he declared with a big smile. "I seed me an angel. Abel, Abel Smithy, dats me," he added, holding out his hand to her. "Darlin' how you called?"

"There'll be none of that," Hattie warned before Bessie could answer. "We don't mean to be unfriendly, Mister, just cautious."

"Sho', ma'am. Ah understand." He nodded and stepped back. "Iffen' you all need any hep, you jes call me. Ahz pretty handy with most anything.'"

"Handy and pretty, too," Becky whispered in my ear. "I think Bessie just got an admirer."

"Ah shore admire yo' spunk," Abel grinned. "I kin hardly wait 'til Mesta Morley shows up."

"Why? Do you think he won't let us join up?" I asked.

"Don' rightly knows. Ah do know we never had just a wagonload of sportin' women wantin' to join." He swapped a fly off his arm.

Six Women West

"Let's get one thing straight," Hattie snapped, steppin' up to him, waving her finger in his face. "We aren't sportin' women, and the next jackass that says that's gonna get a load of buckshot."

"Excuse me, ma'am. Ah'm powerful sorry ah mistook you for dem women. Please forgive me, ma'am."

"Okay, Abel, I guess you can't judge by lookin'," Hattie said in a somewhat softer tone. "C'mon, girls, let's get the stock taken care of. Don't unharness them, and Sara, don't unpack until we talk with the wagon boss."

Sara pushed back the box that she was pulling out of the wagon.

"We have to be accepted and pay our fare first," Hattie explained.

"What do you mean pay our fare?" Sara asked.

"Well, hell, you don't think the wagon boss works for nothin', do you? Plus there's a guide." Hattie shook her head, looking disgusted.

"Of course. I don't know what I was thinking," Sara replied, blushing. "Shall we go ahead and make the coffee and have lunch?"

"That would be okay. Ask Abel if we can use his campfire for coffee. Sorry, Sara. I'm just on edge."

"Ah'll ask him, ma'am," Bessie volunteered. She strolled over to where Abel was standing next to his wagon. I didn't hear what she said, but I could hear his response.

"Why, shore, Miss Bessie. You sho' nuff welcome to mah fire," answered Abel.

"I'll bet he's not just talkin' 'bout the fire on the ground," Becky whispered, grinning mischievously.

"Oh, Rebecca O'Brien you've got a naughty mind for someone so young," I scolded. "C'mon, let's take care of the stock."

After a lunch of bread, venison, cheese, and fresh coffee, we settled back to wait for the wagon boss. Abel had refused our invitation to join us, saying he'd already eaten.

"But ah won't be refusin' a cup a coffee," he said, grinning widely, his eyes on Bessie. She smiled shyly and handed him a cup. He started to sit next to her but at Hattie's frown moved to the other side. "Here come da boss man," Abel said, pointing at a man on a big black gelding. "Mista Morley, Boss, these hyar folks are fixin' to join up," he called to the rider.

"That right? I'll need to talk to your men folk. Where are your men folk, ladies?"

"There ain't any," Hattie said, standing up straight and looking him in the eye.

"What you mean?" he asked "Oh I get it…" He stared at each of us curiously. "You're not dressed like the ones I've run across before, but, well, I'm sorry, ladies, I don't need the kind of trouble you'd cause." He swung out of the saddle.

"You figured wrong, Mister," Hattie said. "We're God-fearing women who just want to get to Oregon." She held out her hand. "I'm Hattie Brown."

"Pete Morley." They shook hands. "Now, ma'am, I shore don't mean to dash your plans, but I can't see takin' on a bunch of women with no men to…"

"To do for them or keep them in line?" I interrupted sharply, finishing his sentence.

"Why, no, ma'am." He looked at me then turned back to Hattie. "I'm just sayin' it's a long hard trail to Oregon. There are all kinds of things that can go wrong. I just don't think women are up to handlin' it."

"We carry our weight and then some," Hattie said. "Don't worry about that."

As they talked I looked Pete over. He was a stocky man, not as tall as Abel. His smooth shaven face was tan, filled with lines that revealed either worry or experience. Probably both. I figured him to be in his forties. With a head full of salt and pepper hair and crows' feet around his hazel eyes, I judged him a good-looking man. He came across as a person you could trust to do what he said.

"Well, Mr. Morley, if you'll just give us a chance, I think we can prove we won't be any trouble to you. Believe me—we can take care of ourselves."

"Well, ma'am, I don't know. Why don't you tell me a bit about yourselves and what you're planning?"

"We've traveled from West Virginia and handled the trouble that came our way. That's over seven hundred miles. Martha and I do most of the drivin'." She nodded toward me. "That there's Martha. Those two there, Becky and Charlie, well, they do the huntin'. Sara and Bessie," Hattie pointed to where Sara and Bessie leaned against the wagon, "they do the cooking and washin'. We all drive, shoot, and ride. We got five good mules and five riding horses. We've got guns and rifles and ammunition."

"Well, ma'am, that all sounds real good, but if you're fixin' to join the wagon train, you're gonna need another wagon. This one's small and probably overloaded with the junk you women bring. There's obviously no room for supplies." He shook his head and turned as if the conversation was ended. "No way, ma'am," he walked away mumbling, "I ain't takin' a wagon full of women. Darn fool females. Don't they know this ain't a Sunday picnic?"

Placing her hand on her hip, Hattie stomped her foot. "Now you wait just a gall darn minute, Morley. Why won't you give us a fair chance like you would a man?" She motioned for Becky to hook up the wagon. "Go ahead," she urged. "Take a look inside our wagon. You'll see we mean business."

Morley turned around with a look of exasperation. "Alright, I'll take a look." He went around to the back of the wagon and pulled back the canvas flap. Sounding surprised, he said, "No rocking chairs. No mirrors. No horsehair mattresses or hope chests." Grinning, he shook his head. "Looks like you gals didn't bring your granny's heirlooms. Nothing here except supplies, a tent, bedrolls, and a couple of carpetbags. Hope you have the funds to outfit your wagon."

He walked over and picked up Randy's leg, examining the hoof. "They all shod?"

"Yes," Hattie answered. "We had that taken care of early on." Chuckling, she added, "Lucky you didn't touch Rowdy. He's a mite sensitive." She moved next to the mule and scratched his ears.

Pete walked over to where I was standing near the three fillies. "Thoroughbreds?"

"Yes. Virginia bred," I replied.

"How'd you manage to keep them away from the army?"

"We did a lot of hiding," I admitted, adding, "We were pretty lucky, I'd say."

"How was the trail coming across Missouri?" asked Pete, turning to Hattie. "Run into many troops?"

"Not many. We kept a point rider and rear guard and tried to avoid any contact. Saw plenty signs of the war, though." Hattie shook her head, frowning. "Burned out farms and graves all over. It was pretty awful."

"It's ready, Hattie," Becky said.

"Thanks, Becky. Come on, Pete," Hattie requested. "Climb up. I'll show you I know what I'm doing." She scrambled up on the wagon and smiled down at him.

Pete laughed. "I'll humor you, woman, just because I like your style. Don't have anythin' else to do right now, so I might as well go for a ride with a pretty lady."

I swear Hattie blushed. The girls and I grinned at each other.

"Oh, Lord," Becky groaned. "First, Bessie and now Hattie. Who's next to be bitten by the love bug?"

"Honestly, Rebecca. Is that all you think about?" I asked, shaking my head.

"Well if she doesn't scare him to death, he just might sign us on," Charlie said as we watch them take off.

Hattie cracked her blacksnake whip in the air over Rowdy's ear and the team moved out at a brisk pace. In a few minutes she had the mules dancing back and forth with only a flick of the reins. She made them start and stop just using the reins and a click of her tongue. It was a sight to see.

"My goodness," Sara remarked. "I didn't know she could do all that."

"Well, she did tell us she was a muleskinner," I reminded her.

Hattie finally pulled the wagon to a stop at the campground. Several of the members of the wagon train who had been watching cheered and clapped at her ability to drive a four-up.

Pete climbed down off the wagon, slapped his hat against his leg, and exclaimed in a loud voice, "Where the hell did you learn to drive like that lady? I ain't seen a man handle mules like that, let alone a woman."

"Well, I drove four-up twelve hours a day when my husband was alive. We had Brown's Freight. We hauled from Independence to Fort Bridger." Hattie couldn't quite hide a smirk. "And, for your information, this won't be my first trip to Oregon."

"You've crossed the trail before? Why didn't you say so? Okay you're in. But no special favors. You girls keep away from the married men. Abel can help you get your wagon fixed up. And I'll get you a list of the supplies you'll need."

"Thanks, Mr. Morley," Hattie said, climbing down from the wagon. She held out her hand to him, and he shook it. "You don't have to worry none. Me and the girls won't give you any trouble. You won't be sorry."

"I'll hold you to that, ma'am." He smiled. "I'll let you know the fare when all the wagons gather." As he walked away, he stopped next to Abel. "She'll do to ride the river with. Hope the other gals are half as good." He mounted his horse he rode off.

"Good work, Hattie," I said. "You got us on."

"Yeah," Becky chimed in. "You purty near charmed the pants off him."

"You mean scared the pants off him, don't you?" Charlie laughed.

Hattie responded with a grin.

"Well," I said, turning to Abel, "You're a blacksmith. If you meant what you said about helping us, I'll need our wagon completely rebuilt with bigger wheels and two feet added to the box." I paused and looked at Hattie. "We still want two more mules?"

"Y'all gwana drive a six-up?" Abel's eyes were round with surprise. "Ah knows of a farm up north o' town dat has mules for sale." We can git de lumber afta' ah sees what ah needs."

"Fine now, let's get our stock taken care of. I imagine it's alright to rope off a corral?"

"Sho is. You wants me ta help pick yor place?"

"Yes, thank you. Would you share supper with us tonight?"

"I'd be right proud to." He glanced at Bessie. "Real female cookin'." Chuckling, he added, "I sho nuff be dere. Uh huh. Miss Bessie be dere?"

I laughed. "She'll be there."

"Ah'll be drivin' behin yall on the train," Abel told us. "So, iffen y'all need help, jes holler. Ahz thinkin' mebbie we could do some tradin'?"

"What do you mean?" Hattie asked.

"Well, ah takes care of yo wagon," he grinned, his teeth showing white against his dark skin, "an y'all take care of me. Ahz talkin' 'bout cookin' and washin'."

Hattie busted out laughing. "She turned to the five of us. "Whatta ya' say, girls? You want another mouth to feed and dirty clothes to wash?"

"I don' mind," Bessie said. "Sho' don' like greasin' wheels or smearin' pitch." She wrinkled her nose and rolled her eyes. The rest of us nodded in agreement.

"It's a deal, then," Hattie said, holding out her hand to Abel.

"You donate your food supplies and help haul, and we'll see you have good meals." They shook hands. Abel went to his wagon, and we got busy settin' up camp.

During supper I couldn't help notice how Abel's eyes watched Bessie's every move. It seemed to me she swayed her hips a bit more than usual, and there was a look in her eyes that matched Abel's.

He grinned widely when she offered him an extra piece of pie.

"Dis sho' is good pie, Miss Bessie," he said, smacking his lips in obvious pleasure.

"Jes pie," Bessie murmured, shrugging her shoulders.

Maybe this would work out good for her. I decided if they were to start courtin', we should find out more about him. "Abel, how does it happen that you are going to Oregon?" I asked.

"Ah done save my money from doin' blacksmith wuk," he said, smacking his lips over the last bite of Bessie's apple pie. "Done saved it soze I could buy mah freedom."

"How'd yo come by the name, Smithy?" Bessie asked softly.

"Well, reckon you know slaves don' got no las names, 'ceppin de massa's. So ah done took Smithy 'cause me bein' a blacksmith. Abel Smithy, dat's me," he said proudly.

"It be a nice name," Bessie said.

"Yessum, thank ya, Missy. Ah figgers ah has to get clear outta de sout 'fore ah be truly free." He frowned, shaking his head. "Free black man still gets treated like a slave in de sout."

"Why Oregon?" Sara asked.

He sighed deeply. "Ah figgers ah kin be free like a white man in Oregon. He sighed again. "You figger ah right, Miss Martha? Or do ah havta go on to the Canada?"

Smiling, I nodded. "We're all lookin' for a fresh start, Abel. We're all praying we'll find it in the west."

"Turn in early, girls. Big day tomorrow," Hattie said. Leaving Bessie and Becky to clean up the supper dishes, Sara, Charlie, and I decided to scout the area.

Tag led the way and then ventured off in another direction. The campground was situated along the Missouri River and surrounded by a large grove of tall oak trees full of hanging gypsy moss. The ground was covered with thick green grass but would soon be trodden into dirt.

We stopped and visited with several families. All the men seemed excited and anxious to get started on the trail. Most of the women seemed more nervous and fearful of what lay ahead.

As we walked along the riverbank, we watched a beautiful sunset of red and gold. The river looked as if it was made of blue silk with cascades of white lace. I wondered how deep it was and if the fishing was good. I was sure to find out while we were here.

Six Women West

Three little girls ran up and started petting Tag. Their Mother calling to them to be careful. I turned and said, "He won't hurt them." She introduced herself as Velma Johnson. "I'm a school teacher. We're from Pennsylvania. I hope to hold classes, and everyone will be invited to attend." It was getting dark, so we went back to camp. We visited awhile around our campfire as the stars came out one by one. Then everyone drifted away to turn in for the night.

> **Comment [CJH]:** This is never mentioned again.

Sara walked out of the tent. She stretched and yawned. "That coffee sure smells good. That's what woke me up. Looking toward the Missouri River, she remarked, "The white mist over the water reminds me of cotton fields in full bloom back in Georgia. Good morning Bessie, Martha."

"Morning, Sara," I said, as I filled our coffee mugs.

"Good mornin', Sara," said Bessie, "Ah thought ah'd let you sleep in. Since we're camped we can take it easy. Ah bin meanin' to ask if you could help sew some bloomers."

"Of course Bessie. We'll go into town while we're here and get material. I bet all of us could use a couple pairs."

After our breakfast of buckwheat cakes, Hattie and I walked down to the picket line. Becky and Charlie's animals were gone. We ventured to guess they had gone hunting. "I hope they bag a deer. We need meat," I said.

"It would also show Pete we can do our own hunting," said Hattie. We saddled our horses and walked back to the wagon. Bessie was cleaning up the camp, and Sara was washing dishes. "Has Abel had been around yet?" asked Hattie.

"He be back direckly. He's gone down to the river to wash up." She smiled shyly.

"Need any supplies?" I asked.

"Sara and me are gonna walk to town later."

"It's three miles. You drive the wagon. Hook up Jenny and Judy. There's no need to walk."

"Thanks, Martha, we'll do that."

"Hi Abel, ready to go for a ride?"

"Good mornin' Miss Martha, Miss Hattie. Are you ready to go on a mule hunt? Reckon the Wiggins place is the best place to go. That's four miles north of town. He sells mules, good mules. Da ones in town are worn out."

"Well let's swing a leg up, Hattie. You ready? Let's go."

The three of us set off for the farm. It was an overcast morning with slate-gray clouds and looked like it might rain before night. Hopefully it would burn off. We rode for an hour down a road lined with tall oak trees full of hanging mistletoe. The fields along the road had freshly planted crops. Hattie shared her knowledge and experience from former trips—the conditions we would encounter and what supplies we would need.

"Pants for me, that's what I'm a wearing," I said. "They make more sense than skirts when you're climbing in wagons or astride a horse."

Hattie said, "For this trip, they're the only thing to wear. I've been wearing them for years. You walk, you climb, you crawl. Who needs skirts? They're too long and too bulky."

"Well, ah don' know about de res o' the men, but ah thinks all you ladies looks fine in dem britches," laughed Abel.

"Well, just you watch," said Hattie. The women, they start out in skirts and before long they'll all be wearing their men's britches. The prissy ones will wear a skirt over the britches."

Six Women West

We arrived at the Wiggins Farm. I sat on my horse as I overlooked the farm. It was well laid out with a huge farmhouse and a grove of large oak trees off to the side. The sunny side had a large garden. It had a sturdy barn with plenty of roomy corrals.

A heavy-set man wearing coveralls and chewing tobacco met us in the yard. "Hello. Step on down. I'm Jessup Wiggins," he said and then spit a stream of dark tobacco juice, wiped his mouth with his shirtsleeve, and then stuck out his hand for Abel to shake. "How about a cup of coffee?"

Abel looked at me. I answered, "Sure would be good, thank you." The coffee was strong and black, had a bite of chickaree, and tasted real good after our chilly morning ride.

"The blacksmith in town said you got some mules for sale," Abel said. "We might be interested in a team."

Mr. Wiggins rubbed his whiskered chin. "Yeah, I have a couple of teams. A matched set of blacks there, green broke about three years. The other is a brace of six-year-olds. Real calm pair who'll work the lead or pull position. They're big roans, Missouri bred. Let's walk down and take a look."

While we walked down to the barn, Hattie asked, "What are you asking for each team?"

"Are you women doin' the buying?" Wiggins asked. "I ain't never sold mules to no women."

"You ain't got nothing against selling to women have you?" smiled Hattie.

"Don't matter to me who buys. Money is money. Just wonderin', that's all."

"Yeah, thez des knows mules well as any man," said Abel. "Deh picks mah stock any day."

Mr. Wiggins's opened the corral, and we went in. Hattie and I checked over each mule. We both decided on the same team. "Well, Mr. Wiggins, we'll take the roans. Would thirty dollars each be a fair price?" said Hattie.

"That's a fair price," said Mr. Wiggins, "but I could let you have the blacks for twenty-five each."

"We have a long way to go and no time to train green mules," said Hattie. "We need a steady set."

Feeling satisfied about the deal, we walked back up to the house leading our mules.

"Your man is right. You women know your mules. You bought the best team for a long haul," Mr. Wiggins said. "You're going to California?"

"No sir, were heading for Oregon," answered Hattie.

I dug in my pocket for six ten-dollar gold pieces for Mr. Wiggins. Looking up on the porch, we saw an ample lady with snow-white hair. I presumed she was Mrs. Wiggins. "Do you have any vegetables for sale?"

"I have potatoes, onions and carrots, and maybe a few beans. Two-bits a sack," said Mrs. Wiggins.

"We'll take two sacks of mixed, thank you."

Mrs. Wiggins yelled, and a young black girl came running. "You get them two sacks of mixed vegetables. Be right quick about it."

Hattie handed her a half dollar. We mounted up and headed for camp. We were in a good mood and happy with our mules.

"I hope Becky got something good to eat today. A wild turkey would be good," I said.

"If not meat, Bessie will have more beans and rice. You can all ways count on that. Even a sage hen would make a nice stew."

Abel laughed, "Y'all wait 'til you're out on the trail. Beans ever night fo' a week. Yes, sir! Beans! Beans! Beans!"

"Well, with Charlie and Becky around, if there's game, we'll have it. They're good hunters. Since you eat what we do, you better hope so, too." We all laughed.

CHAPTER TWELVE

May 14, 1864

"Let's stop at the blacksmith's barn to brand our stock. We need a branding iron made," said Hattie.

"What brand?" I asked. "Oh, we could use your **B**," I suggested, since it's a registered brand and we won't have to file for a trail brand. After ordering the branding iron, we returned to camp. We tied the mules to the wagon wheel and settled down for a glass of lemonade.

"Heard you bought a couple of Wiggins' mules," said Pete. This is Guy Richards, our guide.

"We had to come and take a look. Everybody has talked about his mules."

"Glad to meet you Guy," I said. "The mules are tied to the rear wheel. Come on and take a look."

"I've heard the Wiggins mules are the best trained in the country," said Pete.

"Well, if I'm any judge of mules, he done a good job," said Hattie "They're well-built critters with good dispositions."

"Good grief, look at the chest on that fellow," expressed Guy. "Pete, he looks like he could pull a wagon by himself. I'll bet he's fifteen hands, big son-a-gun."

Bessie looked around the wagon and yelled, "Supper ready. It's rabbit stew. Ah'm sure y'all will be stayin'. Come and get it while it's hot."

The talk was all about mules and different breeds. After they finished, the men praised Bessie's cooking. They excused themselves and drifted away.

Sara and Bessie shared their trip into town. "We took your advice," Hattie, "and decided to stick with the britches. You're right. They'll be better for traveling, so we each bought a pair," said Sara.

"But ah don't know if ahz got the nerve to wear dem. Miss Sara's so little, like a little boy, but you should see the view of my rump," laughed Bessie.

"Bessie, those pants will come in handy when you ride your mule. Nobody will see your bottom settin' on a mule."

"Miss Martha, that little mule you got for me, I hope he don't bounce."

"I hope you bought two pair so you'll have a change," I laughed. "Once you wear them, you won't want to take them off, but you can wear dresses while we travel like most women do."

"Did you see an apothecary in town?" asked Charlie.

"Yes," answered Sara. "There's one at the far end of town across from the doctor's office. Down the side street, I saw a Chinaman's sign if you need anything from him."

"Good. I'll go there to replenish my nursing supplies," said Charlie.

"Oh, Hattie, I took the liberty of leaving your address at the store so if my brother returns, he will be able to find me."

"That's fine Sara," Hattie said. "I should have thought of it."

"We have heard there will be dances at the forts, so we bought material for a new dress for each of us. We'll sew on the trip," said Sara. "We saw a treadle sewing machine. The man showed me how to use it. It is the most wonderful machine. It puts the stitches into the material. Someday I'll have one and open a dress shop."

"We talked to the shopkeeper about vegetables. He said we could buy them canned, but they're costly. He has quite a few things dried. What do we want to do?" Sara asked. "Does it make a difference to anyone?"

"Get all you can that's dried and the rest in cans. Take it easy on the cans as they're more weight.

Bessie, you're in charge of the cooking, and we trust your judgment. Sara you're in charge of our money, so buy what you need. Just be sure to get some canned peaches," said Hattie. "Lots of peaches, and you'll want to buy good strong hats that'll protect your heads from the rain. What you're wearing is alright for nice weather, but in a storm you will need a leather hat."

"Make sure we all get a heavy coat and gloves, and get six extra blankets and a dozen pair of wool socks," I said.

"Sara, we need rain slickers with hoods. We'll be facing fierce northern rain and wind," Hattie continued. "Don't buy any flour in town. We'll order it from the gristmill a few miles from here. That way it will come in barrels. Be sure to get eggs though."

"I'll go into town with you first thing in the morning. I want to get the lumber," I said. "I'd like to see that thing you called a sewing machine too."

"We better turn in and get some sleep," said Hattie. "We have to finish up everything this week before we pull out."

Sara and I drove into town early next morning. Our first stop was the Red Ball Mercantile. At the counter Sara said, "I need this list of supplies."

"Why certainly, Miss. This is a big list. It will take a few minutes. You look around, and if there's anything I can help you with, just let me know."

I was trying on some leather gloves. "Sara, are your leather gloves still good, or do you need another pair?" I asked. "and look—here's a hat for you."

"Martha, I really don't want a hat. I have conceded to wearing boots and men's britches, and I've strapped a gun to my side, but I'm not a man. I just draw the line at my bonnet. We're safe now. Can't I just be a woman?"

"You'll need a hat. Hattie said so, and I agree."

Wanda Reed

"Well, I'm not going to wear a hat. I've always worn a bonnet. I don't want to hear any more about it. In fact I'm thinking of making a new one. This abominable war has bonnets so expensive I have to make my own. Do you know that a bonnet is over five dollars? I can't believe it. It's outrageous!"

> Comment [CJH]: Changed from $50

I was glad the clerk returned to the room. I had never seen Sara act this way. I wasn't quite sure what to do.

"Ma'am you order is ready. There are several boxes. Would you like for me to put 'em in the wagon?"

"Thank you, we can manage," I said. On the counter sat four large boxes and several packages.

"Sara, you settle the bill. I'll start carrying boxes out." At the door I did a balancing act that almost upset the peaches. Crossing the boardwalk, I nearly knocked down a lady. I set the box at the back of the wagon and opened the tailgate and then pushed the box inside. Returning to the store, I picked up the second box which was larger. I said cautiously, "Open the door for me please, Sara." Passing through the door easily and with Sara watching for me, I fell on no one.

"Let me lower the tailgate, Martha. Oh it's already down."

"I'll go get the other box. Stay at the door to let me out. Do we need all these things? Looks like we bought the whole store?"

"Do you doubt my judgment of what to buy? Well, you can take over this job anytime you want to. I'll gladly step aside and let someone else do the shopping."

I decide not to answer. With the mood Sara was in, I decided to get the lumber later. I climb up on the seat and offered to help her, "Can I help you up, Sara?"

"No, thank you! That's why we're wearing trousers. It's easier to climb. After all, men don't need help, and that's what we're trying to be."

I didn't reply. She sure was testy. While driving back to camp I asked, "Sara, is there something wrong? You don't seem yourself today."

"Martha, I guess I'm just being a woman. My insides are all full of butterflies, and I feel like crying, and it's my time, and I'm tired. I'm so tired. Oh, I don't know." And she started crying.

"When we get back to camp, you lie down and rest for awhile," I said, "and I'm going to make sure you do."

"Thanks, Martha. Thanks for understanding."

Shortly after that, we pulled into camp. I told Sara to go into the tent and nap. There was a prairie schooner parked near us. Walking over, I asked, "Waiting for Pete?"

"Yes, I hope he comes soon. I'd like to get camp made. My name is Ted Crane, and this is Mary Louise. We're from upstate Illinois, and we'll be traveling to Oregon."

"Hello," said Mary Louise." Do you have children?"

"No, none of us is married."

"We have four boys—Matthew is seven, Mark is six, and Levi and John are four."

I stood there staring at them. Each looked like the other—dark hair, brown eyes, freckles across the nose. One was just a little taller or shorter. All dressed in blue pants and blue shirts. Finally I got my voice and asked them over for a cup of coffee, which they eagerly accepted.

Becky and Charlie rode in from hunting and dropped off a nice four-point buck. "That's Charlie's kill," said Becky.

"Bessie, could you get Mr. and Mrs. Crane a cup of coffee and the boys a piece of bread and jelly

Wanda Reed

while they wait for Pete? I'll be back. I got to catch Becky. Sorry, I got to hurry. See you later."

I hurried to the corral. Becky was unsaddling her mule. "Would you ride into town and help me buy them girls hats and leather gloves?"

"Didn't they buy hats?"

"No. Sara said she didn't want one, but they'll need leather hats once they're in blowing wind or scorching sun."

"Okay, let's ride into town now and get it over with. I'll need to ride one of your animals. Mine is done in. Sometimes those girls are so prissy." We walked into the corral and saddled Boots.

"What would you think if we got that sewing machine for Sara?" I asked.

"I think she'd like it just fine. I'll help buy it. I can cash in some nuggets. I need cash money for the trail."

"Thanks, Becky. Let's see what it costs. It's at the Red Ball."

We roasted the deer Charlie shot. There was potluck around the campfire that night. Everyone brought a dish. I invited Pete, Guy, the guide, and the Crane family who brought Henry and Bert Davis and their son Ray and daughter Ruth. They were a delightful family. The Johnsons came with their three little girls. It was a time to make friends. We were going to be together a long time.

After dinner Pete said, "There's going to be a meeting up at the supply wagon. I've got to go. Tell everybody to be there in a few minutes."

We joined the crowd as Pete climbed upon a barrel so he could be seen. "Well folks, we'll be leaving in a week. I want your wagons ready. If you need help getting ready, see Guy or me and we'll get you help. Everyone will be required to have two hundred pounds of flour for each person, ninety five pounds of bacon, twenty pounds of coffee or more, fifty pounds of beans, fifty pounds of sugar,

Six Women West

twenty five pounds of dried fruit, fifty pounds of jerky, and plenty of yeast, salt, and pepper for each person in their wagon. I want you to understand that's for each person. Half that for young ones over the age of four. I'm going to suggest you take some canned vegetables if you have them. You can order your flour at the mill. No wagon will go if they're short of supplies. I want an extra wheel on each wagon with two shovels and three hundred feet of rope. Have a well-stocked toolbox. Have some good boots for walking. Most of you will walk to Oregon. Take extra animals if you can. Watch the weight of your wagons. I don't hold with over-loaded wagons. Now folks—a word about Grandma's heirlooms. I know they're special to you, and I can't stop you from taking them, but my advice to you is to sell them here. They'll overload your wagons and kill your stock. And you will end up leaving those heirlooms on the trail to Oregon. Don't take anything except what you need to stay alive. I say again—don't overload your wagons."

Bessie and I were walking back to our wagon. Abel did a double-step to catch up with us.

"Miss Martha, your wagon nearly finished, and dem water barrels is ready. Ah kin put them on tomorrow. Ah done got the new mules and horses all shod, and ah has extra shoes for dem all."

> **Comment [CJH]:** I added "new" before mules since they had made a point of telling the boss that they had already been shod for the trip to Oregon.

"Thanks, Abel. Tomorrow would you go to the Red Ball and pick up the sewing machine? And don't let Sara see it. We bought it for her. How is the wagon coming along?"

"Okay, Miss Martha. Ah gots to pitch paint and peg the hides down. Tomorrow I'll do dat. Miss Bessie, would you go for a walk along de river wid me?"

"Yes. Abel ah would. It's sech a beautiful night."

I watched as they walked along the riverbank and out of sight. The sun was starting to set. Above the white bonnets of the wagons, the scarlet and

147

white clouds mixed with the blue sky as the sun setting slowly made a painting in the sky. I walked slowly back to the wagon thinking of the problem at hand.

Pulling back the flap on the tent, I said, "Hattie I think we may have come upon a problem."

"Yes, I know. I been doing some ciphering, and we come up overloaded," Hattie said. "We can use a couple of the mules as pack animals or get another wagon. We're looking at twenty five hundred pounds with no extras—like a sewing machine, tent, or trunks."

"There's another way—we could ask Abel if he would haul some of our supplies, He only has about four hundred pounds in his wagon," I said. "Maybe some barrels of flour and share his tools? In turn we could buy him a team."

"Let's talk to him about it. Otherwise, we'll have to get another wagon, and I'm not partial to that idea."

"We'll have to do it tomorrow. He's out walking with Bessie right now. I'm going slip down to the river and get a quick bath."

Long after everyone was asleep, the sky danced with lightning. The tall oak trees were silhouetted against the night. The sky opened up with a deluge of rain. In a short time there were small streams that flowed to the river. We were lucky we had the tent to sleep in. It gave us plenty of room.

Right after daylight, Pete stopped by for a cup of coffee, "I looked at the river this morning. It's up near a foot. Hattie, I need to ride over to the mill and turn in orders for flour." He sat down on one of our barrels.

Would you like some breakfast, Pete?" asked Bessie, as she handed him a cup of steaming coffee.

"I sure would Bessie. It smells delicious. Hattie, about the extra provision, would you go into town...."

Six Women West

While they were talking, I went to find Abel. He was currying his mules. "Abel would you consider helping us carry some of our provisions if we buy you a team of mules to help haul with?" I asked.

"Why, shore, Miss Martha. Miss Bessie can ride with me too, if she want to. Les jes say our wagons kin work together."

"Look around and buy a decent team of mules, and don't pay more than thirty dollars each."

"I'll get us a good set of mules for that price. Miss Martha, we gonna put the contraption for Sara in your wagon?"

"Yes, we'll sneak it in while Sara's down by the river. Here's the money."

When we saw Sara returning, we all found somewhere else to be so she could discover the machine by herself. After about twenty minutes we returned. She had red swollen eyes and hugged and kissed us all and cried again.

For the next three days Becky and Charlie went out after meat and never complained. It was a ten mile ride to where they could get game every night. They brought in one or two deer to be jerked. We were trading fresh meat for jerky with the butcher in town. We'd needed lots of jerky for six people. I went with them several times.

Pete called another meeting. He climbed upon a box and motioned for quiet. Then he placed his hands on his hips, and his voice boomed out, "It looks like we got about fifteen wagons gathered to go west. That means fifteen families must work together and live in harmony. You'll have to depend on each other for help crossing rivers and climbing mountains. There will be scorching days and colder nights, days of rain, and all elements of hardships. Some will make it. Some won't. There will be sickness, accidents, and snakebites, food poisoning, and bad water. It will be hard. If your loved one dies, bury him beside the trail and go on. It will be hard, but you just do it. So be ready to roll come daylight. Check your wagon. Check your supplies twice. Don't overload your wagons. Use pack mules if you need to."

I was currying my gray mare between Abel's wagon and our wagon. Tag was nearby chewing on a bone. Hattie and Bessie were sitting in chairs snapping beans while they waited for the bread to rise. Bessie said she wanted to get several loaves baked and asked if anyone got some rice.

"Charlie got fifty pounds at the Chinaman shop," Hattie said.

About midday, another wagon pulled in. A prairie schooner loaded with utensils hanging off the sides pulled up near us. Four grown boys rode beside it. A horse and goat trailed behind. The driver, an older man with whiskers, announced, "The name is Riley. Where's the wagon boss?"

"Go down by the far wagon and wait. He'll be down to see you shortly," said Charlie. When they rode off, she turned to Hattie and added, "That looks like a rough bunch of Georgia crackers if you ask me."

"You're right," answered Hattie.

I stared at the man. He looked hard and cruel. The old man had a mass of unruly dark hair and heavy wrinkles. He was lean and gaunt with a pointed chin and cold hard eyes. Two of the boys looked like a younger version of the old man. The two others had light hair. The youngest smiled. I didn't see any women. Thinking they reminded me of Abner, that brought back a flood of memories I would have liked to forget. Near an hour later, I nodded to Guy Richards as he approached our wagon. "Looking for Sara?" I asked. He was sweet on Sara. He was a handsome fellow built on the slim side. His hair was sun-streaked, and he had a face wrinkled with smile lines. He was tan and had flirty blue eyes. I hoped his intentions were sincere regarding Sara. It was hard to tell as he was always friendly.

"Mornin', ladies," he said as he dragged a box up near the fire and sat down. Then he pulled out his tobacco and rolled a smoke. "Just thought I'd better alert you ladies about the new wagon that joined the train. Could be trouble. I advise you to steer clear of those men. They look real rough. Don't figure they have much respect for women." He drew in on his cigarette.

"Pete tried talking them into goin' upriver to the other outfit that's leaving next week. They said they're ready to go now and already picked up their supplies."

"Guy, I seen the boys when they pulled in," Hattie said, getting up to pour him a cup of coffee. "That new wagon got any women or kids on it?"

"Thank you, ma'am," he said, taking the cup. "The wife's named Ruth, and there's a baby. The woman's face is bruised, and she's sportin' a dozer of black eye." He shook his head. "Don't have any use for a man who'd hit a woman. I don't trust those boys, either. Quite obvious they don't stick up for their ma." He inhaled deeply. "Well, consider yourselves warned. Don't get caught alone with them. If they give you any trouble, let me know." He finished the last of his coffee and set the cup down. "Thanks."

"Thanks, Guy," Hattie said. "I'll tell the girls to stay in pairs and be careful." She wiped her hands on her apron, muttering. "Can't say for sure where they're at right now," then muttered, "Like trying to keep track of rabbits."

I saddled Gray Lady and went into town to do a little shopping for myself at the lady's shop. I had a desire for some lilac soap that smelled like Ma use to have, and I needed some personal undergarments and a new shirt. After I finished with me, I went to the leather shop and said hello to the old man. I got a bridle for my horse and some stirrup covers for my feet. Then I stopped at the Red Ball and got a sack of peppermints. It was getting on near dinnertime when I returned to camp.

"Miss Martha! Come look at de mules we got."

I came out of the tent and came face to face with two of the reddest mules I'd ever seen. A grinning Abel sat astride one of them.

"Wow, Abel! They're somethin' alright." I walked around them, admiring their size and obvious good health. Their left hips carried the brand of the U.S. Calvary with an X across it, designating they had been sold.

"Miss Martha, ah done checked 'em good and hooked 'em to a wagon. Dey pulls jes fine. Der was no problem wit ridin' 'em. Man say dey be all round good animals. They been in battle, and dey jes don't like gunfire. Oh, here's da bill uh sale."

"You sure did good, Abel. Brand them with your brand and give them an extra scoop of grain." I patted a large rump. "And tomorrow they start earning their keep."

After supper we were invited to the Johnson's wagon for a sing-a-long and a cup of hot buttered rum.

As the fire burned down to embers, we all held hands and John Johnson led us in a prayer for a safe journey. Good nights were said. As we walked away, Guy showed up.

"Just want to make sure you ladies get home safe," he told us, looking at Sara.

"Why, thank you, Mr. Richards," I said, trying to hide a smile. "I think we'll be safe enough with Tag along, but Sara always likes a short walk before turning in. Think you could keep her company in my place?"

Guy's face lit up like a sunny day on the lake. "That okay with you, Miss Sara?"

Six Women West

"I think that would be nice," she murmured. Taking his arm, she strolled off with him in the direction of the river.

"Ah, ain't that sweet?" Becky remarked in a low voice that sounded a bit envious to me. I could relate to that. "I'll see you later."

I walked over and sat on the wagon tongue and stared up at the blueberry sky filled with twinkling stars, wondering if these same stars could be seen in Oregon. Just a few short years ago, I thought I would live and die in Manassas. Now here I was, alone on a wagon train going to Oregon, wondering where life would take me. No, not truly alone. Just with a different family. "Oh Pa, I miss you so much!" I whispered. My eyes filled, and it was all I could do to keep from crying. Brushing away the tears, I crept back to the tent, lit a button candle, and crawled into my bedroll. I opened my journal and began to write: *Everything is ready. Tomorrow is the big day. We leave for Oregon. I am anticipating the trip and scared at the same time. May God watch over us!*

Just at dawn I walked out of my tent and breathed deep. The sky was dark blue, dotted with cotton-wool clouds. The sun had just started to peek through, making some of the clouds pink. What a beautiful sight! Exhilaration rose to fill me. I tied my hair back with a piece of rawhide as Moe started beating out the wakeup call that brought the camp to life. I picked up the coffeepot and filled it from the water barrel. Our first day of going west! I stoked up the hot coals in the fire pit, threw a stick of wood in, and set the coffeepot over the small fire. Then I laughed, sticking my head in the tent and yelling, "Wagons West!" I ran to saddle the horses, and when I got back Bessie had biscuits and gravy ready with slices of ham.

"Girl, you screamin' in the tent like that near skeert me to death," scolded Bessie. "I'm gonna Wagon West you!"

Quickly, I ate my biscuits and gravy and then wrapped three biscuits and some ham in a kerchief and put the bundle in my saddlebags. The camp was in erratic motion with everyone busily harnessing their teams to roll. To my surprise all the drivers took off, each one on his own, south across the Blue River at Red Bridge. All Pete's orders went to hell in a hand basket. What'd happened to the line of order? You were lucky if you didn't get run over. Lucky for us, Hattie held back and avoided the rush. At Fitzgerald Mill everything was a jumble trying to load our order of flour. Continuing on to Elm Grove, the wagons pulled up to camp with much confusion. Wagons were parked every which way. No one was in a circle or in their place.

Hattie and I took the stock down to river for water. "So this is what it'll be like on the trail," I mused. The mule waded into the water while I held the rope. He drank his fill of the cool water.

"I don't think so," chuckled Hattie. "I'm sure we'll hear from Pete about the disorder. If we don't, he's not the leader or man I expected." She sat down on a large rock beside a shade tree that protruded over the river.

"It was quite a mess," I chuckled. "Everyone wanted to be first. These mules are finished drinking. They just want to eat this tender grass by the river bank."

"Yes, and they didn't circle up tonight. Pete should rake 'em over the coals. I'm so glad to have Abel. He's a special gift. He's done a fine job on the wagon, and those new skins make it right comfortable. Did you know that Sara put some bed cotton on the seat before she covered it? Now it's soft as a feather bed," laughed Hattie.

"Did you see the last skin Becky cleaned? It's so thin you can see through it. She gave it to Bessie to wrap bread in. Said it will keep it soft."

"No, I haven't seen it, but if it does help keep the bread, that's good."

"We better get back. Those horses should be cooled down and want a turn at the water."

Right after sunset Guy stopped by the wagon and announced, "The wagon boss is holdin' another meetin' in about ten minutes."

"Now what?" snipped Sara. "There sure are a lot of meetings."

"Sara, I'd tell you," he said smiling, "but then I wouldn't get to walk with you to and from the meeting."

"Thank you, Guy. That's nice of you." She smiled.

"It's been a long, hard day. You'll get used to it."

When we all arrived at the meeting, Pete climbed up on the tailgate of the wagon. He shouted, "The order of departure this morning was a disaster. The only thing worse was how camp was made tonight." His voice boomed out, "I am only going to say this once, so pay attention to me. I have assigned everyone a place in line. You have a number somewhere between one and seventeen." He paused to see if there was any objection and then went on. "When we get out on the prairie you can fan out or split up. At night we circle up, and that's wagon tongue to tail gate. Starting tomorrow night, I'll teach you how I want it done. There are rules on this train. I'm the law, and the rules will be followed by everyone. We circle up for a reason. It's to protect the stock and us from an attack. You asked me to be wagon boss. If you're not happy with me, say so and get someone else.

"Now folks, we have two thousand miles of hell to go through, and the lucky ones will make it. Some of you will turn back. Sorry to say some will be buried along the trail. If you're told to lighten your wagons, you will. If you're told to share your food with a neighbor, you will. Now we are only one day out. Anyone can't or won't obey these rules, it's best you turn back and join another train."

Mr. Riley called out, "I don't like bein' last in line. I want to be closer to the front."

"Well Mr. Riley, you were last to come into camp. That makes you last in line. If I want someone, I want to know exactly where to look for them, and I won't know that if everybody keeps moving around.

"Like I said, everyone stays in line. If you have trouble with me or don't like the rules, now's the best time to turn back. Remember your number. If you can't remember it, paint it on your wagon and pull out in that order. Meetin' over. Everyone get some rest. We'll roll at first light."

CHAPTER THIRTEEN

May 16, 1864

Under the orders of our guide, Guy Richards, and the brothers, Billy and Tommy Smith, the wagon line was formed. Moe, the old man in charge of Pete's chuck wagon, was in the lead. Mac, also on Pete's crew, came next with the supply wagon which held emergency equipment. Fifteen wagons, including ours, lined up behind Mac. There were many single men traveling with just their horse and pack mule. After them came the loose stock.

That evening several of us gathered around the campfire, sitting on camp chairs, logs, or a blankets on the ground. The women kept busy with mending or knitting while the men smoked their pipes and told stories.

"Enjoy it while you can," Hattie said, glancing at me. "These kinds of times don't come often."

"You know, Hattie, with everything that's happened to me in the past year, I've come to really appreciate when good happens. Before, I just took it for granted." I scratched Tag's head as he slept beside me.

Hattie reached over and patted my shoulder. "We all pretty much do that until life takes a hard turn, and you had your share." She tilted her head upward, and we both gazed up at the sky. I was sure that one star winked at me, just like pa used to do.

"How many stars you think are up there?" Sara whispered, sitting down next to us.

"Well, I counted at least a million," Guy said, smiling down at Sara. "Sara, would you walk a ways with me?"

"Yes, Guy," said Sara. "I'll be back shortly," she added, looking at me with a shy smile.

Becky grinned and nudged Charlie. "Betcha he kisses her."

"Now, Becky, Sara wouldn't allow that."

"Alright, girls, no gossiping. Get to bed," Hattie ordered. "Daybreak comes mighty early."

Some of the others were calling goodnight. "Big day tomorrow," Pete said, walking away.

"You weren't gone very long," I whispered when Sara crept into the tent shortly after we had all bedded down.

"Is everyone still awake?" She asked, carefully making her way over me.

"Are you kidding?" Charlie giggled. "Think we could get to sleep before hearing what happened with you and lover boy?"

"Charlie! It wasn't like that," Sara sputtered. "Guy just wanted to give me some advice."

"Sure," Becky teased, "Advice on kissing?"

"No. Don't be silly Becky," Sara scolded. "He told me we should stay close to camp and stay in pairs." She snuggled down in her bedroll.

"Seems kind of odd he'd have to take you for a walk to tell you that," Hattie growled.

"Well, he did ask me to go riding with him," Sara admitted shyly. "I can't believe he noticed me!"

"Why wouldn't he notice you?" I put in my two cents. "You're pretty, you're smart, and you're really nice." *Blonde and dainty too, just the kind men like*, I thought, remembering Ma's remarks. "Sara, you can use the side saddle and ride Boots."

"Oh, that's sweet of you to say, Martha, but I have a mirror. I see this ugly scar, and I wonder how anyone could call me pretty."

"Sara, that scar hardly shows," Hattie said firmly. "No one notices it. Don't worry about it and no one else will."

"She's right," the rest of the girls chimed in.

"Now get some sleep," Hattie ordered. "Daybreak comes early." Soon the only sounds in the tent were those of Tag snoring and the deep sighs of sleeping bodies.

Six Women West

Yes, daybreak came early, and we rolled. The drivers learned to stay in line and not to crowd the wagon in front. Pete yelled all the time at someone. If it wasn't a loose wheel, someone's child had wander off or some mule threw a shoe, and he yelled some more. We kept moving.

We were three days out of Independence. We were close to Alcove Spring, and then we would cross the Big Blue River, Hattie said. It was midmorning when Pete halted the wagons so we could all visit Alcove Spring. It was beautiful—an eleven-foot waterfall and clear sweet water. We filled everything that would hold water. Then we gathered for a prayer for the Donner Party and Sara Keyes. Mrs. Keyes had died there 18 years before. We moved on toward the Blue River with a slight rain falling. It was getting late, and we made camp two miles from the Blue.

> Comment [CJH]: I added this.

Loud rolls of thunder awakened me. Frightened, I sat straight up in my bedroll. The thunder took me back to the farm and the roar of cannon fire at Manassas. I pulled back the flap of the tent and looked up at the black sky. Bolts of lighting flashed across the night, lighting up huge oak trees like giant skeletons. Rain began to pound on the tent, waking the others.

"What is it? What's happening?" Bessie called out in a sleep-sodden voice.

"Go back to sleep. It's just a summer storm," Hattie said, coming to sit beside me. She put her arm across my shoulder. "It's alright, Martha. Nothing to be feared of. It's only thunder. It will pass."

"I know. I'm sorry. It's just that the sound took me back to the day we left the farm." I couldn't stop trembling as the incidents of the past year filled my mind. Hattie patted my back in an obvious effort to calm me.

"Now, now, it's not a bad thing to be scared. Hell, we all get scared sometime. Try and get some sleep."

I crawled back in my bedroll and tried to black out the memories, but I lay awake a long time.

It was still raining hard at daybreak. Sara pulled our rain slickers from the trunk and passed them out. Pete told us to roll without breakfast, so Bessie passed out biscuits left from the night before.

"Fine thing," Becky complained, "Here it is the middle of May. Think we'd have sunshine, for goodness sake."

"Oh, stop your whining, Becky," Charlie growled. "C'mon, let's get saddled up."

"Sara, you ride Sugar. Bessie, you ride Flower," I said, starting towards Gray Lady.

"Lawd, Miss Martha, I be ridin' in the wagon," Bessie told me, as she began breakin' camp.

"Nope, Bessie. Nobody's ridin' in the wagon today. Too hard on the mules." Hattie's tone suggested she wouldn't be doing any negotiating. You either ride your mule or walk. I'll only be ridin' on account I'm doin' the drivin'." She pulled her hat down around her face. "We could end up pushin' this wagon."

"Oh, Father in Heaven," Sara moaned. "What have I got myself into?"

Pete and Guy rode up, shouting above the rain that we were ready to roll, and roll we did, until around midmorning. Hattie climbed down from the wagon and joined the rest of us in the back-breaking, dirty task of keeping the wagon moving forward. We inched forward through the thick, stinky mud. The mules pulled. We pushed. With every step forward, we slid several steps backward.

I looked over at Bessie who worked beside me. Her straw hat drooped pathetically over her face. I reached into the wagon and handed her one of the

Six Women West

leather hats I bought at the mercantile store in Independence.

"Guess y'all were right about my straw."

> **Comment [CJH]:** No comment was made in reference to Bessie's straw hat before this.

Pete came riding up, covered with mud from head to foot. "You gals doin' alright?" he asked.

"We're doin' just fine," Hattie called from the other side of the wagon. "No need to worry yourself about us."

Pete smiled, his teeth showing whitely in his muddy face. I knew I didn't need to worry about you, Miss Hattie. We won't be stoppin' for awhile yet. We'll keep movin' 'til we reach the river. Think you can hold on?"

"We'll hold on." Hattie's voice and meaning were loud and clear. "We might be female, but we're sure as hell not helpless."

Just as I thought I could go on no longer, I heard the sweetest words I'd ever heard.

"Pull up!" Pete yelled. "We'll camp here."

I had been pushing with my head down for so long I didn't realize we had reached the riverbank. I suppose I'd heard the sound of the river and just thought it was more rain.

Actually, the downpour had slowed to a light drizzle. We were wet clear through. I fantasized about a hot bath and warm clothes but knew I was in for being wet and miserable for a long while yet.

Pete directed, and the train lined up haphazardly along the riverbank. There wasn't any way to circle everyone trying to get out of the mud. Hattie maneuvered us into a site next to Abel. Except for Hattie, we all slumped down on the rocks, sighing with exhaustion. I heard a splash and looked up to see Tag taking a swim. *Lucky dog*, I thought enviously. The river was running rapid and high with a few green bushes along the edge. I look at it with pure anticipation of washing this mud off.

Hattie climbed down from the wagon and began issuing orders. "Charlie, you fetch the bucket of hot coals and get a fire going. Sara, you and Becky set up the canopy. Bessie, you get the food out. Martha, come with me. We'll tend the stock. We got to get the mud washed off the stock. Once we get camp set up, we can find a place to wash this mud off ourselves."

Groaning loudly, we helped each other up. "Slave driver," someone mumbled. I can't honestly say it wasn't me.

"We can do it," Charlie said.

"We gotta do it," Becky declared. "We told Pete we could hold our own. We can't back down when the goin' gets tough."

"You're right, Becky. Come on, let's show the rest of them just how strong and self-reliant we are," I said, feeling my spirits and my energy lift.

We got the chores done in record time, even for us. By the time we'd finished, Bessie and Sara had the spider-cooker up and Dutch ovens full of beans and rice. They had washed up and had a kettle of water heating for our use.

"You can wash what you have to now and do the rest later," Sara said. "I don't know about you all, but I'm starving."

"Golly, that smells good," Becky groaned. "My belly thinks my throat been cut." We all agreed and hurried to wash up and then unloaded a couple of camp chairs to sit on.

"You want to call Abel, Bessie?" Sara asked.

"Don't hafta bother 'bout dat," Abel said, walking up to them. "I done smelled da stew." He shook his head. "My, my, it sho' smells fine." He licked his lips. "Lawdy, what a day. Pete say we only made three miles. Sho' felt like a hundert." He stepped closer to the stew pot and sniffed. "Ah sees you gals done fine without no hep. Ah wanted to hep you but sho' was busy pushin' my own wagon. Miss Martha, I sho' does like dem mules you done got to hep out."

Big Blue River. This was to be our first major river crossing. "The river runs about four feet deep and has a strong current," Hattie told us, "so stay alert."

The river was pure and fresh, lined with cottonwoods and wildflowers. It was so picturesque, it reminded me of a painting.

Pete and Guy scouted out a natural crossing. With outriders in case of trouble, we watched as the chuck wagon slid down the bank and crossed with no problems. We were fifth in line. When it was our turn, Hattie cracked her whip over Rowdy, and he plunged the team forward. Charlie, Becky, and me followed behind on our horses. I could hear Hattie cussing as she urged the mules across. The wagon swayed with the current and started drifting downstream.

Bessie was riding beside Hattie, hanging on for dear life. She screamed and began praying in a full voice. "Save me, Jesus. Save this hyar sinner," she moaned, rocking back and forth, as the wagon continued its descent downstream.

I yelled for Charlie's help and brought my gray in close. I felt Lady braced her feet against the swift current as I threw a rope on the tool box on the side of the wagon. Pulling it taut, I managed to steady the wagon and halt its progress. Charlie roped the back end and held it straight as we crossed. Sara yelled out the back. "You're doing great."

"Nice work, girls," Hattie said. "You can hush now, Bessie. Jesus and the girls saved you this time."

By four that afternoon the rest of the wagons had crossed with only minor problems. Pete had given the order to circle up as we crossed. After everyone was across, he stopped by to speak to us. We had our camp set up and were starting our chores.

"Howdy, ladies," Pete said. "Nice job of crossing. You handled that well." He smiled at

Wanda Reed

Bessie. "Miss Bessie, I'm right glad to see the Lord delivered you safely across the river." He nodded to Hattie. "We'll rest up and leave tomorrow after church services. If you've got things that need to be done, now would be a good time to do 'em. There's gonna be a dance tonight." He tipped his hat and rode off.

"A dance!" Sara exclaimed. "What fun. Goodness, what will I wear?"

"I don't think Guy will care what you're wearing, Sara," I teased. I wasn't sure I wanted to attend the dance. I supposed I would be a wallflower sitting on the sidelines watching the others, plain as I was. "Come on, let's get down to that beautiful river and get some washing done." This was our first rest stop since we'd been on the trail four days. How we needed it! We were down to our cleanest dirty shirts.

We walked past Bert, Jewel, and Victory who had already started their wash on the banks of the river. We took time to talk a bit with each one. I carried our basket of dirty clothes, and Sara carried the tub. We went downstream, setting them on a sandy bar to fill our buckets. While Sara gathered some small wood to start the fire, I walked to the Reece's wagon and borrowed hot coals from Jodie. She was smearing some salve on her son Sy, who had gotten into some poison oak. Soon we had a roaring fire. While the water heated, we stretched a rope between two trees to hang our clothes. "It sure is a pretty river once you get across," Sara said. "It was scary crossing. I was sure we'd be killed."

"I'm glad I didn't have to ride the wagon," I admitted. "I thought Bessie was going to jump straight up to Heaven. Her eyes were as big as dollars. She was prayin' for all she was worth," I laughed.

> **Comment [CJH]:** Only time this name is mentioned

"And Ma Brown yelling and cussing them mules. It's sure funny now," Sara said, giggling. "One was praying and one was cussing."

"If Hattie hears you calling her Ma Brown, she'll skin you alive," I said. "We better get to work and get this wash done. Do we have any dirty trousers for Becky?"

"Yes. I wish I had bought one more pair of britches," said Sara. "They don't get as dirty as a dress."

We filled the tub. I grabbed the lye soap and began scrubbing the clothes.

"Have you heard that Ruth Riley is sick?"

"Yes. We should go by and see her."

"That's a good idea. After we finish our wash, let's do that." Sara lowered her voice. "I finished Becky's dress. She can wear it to the dance if she takes a bath."

We were almost finished hanging the wash when Mary Louise walked up. Her family was in the wagon just behind Abel's. "I just picked up Ruth's baby, Polly, crawling near the riverbank. Just lucky I saw her or she would have fell in. She is awful dirty, and her diaper hadn't been changed in awhile from the smell of her. I carried her back to their wagon and woke Clem. I told him she needed to be bathed and changed and then fed and put down for a nap. If Ruth is too sick to tend to the baby, we better look in on her, don'cha 'spose?"

"Martha, you go. I'll finish here," Sara said.

"Alright." I didn't like the thought of going around the Riley men, but as long as there were two of us I didn't mind so much.

When we arrived at the wagon, we found Polly tied with a rope playing in the dirt while Mr. Riley sat sleeping in a chair propped against the wagon. It was obvious he had not tended to her. Her blonde curly hair was matted, and her little body was covered in dirt. Her potty was dried on her legs. Her big eyes, blue as cornflowers, stared up at us.

I knelt down beside her. "Hello, Polly. We'll get you changed in just a minute, alright baby?"

Polly nodded, smiling shyly.

Mary Louise took hold of Clem's outstretched boot and shook it. "How is Ruth feeling today?"

He slowly opened his eyes and replied grumpily, "She's poorly, been that way for awhile. Can't get up and 'round to do her chores."

You old carbuncle, I thought. *It wouldn't hurt you none to get off your bony behind and help out.* I didn't say anything as I was afraid it would just make things worse for Ruth.

"May we see her, Mr. Riley?"

"Yeah, go on in. If she's awake, get her up."

When we opened the back flap, a horrible odor hit us in the face. It was the smell of sickness, body odor, and filth. Ruth obviously was in bad shape.

"Ruth, may we come in? We're here to help you," I said.

A low moan came from the direction of her bed. "Polly? Where's Polly?"

"We'll take care of Polly, Ruth. Don't worry. We'll take care of you, too," Mary Louise said.

"I'll put some water on to heat, if you want to stay here with her," I offered, and went outside.

"She gittin' up?" Riley growled.

"No, Mr. Riley, your wife is very sick. She needs care. She needs a bath, so I would appreciate it if you would put a kettle of water on to heat." I shook my head in disbelief that a husband could be so uncaring. "I'll take Polly to my wagon and leave her with Sara. That is, with your permission, of course." I couldn't keep the sarcasm out of my voice.

"I don't care what y'all does with the kid. You can throw her in the river. Don't make no mind to me." He got up and started to walk away as if he didn't have a care.

"The water, Mr. Riley?" I called.

He turned to me, "You get it yourself, you damn woman trying to act like man. You need a man to put you in your place. Not that you could find one that would have you." He waved his hand and kept on walking.

I found a bucket, filled it with water at the river, and then ran back to the fire. Polly stared at me, her eyes filled with questions.

"Come on, little lady, let's find you some clean clothes and take you to Miss Sara. Okay?"

Sara, she's in bad shape, and that husband of hers..." I shook my head in disgust.

"You go ahead. I'll see to Polly. I've got Bessie to help me."

Back at the Riley's, the water was hot enough and I brought it into the wagon. Mary Louise had moved Ruth from the urine-soaked bed into a chair. Ruth seemed barely conscious, not speaking or offering help or resistance as we bathed her.

We slipped a clean shift over her frail body.

"We should try to get some food and liquid down her," Mary Louise said.

"I'll run and ask Bessie for some soup. I think she has some beef broth."

"What did you do with Polly?" Mary Louise asked softly.

"Polly? Polly?" Ruth cried out, startling us.

"Polly's just fine, Ruth. She's with Sara," I told her, leaning over to stroke her hot forehead.

"Are you in pain, Ruth? What can we do for you? Would you eat some broth?" Mary Louise questioned.

"No, no food." She put her hand on her stomach. "Hurts, hurts real bad."

"I'll bring Charlie back with me," I decided aloud. "She knows something about doctoring." I grabbed up some diapers and a dress for Polly and, saying I'd be right back, I took off for our wagon.

On the way, I stopped at Lucinda's. Quickly I told her what was happening and asked for her help. She said she'd get some of the other women, and they'd take turns caring for Ruth.

Sara had washed and diapered Polly, using some soft cotton. She was holding and rocking the child as if she had been doing it all her life. Polly's eyes were closed, and she slept like the baby she was.

I started off across the campground looking for Charlie. I located her at Pete's wagon. "Oh, Charlie, I've been tryin' to find you. Ruth Riley is real sick. Could you take a look?"

"What seems to be the matter?"

"She's complaining about her stomach. Says it hurts real badly."

"Okay, we'll need to stop and get my bag. Clem didn't beat her again, did he?"

"I don't know, but there's no marks on her face. I haven't looked at her body. He's mad at her for being sick, and he just took off when I ask him to get a bucket of water."

"Well, I don't know much about the insides of a person. All I know is births, stitches, and settin' bones. Just a little about stomach poison and the flux. It's a shame there isn't a doctor on the train."

We picked up Charlie's bag and hurried to the Riley's wagon.

"She's asleep," Mary Louise told us.

"I hate to bother her. I'll be real careful." Charlie put her hand on Ruth's forehead. "God, she's burnin' up. Get some water from the river. We'll try and bring her temperature down with a sponge bath."

I hurried off to get the water. When I got back, Ruth was conscious and moaning.

"She woke up when I started pokin' her stomach. I think she's got appendicitis or is hurt inside. Ain't nothin' I can do except maybe give her some licorice tea to help ease the pain. We need some laudanum. Maybe I'm wrong. I sure hope so!"

We applied cold wet cloths to Ruth's body, but the fever didn't go down. Charlie made the tea, and we spoon-fed her, hoping it would help.

"Polly's with Sara. We'll keep her until..." I hesitated. "Well, for as long as needed." Charlie and I left with a promise to return around nine o'clock.

After supper, sitting around the campfire talk turned to Ruth and who would take care of Polly.

"I asked the old man if I could bring Polly to our wagon. He told me in no uncertain terms I could throw her in the river." Everyone was shocked and angry.

"Why, that old jackass!" Becky swore. "I'd like to throw him in the river and hold him down for 'bout an hour."

"If there are no objections, I'd like to take care of Polly while Ruth is sick, and if the worst comes, I'll raise her," Sara volunteered shyly, holding the now shiny clean baby in her lap. Polly was occupied with patting Tag, who was lying as close as he could get to Sara. He seemed to be in heaven.

The talk turned to the dance and what we would wear and who would dance with whom.

"We better get busy. With six of us in that tent getting dressed all at once, we'll need extra time," Sara reminded us.

"You girls do what you have to. I'm goin' just like I am. This here ridin' skirt will do just fine," Hattie said. "I'll walk over and check on Ruth."

Sara had several dresses and loaned Charlie a scoop-necked yellow one, which really made her brown eyes sparkle and called attention to the fact she was well-endowed. I took out my blue summer cotton. I didn't know if it did anything for me, but I felt comfortable in it. Becky watched silently as we dressed. She stared at our colorful dresses. There was an expression of longing on her face.

"Becky," I said, "Your dress is on your bedroll. You put it on and see if it fits." I winked at Sara, who was trying not to smile. Waiting for Becky's reaction, it was hard to keep a straight face.

She went to her bedroll and picked up the dress, ignoring the camisole and waist cincher. "This is for me?" She shook her head. "It's real pretty. It's too nice for me."

The dress was mint green cotton with full sleeves and a sweetheart neck line. The sleeves, bust inset and bottom ruffle had green and white stripes. Sara and I had agreed it would look great with Becky's flaming red hair.

"Don't be silly, Becky. It's just right for you. It will look beautiful on you."

"It's too nice. I can't borrow it. What if someone made fun of me and I got in a fight and it got it tore?" She shook her head vehemently. "No, I can't wear it."

"You must wear it, Becky. I made it for you," Sara insisted. "It's yours to keep and don't worry about fighting—you won't. Ladies don't fight."

"Mine? You made it for me? Oh, Sara!" Becky's green eyes filled with tears.

"Now, now, don't go making a fuss. It's just a dress," Sara said. "I'm making one for everyone. So hurry and put it on."

Holding up the camisole and waist cincher, Becky asked, "What's these? I can figure out the dress, but what's these other doodads for?"

"The camisole covers your breasts and the bloomers cover your legs. The waist-cincher gives you a small waist," Sara explained.

"Well, I'll cover my breasts, but I ain't wearin' that thing," Becky declared, throwing the cincher on the bed.

Laughing, we helped Becky dress. "It's a beautiful dress. First I ever had," she whispered, stroking it softly.

Six Women West

After she had changed into the dress, the image of a boy was gone. "You look beautiful in it," I said. The cut of the dress made her small breasts seem larger, and her naturally curly hair had grown 'til it brushed her shoulders. She looked every bit a woman. I was curious to see the reactions of the young men at the dance. They were in for a surprise.

Polly had fallen asleep on Sara's bedroll. Picking her up gently, Sara moved the sleeping Polly into the wagon. Tag jumped in and settled down next to her. Bringing her Sunday shawl of lace, Sara rejoined us. Bessie stopped and picked up a dried apple pie for offering.

"Tag will watch over her," I said. "Let's go." We walked across the grass circle to the center of the wagon circle where the men had built a large bonfire, put up lanterns for light, and set up a makeshift table under the only tree in the circle, laden with food and a bowl of punch.

The men had brought out their banjos, squeezeboxes, fiddles, juice harps, and anything else they played. There was a washtub with a board and strings they were warming up to play music. Loud and lively, it gave a little bounce to our steps as we hurried to join the others. Everyone had come. The women were in clean dresses, and some of the men even wore ties. Those who had chairs brought them, and barrels with boards across made benches to sit on. Some had spread blankets around. There was a barn dance atmosphere. I was both excited and nervous. Ma taught me to dance, but I'd never danced with a boy.

"What if someone asks me to dance?" I whispered to Sara. "What will I do?"

"Why, say yes, silly," Sara giggled.

The music stopped, and Mr. Crayon stepped upon a box and began to clap his hands and stomp his foot.

"Find a pardner. Form your squares. "

> **Comment [CJH]:** Speaking as a mother, leaving a crawling baby where she could fall out of the wagon seems irresponsible. You might consider having someone stay behind to watch her in addition to Tag.

Guy ran over and grabbed Sara by the hand, bringin' her to the center that had been formed for the dance floor. Pete pulled Hattie into the square, and Abel took Bessie's hand and urged her to join the group.

"Becky? Is that you?" Tommy Smith asked, staring at her with round eyes.

She nodded and took his outstretched hand. "I never done this before," she admitted.

"It's okay. You look pretty. I'll help you," he said, grinning widely. "Just keep walking forward."

Some fellow grabbed Charlie and pulled her into the square. I was wondering if I would get to dance when Billy Smith reached for my hand. "Come on, Miss Martha."

I held back. "I don't know..." I stammered.

"Aw, there ain't nuthin' to it," he said, coaxing me into the square.

"Don't be bashful. Jump right in," Mr. Crayon urged. "Okay, here we go. We got four squares." He was patting his hands and tapping his foot.

"All join hands and circle to the left. Circle back to the right. Gents to the center with a right hand star. Pick up your lady and star promenade. Chicken in the bread pan pickin' out dough. Grab your pardner and do si do. Swing her high, swing her low. Swing your corner and do si do. Throw her out, catch what you can, and promenade around."

Dresses were swirling about in a rainbow of colors. With Billy's strong hand on my waist, I had no trouble following the calls. "Goodness, this is fun," I confided.

"See? I told you there was nuthin' to it," Billy said with a wink.

When the square dance ended, he brought me back to the edge of the dance floor where I'd been standing. "Thanks, Miss Martha. Now I best give the other girls a whirl."

"Thank you, Billy." Feeling flushed, I walked around the dance floor to the tree where the punchbowl was set. Several people were standing around, obviously enjoying the music and the punch. Three of the Riley boys stood a few feet apart from the rest of us, smirking and making crude remarks. It was obvious they'd been drinking something stronger than punch.

Pete went up and spoke to them. I couldn't hear what was said, but their faces turned red and they left the dance. I was glad to see them go.

"How's your father-in-law holding up to the trip?" I asked Jewel.

"You know how old men are," she answered. "He's fit when he wants and sick when he don't. At the age of seventy four, I guess you just put up with 'em."

"They're startin' the Virginia Reel. I got to go find Boyd. Thanks for askin'."

"May I have the privilege of this dance with you Miss Martha?" asked Mr. Crayon. He took my hand.

"Most certainly, sir," I replied.

As the evening wore on, I watched as Sara and Guy danced every dance together. When the music stopped, they came over to me. "We're going to check on Polly," she whispered, smiling. They reminded me of a couple married and very much in love. Hattie seemed to be enjoying the attentions of Pete, who took time out from dancing with the single ladies to bring her punch. It became obvious that Abel was courting Bessie. I couldn't help but smile as I watched him outmaneuver those that tried to get a dance with her. I was really pleased that people accepted the only black people on the train. *Of course*, I thought, *it would be awfully hard not to like either of them.* As far as I could see, everyone seemed to be paired up except me, Charlie, and Becky.

I was about ready to leave when Gus asked me to dance. "Figured I could manage one of these

Wanda Reed

h'yar slow ones," he told me. Mo was waiting when the waltz was over and the musicians began a Virginia Reel for the third time.

"Now you done with that old man, I'll show you how us young 'uns dance," he joked.

"I don't know," I ventured, as he took my hand.

"Jes foller my lead." We joined the line, and I discovered I was able to do the steps easily. Something Pa had told me long ago popped into my head: *We Irish are born for music. Dancing and singing just come natural to us.*

"You're a fine dancer, Miss Martha," Mo said, squeezing my hand

"Thank you, Mo. I enjoyed it." He left to rejoin Gus, and I smiled. Both men were old enough to be my Pa and just "titty high," as Bessie would say.

I strolled over by the front of the wagon and stared up at the sky, looking at the stars—more than I had ever seen before. Hearing the laughter and the music in the background, I had never felt so alone. Would there ever be someone for me like there was for Sara and Bessie? Why did I have to be born so tall and plain? My thoughts wandered back to Pa and the things he told me after Ma had gotten on me.

If you could see yourself through other people's eyes, you would see a lovely person, Lassie. Your ma has her own notions of what a woman should look like, but that's not everybody's feelings. You have a bright mind, and you're polite, helpful, and honest. He'd stroke my hair. *Your hair,* he'd say, *is like my own dear ma's. As rich and shiny as a freshly groomed chestnut horse and, lass, those tears you be sheddin',* he'd continued, *make your green eyes sparkle like dew on a shamrock.*

"Oh, Pa," I whispered. "It didn't help when I was growing up, and it doesn't help now. Besides, what are my chances of finding a man who wants a wife six feet tall and as strong as he is?" I sighed. "Sure, about as much chance as catching a falling

> **Comment [CJH]:** N.B. Throughout when Martha thinks, prays, or remembers something like this, I put it in italics instead of quotes. Before it was sometimes in quotes and sometimes italics.

star." A tear slid down my cheek. I rubbed my eyes, the sound of music and laughter ringing in my ears. Throwing back my shoulders, I said to myself, "Martha get off your poor-me pot. You're going to Oregon." I walked back to the dance.

Sara and Guy were back, dancing and gazing into each others' eyes like two lovebirds. Charlie and Becky were taking turns dancing with Billy and Tommy. Bessie and Abel finished dancing and disappeared into the shadows of the night. Would they kiss and say sweet words to each other? I managed to swallow the pangs of envy I felt.

Families had started leaving, heading for their wagons. I waved goodbye to Sara and Guy and headed for our wagon. Tag jumped out of the wagon to greet me. In our tent I changed into my trousers and slipped my gun into my waistband. Since the Riley boys were liquored up, I felt safer armed. Starting toward the Riley's wagon I said to Tag, "Good Boy. Stay here. I'll be back." I hurried over to the Riley wagon to relieve Jo.

Josephine Tanner stood outside the Riley wagon looking across the circle at the people dancing and clapping her hands lightly to the music.

"Hi Jo, how's Ruth feeling?"

"Her fever's high and she's been moaning a lot, holding her belly. Glad you're here. I've got to go and tend to Boris. He's got the trots."

"Okay. Thanks for sitting." I stood there feeling the night air, looking up to the starry sky. It was a beautiful night, the frogs croaking in the background creating their own music.

I climbed into the wagon and knelt beside Ruth. Both she and the wagon's interior smelled a lot better, though the odor of sickness still lingered. Ruth moaned softly. I touched her forehead. She was burning up. I poured a healthy slug of moonshine from a nearby jug and held the cup to her lips. "Drink this. It'll help the pain."

She fluttered her eyelids. "Oh, it hurts. Where's Polly?" she whispered, pushing the cup away.

"She's with Sara. She's fine." I assured her.

"Sorry I'm late. I had to change," Charlie said, crawling in beside me. "How is she?"

"She's in severe pain. I tried to get her to drink this moonshine. I thought it would help ease the pain."

"Martha, take this sheet down to the river and soak it good and hurry back. We got to get her fever down, and this is the only way I know with what we've got to work with."

Ruth barely protested when we stripped her down and wrapped her thin body in the cold wet sheet.

"Did you notice those awful bruises on her body?" I asked, feeling pretty certain as to how she'd gotten them.

"Yeah. That dirty bastard. I'd like to take Hattie's whip to him," Charlie muttered. "You'd think one of them would ask about Ruth. They're a strange family."

Throughout the night, Charlie and I spelled each other while the other took a turn at caring for Ruth. She was getting worse. Her fever was still high, and by dawn she was delirious.

"Mary, she is a lot worse. We'll stay with her. I'm afraid she may not have long."

We jumped at the sound of an ear-piercing scream from Ruth, a scream of terrible pain.

"I'll bet her appendix ruptured," Charlie said, as we rushed to climb back in the wagon. Charlie and I knelt down next to Ruth. Charlie touched her forehead and quickly pulled her hand back. "Heavens! I never knew nobody could get so hot!" she exclaimed.

"Ruth? Ruth?" I didn't know what to say or do.

"Martha?" she whispered.

"Yes, Ruth, it's me."

"Martha, Polly. She's not Clem's." She shivered, and it was obvious it took all her strength to speak. Her eyes opened wide.

"Tell Sara to take care of her. Keep her. Please. Clem mustn't…" With a shuddering gasp, she collapsed.

Charlie put her ear to Ruth's heart, "She's gone," she said sadly.

"Go with God," I whispered, reaching down to close her eyes. Charlie and I stood in silence, each with our own thoughts. I was trying to understand what Ruth had said regarding Polly. That would explain Clem's attitude towards the child.

Walking up to the fire circle which was out completely, we heard Clem. "Damn! No fresh coffee! Who let the fire go out? Damn women all over the place and no coffee."

"I'll tell him," I said to Charlie. "I don't think you can hold your temper, and there's no use getting him riled up." I climbed down from the wagon.

"I'm sorry. Ruth's dead. We did everythin' we could," Charlie began.

"Her price of sin is paid. I'll tell the boys. They can dig the grave."

He didn't seem at all upset. *As if this wasn't the woman he had once loved and married*, I thought. *Or had he ever loved her?*

"If it's alright with you, we'll prepare Ruth for burial and speak to Pete about a service," I said, trying hard to keep my disgust for him out of my voice.

"No need. Just wrap her in a blanket. We'll bury her right away. Don't need no service for the sinful."

"But…" I protested. He turned his back and started building a fire.

"No use talkin' with the old jackass," Charlie said. "Come on. We've done all we can here."

We started for the tent, "Let's talk to Pete," Charlie said.

"Good thinking."

"He doesn't want a service for her," I complained, after telling him of Ruth's passing.

"Well, Mr. Riley doesn't have the last word around here. Ruth will have a service whether he likes it or not," Pete stated firmly. "I'll tell him. Girls, spread the word—we stay here tonight."

Relieved, Charlie and I went to our wagon to tell the girls.

The grave was situated under a white oak. I wondered whose decision that was because it seemed like a nice place, and I couldn't imagine Clem choosing it. There was no coffin. Ruth was wrapped in an old gray blanket. Pete recited the Lord's Prayer and we sang "Rock of Ages." "Anythin' you want to say, Riley?" Pete asked.

"It's over. She paid the price for her sin." He got on his horse and rode away without looking back. The four boys stayed to pile rocks on the grave, and the rest of us returned to our wagons.

Sara and me were seated on a blanket in front of our wagon playing with Polly when Ted, the youngest Riley boy, rode up and handed Sara a pillowcase stuffed with clothes. He had a little boy look to his face with the blue eyes and light brown, curly hair.

"This here's Polly's and Ruth's clothes in case you need them." He smiled shyly. "I'm real glad you're takin' Polly, Miss Sara."

"I'm happy to do it," Sara said, hugging Polly to her.

The boy seemed reluctant to leave. "I carved her name on the tree, like a headstone," he said, looking as if he were embarrassed at showing sentiment.

"Step down, Ted," I interjected. As he dismounted, Tag went over and pranced around his boots, hoping for a pat or two. "That was very thoughtful of you," I said. "I'll bet you chose the gravesite, too, didn't you?"

"Yeah, Ruth was mighty nice to me. My ma died when I was eleven."

"I'm sorry. It must have been hard for all of you." I paused. "Your pa didn't seem too heartbroken about Ruth, if you don't mind my saying so," I said.

"Naw, Pa just married her for a housekeeper. Her family was killed in the war. She was down on her luck and lookin' for work. Pa ran across her outside a saloon and hired her to cook for us." He paused, frowning. "Course, the boys started sparkin' her, so Pa upped and married her himself. She was mighty pretty then. If Ruth talked or was nice to any of us boys, Pa would slap her. Don't think Ruth was ever happy with us, though, especially after she was attacked."

"Attacked?" Sara and I both looked shocked.

"Well, she didn't actually get herself attacked. I mean, it weren't her fault. Pa blamed her, I think. He didn't want admit he was wrong to leave her alone in town on a wagon in a town full of drunken men."

"My goodness! How awful," Sara exclaimed.

"Poor Ruth," I said. "Is Polly. . .?" I glanced at the baby asleep in Sara's arms.

"Yep, the way Ruth told me, three of them bastards...." He blushed and stammered, "Sorry, ladies." Looking down, he vigorously petted Tag.

"It's okay, Ted, go on with your story," I urged.

"Well, she weren't flauntin' herself as Pa made out. Three varmints pulled her out of the wagon, beat the hell out of her, and had their way with her. When she found out she was carryin' a babe, Pa just treated her terrible." Ted shook his head. "Me? I figure he was to blame for leavin' her. He got to shouting all the time 'bout the price of sin. Sometimes he accused us boys for gettin' her in the family way. Shore got tiresome listenin' to him rave."

"That's awful!" I said. "Best of luck to you, Ted. You're a good person. Maybe we'll see you at Fort Kearny."

"Thanks, Miss Martha. I hope you all have a safe trip." He started off and then stopped and turned back. "Miss Sara, the old nanny goat was Ruth's. You better take it so you'll have milk for Polly."

"Thank you, Ted. We'll go get it when Polly wakes up." We waved goodbye as Ted rode off.

"It's a shame when a family tears apart in bad times. It's hard to understand why he married her. Was it free labor or to keep one of his boys from marrying her?"

"I don't think he was ever a warm, caring person," Sara commented. "He seemed heartless with his boys, too. He's a deranged man."

"I'll go check on the horses." I walked off and left Sara curled up with Polly. Tag stayed on the blanket and seemed to be keeping one eye on Polly. Obviously, he thought of her as his own personal responsibility.

CHAPTER FOURTEEN

Breaking camp at dawn and traveling 'til dark with only short rest breaks for the mules, we covered many miles alongside the Little Blue. Pete rode up beside us, calling out, "We're coming up on the Platte. Circle up, ladies. We'll make camp here and cross in the morning. Becky-girl, you spread the word."

Moe slowly formed a circle with Pete yelling for them to close up ranks. "Make sure everythin's tied down tight. You wouldn't want to lose anythin' in the Platte."

Hattie got us a good place to camp with our back side to the north wind. Once we were unhitched, we dragged out the tent, put down the groundcover, and got the tent up. I worked fast and soon had a small fire going underneath the canopy. Bessie had coffee brewing when Pete rode up and slid off his horse. He seemed in good cheer in spite of the griping over crossing the Platte.

"Howdy, Miss Bessie," said Pete. "How's chances of gettin' a hot cup of coffee?" Looking at Hattie, he said, "Decided to stop at Fort Kearny for those who need supplies. Some forgot their salt and pepper. Why is it some always leaves short on supplies?"

"Sho, Mr. Pete. Hunker down there on that barrel close to the wagon. It's mostly cool there. I'll fetch yo coffee."

He took a big swallow of coffee and smiled appreciatively at Bessie sitting on camp chair. "You sure make good coffee, ma'am."

Bessie grinned and kept on peeling potatoes.

"We sure got lucky when Bessie decided to join up with us," Hattie remarked, picking up a knife to help pare the potatoes.

"Might not have her long if Abel has anythin' to do with it," Pete said, winking at Hattie.

"Well, he'll have to fight us for her," Becky said, coming around the wagon with Charlie. "We got the tent up and the bedrolls out."

"Boy, it sure is hot. That wind near blew us away," Charlie said. "The tent's tied real sturdy." She wiped her face and reached for a mug. "Polly awake yet?" she asked, as Sara climbed down from the wagon.

"No, she's still asleep." Sara smiled widely. "She's such a little angel. I'm so happy she's with us." Shaking her head, she added, "Tag thinks he's her personal protector."

"Yes, I noticed that," I said. "I think I lost my dog," I chuckled. "Charlie, how about you and Becky help me go drag up a log? We can sit on it and then burn it when we need it."

"Just as soon as I have some coffee," Charlie said.

"Well, ladies, thanks for the coffee. I got to go check on the tenderfeet," Pete said, rinsing out his cup. "They're slow as molasses makin' and breakin' camp."

"Not findin' fault with our bunch, are you, Pete?" Hattie asked, with a frown.

"Not a chance, girl. You gals put the big boys to shame." He grinned. "But, unlike you, most of 'em ain't in shape to pull fifteen or twenty miles a day." He shook his head.

"Well, Pete, keep in mind this is just the first three hundred miles. They'll start to toughen up," Hattie reminded him. Turning to Becky and Charlie, Hattie said, "Better pull up a couple of logs."

"Say, Pete, supper's gonna be ready soon. Why don't you join us when you finish your rounds?" I asked, feeling it would please Hattie.

"That's right nice of you, Miss Martha. Be glad to." He glanced at Hattie, who avoided his eyes. He climbed on his horse and turned to move away, but Henry Davis came running up.

"Pete! Pete!"

"Yeah, what is it, Henry?"

"Damn thievin' varmints are at it again," Henry said in a controlled anger. "My supper just disappeared off the fire. Our whole pot of stew's gone. Bert's mad as hell, and I ain't got any supper."

"Consarn it! That's one every night since we left the Big Blue. Somebody's out of supplies or too lazy to cook," Pete growled. "Moe will give you some stew for your supper. Tell Bert not to worry. We'll find your pot in the mornin' if it's like the others."

"Thanks, Pete," Henry said and took off running. Pete left too.

"I think we know who the thieves are," said Hattie. "It started when Ruth died. Everyone I've talked to figures it's the Riley boys. Why can't we set a trap for them?"

"Good thinkin'. Got any ideas?"

Mary Louise Crane walked up to our fire with a worried frown on her face. She went straight to Hattie, very upset, saying, "All my coffee is gone. I don't know where it went. Could I borrow enough to get us through to the fort?"

"Mrs. Mary, I get you some coffee," said Bessie.

"I'll report it to Pete," said Hattie.

"I'm sure he can replace it from the supply wagon," I added.

"Thanks. I don't know where that coffee went, but I got my ideas. Bye. Tell Pete I'll be waitin' for him. I know someone was in my wagon prowling."

"Boy, I'm glad somethin's finally gonna be done 'bout those lazy thieves," Charlie said. "This is gettin' bad—stealin' food."

"Yes. I don't feel safe with them in camp. I don't trust them," Sara said.

"Don't worry, Sara. We won't let anything happen to you or Polly," I told her firmly.

"Speaking of Polly, don't I hear her?" Becky asked, glancing toward the wagon.

"Yes. She's probably hungry." Sara opened the flap and turned to Charlie. "Would you get the goat so I can milk her?"

"Sure," Charlie said as she left, "and I'll milk her for you.".

After the goat was milked and Polly had been changed and fed, we took turns playing with her 'til supper was ready.

"Just followed the smell," Pete said as he rode up with Abel close behind him. They dismounted and entered the tent together.

"Watch Polly for a minute, will you, Martha?" Sara whispered. "I have to go to the brush."

"Sure. Take Tag with you. " I took Polly, enjoying the clean, sweet smell of her, so different than when I pick her up at the Riley wagon. *Life was so strange*, I thought. *If the war hadn't intervened, I might still be in Manassas holding my own baby. Ma would have liked that.*

"Y'all take a plate and help yoselves," Bessie said. "Der's butter in a dish yonder."

"Sho' will, Miss Bessie," Abel said, taking the pie tin she held out.

"Don' wants the biscuits to get cold. Dis butter Miss Charlie done milked from one of dem cows."

Sara came running back into camp, obviously distraught. She rushed up to the group near the fire followed by closely by Tag, "Oh, Hattie," she began, and seeing Pete, turned to him. "Pete," she stammered. "Jed and Cleo stopped me as I was coming out of the brush. I was so scared. I just froze, but Tag got between us and bared his teeth, growling."

"My goodness, Sara. Are you alright?" I asked, putting my arm around her trembling shoulders. "What did they say?"

"They want money!"

"Money?" Pete bellowed, putting down his cup.

"Yes. They said they would take Polly away from me if I don't give them one hundred dollars." Sara broke into tears. "Pete, I don't have much money. Can they take Polly away from me?"

Hattie stuck out her chin. "Honey, they ain't nobody gonna take Polly. We'll take care of those varmints."

"That's the last straw," Pete declared, shaking his head. "What the hell's wrong with that bunch? Good for nuthin' hooligans! No, Sara, they ain't takin' Polly. In fact, they ain't gonna be around no more."

He turned to Abel. "We'll get Guy and have a word with them boys. Hattie, get the girls in the tent. I leave it to you to watch out for them." The two men left the tent.

"Becky," I whispered, motioning to her. "Let's follow them. We'll stay close enough to help if they need it."

"Now you two be careful," Hattie warned. "No tellin' what those no-goods will do if they're cornered."

Becky grabbed her rifle, and we stayed a short distance behind Abel and Pete as they hurried towards Guy's wagon. We watched and listened as the three men discussed what needed to be done.

"The lazy thieves have given this train enough trouble," Pete stated firmly. "I'm goin' to kick 'em off. I may need you two to back me up in case they don't take kindly to it."

They all three started for the Riley's wagon. Becky and I stayed in the shadows close behind.

"Jed! Cleo! Get out here! I want to talk to you!" Pete yelled.

"Yeah, what you want, Mr. Wagon Boss?" Jed asked sarcastically as he climbed from the wagon.

"Git your brother out here. What I've got to say is for the both of you."

"Hey, Cleo, the big man wants to talk at you," Jed called.

"I'm comin'. Jes' hold your horses." The younger man joined his brother beside the wagon. He wiped his face with the arm of his shirt. They stood with arms crossed, staring defiantly at Pete. The air smelled heavy of stew.

"Okay, we're here," said Jed.

Pete stood about two feet in front of Jed. "First of all," he began, "you got no business askin' Sara for money for takin' care of your sister. She's doin' what's best for Polly," Pete told them.

"Well, hell, boss, she's our sister. We got a right to get somethin' for that woman takin' her from us." Jed rolled his eyes and tried to look pitiful.

"That's right," Cleo interrupted. "I bet you a lot of people would be happy to pay for her." Sneering, he added, "Maybe even the Indians."

"You low-down coyote!" Guy roared. "I'd like to kick your ass from here to Kansas."

"Hold it, Guy," Pete cautioned. "We won't get rough unless we have to." He glared at Jed. "Ruth's last wish was that Polly stay with Sara, and that's where she's gonna stay. There were several witnesses to that."

Staring Jed in the eye, Abel said quietly," You don' be botherin' Miss Sara no mo'," his tone threatening.

"Hey, nigger, you don't be threatenin' us," Jed growled, starting toward Abel, who stood his ground.

Becky and I hunkered down behind the Riley wagon, watching and waiting. Becky seemed calm enough, but my heart was beating fast, and I wondered what I would do if things got nasty.

"We'll have none of that," Pete said, stepping in between the men. "I want you off this wagon train. Now! Pack up and go."

"What if we don't wanna leave, Mr. Wagon Master?" Cleo put in, smiling confidently.

"It don't matter what you want," Pete said. "You've caused enough trouble. I want you gone before some of the folks decide to string you up."

"Shut up, Cleo," Jed ordered. "Will it be okay if we leave at sun-up, Pete? We don't want no trouble."

"Fine, but, I'll be here to make sure you do. Come on, fellows. I don't think they'll give us any more trouble. Let's go, Guy, Abel."

When they were out of earshot, Pete said, "Something's wrong. This is too easy."

"Seems they are goin' too easy," remarked Guy, as they passed Becky and me hiding in the shadows.

"They sho' acted agreeable," Abel said. "Bet they up to somethin'."

When they reached the supply wagon, we took off for ours, hoping to get back in the tent before they got there.

"Dangit!" Becky swore. "They didn't need us." She stroked the butt of her handgun. "I was itchin' to use this."

"Oh, Becky, you wouldn't really shoot anyone, would you?"

"Damn right, I would. Done it before when it needed doin', and I ain't afraid to do it again." We managed to get back to the tent ahead of the guys and then tried to look as if we'd never left.

"Hattie, it's Pete. Okay if we come in?"

"Come on. We've been waitin' to hear what happened," Hattie said, looking up at Pete from her bedroll where she sat.

"Didn't the girls tell you?" Pete asked, coming inside, looking at me and Becky. Abel and Guy were right behind him. Guy went over to Sara and whispered, "You alright, Miss Sara?"

Wanda Reed

I didn't hear her answer, but I saw her smile. *He would make a good father for Polly*, I thought, *if things worked out that way.*

"What do you mean?" Hattie asked, pretending ignorance.

"You know what I mean," Pete said, laughing. "You think I been a trail boss all these years without knowin' when I'm bein' followed?"

We all laughed, and Becky said," Durn skunks, I was hopin' they'd put up a fight." She took her gun out of the holster and twirled it standing near the tent flap.

"Why, Miss Becky," Pete grinned, "you're a real bad'un, ain't you?"

"Only when I have to be," Becky replied.

Bessie stood up from her bedroll and interrupted, "How would y'all like a piece of shoo-fly pie and coffee?" She smiled at Abel. "Ah jes' made it."

"Yes," we answered in unison. We all moved from various positions of sitting to hurry after Bessie for pie and coffee. We ate our pie and talked of the weather turning so cold 'til very late. When the men left, we rolled out our bedrolls and readied ourselves for bed, feeling relieved that the problem of the Riley boys had been taken care of.

"Hate to eat and run, but we're going to cross the Platte and stop at Fort Kearny for an hour to get any supplies," said Pete. "I have advised several parties to sell some heirlooms."

> **Comment [CJH]:** IMPORTANT: It sounds like the stop at Fort Kearny is imminent, but it doesn't happen for another 32 pages. Is there some minor place they stop for supplies that isn't mentioned? This paragraph could probably just be deleted.

Six Women West

CHAPTER FIFTEEN

Dawn broke and the smell of fresh coffee lured me to Moe's chuck wagon. Moe and Pete were standing by the campfire with steaming cups.

"Looks like we got a sprinkle of rain last night," Pete commented, handing me a cup.

"Yes, it's pretty, but cold," I said, holding the hot cup with both hands. "Think we can roll today, Pete?"

He nodded. "We'll try. Just as soon as I see…" He stopped midstream as Mrs. Roberts came running up. "Good mornin, ma'am," he greeted her.

"No, it's not," the woman snapped. "Elmo's not in from watch, and I'm worried."

"Now, Mrs. Roberts, most likely he fell asleep. Go see if you can find him," Pete said, turning to Tommy Smith, who had just joined us from under the supply wagon.

"Yes, Mr. Pete." As he walked towards the picket line, he buckled on his holster.

"Have him look for Mac while he's at it," Mrs. Macintosh declared, striding up to stand in front of Pete. "I haven't seen him since last night."

"What do you mean? Wait a minute Tommy."

"Well, he heard something late last night and went to check on our stock. He wasn't under the wagon this mornin', and nobody's seen him. She shook her head. "Somethin's happened to him. It's Indians—I just know it."

"Now, try not to worry, ladies. I'm sure both men are alright. Probably just fell asleep somewhere. They couldn't go far out here on the prairie. Now go on back to your wagons. I'll take care of it." He smiled and they headed back towards their wagons.

When they were out of hearing range, he turned to the rest of us. "This doesn't sound good." He frowned. "Billy, Tommy, get your horses and some

> **Comment [CJH]:** There are two different characters named Mac—the one on Pete's crew and Mac Macintosh. One of them should probably have a different name. Maybe the one on Pete's crew since Mac Macintosh is quite memorable.

help from the other men and see if you can find Elmo and Mac. Me and Guy are goin' to check the Riley wagon."

"Right, Mr. Morley. We'll find 'em." The boys ran over to saddle their horses.

"What's the matter? You don't believe they just fell asleep?" Guy asked, strapping on his gun.

"No, I don't. I have a gut feelin'...."

"You suspect the Rileys, Pete?" I interrupted, thinking they could be behind the men's disappearance.

Before he could answer, Tommy rode up. "Mr. Pete! Mr. Morley," he shouted, "We founded them in the remuda tied and gagged. They're okay but madder'n hell. They was in plain sight. It was them Riley boys that done it, and they stole some horses."

"Yeah," Billy added. "They took two of the best horses. One of them was mine. Dirty cur dogs!" He tipped his hat to me. "Beggin' your pardon, ma'am."

"It's alright, Billy. They're skunks," I agreed.

Mac and Elmo stumbled up, rubbing their heads and cursing. "They came up behind me and hit me in the head," stuttered Macintosh. "Little bastards. If I had seen them first...." He shook his fist angrily. "When I come to, I was trussed up like a pig with a gag in my mouth. They took my money belt. What'll I do for supplies?"

Here, fellows. Settle down and drink a cup of coffee," Moe said.

"I gotta get back to my wagon," Elmo said, refusing the offer. "The Missus will be worried."

"Yes," I agreed. "She was here asking about you. She'll be greatly relieved to see you're alright."

Mac took the cup from Moe. "Thanks. We goin' after them thieves?" he asked, looking at Pete. "I'll be needin' my money."

"Afraid not, Mac. Much as I'd like to see them boys hang, we don't have time to chase after them. We'll sell their wagon and mules at Fort Kearny to get your money back. Boys," he added, turning to Billy and Tommy, "hook up their wagon and get a man to drive it. Martha, maybe you'd let the rest of the camp know we roll in thirty minutes!"

"You just going to let them get away with it?!" Mac fumed.

"Not if I can help it," Pete assured him. "I'll have Guy go after them and bring 'em back to Fort Kearny. We'll turn them over to the post commander there. He'll see they're brought to justice."

"Justice, be damned!" shouted Mac. "I want five minutes with those scrawny Georgia peckers. I'll show 'em justice."

"Now Mac, we can't all go chasing cross country. We got to take these wagons across the Platte this morning."

"Mac, your Missus was here asking for you. She's been worried. You go on home and let her take care of that cut," I suggested, attempting to calm him.

"Yeah, suppose you're right, Miss," he mumbled, shuffling off in the direction of his wagon. "You take care of it, Pete," he called over his shoulder.

"Thanks, Martha," Pete said. "Thought the old guy was really gonna blow his top." He smiled. "You'll let the others know we're hitting the trail right away?"

"Sure, Pete, I'll do it now." We crossed the Platte River and kept moving. The rain was steady and kept coming. The trail was wet and soft but passable. Then about early afternoon the rain turn to a cloud burst. You couldn't see for the rain.

Pete rode up to our wagon. "We'll hold up here rest of the day. Do some hunting. This damn weather is impossible."

"Pete, we're already behind," Hattie reminded him.

Wanda Reed

"I know, Hattie. I know. The wagons are loaded heavy 'cause the tenderfeet brought everything they ever owned. The ground is soaked, and the damn wagons bog down. It takes all day to pull 'em out of the mud."

"We can't afford to lie up too long," Hattie persisted.

"Doin' the best I can, Hattie-Girl. You stop the rain, and I'll move ten hours a day. I got to spread the word. I'll be back later. Keep the coffee hot. Send the girls out hunting to stock up on meat. There won't be any stops if the weather breaks."

"Sure, Pete, but I got a bad feelin' about this stoppin'." She slapped her hat across her riding skirt. "Becky! Charlie! Go get us some meat!"

In the rain Becky and Charlie rode off without a word of complaint, leastwise not so we heard it. Hattie was still fretting.

"Now, Hattie, calm down," I said. "We'll get to Oregon. Look, there are a few trees over there. I'll go see if I can pull a log up."

"I'm calm. Just hope we can cross the Rockies before the snow flies. If only they would lighten those wagons. These Nebraska plains are so damn unpredictable."

For the next three hours, Sara and Bessie busied themselves with sewing and cooking. Polly and Tag slept in the wagon. Hattie and me checked the stock over head to hoof and doctored some harness sores. Hattie told me the jenny slipped her foal. In a few days we could put her back on the wagon. The rain had let up for now, and everyone was out drying clothes and taking care of their stock.

A thunder of hoofs brought us all to our feet as Becky and Charlie came riding into camp, hell bent for leather, leading two extra horses. One had a deer slung over the saddle. They pulled to a sliding halt in front of us. Everyone came running to see what the commotion was.

> **Comment [CJH]:** No mention before this of the mule being pregnant. You might consider just leaving this out.

"Becky, Charlie, what happened?" I asked excitedly. "Aren't these the stolen horses?"

Becky jumped to the ground and was working to catch her breath, bent over with one hand on her knee while with the other she waved for us to wait.

"What happened? How'd you get the horses?" Hattie yelled.

"It was scary. Uhoo. It was the Riley boys. Uhoo They. . . Uhoo. Here," Charlie dismounted and handed the money belt to Hattie. "Let me catch my breath. Water."

I brought a dipper of water. She took a swig and handed it to Becky. "Get Pete. He'll want to hear."

"I'll go," Bessie said and took off at a run.

Abel led the horses aside. He motioned to Tommy who was among those up close. "Hep me with this deer, Tommy. It's gotta' be hung and gutted right away."

I looked up, and Pete was running toward us with Bessie right behind him. "You girls okay? You're not hurt, are you?"

"We're okay," Charlie assured him.

"Good. Can you tell me what happened? How did you get the horses?"

"You tell 'em, Becky," Charlie said, "I'm still tryin' to catch my breath."

"Well, about nine miles upstream," Becky began, "there's a nice clearing, just perfect for deer. We separated to wait. Charlie went up the right side and I took the left." She took a deep breath and wiped her forehead.

"I settled down in the crook of a fallen tree to wait, listening and watchin'."

"Becky, get to the story," interrupted Pete "Ain't got all day. It'll be rainin' again before long."

"Okay. Okay. Well, five deer come to the edge of the clearing, stopped, waited, and then walked into the meadow. I got the buck in the sight and fired. Clean kill—a nice four-point," she smiled.

"Go on," Hattie urged. "We already know you're a good shot."

Becky shrugged and continued. "I went over to bleed him, leaned my rifle against a log, and bent over to get my knife out of my boot. I heard a voice from the brush behind me."

"Good shootin'," it said, and I recognized Cleo's voice.

"Oh, Becky, how awful," Sara whispered.

"It was scary," Becky agreed. "Especially when he said, 'it's the little lady who likes to play with guns.'" She shook her head. "I turned around, and there stood Jed and Cleo." She clutched at her shirt. "I swear, my heart stopped. I knowed I was in trouble."

"Where was Charlie?" somebody asked.

"I was on the other side of the meadow. I come a runnin' when I heard the shot. Then when I saw what was happenin', I waited. I wanted to see if they'd give me a reason to shoot them."

"That was the only thing that kept me from bein' scared to death. I knew Charlie wouldn't let 'em hurt me."

"Okay, go on, girl," Pete urged.

"Well, it gets kind of embarrassin'," Becky said, lowering her eyes. "Cleo says to me, I got somethin' you can play with. He grabbed his privates and jiggled his pants. 'I got a look at you at the dance,' he says, 'and you're a whole lot of woman under them pants.'"

"The bastard," I muttered, surprising myself. *There was more than one Abner in the world*, I thought, wondering how many more I'd run into before I got to Oregon.

"Yeah, but I had a knife in my boot. I weren't about to let 'em get me—not without a fight. I just stared at them, hoping Charlie was nearby."

Six Women West

Then Jed laughed and started towards me, threatening to take off my pants. Then Cleo said they would take me to their cave to be their woman.

"They were going to kidnap you?" Sara said, "Oh, those horrible men."

"Pete, I better skip this part. I don't know if I should say what they said," Becky said, blushing.

"It's okay, Becky, you don't have to tell anyone but me. Just talk low."

"I can tell you, Pete, but it'll embarrass the ladies."

"That's okay. If they don't want to hear, they can plug their ears."

"Okay. Well, Jeb said it would serve me right." Her voice lowered so I had to strain to hear her.

"Speak up, girl," some man hollered. "We can't hear you."

"You don't have to hear her," Pete hollered back.

"Thanks, Pete," she sighed and continued. "Anyway," she whispered then, "they said they would take turns bugger'n me." Becky stopped for another sip of water. Her face was beet red.

Charlie took over and continued their story. "Like I said, I was on the other side of the meadow. I heard the shot and started for Becky. When I saw them, I hid and waited. When Cleo reached for Becky, I took aim and shot him. I hit him in the arm. He grabbed his arm, twisted around, and slumped to the ground howling in pain. Becky picked up his gun and pointed it at Jed. He started to run."

"I yelled, "Stop, Jed! Run and I'll shoot.""

"You bet I was mad," Becky chimed in. "I wanted to shoot 'em both, but I wanted to humiliate them first. Cleo was still layin' on the ground whimperin' like a big baby. 'Take off your pants and boots, boys,' I said. 'I want to see what you got.'"

"Cleo started whining," Charlie said. "They said they was just funnin'. Said I didn't have to shoot 'em." She slapped her thigh. "Hell, he's lucky I didn't shoot him in the privates."

"They took off their pants, right down to their red under drawers." Becky laughed. "Boy, that was a sight to see. They're lucky I let them keep the drawers."

Charlie was laughing so hard she had tears in her eyes. "I didn't know Becky had it in her," she said, "She told them varmints to start running afore she shot their asses off."

"They took off with their drawer flaps flyin'. They were outta sight in minutes." Becky wiped her eyes and continued. "We took the money belts and the pocket money and threw the pants and boots up in a tree. We slung the deer on the stolen horse and headed for the wagons," she shrugged, "and here we are."

"Good work!" somebody yelled, and everyone broke into clapping.

Elmo and Mac came over to Pete and collected the money the Rileys had stolen.

"Thanks, girls. You did a fine job of getting out of that scrape," Pete laughed. "I'd like to have seen those skunks running through the woods without their britches."

"They'll think twice about coming around here," laughed Hattie. I know Bessie just made a fresh pot of coffee. I think we could all use some. If we talk real sweet to her, maybe she'll let us have some of those bear signs she made earlier." Hattie looked at Bessie, and Bessie nodded.

"Sounds good to me," Becky said grinning.

"Me too," agreed Charlie. "Come on, Martha. You can eat a bear sign or six, can't you?"

"You know I can."

"Can we get in on this, too?" begged Abel and Tommy.

"How about me?" Pete echoed. "Tommy, after your bear sign, track Guy down and tell him the Riley boys have been taken care of."

"I know I should've never said bear sign," laughed Hattie. "Hope you cooked up a bunch, Bessie."

"I sho' nuff did," Bessie assured us, grinning widely.

Wanda Reed

CHAPTER SIXTEEN

Pete rode around to each wagon telling people to unload any heirlooms. The next morning brought clear skies and a call from Pete to get ready to move out. The weather stayed cool but clear, allowing us to travel an extra two hours each day. Summer had finally arrived, turning the grass and shrubs green. Everywhere there were fields of purple, yellow, and white prairie flowers. The land stretched on as far as the eye could see, and the sky met the land.

We'd been on the trail a few hours. I was riding point with Pete along the foothills of Windlass Hill. Around midmorning, Pete said, "Rider comin' in. Looks like Guy." He had gone ahead to scout the area.

"Howdy Pete, Miss Martha," he greeted. "I ran across a family. They're broken down 'bout five miles out. They got a busted wagon wheel. They need some help."

"Well, we'll do what we can," said Pete.

"He's got the wagon turned crossways blockin' the trail. They're real young kids, real tenderfeet."

"Well," Pete laughed, "guess we'll have to help, won't we?"

As we approached the wagon, Pete called, "Hello! You in the wagon."

The barrel of a rifle was thrust out between the wagon flaps and a man's voice demanded, "Who are you?"

"Pete Morley. We're from the wagon train," Pete said. "We're here to help. Looks likes you broke a wheel."

A young man climbed down from the wagon. "Howdy. I'm Mark Price. Sure glad you came along. My wife and me, we're from Illinois. We've been here for a week. I couldn't go for help because my wife's expecting." He sighed.

> **Comment [CJH]:** I thought he was encouraging them to sell them at Fort Kearny. Maybe leave this mention of heirlooms out.

> **Comment [CJH]:** Changed from spring to summer since it was June.

Six Women West

Pete shook his head. "Soon as I get a wagon here, we'll get the wheel changed."

"I don't have a spare wheel," he said, lowering his eyes.

"You left Illinois without a spare wheel?" Pete roared. "And with your wife in her condition? What were you thinkin', man?"

"I don't know. It was real stupid of me. Well, the man who sold me the map told me I didn't have to worry about going alone. He said the trail was all laid out and was safe."

"Let's offload the wagon while Guy rides to our wagons to get a wheel," said Pete.

"Let me help my wife out of the wagon. She don't get around too good right now."

"I'll take care of her," I said. "Mrs. Price, hand me a quilt, and I'll fix you a place to rest here while you wagon is being fixed."

"Call me Cathleen," she said, obviously grateful for the help.

It was an hour before Abel arrived with Mac and Harry to fix the wagon. It didn't take long for the men to change the wheel. Guy arrived just as we reloaded the last of the Price's belongings. Pete told them to circle up. "We'll noon here," he added. "Eat and stretch your legs. Give the stock a rest. We'll roll in two hours. The Prices will be joinin' us."

I sat with Cathleen, and she was having pains. I told her I was going to get Charlie.

"No, I don't want a man. Isn't there some woman among you who's helped with birthin' babies?"

"I'm sorry," I smiled, "you couldn't know. Charlie is a woman, and she knows all about birthin' babies. She's a midwife."

"Oh, good," Cathleen sighed, arching her back. "My goodness, that's a sharp pain. I must have pulled my back getting in the wagon. It's really hurting now." Her face wrinkled and she grabbed at

> **Comment [CJH]:** I made some minor changes to the labor sequence below. As the mother of six, this is an area where I have some expertise. ☺

her stomach. I was sure that baby was going to be here soon.

"Oh, somethin's wrong. It's the baby isn't it? The baby coming?" she cried.

"I don't know. Charlie can tell us. You try to stay calm while I run and get her."

I took off to where the horses were picketed. Charlie was there currying her horse. "Charlie," I called. "Mrs. Price is very pregnant. I think she might be in labor."

Well, let go see if we can help her," Charlie replied.

"Charlie," Pete said, "do you know how to birth babies?"

"Don't worry, Pete. This will be fourteen. I can handle a normal birth."

"Sounds like you can handle it, alright. I'll leave it in your hands. I'll let the rest of the wagons know we'll be stayin' the night. Have someone call me if you need me."

"Why don't you take him with you?" Hattie asked, tilting her head towards Mark.

At that moment, an anguished cry came from the wagon. Bessie stuck her head out. "Y'all betta' come. Her water done broke."

Charlie climbed in the wagon. After a few minutes she came out. "With good luck, we'll have a baby before mornin'."

"Is my wife alright?" Mark asked.

"She's doin' fine," Charlie assured him. "You go ahead with Pete. We'll call you if we need you." She climbed up in the wagon.

Mark slowly and reluctantly headed away from the wagon.

Turning to me, she said, "I see Hattie's got water heating. We'll need rubbing alcohol. Whiskey will do if you don't have any."

"I'll ask Pete. He'll know who has some."

Another scream from the wagon filled the air, which caused Mark, who had only gone a few yards, to halt in his tracks. He came running and attempted to climb into the wagon.

Charlie pushed him back. "There's nothin' you can do right now."

A couple hours later, Charlie announced that Cathleen Rose had delivered a healthy boy.

"Mark! Mark!" I yelled. "You have a son!"

Mark came out from under the wagon so fast he hit his head and nearly fell. "A son! I have a son? Is she alright?"

"See for yourself," Charlie said, coming out of the wagon with a bundle in her arms. "He cleaned up real nice." Smiling, she held the baby out to Mark.

"Oh, my gosh," I whispered, leaning over Mark's shoulder to gaze upon the tiny red face, topped with thick black hair. "He's beautiful." He was the first newborn I'd seen.

"Yes," agreed Mark in a hushed voice. "Can I see Cathleen Rose now?"

"She's waiting for you. Don't be too long. She's awful tired."

Mark went into the wagon with his son. Sara came out, looking sleepy and worn out.

"I think we can all use some sleep," Charlie said. "It's been a long day."

We need the tent set up for Rose and the baby. He stills need a bath."

"I'll go let Pete know," I said and hurried off to tell him.

After Mark and Cathleen visited for awhile, Charlie and Bessie made pallets in the tent for Cathleen, the baby, and themselves and went to sleep for the night. The rest of put our bedrolls outside to sleep.

After breakfast, Charlie checked on Cathleen Rose and declared she was fit for travel. She and the baby would ride in their wagon. We were on the move again. Bessie rode with the Prices to help out. When we stopped at noon, Charlie looked in on Cathleen Rose, reporting that she was holding up okay. Unexpectedly, a line had formed at the wagon. Everyone wanted to get a look at the newest addition to the wagon train, and some had even brought a small gift.

"All that bouncin' ain't doin' her any good," Charlie told us, adding, "It can't be helped though. We gotta' keep movin'."

After we'd traveled about twelve miles, we camped for the night. Pete and Mark set up our tent so there was more room, and Cathleen Rose and her baby—named Maxwell Charles—would be more comfortable.

"Maxwell is for my father," Mark had explained, adding, "Charles is for Charlie. We wanted to show her we appreciate what she did."

In the tent, Charlie got the new mother up to walk and had her sit in the chair while nursing little Max. When the baby finished feeding, Sara took over, changing and dressing him. She had temporarily given up custody of Polly to Becky and Tag.

After supper, we all settled in for the night. When he finally left, we gathered around Sara, who had made a ritual of reading to us whenever possible. "Well, what is your choice for tonight? Dickens, Browning, or the Bible?" she asked, holding the books out to us.

"Instead of reading tonight, why don't we each tell our own stories?" I asked. "I know we already know a lot about each other, but I'd like to know more, wouldn't y'all?"

"I would," Becky said. "It will be fun. Sara, you go first. I wanna hear how people live who have money and upbringin'."

Six Women West

"Becky, try to use the words I have taught you. You should say, 'I want to hear how people live who have money and upbringing.' But to answer your question, there's not much to tell." Sara reached over and patted Tag, who was lying as close to the sleeping Polly as he could get.

> **Comment [CJH]:** This sounds awfully snooty.

"Start from the beginnin'," urged Becky. "You know, from when you were one of them southern belles."

PART THREE

CHAPTER SEVENTEEN

SARA'S STORY

"Our plantation had been in our family for generations. It was one of the earliest in Georgia. It was magnificent. The house stood three stories high with an eight-foot-wide front porch going all the way around. Four white columns supported the verandas to the second and third floors. Giant windows that could be used for doors were at the end of each room so you could walk out on the verandas."

"Holy Moses!" Charlie exclaimed. "What would you want with all those rooms? How'd you keep 'em clean?"

Sara ignored or didn't hear Charlie's question. She just continued recalling her past.

"Oh, how I miss that beautiful house. There were twenty four rooms, eight on each floor. The hallway landings on each floor four feet wide and beautifully furnished. On each side of the long drive were four oak trees hanging full of gypsy moss. Great-grandfather did everything by the number four. He said it was because it took him four weeks to make the passage from England.

The rooms on the ground floor had doors that folded back to make a gracious ballroom. We always had plenty of room for guests and parties. Such wonderful parties! I had beautiful gowns of all colors and styles. Mama had a seamstress come several times a year and sew for us both. That's how I learned to sew."

As she described the parties and ball gowns, I could picture the dresses of beautiful colors twirling around the floor as the musicians played waltzes.

Six Women West

"There were gardens filled with the sweet smell of magnolias and jasmine," Sara smiled. "That's where you and your beau would go strolling when you wanted to be alone."

"But, how did you take care of all that?" Charlie persisted.

"Why, we had slaves, of course. I had two personal slaves all my own to take care of my needs," Sara explained, glancing at Bessie in obvious embarrassment. "We didn't know better, Bessie. I'm sorry."

Watching Sara's face in the firelight, seeing how it glowed with pride as she talked about the memory of her home and family, I knew she must miss them very much. She took a deep breath and continued.

"Papa hired a teacher to tutor me, and he stayed for six years. Papa taught me to keep the accounting books for the plantation, and Mama taught me to manage the household and become a lady. She believed that the mistress of the house must know how to do things herself in order to know if the help was doing it properly."

"Sounds like a good idea," Hattie said.

Sara nodded. She smiled as she continued, "We had parties that often lasted for days. Friends came and stayed for a week or more, and relatives sometimes stayed for months. We had over a hundred field slaves and dozens of house servants. Since we had plenty, guests were never any trouble no matter how long they stayed.

"When I was about fourteen, Papa and my brother, Jeffery, had a strong disagreement, and he was disinherited. I heard nothing about him for years until I got word about the leather shop," she said, turning to me. She shrugged. "I thought I'd be staying with him. Anyway, Papa said I had to learn to run the plantation, and when the time came he would help me pick a good husband. By the time I

> **Comment [CJH]:** Changed name from Jonathan to match the brother whom she expected to find in Independence.

205

was fifteen I was in full charge of the breeding book and the young slaves."

"Goodness, that seems like a lot of responsibility for a young girl," I commented.

"Well, it was a lot of work, but it made me feel grown up. Since the plantation was supporting several hundred people, there was always a lot to do." Sara glanced at Bessie. "We couldn't have done it without the slaves."

Bessie nodded. "Yessum," she agreed softly.

"Once Papa brought five new darkies from New Orleans and later found out they had small pox. When it started to infect the others, Papa had to kill a lot of the infected slaves." She looked at Bessie apologetically. "He had to, you know, to stop the sickness from spreading. As it was, we lost two thirds of our slaves. Papa borrowed money from the bank to buy the slaves he needed to work the crops."

Polly cried out in her sleep, and Sara immediately got up and went to her. "It's alright, baby. I'm here. Go back to sleep." We waited as she calmed the child. When she rejoined us, she smiled and asked, "Are you sure you want to hear more?"

"You bet," insisted Becky. "I wanna know why you left all that."

Sara sighed. "Alright, you see Papa decided to try and sell off all the young blacks for cash so he could buy field hands, but no one would buy them because they were marked from the pox or men were afraid they might have smallpox. Papa was desperate. Without our slaves, we could lose everything. We would have to take out a mortgage." She paused and Becky filled our coffee cups and laid another piece of wood on the fire.

We sat quietly, waiting for Sara to continue. Her expression grew solemn. "One day, just after I turned seventeen, Papa sent for me to join him in the library. I could see the anguish in his face. 'I've

> **Comment [CJH]:** IMPORTANT: I don't find this believable. Separate them from everyone else, yes. Kill your valuable "property" even if totally heartless? No.

Six Women West

arranged for you to marry Jerome Dale. The wedding will take place the end of summer,' he said. He said he was sorry, but it was necessary to join the two families in order to save the plantation. It felt like a boulder dropped in my stomach. I could hear Papa talking about Jerome, saying he was attractive and well-bred. He said it wasn't like I didn't know him. I felt like I was in a dream when I said, 'Yes, Papa. I'll marry Jerome.'"

"Damn!" Becky exclaimed. "Couldn't you just tell him you didn't love the guy?"

"No, Becky. In good southern families, marriages are often arranged. Love doesn't enter into it. Often it's done to merge plantations."

"Rats!" Becky retorted.

"Of course, I was unhappy about it, but I had to face reality. The plantation was my inheritance as well as my family's livelihood. So many people depended on us."

"Was there someone you were in love with or wanted to marry?" I asked.

"Well, there was someone, but we had not been properly introduced. I had been hoping to meet him when the season started."

> **Comment [CJH]:** I could find no reference to a season such as the winter season in London in the antebellum South. This may not be important though.

"What do you mean? Which season?" Charlie asked, frowning.

"Oh, that's when we have the most wonderful parties and all the young girls dressed in their finest gowns and looked for beaux."

"I thought you said the marriages were already arranged by the fathers," Becky reminded Sara.

"Yes, but that needn't stop the girls from looking. Many times their choice would be acceptable to the families."

"I see," Becky nodded.

"Our engagement was announced, and Papa hired a seamstress to come and stay with us and make my wedding dress and trousseau. Jerome and I attended all the parties, and I found myself liking him. It would be alright, I told myself."

"So you forgot about that other fellow?"

"Not entirely. I was finally introduced to him and thought him quite wonderful."

"You ever think about just running away with him?" Charlie asked.

"Heavens, Charlie. I don't think I even considered it. Nice southern girls don't do things like that," she smiled shyly. "I did let him kiss me when he followed me out to the garden one night. I never saw him again." Her smile disappeared. "I heard later he was killed in the war."

"The wedding took place as scheduled," she went on. "The celebration lasted for three days. We honeymooned in Atlanta, and Jerome was very sweet. I was beginning to think Papa had indeed made a wise choice. We returned from Atlanta to live at Jerome's family home where I was made welcome.

"Several months later, I was with child, which pleased my husband and both families. One day, after about six months I was out walking against Jerome's wishes, and I fell, causing a miscarriage. The doctor told us it was a boy. I was heartbroken." She paused and swallowed. "Even though it was an accident, I felt Jerome blamed me."

"When the war started, Jerome went to fight for the South." She grinned, adding, "He did look handsome in his gray uniform with the gold sash. His family insisted I remain with them while he was away. I would have preferred to be with my own family, but I didn't argue about it."

Hattie yawned, covering her mouth quickly. "Not the company," she sighed. "Go on, Sara. Your story is mighty interestin'. I never knew much about southern gentry or slaves."

Sara looked at Becky. "I think what I tell you now will be the exciting part. At least, if one hadn't had to live it. For us, it was tragic, including the slaves."

"Yessum," Bessie agreed, nodding energetically.

"The slaves had started a revolt, killing and burning. One morning a neighbor came by to tell us that my family's plantation had been burned to the ground and my parents murdered."

"Jumpin' Jehoshaphat!" Becky exclaimed. "That wasn't the kind of excitement I wanted to hear 'bout."

"It was awful," Sara said, her eyes misting. "It wasn't just my parents. Most of my aunts and uncles had come to stay until the war was over. We learned later that the doors had been barricaded so no one could escape."

"Lawdy, Miss Sara. Yo' own darkie done dat? Ah'm sho' nuff sorry, Miss Sara," Bessie stammered.

"It's this war, Bessie. People do reprehensible things during wartime," Sara said, reaching over to pat her hand. "The slaves began running off, taking what they wanted. We couldn't stop them. Finally my in-laws, in fear for their lives, left for Europe. The houseboy and the cook remained, and so I was able to stay on. I had nowhere else to go. Besides, when Jerome came home, he'd want me there."

"Did he come home?" Becky asked.

"Yes, he came home on leave, a changed man. He had always been a gentle person, but now he seemed hard and bitter. It was understandable, I thought. I had never known him to drink to excess, but now, he poured his first drink before breakfast and continued throughout the day. He raged on and on about the war, cursing Lincoln and the Union. I was actually quite relieved when he returned to duty. He also became very verbal about his thoughts of me."

"War is terrible. You'd think as smart as men think they are, they could figure out a better way to handle things," Charlie remarked.

"Yes, but we all know they're not as smart as they think, don't we?" I said. Everybody smiled and nodded.

"Shortly, I discovered I was again with child. I was hopeful this would make a difference in my marriage, and it might have if Jerome hadn't been injured. He was hit in the leg by a Minié ball, and they sent him home. Gangrene had set in, causing him a great deal of pain. Eventually, he had to have his leg amputated. He took morphine, which helped, but he continued to take it long after the pain was gone. He learned to walk with his wooden leg, but he was consumed with self-pity and bitterness."

"My, he must have been awfully hard to live with," I said, imagining how it must have been for both of them.

"Yes." Sara nodded. "He drank and took the drugs, which made him angry and intractable. The two house slaves ran off when he threatened to kill them. He beat me twice before I learned to keep out of reach. After the last beating, I delivered the child, but it was too early and the baby was stillborn. The doctor said I couldn't have any more children."

"Oh Sara, how awful. You're such a good mother," Becky told her.

"I do love children," Sara admitted. "Jerome taunted me, saying a barren woman was useless as a wife. I was too weak to get away from him, and he struck me in the face." She reached up and touched the scar on her cheek. "He was wearing a big ring. That time he couldn't be bothered to say he was sorry."

"Bastard!" Becky roared, expressing the feelings of the rest of us.

"How did you manage with no slaves?" Hattie asked.

"It was hard." Cathleen's baby awoke and began to cry. "Let me take care of little Max, and then I'll finish my story," Sara said. She changed his wet clothes and took him back to Cathleen. "Max is hungry," she told her, and placed the baby next to her breast.

Hattie took the opportunity to pass around bread and jam and fill our cups with hot coffee. It was getting late, but no one seemed to be ready for sleep. Sara's story had us enthralled. Becky put more wood on the fire and Sara returned to continue her story.

"The Confederacy was losing the war, and the Confederate dollar had no value. We were destitute. Jerome sold his mother's silver and bought morphine. He'd sold all my jewels except for a ruby ring encircled in diamonds that my grandmother had given me. I had hidden it from him by sewing it into my camisole."

"Smart," Charlie said, nodding.

"I was saving it just in case I had to run away from Jerome. He took a job with a friend of his father's, but he really didn't want to because of pride. He considered the job beneath him." She raised her eyebrows. "Southern men have a lot of pride. Anyway, he stayed drunk. After he beat a slave to death for no reason, he was asked to leave his job.

"By now I was completely devoid of feeling for him and was losing my own self-respect. I wanted to run away, but I had no place to go. Still, I was determined to escape, and I knew I would if we got to a town or train where I could get away." She paused and ran her fingers through her hair.

"We arrived in Charleston, West Virginia, without even money for a room. He got me a job at the hotel saloon, telling me I could work as a waitress and they'd give us a room." Her eyes filled with tears. "Then, right in front of me, he told the barkeeper I would whore because I couldn't have a child. I was astonished and mortified. I screamed, 'No!' I said, 'Waiting tables is what you said. I'd never sell myself for money. There's a mistake.' I was crying. Jerome twisted my arm and told me, 'I'm you husband, and you'll do as I say. We need the money. It won't hurt you.'"

"A man standing at the end of the bar laughed loudly and called Jerome low-life southern trash. He said any man who would sell his woman was no better than a dog. Jerome acted as if he didn't hear him, but the fellow kept taunting him, making nasty remarks about slave owners and so-called southern gentlemen."

"Good for him," Becky said. "I hope he knocked him for a loop."

Sara grinned and shook her head. "I'm afraid he did worse than that. Jerome finally started raging at the man, blaming him for the fact he was crippled. He roared that all Yankees should die, and he was going to kill this one. Jerome drew his gun. I pulled at his arm and screamed at him to stop."

She sighed along with the rest of us. "I guess I fainted. I awoke in a strange bed. The man standing over me told me he was a doctor—Dr. Randall was his name—and I was there because I had fainted. I asked about Jerome, and he told me Jerome was dead. He said the man at the bar shot him and had left me twenty dollars."

"My kind a man," Charlie exclaimed. "Suppose he's still around somewhere? Sure like to meet up with him."

"Oh, Charlie," I said, shaking my head. "Go on, Sara. What happened next?"

"Doctor Randall told me I was suffering from malnutrition. He insisted I stay at his house while he nursed me back to health. After a couple of weeks, I was feeling quite well and he introduced me to the owner of the local dry goods store, who gave me a job." She stopped and looked around the tent. "That's where I met Martha."

"I would have liked the job if the owner could have kept his hands to himself."

"Men!" Becky muttered.

"Yes. I'm beginning to wonder if there are any nice ones," Sara said.

"Guy seems awfully nice," Hattie commented.

"We'll see," Sara said. "Anyway, I had sort of a bad reputation because of the circumstances of Jerome's death. Of course, this ugly scar on my face didn't help matters." She touched the scar and shrugged. "Martha helped me get over letting the gossip bother me. She assured me it didn't matter what others thought as long as I knew the truth."

"Good for you, Martha," Charlie said.

"Yes, Martha has been a good friend." Sara reached over and patted my hand. "I don't know what I would have done without her. With her help I began my journey to Missouri to live with my brother." She sighed. "Well, as you know, that didn't work out, but I'm glad. I would have missed all of you, and this way I'll be able to make a fresh start in Oregon. My deepest regret is I'll never have a child of my own. Still, I have Polly. I'm very grateful for her. She is such a delight." She wiped her eyes. "Well, that's it. That's my story."

"Sound like you was a slave, too, Miss Sara," Bessie murmured. "Guess'n you don' has to be black to be da white man's slave."

"You're surely right about that, Bessie. I don't know about black men, but the white men I've known didn't treat me as good as they did their horse," Charlie confessed bitterly.

"Course, ah never knew no different. Ah was born a slave. Ah never had no say over my own sef." Bessie stood up and thrust out her chin. "But now ahz free, and ah'll die free."

"Well, don't die for awhile yet, Bessie," Becky said, grinning. "We'd all starve to death before we got to Oregon if'n you did!"

Wanda Reed

"Ladies, we'd best call it a night," Hattie said. "We got another long day tomorrow."

Before long the sound of snoring filled the tent. I prayed I would never fall in love with a man capable of beating me.

CHAPTER EIGHTEEN

We woke up to a deep blue sky streaked with scarlet breaking through the night. We'd just finished our second cup of coffee when Pete rode up.

"We roll at first light," he told us, glancing around.

"Pete, I need to talk to you," said Sara.

"Okay, Sara. I have a few minutes. What can I do for you?"

"About the Riley wagon, I'd like to have it please. The men got their money and horses, so it doesn't have to be sold. After all it belongs to Polly."

"It's yours alright, but you'll have to hire a fulltime driver—maybe one of the single men," suggested Pete.

"Thanks, Pete."

"Looks like you're ready." He tipped his hat to Hattie.

"Been ready," Hattie snorted.

"Yep, well, I plan to make twenty miles today. Think you can handle it?"

"Don't worry about us. We'll keep up."

"I'm countin' on you to keep the stragglers movin," Pete said, turning to Becky and Charlie. "Watch the Price wagon. They only got two mules. If they drop behind, we'll hook up two more."

"We'll keep right on their tails," laughed Becky.

A few minutes later we heard "move 'em out." Whips cracked and wagons groaned and slowly moved. The column moved across the prairie for several hours without problems. Becky and Charlie worked hard making sure the back wagons didn't lag behind.

Pete had told us earlier that we'd be crossing a river and sent Guy to scout ahead to find the easiest crossing. I was riding with Pete when Guy rode in around four o'clock with his report.

"The old bridge is gone," he said. "It looks like it's been blown up."

"Why in the hell would anybody do a thing like that?" Pete roared.

"Beats me. All I know is we're gonna have to find another way to cross."

"Shit," Pete swore. "I'll take a look-see. Maybe it's fixable."

"Can I go with you?" I asked.

"Sure."

"Where you goin'?" Becky yelled, riding up close to me.

"We're going to the river," I told her. "You know, the one Hattie told us about."

"Can I come?" she asked, directing her question at Pete, who nodded assent.

"Let's go before the crowd gets any bigger," laughed Guy.

It was near three miles to the river. The cottonwoods grew thick along the steep banks, hiding the river from sight. However, the smell, a mixture of rotting vegetation and carcasses, left no doubt it was there.

"Whew!" I said, holding my nose. "Looks like the bridge killed several animals when it blew."

"Smells worse than the outhouse in the city," Becky volunteered.

"Well, get used to it, ladies," Pete said, grinning. "You'll smell it for awhile."

The trail ended at the riverbank, which was strewn with debris. What had once been a bridge was now a pile of logs.

"Looks like you're right, Guy. Either some damnable idiot blew it up, or there was a hell of a flash flood," Pete growled. He looked at me. "You and Becky go upstream. See if you can find a crossing place. Me and Guy will go look downstream. Don't dawdle. This is no time for sightseein'."

"Okay, Pete. Let's go, Becky."

We followed the river about a mile upstream and finally found a spot that seemed like it could be used with some work. We hurried back to make our report. Pete and Guy were waiting for us.

"Any luck?" asked Pete.

"Yeah, I hope so anyway," I frowned. "It'll take some fixing though. It's about a half mile away. It still stinks just as bad but has good clearing for the wagons."

"We'd have to clear the trees to make a trail, but the bank there ain't so high," said Becky.

"Well, there weren't nothin' downstream, so let's see what you found," said Pete. "Anythin's better than backtracking to the Blue." At the spot, he nodded. As he studied the riverbank he agreed, "It'll be a lot of work, but it can be done."

Guy nodded, "Yep, we can do it. Hell, we gotta do it."

Back at the wagons, Pete explained it briefly to Moe. "We got our work cut out for us. I'll tell you the rest of the details when the wagons get here. No use chawin' it twice." He turned to Becky and me. "You gals go tell all the men to join us here."

We did as we were told, and within a half hour all the men and most of the women were gathered around Moe's wagon.

"I know you're tired," Pete began. "Twenty miles can take a lot out of anybody. I'm proud of you all. You stayed right with us, and nobody whined about it." He stopped and focused his gaze on his audience. "Now, I'm gonna ask more of you. The bridge we planned on crossing has been destroyed. We're gonna have to build a new trail. The girls here," he pointed to Becky and me, "found a spot we think you can use. It's gonna take hard work, but it's either that, or we turn around and go back to the Blue, where we ferry across." He shook his head. "That would put us way behind. So, I'm for building a trail. Are you with me?"

Everyone started talking at once, but Matt Holt's voice came through over the noise. "We can do it," he said. "Let's get started."

"That's what I want to hear," Pete said, smiling widely. "I figure we split up. Some of you start making a trail on the other side of the river, and the rest will work on this side."

"Sounds good," Frank Warren agreed. "Best if we get right to it and get as much done as we can 'afore dark."

"Okay, lets head for the river," Pete said.

"The women can fix a potluck supper and plenty of coffee." Hattie told him, turning to leave.

"Good thinking," Pete said. "We'll need plenty of it." When everyone had reached the area, we circled the wagons, and the men got right to work. The women and children who were able began to gather wood for the campfires.

"Martha, you and me can help the men. We'll use our horses to drag the trees" Hattie said. "The young boys can help drag off the saplings, but no one under the age of twelve."

We worked as a team, trying to ignore the stench of the river and doing our best to stay out of the black mud, which stuck like molasses. The men ate and took time to rest a spell and then returned to the work. By dark there was a wagon train full of very tired people, but there was a trail to cross with a log bottom for the wagons and up the other side.

The sun barely up and with bacon and biscuits for breakfast, we began crossing with Mac in the lead wagon and Moe right behind him.

"The rest of you, get ready," Pete yelled. "As soon as the wagon in front of you hits the far bank, start your team."

Six Women West

When it was our turn, Hattie cracked her whip and the mules moved into action down the muddy slope. Holding Tag across my saddle, I followed, trying to keep my legs up and out to avoid the mud. Unfortunately, Gray Lady stumbled, my legs came down, and I lost control of Tag who fell into the muddy water. It was all I could do to keep from falling from Gray Lady as I pulled Tag back to safety. We both were covered in the sticky, smelly stuff.

The following wagons kept up the cries of "keep moving," and the crack of whips filled the air, leaving no time to clean myself off. Tag struggled up the bank and tried to shake himself clean.

Everything was going good until the Rogers wagon entered the water and bogged down. Guy hitched another team to it. The wagon was so overloaded, it made it impossible to pull free.

"Throw some of that damn furniture off," Pete ordered. "You're going to have a new life in Oregon. No need to drag the past along."

Despite the protesting moans of the women, several pieces were thrown on the riverbank. With the wagon load lightened, they finished crossing. The Davis boy, Ray, stood up in their wagon, lost his balance, and fell in the river. Moe fished him out and said he'd need a bath, but he wasn't hurt.

> **Comment [CJH]:** I changed the name from Moses to Moe, assuming that is who was meant.

Four wagons had crossed when Pete told Guy and me to take the wagons a few miles down the trail. "See if you can find a campsite alongside the creek," Pete said.

Luckily, we were able to find a creek running into the river. While the wagons circled, I slipped off down to the creek and washed the mud off Gray Lady, Tag, and myself. I found an old rocker in the bushes and carried it back to the wagon. Taking it to Sara, I asked, "Can you use this? It's worn, but it seems sturdy."

Wanda Reed

"Oh, my yes," Sara said, taking it from me. "Polly will love it."

"Don't let Pete see it," I warned, "He'll make you toss it."

"Thanks, Martha. I'll put it inside," she said, disappearing into the wagon.

It was late afternoon when Pete brought in the rest of the wagons. "You two did good," he said, greeting me and Guy. "This spot will do just fine. Plenty of trees and a fresh creek. Now let's gets the rest of the wagons circled." He glanced up at the sky. "Looks like a storm's brewin'," he said, pointing out a clump of huge black clouds.

We hurried the wagons and soon had them all in the circle. The men began unhitching the teams. A strong north wind blew up, accompanied by hail and then rain.

"Dey was plentiful beans and cornbread left," Bessie said.

Abel smiled. "That sho' sounds tasty, Miss Bessie."

"Hattie," I said, "How are we going to feed our stock? We walk out there with feed, and we're going to get trampled." [Comment [CJH]: Why?]

"The horses are tied to the picket line in the trees. We can put nosebags on them. Let's tie the mules to the back of the wagon 'til they eat and then turn them loose again." We put a handful of grain in our pockets and went out to bring our mules over to the wagon.

The tent was as warm as possible under the circumstances. We bundled up good and huddled together, determined to make the best of it. Sara had brought the rocker out of the wagon.

"Come, dear," she coaxed, holding out her arms to Polly, who was obviously enjoying her bottle of warm goat's milk with her toes curled in Tag's fur. Tag, as usual, lay next to her. "Mommy will read you a story."

Six Women West

The rest of us drew closer, as much for warmth as to hear the story. Sara's voice was soft and melodious. I dozed off. Abel's voice brought me upright.

"Jus' me, Abel," he said, raising the flap, letting in a gust of freezing air.

"Oh, Abel, close the flap quickly," Sara urged, holding Polly close to her.

"Yessum." He dropped the flap, securing it tightly. "Brought you womenfolk some mo' wood. Figured you'd need it."

"Thanks, Abel. That's really nice of you," said Hattie. "Come on in and set a spell. Sara's readin' from the Good Book."

"Thank ya, ma'am, but I gots to get back." He glanced at Bessie. She smiled shyly and nodded. "Well, good night y'all."

When Sara stopped reading, we bundled up so we could share our blankets, pulling our bedrolls close to the fire. Just before I fell asleep, I heard Sara whisper, "I hope Max is warm enough."

Bless her heart, I thought. *She's a born mother.* I prayed she would find a good man in Oregon and create the family she deserved.

We were awakened by Hattie yelling for us to rise and shine. Shivering, we rolled out of our blankets. Bessie started grits, biscuits, and bacon. Sara took care of Polly. Hattie and me took care of the stock. After breakfast we hitched the team while Charlie and Becky rolled up the bedrolls, took down the tent, and loaded the wagon. Polly, her cheeks rosy with the cold, was having a great time playing with Tag.

Pete called to us to get in line. Sara loaded Polly in the wagon, and Hattie climbed aboard, taking the reins. Clicking her tongue, she urged the mules forward. The wagons creaked, but the usual sound of the wheels crunched on the frozen ground. The icy wind continued to blow, causing those in the

> **Comment [CJH]:** The fire is inside the tent? This is explained much farther on when Morgan offers to open the smoke hole in the tent, but perhaps an explanation now would be helpful because I was confused until I came to the explanation about having fire in the tent.

open to pull their coats closer and wrap their faces in mufflers. The stock suffered too. We had to stop several times to clear the ice out of the noses of the mules. Pete came by to tell us we wouldn't be stopping for a noon break but would continue on until we camped for the night.

It was late afternoon when Pete gave the order to circle up near a small grove of trees. The men roped off the trees, making corrals. We picketed our horses, brushing the frost off the grass for them to graze. Later, after their ration of grain, we planned to put them inside the corral. Clearing a space beside our wagon, Becky, Hattie, and I set up the tent. Afterward they went to gather wood while I dug a fire pit inside to get the tent warm and started a cooking fire under the canopy.

Sara set a bucket of water on the fire to melt. "I've got to wash Polly's diapers," she explained. "Charlie, Polly's out of milk, would you milk the goat?"

"You tend to the washing," Charlie said. "I'll get the milk."

"Need some help with supper, Bessie?" I asked.

"You could git out de jerky. Dat's 'bout all we got. Ah be makin' burnt gravy and rice wit it."

Guy and Abel rode up. "We're goin' huntin', ladies," Guy said. "Anythin' special you'd like me to bring you, Miss Sara?"

She smiled shyly, "I don't suppose there would be a deer out there?"

"Can't say for sure," Guy said. "But, if there is, I'll get him for you."

"You want a couple of us to go with you?" Hattie asked.

"Not this time," Guy shook his head, his gaze still on Sara. "We got three hunting parties goin' out. Pete wants the rest of you to stay in camp. It's easy to get lost in this weather."

> **Comment [CJH]:** IMPORTANT: Isn't it still June? Why so cold in Nebraska in summer? It would be good to have some more mention of place and time every few chapters or even at the beginning of each chapter.

> **Comment [CJH]:** Another item about goats—she would have to be milked regularly once or twice a day to stay in milk. It couldn't just be whenever Polly was out of milk. Perhaps Charlie could agree to do it every morning as part of her regular jobs.

> **Comment [CJH]:** Would anyone really ask this? Wouldn't they just get any game they could? If you want to leave it in, maybe Becky could roll her eyes at the lovebirds.

"Well, good luck. Hope you get a deer. We sure could use some fresh meat for supper," Hattie said.

"Sara," Guy said as he looked into her eyes, "would you check on the Prices? Ask Pete to make a box of supplies for them, but you and one of the other women take it over. It will go down easier coming from a woman."

"Yes, I'll do that, and I want to check on Max too."

"Whatever we get has to be shared with everyone," Guy said, adding, "Don't reckon we'll be back in time for supper."

"Ah be savin' you some gravy and rice," Bessie promised, flashing a smile at Abel.

"I'd sho' be grateful, Miss Bessie," he said, grinning widely.

The men rode off, and we went back to our chores. Sara finished her wash and hung it in the wagon to dry while Tag and I watched Polly. Sara went with Hattie to see Pete about supplies for the Prices. He sent supplies enough for a couple weeks.

Bessie had added wild onions to the deer jerky, making tasty gravy which we poured over rice. As usual, she made biscuits, and thanks to Charlie we had butter to go on them. We filled our plates and gathered in the tent. As we made ourselves comfortable around the small fire, I turned to Bessie.

"This is delicious, Bessie," I smacked my lips, "Where did you learn to cook like this?"

"Yes," Sara chimed in. "It's very good." She tilted her head, gazing at Bessie. "You all know my story. Would you feel like sharing yours now, Bessie?"

"Oh, please say yes," I urged. "I know you have a great story from the bits and pieces we've already heard."

Bessie wiped her mouth and looked around the tent at each of us. "Alright, ah'll be tellin' you whets

Wanda Reed

I   'member."

CHAPTER NINETEEN

BESSIE'S STORY

"Me, and my mama lived in a cabin on a cotton plantation in Mississippi. Ah member ah was bout knee-high to a grasshopper when de masta come to da cabin with another white man. I was skeert, thinkin' they was gonna whoop mama. Ah don' 'member what they said, but mama took her clothes off an just stood there neked." Bessie picked up her plate and dipped up spoonful of gravy. She swallowed hard.

"Bessie, if this is too hard for you, you don't have to tell us," I said, sensing the pain she was feeling.

She shook her head. "It's alright, Miss Martha. Ah needs to give my 'count why ah'm on this here train."

"Dat man jes put his hands right on mama, feelin' her all over. He even looked in her mouth. Yessum. He axd how many suckers she had. Masta said jes dis one, and he point to me. That man look me over. He said he would take Mama. Say she got nice color and gets high yeller suckers. That man gave money to the masta. Mama took my hand, but Masta pull me away. He says, 'No, she don' go.' Mama scream and beg, but he jes' tol her to shut up cuz she done been sold. Masta call old Joe to take me to the chillun's kwatuzs." Bessie sighed deeply and shook her head. "That be the last time ah seen mah mama."

"Oh, Bessie, how awful," Sara whispered, wiping her eyes. She wasn't the only one shedding tears. I think we were all thinking of the family we had lost too.

Wanda Reed

"What did you do? How did you manage without your mama?" I asked, remembering how much I'd needed my mother.

"You sees, Miss Martha, the masta didn't leave us slaves much time for grievin'. Ah cried at night on a bed of straw with de other pick ninnies. We wus up at the crack o' dawn doin' the work the old slaves didn't do. I don' know which was worst—pullin' seeds all day in the cotton house or pullin' weeds outside in da heat." She paused and grinned. "Workin' in the garden was good 'cause you could eat sumpin' or steal it fo' later."

"When I was titty high, the old mammy started learnin' me how to work the spinnin' wheel."

She stopped and looked at each of us. "I knows none of y'all been slaves," she began, and was interrupted by Charlie exclaiming, "I sure as hell felt like one."

"Yes, but you had a choice, Charlie. Slaves don't," Sara frowned. "We had slaves, and they either did as they were told, or they were severely punished or sold. Even kind slave owners treated slaves like quality livestock. If they did rebel, they were often maimed or killed." She shook her head. "It's a terrible way to treat other human beings."

"Ah'm shore you treated you slaves kindly, Miss Sara," Bessie said softly, placing her hand on Sara's shoulder for a brief moment.

"We wasn't all treated poorly," Bessie continued. She seemed anxious to explain her life. "The house slaves done got the best jobs. Mos' all wanted to work inside. The men, they like workin' in de barn or smithyin'," she paused, "like Abel. They done made shoes. The womenfolk done the sewin' an weavin'. Bein' the cook was the best, tho'."

Breathing deep and yawning, she continued, "By gum, de cook, she was 'bout as 'pow'ful as de masta, or so it seemed. Ah was lookin' to be cook's

Six Women West

helper soon's I growed enuff." Yawning again, she said, "That's enuf for tonight. Ah'll tell y'all next time when ah became a woman. Ah's got to get these dishes done afo I fall asleep on my feet."

We all pitched in and got thing washed and put away, banking up the small fire good. We were soon asleep as the nor-eastern blew and the snow flew. When morning came, we found four inches of snow.

> **Comment [CJH]:** Again, could this happen in June in Nebraska? If it's possible but unusual, consider having someone comment on the unseasonable weather.

The next night after taking care of the stock and gathered wood, we stayed close to camp while the wind and snow continued. Right after supper, Sara sat in the rocker with Polly, and Bessie sat in her chair to continue her story.

"I'd just had my first bleedin'. Flower, de midwife, said ah wus a woman now. One of the houseboys comes to fetch me up to the big house. Scared an excited, ah went to the backdoor to the Cook, Sophie Mae.

"'You gonna see the masta,' she sed, 'but fust ah gonna scrub yo' musty ass. Git yo'sel in this here tub of hot water so's I can scrub you with dis soap that smell like flowers.'

"'Is ah gonna be a house nigger?' ah asked, but Sophie Mae, she doesn't say nuffin'. She jess scrub an' scrub some more. Den she poured a bucketful over my head to rinse me off. Den Sophie Mae, she say 'You git yo sef out of da tub and wrap dis round you, now chile.'

"Ah ask again, 'Sophie, is ah goin' be a house nigger?'

"'If you smart, you gonna do as you tol', thass all you do,' she said, handin' me a bowl of stew, a biscuit, and milk. 'Now eat this,' she said.

"By golly, that stew was good! Ah never had anything tasted so good. There was big chunks of meat in it. The only time we had any meat in the kwatuzs was on Christmas or if someone stole somethin'—or once in awhile an old milk cow died, and de masta would give it to de kwatuz. Anyway, Sophie give me a soft cotton shift to put on and combed mah hair into braids. Den she led me upstairs. Den she took me by the shoulders and looked right into my eyes and said, 'Now you set you' sef in dat chair an wait til de masta come for you. An you do as he say, you hear me chile? You do as he say.'

I listened closely as Bessie's pattern of speech changed as she told her story from plantation dialect to the teaching she had in New Orleans. Sometimes she used the English she had learned from Sara.

"Ah sat, afraid to move. Ah looked around the large room. Dey was a massive bed, wit high posters and a stepstool next to it. Mercy, I was so skeert. Ah never knowd there was things like this. Ah slid off the chair and went over and touch de bed. It was real soft. Ah stared at the tall dresser with the big mirror over it, and if ah stretch real high, ah could see part of my head. After awhile, ah couldn't help it, ah stood in the chair and saw myself in the mirror. Fo' the fust time, ah got a clear look at myself. Ah looked like my mama. I was honey colored. I was a high yeller. Oh, ah was skeert. Dem women in the kwatuzs said dats why mama got sold—cuz she was yeller. Would ah be sold too? Was that why ah was here, to be sold? No, ah wasn't gonna be sold. Ah was too young. Ah was gonna have a job in de big house an' have pretty clothes an lots to eat.

"Dey was a colorful braided rug lay on de floor. Ah lean down an saw a piss-pot under the edge of the bed. Ah sure did need to use the outhouse, but ah was afraid to leave the room. Ah waited and waited. Ah had to go pee so bad it hurt my belly. Ah got up, looked out the door an up and down the hall Ah didn't see nobody, so ah used the pot an put it back under the bed. Ah got scared I would be in trouble for using the pot, so's ah poured it out de window then pushed it far back under de bed.

"Ah sat on the chair 'til ah was so tired, ah fell asleep, almost falling off de chair and woke up. Ah laid down on de rug.

"Why din de masta come, and tell me what my job is? Daz ah stay here all night? I sure would like to know if ah gits to be a house nigger. Life would be grand if ah could be a house nigger. The house nigger git to wear nice clothes and got a plenty to eat. 'Will this be my room?' I wondered, and then ah fell asleep agin.

"Way in the night de' door open. Ah could hear de masta's footsteps as he crossed the room. Then ah felt a kick in the butt. I jumped up quick as I could. Ah stood up rubbing my face, and I could smell the corn whiskey.

"'Let's have a look at you,' he said in a slurred voice. Ah stood in front of him, too skered to talk. 'Do you know why you're here? To be broke in for suckers, and we gonna put one right there tonight.' He reached out and patted on my cotton shift.

"Ah nodded my head. Ah didn't know what he meant. Ah don't know if ah was too shy to talk or just plain skeert.

"'You been messin' with any them boys in the kwatuz, girl?' he asked.

"Ah shook my head no. Ah was trembling head to toe.

"'Girl, you wouldn't lie to the masta would you?' he asked.

"Ah shook my head. Ah was skeert through an' through.

"'Let the masta see what you look like. Take that shift off.'

"Ah was so skeert, ah was jes froze.

"He repeated, 'Girl takes that shift off.' Then he reached out and took my shift by the neck and ripped it off. 'Well, your color is a real nice yeller.

You sho' skinny as a rail. Got no tits, but you'll fill out.'

"He put his hands on my body. Ah jumped at his touch, jes skeert so bad I wuz shakin' all over. Wantin' to run, de tears run down my cheeks.

"He growled, 'Open your legs.'

Bessie closed her eyes as she told the tale as if to see the pain she suffered as a child.

"He held my arm with one hand as he pushed his other hand between my legs. He rammed his finger up inside me. That hurt, and ah screamed and cried out in pain. He slapped me then an' threw me on the bed. Ah fought an got loose an run, but in that room there was no way out. He grabbed me then an he hit me several times and threw me back on the bed. Then he held me down and took me roughly. At that time ah didn't know what was happinin', but now ah know. It didn't last long 'til he finished with me. Ah heard snoring, an ah pulled away from him.

"Ah got down on the rug and cried. Ah jes lay there 'til morning. When he woke up, he washed and left the room. Ah lay there afraid to breathe, hopin' he wouldn't touch me no more. De water he left in the basin ah used to clean up with. Dey wuz blood between my legs. I hurt real bad. My body done hurt all over, he had beat me so bad. Ah stood on the chair and looked at myself in the mirror. Ah had a black eye an' a bruised cheek. My face was all swelled up. Ah felt ruined an' alone. Helpless tears done overflow the brims of my eyes. Ah never wanted my mama so much as ah did right then. Ah wished ah was back to the cotton house. Ah never wanted to come to de big house no more. Ah didn't ever want that to happen again, an' I hated the masta. Ah pledged myself someday to get away. Den ah wrap my shift around me. Ah whimpering as I crept down the stairs to the kitchen.

"'Oh chile, why you do this,' Sophia said. 'Shut up, it be over with. Now drink dis. Chile, why you fight de masta?' She handed me a cup of strong hot tea laced with rum. 'You gits tough, girl, or you die. De fus time iz de worst, chile. Ah tel you chile, jes lay still and let the masta do wat he do.'

"She handed me a clean homespun shift to wear. 'Ahz gonna get tough,' ah said, 'and someday ah gonna leave here.'

"'Don't you go let de masta har yo talkin' like that. Wash, eat, and help in the kitchen. Dem bruises will fade. Wit time, yo heart wil git hard. Jes don't fight him, chile.'

"I spent my day with Sophie and learnt about cookin'. That was the only good that come from the big house. After supper, Sophie handed me a bit of soap. 'Go bathe an put on a cotton shift. Den go up to de masta.'

"Big tears come swelling up in my eyes. Sophie said, 'Honey that won't do no good. You jes make de best of it and let you mind take you somewheres else, and it soon pass. Honey-chile, don't fight him, jes lay there.'

"Before ah left, she give me a cup of tea heavy with rum. Ah said, 'Thank ya, Miss Sophie. She handed me a peppermint leaf to chew. I was mos' thankful for the rum.

"After the first couple nights, ah let my mind forget what was happenin'. Ah work so hard all day, there was no feelin' left at night. Ah learnt to just lay there, and he would soon be done with me. And if ah didn't resist, he didn't hit me. Ah was unhappy and wanted to run away, but ah knew that I would be caught an beat. Ah had seen them beatins. Dey don't kill you, but you wished dey did.

"Sophie had told me dat soon da Masta would tire of me and send me back to the kwatuh. It had been most a month, and ah was waitin' fo him. He come in all liquored up. After he took a swing at me, he fell down. Then yelled for me ta git my wuthles lazy ass outta there an down to the kitchen. Ah took off runnin'. After that, ah worked in the kitchen with Sophie Mae and slept on a pallet aside her bed. The smell of the cookin' started makin' me sick, so Sophie sent me back to the kwatuh.

"Later, ah kept gettin' sick, so Flower told me to come see her. She told me ah was with child. Ah was moved to the sucker house, where the pick ninnies is kept. De women that's wit child work there, takin care of the little ones so's their mammies can work the fields. Sometime de mother quits comin' to see her baby. Sometime maybe she don't want the chile, cuz it might be sold and she don't wanna get attached. Ah was real sickly, but ah carried my baby an went into labor. Ah was sent to the birthin' house where Flower, the midwife, was to help me birth. I was havin' a hard time, so da masta done come to see me. He come and told me what a good girl ah was. He said he would give me a gold dollar if the baby be a girl.

"Ah screamed to keep myself from scratchin' out his eyes. Ah wanted to spit right in his face. Ah hated him. Bein' built small and as young as ah was, ah didn't weigh no more den a sack of cotton. Givin' birth to the babe near kilt me, but it was the babe that died. Ah was glad it did, not cuz ah hated it but cuza how it got here and how it would haftsa live. And knowin' what happened to me would happen to her. It took near two month for me to get well. Ah was scared ah would have to go back to the big house. Maggie told me, 'You yella, so ah'm not shore, but most times gals only hasta go der once unless you're a frisky gal and de masta has a gentleman friend who wants a bed warmer.'

"When ah got well, ah was told Buck was to be mah man. When ah wuz told this, ah thought ah wuz jes like a hound dog an' they wanted a litter of pups to sell. He wuz big and strong an the color of coffee with cream. Masta said dat we'd make some fancy pick ninnies. We wuz to live together. He tried to make me a baby for six months, but none ever come. Ah prayed there never be any suckers. Masta said Buck had made a lot of suckers, so de Masta told me I was worthless. Finally, Masta sold me. Den de new masta sold me. Ah wuz sold again and again. Ah went from place to place. Each time I had a new masta, ah was forced to sleep with him or de men folks in the family 'til they found out ah didn't make suckers.

"Ah was sold again 'til ah was sold to an owner of a coffle of slaves goin' to New Orleans. Ah was gonna be sold on de auction block. I had heard dat was de bottom for a slave. Ah was at de point ah din care. Most female sold at auction goes to de cribs on de waterfront. Down in de cribs, they die quick, full of sickness.

"Ah stood neked in front of dem white folks, and de men come an' look me over and put their hands all over me. De auction man say all kinds of lies about me, but one man stand up and shout, 'I owned her afore. She's dry as a bone an' cain't breed suckers.' And the interest stopped.

"They called me 'The Yeller.' Some touched me between the legs and lifted my breast and look in my mouth at my teeth. A woman dressed fancy walked up near the block and look me over. She didn't touch me. She told de men, 'If you ain't buyin', keep your hands off. After today you'll only see her at Rosie O'Day's Place.'

"She had a hat full of feathers and a silk dress. She had rouge on her face and paint on her lips. When the biddin' started, the woman bid one hundred dollars. Ah heard, 'Sold to Madam Rosie O'Day.' That was the only bid.

"She bought me. I was taken back to the stable and chained there 'til supper time. Then a black man put me in a wagon with two other men slaves.

Wanda Reed

Ah was delivered to a beautiful house. I was introduced to life in a bordello. I stretched my neck to see the house. It was a large white house. They call it French. Ah was brought in de back door where a black woman said, 'You follow me. I stared around. Everything was so grand. There wuz a floor you could see yossef in and running water, brightly color pictures, and chandeliers. My mouth jest stayed open. After ah was bathed, fed, and had clean clothes, Rosie called me in front of her and told me she would treat me fair if ah worked hard. My job would be to change beds, clean, and cook. If ah wanted to earn some money, ah could do dat by pleasurin' a man, an ah could keep half de money.

"Ah asked, 'Could ah use de money to buy my freedom?'

"'If that's what you want, I'll sell you your freedom,' she said.

"Over two years, ah entertained every man dat had the price. Ah learned how to talk like Madam O'Day wanted. I learned me to be proud of my body. My yeller color was wanted in de business, and ah learned well. Ah was asked for by name. Ah was a preferred girl. My price went up, and so did my tips. My bag of coins grew heavy. Ah knew my freedom was near.

"Right after de war started, Miss Rosie's house got burned. We wuz all asleep in our rooms. No one knew how it started, but that wuz a bad fire. Most of us got out with jes what we had on. Rosie was out of business. Ah had got my poke out with me and paid her my money, and she promised to help me get north. She sold me my freedom, but she was in no hurry and was takin' her own sweet time. Ah was still workin' for her to pay for my trip. Ah must admit, after ah paid for my freedom, ah didn't feel it was right for her to take half of my earnings. Ah helped myself when ah left.

Six Women West

"Then ah met y'all women where I joined you on the river bank and left with y'all—people who treat me like an equal. You don't care if ah is yeller, or what ah did to get free. Now ah got my free papers, an' ah am goin' north. No one will make me do what ah don't want to again."

We sat in silence when Bessie finished her story. How could a person rule someone's life like Bessie's had been ruled? I had grown to love her. We all had tears on our cheeks, and no one had moved or said a word since Bessie finished. I put some wood on the fire. It was late, and we all retired to our bedrolls.

That night the wind blew and howled. It was a raging blizzard. Looked like we would stay another day. To my surprise, next morning the wind was gone and the sun was out.

Pete rode up and yelled, "Get 'em hitched. Let's roll. We'll see if we can't make a few miles today."

We travel across the plains for the next two days, making good time, and Hattie was thrilled that we were moving.

Wanda Reed

CHAPTER TWENTY

> Comment [CJH]: Who is that?

"Good evenin', Hattie," Pete said, walking into camp after supper. "Say, can you get your girls to push those rear wagons a little faster? They're fallin' behind."

"We better, if we want to stay ahead of the Kirby Jones wagons," Hattie said, laying down a halter she was mending while sitting under the tree we parked close to.

Becky came around the wagon. "Hattie, would you take a look at old Jake? He's pulled up lame again."

"Sure. Come on, Pete. Walk along with us."

Pete nodded and the four of us walked to the remuda with Pete and Hattie in the lead. Tag stood up and shook and then followed at our heels. Polly was sleeping, so I suppose he figured it was alright to take a break.

Becky looked at me and snickered and then whispered, "Pete's sweet on Hattie."

"I know," I agreed. "I think they make a good pair." At the edge of camp, the grass grew tall. Several rabbit-brush bushes with their yellow blooms were pretty but didn't smell so nice. There were several large trees in this area that we had roped off to keep the stock from straying.

"Tomorrow we reach Alcove Spring," Pete said, turning his head to look at us.

"Great," I said. "Will Guy want someone to go with him to check it out first?"

Pete hesitated. "I was thinkin' maybe me an' Hattie would do that." He grinned at her. "What'ya say, Gal? Wanna take a ride with me?"

Becky rolled her eyes and snickered again. I jabbed her with my elbow. "Shush."

"Yes," Hattie replied, "I think I might like that."

"Good. Be ready at sunrise?"

"I'll be ready. Martha can drive our wagon. She's turning into a first-class mule driver." She spoke loudly as if to make certain I heard her.

"Thanks, Hattie," I said, raising my eyebrows. "That's always been my dream."

"Jake's limping on his left foreleg," Becky said, as we came into the remuda. "What's causing it?"

Pete knelt down and looked at the mule's leg. "His knee is swollen. Soak it in a bucket of cold water, wrap it, and see how it is tomorrow."

"I'll do it," volunteered Becky.

"I'll help," I offered. "I'll go get a bucket of water and a rag. Be right back."

Hattie and Pete started walking towards the river. "Do you think we should get another mule at the fort?" I called.

"We'll see," Hattie replied over her shoulder.

"I think she's got other things on her mind right now," Becky said with a grin.

"Lucky her. I'll go get the bucket." When I got back, the two of us managed to get Jake's leg in the bucket and sat there while it soaked. Afterwards we wrapped it with a wet rag. Picking up the bucket we walked back to camp.

"You suppose Pete's gonna get together with Hattie?" Becky asked, as we started back to the wagon.

"That's none of our business, Becky, and besides its obvious Pete likes Hattie for more reasons than what you're thinking."

"Like what?"

"Well, for the same reasons we like her. She's smart, she's funny, and she's kind. She'll make Pete a good partner."

"Yeah, but," Becky still sounded confused, stopping under a tree.

I could tell Becky was interested about relationships between a man and a woman. Becky, not all men are just interested in coupling. "What they're doing, you know, is called courtship." I sighed wistfully. "It's flirting and holding hands and just talking," I paused. "Sometime maybe a kiss or two. It'll happen to you someday." *Me, too*, I thought hopefully.

"Yuck! No boy's gonna kiss me. He tries any manhandling, an' I'll poke him with my pig sticker. I did it before, an' I kin do it again."

Her eyes flared with anger, and I wondered what had happened to make her feel this way. "It's not always like that, Beck," I told her. "Tell me why you think that someone would treat you mean?"

"When men found out I was a girl, they wanted to get all over me."

"They didn't care about you. They just wanted a whore. When you love someone and he loves you, you won't feel that way. You'll change your mind when you meet the right man."

"How will I know he's the right one, Martha? They all pretty much look an' act the same—bastards always wantin' to git my clothes off."

"I honestly don't know, Becky," I admitted. "I'm still waiting for the right one myself." I patted her shoulder. "Maybe we can get Sara to tell us how she knew." I didn't know what to tell Becky, so I started walking on toward the wagon.

"Yeah, but she didn't git the one she wanted, did she?"

I shook my head. "No, but I'll bet she remembers the feeling."

"You think Guy's her right one?"

"Could be," I said, smiling. "Could be."

Guy and Sara arrived at the wagon right after we did. He helped her off her horse, something she could have done—had been doing for ages. Now, she acted as if she couldn't have done it without his help. "See you in the morning" Guy said.

"Good night, Guy. I had a nice time. Thank you. I'll be ready." Guy waved goodbye and rode off.

"Sara's got a feller!" teased Becky. "Sara's got a feller!" she taunted as she danced around just out of Sara reach.

"Becky! I am going to skin you alive. You better behave," Sara warned, flinging her arms out to grab Becky.

Sticking her head out of the tent, Bessie whispered, "Y'all keep yo' voices down. Dis babe's sleepin'."

"Is she alright?" asked Sara, a worried tone to her voice.

"Yessum, Miss Sara, she be fine," Bessie assured her; "I just give her a washin' and rocked her to sleep."

"Good. Where's Charlie? The Warren children have the croup. They need her."

"I'll go get her," Becky said. "I think she's over currying her horses in the remuda." She took off running.

"Sara," I began, "you need to talk to her. She doesn't understand about courting. She teased Hattie about Pete and now with you and Guy." I shook my head. "She has her own ideas of men and their intentions All bad."

"I'm certain she's had some bad experiences with them," Sara said. "Hopefully, she'll meet someone who'll change her attitude." Walking over to the water barrel, she dipped a drink of water.

"She mentioned she used her pig sticker on a man. Do you think that's true?"

"I wouldn't be surprised. A young woman alone with no male to protect her is at the mercy of those with evil intentions."

I sat down in one of the camp chairs, slipping my boot off to remove a stone. "I guess all we can do is pray for her and keep an eye out for her."

"Yes," Sara agreed.

Bessie came out of the tent. "Ah be startin' supper now."

"We'll help," I said. "What are we going to fix?"

"Don't know what to call it. Jes vittles. Dat breeze feels good, don' it?"

Coming into camp, Becky said, "Charlie sent me for her bag." She climbed in the wagon and was out and gone with the medicine bag within minutes.

"Bless her heart," Sara said. "She's a good person. I have to figure out how to tell her about life."

"Amen to that."

Bessie said, "Miss Martha, would you cut this meat and onions up real small? And Sara, would you cook de rice? Ah gonna wash de greens."

Charlie and Becky returned in time for supper, telling us to stay away from the Warrens' wagon for a few days since they had the croup. Abel came into camp. He handed Bessie four rabbits all skinned and cleaned. She laughed and said we were going to have rabbit for supper.

Afterwards, we ate and cleaned up camp and then sat around visiting. The wind soon got stronger, and we hurriedly put everything away and moved inside the tent listening to the wind, which had gotten real strong.

Late in the night the wind howled, and the tent stakes worked loose, causing the tent to collapse on top of us. Everyone woke with a start. Polly began to cry. Tag barked and whined. We managed to climb out from under the tent and take cover in the wagon. Bessie ran to Abel's wagon for cover.

The wind whistled through the canvas, rocking it. I was afraid the wagon would blow over. Inside everything was covered with dust, and we could barely breathe. We hadn't been able to get our bedrolls, so the sand hit our skin and stung our faces. We had no protection from the wind and dust. Reluctantly, I open my trunk and, turning everything upside down, I manage to pull out my two precious quilts, and we spread them over us.

Finally, out of sheer exhaustion we slept. I awoke early to a quiet stillness. Tag was letting me know he wanted out. I moved, and the sand slid off the quilt as the others started to wake. I let Tag out and shook the sand off my quilts and returned them to my trunk.

"Thank God the sand has stopped. Come on Polly, let me get you changed," said Sara.

Starting a fire Bessie said, "We'll have coffee purty quick."

"Give us a hand, and we'll get this tent off the ground and shake out the bedrolls. We'll have to clean out the wagon before we roll. We better get a move on to get it all done," advised Hattie.

Charlie went to check on the Warren family, and me and Becky went to the remuda to see how Jake's knee was and bring the mules back to the wagon to hitch up.

"Jake's leg isn't better, Hattie," I told her, wiping the dust out of a cup before filling it with coffee. "Will we just drive a four-up today?"

"Probably a good idea—give Jake's knee time to heal." She threw a saddle on the gelding. "Do you think Becky would trade me her mule for this horse?"

"We can always ask. She's still at the remuda. Tommy was there, talking to her," I grinned. "I think he's sweet on her, and she kind of likes him too. Only she either doesn't know it or won't admit it."

"That girl's got a lot to learn yet," Hattie said. "Well, see what she says about the mule."

I rode the gelding to the remuda. Becky and Tommy leaned across from each other on his horse. They were both laughing and seemed to be enjoying each others' company.

I smiled to myself, thinking Becky didn't even know she was being courted. Even funnier was the fact that she didn't realize she was responding. She was unknowingly flirting with Tommy, batting her eyelashes in the way I had seen my mother do with the storekeeper. I thought how upset Becky would be if I pointed this out to her.

"Hi. Sorry to break this up, but I need to speak to Becky."

Looking guilty, they both jumped back away from the horse.

"Sure, Martha, what's the matter? We low on meat?" Becky asked. She sounded flustered.

"No, another problem. How would you feel about trading your mule for this gelding?"

"Ain't that Hattie's?" She looked surprised. "Why, he's worth more'n twice what my mule is. Why does she wanna git rid of him?"

"Well, you've seen Jake's knee. He's not able to pull. He needs some time off to heal, and we can't put this gelding in harness with the other mules."

"I don't know if Splash is broke to harness. You can try him. If she wants her horse back later, she can have him."

"Thanks." We switched saddles, and I climbed on Splash. Becky started to mount the gelding, and Tommy immediately tried to give her a foot up.

"I don't need any help," she snapped, glancing at me. I wanted to tease her so bad my teeth ached, but I didn't feel it was the right time. I grinned at Tommy, who looked somewhat bewildered.

"Thanks, Becky," I said and kicked Splash into a trot across the field of grass.

At the wagon I stripped off the saddle and handed the reins to Hattie. "She said you can have your horse back if Splash doesn't work out."

"Well, let's see if he's broke to harness." Hattie put the tack on him. We were both relieved to see he acted like he was born to it. "Go ahead and hitch him to the wagon with the others," Hattie said, handing me the reins. "I'll be goin' with Pete. He stopped by earlier, and I asked him to bring me somethin' to ride just in case Becky made the trade."

"Why Hattie, you know you're welcome to ride one of my horses."

"I know, but I prefer a western horse—a surefooted mountain animal.

"Mornin' ladies. Ready to go, Hattie?" Pete asked as he rode up, leading a black mare. He slid off his horse and picked up Hattie's saddle, throwing it over the range mare. After making sure everything was secure, Hattie climbed on and they took off.

After Hattie and Pete rode off, Guy rode up, and Sara was ready to go with him after promising Polly she'd be back soon. "You be a good girl and mind Bessie, alright?"

"Otay," Polly whispered, smiling shyly.

"There must be something special up there," I remarked to Bessie.

"Ah guess we see when we get there," she replied. "Would y'all mind if me an' Polly ride with Abel?"

"No, go ahead. Tag can keep me company. Come on Tag, we're gonna cross the Little Blue." The river was low, and with a rider in place to mark the way, we crossed with no difficulties. The trees along the riverbanks and wildflowers made me want to stop and camp there for several days. It took about four hours to cross all our wagons.

A few miles later, we made camp on the Little Blue. The tall grass grew belly high to our horses, and the water was clear and cold. We heated some water and did our wash, and then we tied a rope between the smaller cottonwood trees to hang our wash. As it dried, Charlie, Becky, and I walked upstream and dropped our fishing lines in the water. We caught a mess of fish.

Bessie and Sara fixed supper. We had cornbread, fish, and greens for supper. Somehow Bessie always came up with greens. Afterwards we went downstream for our bath and then to wash out the clothes we were wearing. With a limit of three changes, we didn't get a chance to wash them often. It was a pleasant place to camp.

The time along the river went by too fast, soon becoming only a pleasant memory. We pushed hard day after day from daylight to dark for several days crossing the plains. The fields were turning a yellow-brown as far as the eye could see, making the days all the same and the landscape boring. We understood that Pete was pushing hard to make up the time lost due to the bad weather. But as people are, some were unhappy at the fast pace.

We had only one accident. It was when the Reece's wagon hit a rock, breaking a wheel, and threw Jodie and Sy off the wagon. She suffered a broken arm and cuts on her head. The boy was bruised and skinned up, but nothing serious. Charlie set Jodie's arm and tended the cuts while the men changed the wheel. Pete said it was time to break for lunch.

At sundown, about nine miles from Fort Kearny we reached Valley Station, and Pete gave the signal to circle up. We set up our tent near the water trough and the station house close to the tall beechwood tree. We all wanted to bathe before we got to the fort, so I grabbed a bucket and got busy pumping water. I was pumping my fourth bucket of water at the trough when six men rode in and dismounted next to the trough. Five of them were in uniform and one, whom I took to be the scout, was in buckskins. Three soldiers watered the horses and the other two along with the scout walked over to Pete who was a few feet away.

"Name's Morgan," the scout said, holding his hand out to Pete. "This here's Corporal Shiloh Kane and Sergeant Luke Watson." He inclined his head in their direction. "We're heading back to the fort. You plan on stopping there?"

"Yeah," Pete said. "Any problem with that?"

"Hell, no," the one called Luke said. "We're always glad for company."

"Great!" the one named Shiloh exclaimed. "We'll have a dance."

"Good. We'll be pullin' in tomorrow."

My bucket full, I walked the four feet to the tent. Entering, I turned and peered through the tent flap at the tall fellow in buckskins. My heart jumped, landed in the pit of my belly, and bounced back. He was the handsomest man I'd ever seen. He was way over six feet with a powerful frame that didn't seem to carry a bit of extra fat. A stump of bristly beard didn't hide a square jaw and firm, full lips. Thick dark hair fell in waves to broad shoulders that looked as if they could carry the weight of the world. His shirt opened halfway to the waist, revealing a chest of dark curly hair. I had a sudden desire to touch it. I blushed. What had come over me? I'd never felt like this before. I sneaked another look and then went to the tent to take a bath.

Would he be at the dance? I wondered as I settled into the tub of warm water. "Please, God" left my lips without conscious thought from me.

When I told the girls about the possibility of a dance when we got to the fort, they got more excited than I had seen them in a long while.

"A dance, goodness," Sara said, smiling. "I'm so glad I finished all the dresses."

"You sayin' we each have one?" Charlie asked.

"That's right. I wanted to surprise you."

"Whenever did you find the time?" I asked.

"Oh, with the sewing machine it's fast. I did some when Polly was sleeping and when you girls were off hunting. I sure hope they'll fit. I had to sort of guess at the sizes." She went into the wagon and brought out an armful of dresses.

She handed one to each of us. "This one's Polly's," she said, holding up a small pink dress with a round pink collar. The bodice was cream colored with pink rosebuds and a pink gathered skirt.

We all made appreciative sounds. "She'll look like a little doll," I said.

"I used up what was left over from Bessie's dress." Sara explained. She glanced at Becky. "I didn't make another one for you, Becky. You'll have to wear the one you wore at the last dance."

"Why not? It's only been wore once," Becky said. "I like that one just fine."

Sara had obviously given a lot of thought to the personality and coloring of each of us. All the dresses were different colors and styles. With just a tiny tuck here and there, they fit perfectly.

We spent the evening heating irons and pressing dresses as we ooh'ed and ah'ed over each one. Hattie's was dark blue with red roses and a white collar of tatted lace. Mine was periwinkle blue with a six-gored skirt and a gathered ruffle at the bottom. Charlie's was dark green with a scoop neck that would show off her bosom. Sara had sewn herself a light pink, which complimented her blonde hair and blue eyes.

"Abel done axed me to marry up with him," Bessie blurted during a lull in the conversation. "Ah done told him ah would."

"Bessie!" Becky yelped. "You fox, you. I knew you two was up to somethin'."

"Oh, Bessie, we're all very happy for you. Aren't we, girls?"

"Yes, yes," everyone agreed enthusiastically.

"Your dress will be perfect for a wedding," Sara said.

"Yessum, that's what ah was thinkin'." Bessie's smile reached her eyes, making them sparkle.

"When you going to do it, Bessie?" Charlie asked.

"Abel says we be marryin' at the fort iffen dey has a preacher. That be tomorrow, ah reckon." She paused, looking pensive. "Ah'll be movin' to his wagon, but ah still intends to cook for y'all if y'all wants me to."

"Are you kidding? We wouldn't let you get married if you stopped cooking for us," I said, grinning. "Why, you've got us all so spoiled, we couldn't get to Oregon without your cooking."

"I'll get busy and sew you some kind of veil," Sara said, looking pensive. "Maybe one of the women will have something. I'll go ask them right now." Without waiting for comments, she left.

"Sara, it's dark out there. You be careful," Hattie yelled.

"I will," she called back.

"Gee, I hope they have a nice chapel at the fort. A wedding. Gee," Becky mused. "I ain't never been to a real wedding."

"Me, neither," Charlie said.

"Me, neither," I admitted. "How about you, Hattie?"

"Well, I was to my own. No veil, though. Just a preacher and a roomful of people I'd never met, including the groom."

"What!" I exclaimed, all of us staring at Hattie for an explanation.

"Not now," she said, shaking her head. "Maybe one of these nights, when it's my time for story tellin'." It was obvious from the tone of her voice that she wasn't saying anymore.

"You reckon it'll be alright for us black folks to marry in the white folks' chapel?" Bessie asked, frowning.

"Why, I don't see why not!" I exclaimed, not knowing whether or not there would be a problem but determined to see Bessie married in a church.

"We're not in the South, and you're not a slave. Don't give it another thought, Bessie. Just think about how pretty you're going to look and how proud Abel will be."

"Yessum, Miss Martha."

Sara came running in waving a large piece of lace. "Look what I got!" she exclaimed. "Velma gave it to me. It was her wedding veil, but we can borrow it. Isn't that wonderful?"

"That's great, Sara," I agreed, adding, "It can be her 'something borrowed.'"

"We best get to bed, girls. Got to be up early," Hattie reminded us.

The sun was high in the sky when the train reached the Platte River. There we saw a small settlement of Indians camped near the fort. We circled up and kept our stock pastured inside the circle. Then we walked over to the fort to look it over and order supplies.

Fort Kearny was an open fort composed mainly of adobe and sod. It boasted a post office, supply center, officer's quarters, and a small chapel. We walked over to the chapel and met the preacher, an elderly man with a long gray beard who showed us the chapel. It was small with five benches on each side and a large wooden cross hung on the back wall above a long table with candles on each end behind the pulpit. Pastor Benson said he would be pleased to marry Bessie and Abel.

"They're black," I told him.

"Don't matter," he said. "We're all God's children."

We finished what we had to do at the fort and returned to camp.

About four thirty, Becky, Charlie, Sara, and I took off downriver to bathe. We found a spot surrounded by cottonwoods and happily dove into the water, laughing and giggling about the dance and Bessie's wedding.

"Bet Tommy won't let anyone else have a dance with you," I teased Becky.

"Oh, that won't be happenin'. The little polecat tried to kiss me and I punched him," She laughed.

"Becky! That's no way to treat a fella," Sara said, shaking her head. "Becky, we need to have a talk about the proper way to treat your suitors."

"Yeah, we'll talk, and you tell me how to stop them kissin' me."

"I guess Guy will be takin' you," I said to Sara.

"Yes. He asked me early on," Sara smiled, her eyes lighting up.

"How about you, Martha? You got your eye on anyone?" Becky asked.

"Well, I saw this fellow at the station," I hesitated. "He's a scout. I think he's real handsome. I don't reckon he'll look at me with all the pretty girls around though."

"Ah, Martha, you're prettier than all of them," Charlie insisted. "None of them got hair like yours."

"Thanks, Charlie. You're sweet to say that," I sighed as I climbed out of the water. "C'mon. We best get back to camp."

"Charlie, your grammar is improving so much. I am so proud of you," Sara exclaimed.

Later after supper, we helped one another get dressed in our finery. We finished just about the time Abel and Guy came by to escort us to the dance.

"How's my girl?" Guy asked, picking up Polly, who looked like a little doll in the dress Sara had made for her. "Ready to go dancing?" Polly smiled and put her arms around his neck.

"My, don' you look fine, Miss Bessie," Abel said, holding out his hand to her.

"Ah's savin' my new dress for my weddin' day," she told him. "We gonna be married in duh chapel. Da girls done fixed it."

"Oh, Lawdy yes," Abel exclaimed. "I'm gonna take me a bride. Nobody tellin' me ah has to. Jes doin' it cause ah love the woman!" He laughed and took Bessie in his arms and swung her around, ending with a tight hug.

Sounds of music and laughter filtered through the trees. The dance had started. "Come on, you lovebirds," I said. "We best get going. I'm sure there are some eager young men out there who are getting impatient."

Pete joined us on the way, walking next to Hattie. Removing his hat he commented, "Lookin' might fine tonight, Miss Hattie," casting a quick glance at her.

"Is that you Pete? My, you clean up right nice yourself," she replied grinning and fell in step with him.

Inside the fort in front of the buildings the men had built a boardwalk. We bumped into a very tall young soldier with straw-blonde hair and a pencil mustache. "Hello, Corporal Kane. On your way to the dance?" asked Pete.

"Yes sir, Mr. Morley," he replied as he tipped his hat to the ladies.

"Well, you're welcome to join us." Pete turned to Becky. "This here's Miss O'Brien." He nodded at Charlie and me, saying, "Miss Taylor and Miss Patterson." He took Sara's hand. "This is Miss Dale, and there's Miss Brown and Miss Bessie, soon to be Mrs. Smith." He paused, looking at Polly, still in the arms of Guy. "The little one's Miss Polly."

The corporal nodded, acknowledging the introductions, but his gaze was focused on Becky.

"The corporal will be traveling with our train for awhile," Pete said. "Six men are being transferred from Fort Kearny to Fort Bridger in Wyoming."

"Miss Becky, I'd be real honored to escort you to the dance." The corporal doffed his hat and held out his hand to her.

Becky blushed, looking flustered.

"Go ahead, Becky," I said. "We're blocking the walkway." Someone behind us must have been carrying a pie. The air was filled with the smell of cinnamon and apples.

"I'm surely looking forward to dancing with you," he said softly as they moved ahead of us. I was the closest to them and could hear him talking.

"We'll be seeing a lot of each other between here and Fort Bridger," he was saying. "I really want to get to know you. I've never met anyone as pretty as you." He brought his head down close to hers. "Who do I have to see to get permission to court you?"

Sara caught my attention and raised an eyebrow. I nodded, wondering if her thoughts were like mine. Who was this Dapper Dan sweet-talking Becky? He seemed much too smooth for his age, which I guessed to be the early twenties. For some reason, I was reminded of the phrase, 'a fox circling the hen house.'

Hopefully, Becky was too smart to be taken in by his charm. Watching them, I wondered and worried, deciding to discuss it with the other girls later.

Maybe I was jealous, I thought. *Maybe I wanted it to be the scout, Morgan Brooks, sweet-talking me.* That thought sent a shiver of delight up my spine. *Please let him be there*, I prayed silently. *And, Lord, please let him ask me to dance.*

I guess the Lord was listening. As we walked into the soldiers' dining hall, we met Morgan right at the front door. Hattie had already met him, and now she introduced him to the rest of us. My throat was dry as dust, and I could only nod when he asked me to dance. He took my hand and led me to the floor.

I trembled as I floated in his arms. He didn't say anything. Was he waiting for me to say something? I couldn't think. I was feeling very strange, and the sensations I was feeling I'd never experienced before. Heat surged through me, and I was sure he could hear my heart pounding, probably aware of it through his hand on my back.

He looked down at me, and his gray eyes seemed to look into the depths of my soul. His lips were only an inch away. I could feel his warm breath on my cheek. "You fit real nice," he murmured.

I just held my breath, hoping the music would never end, wondering if I had lost my mind. A man was not part of the future I had planned when I left home. The music stopped. Morgan walked me to my seat, thanked me, and walked away. I felt so flustered.

I should have been relieved, glad to be out of his arms. Instead I felt empty. My eyes followed him as he crossed the floor and asked Lorraine to dance. She smiled and took his outstretched hand. They strolled into the dancing area, him with his hand touching her small waist. She appeared even more petite compared to him. I felt taller and uglier than ever. I made my way to the table that held the punch. My throat was so dry.

Everyone had a partner—everyone else, that is. Charlie was laughing with the army officer, Luke Watson, who seemed to be quite taken with her. And who could blame him? She looked very fetching in the dark-green gown, which set off her bosom and auburn hair.

Becky and Shiloh were gazing at one another as if no one else existed. The musicians started another dance, and Morgan walk toward Mary Beth. Sara and Guy sat on the sidelines, obviously enjoying each others' company. Hattie and Pete stood leaning against a wall, talking animatedly. Bessie and Abel danced together as if they'd been doing it forever.

Just as I finishing my punch, Major Peril, a large, burley man with a handlebar mustache and a big belly, asked me to dance. He pulled me up close to him, his belly pushing against my body. I smiled weakly and pulled back. "Sorry, Missy," he said. "Didn't mean any disrespect. Just my arms aren't long enough, I guess."

"None taken, Major," I assured him and move my hands to his elbows. We moved around the room rapidly. We flew past Morgan and Mary Beth. She was holding on to him, looking up adoringly. Morgan wore a strained expression.

None too soon, the dance ended. The major asked me to join him for a cup of punch, which I accepted gratefully. We made small talk, and I did my best to keep my attention on him, but my eyes kept straying to Morgan.

Polly was now with Pete and Hattie while Sara and Guy twirled around the dance floor. Morgan returned Mary Beth to her seat and walked over to Hattie. She smiled, nodded, and handed Polly to Pete. As Morgan and Hattie began to dance, Pete held Polly in his arms and began to dance around the floor. She was laughing and chattering excitedly. *Such a happy little girl*, I thought. *She was lucky to have Sara.*

Would I be a good mother? I wondered as I watched the dancers move around the room. Automatically, my eyes focused on Morgan. He and Hattie seemed to be doing serious talking. *Probably about the trail ahead*, I thought, until they both turned and glanced at me.

Flustered, I looked away, wondering what was being said about me. "I need some fresh air," I told the young soldier who approached me to dance. I needed to be alone and try to sort out my feelings.

Out on the boardwalk, I leaned against a pole and stared up at the sky. "Oh, Papa," I whispered, "what's happening to me? I've never felt this way before. I feel all mixed up." I sighed deeply. "I wish you were here to talk to."

Suddenly, I sensed someone behind me. Turning around, I was face to face with Morgan. "It's a nice night," he said. "Have you ever seen so many stars?"

"No. I mean, yes," I stuttered. "It's beautiful here. I hope it's this beautiful in Oregon." I wanted to ask him what he and Hattie were talking about—if it had anything to do with him being here. I'd be sure and ask her later. Now, I just smiled and waited.

"I don't know. I've never been to Oregon." He paused. "I've heard it's real nice. Lots of water and trees—beautiful country. Do you have folks there?"

"No, my folks have passed away." Nervous, I started talking about my horses. "All I have are my fillies—thoroughbreds. I'm going to have a horse ranch in Oregon. Someday you'll see my horses running in the Derby," I told him, unable to hide the pride I felt.

"That's quite an undertaking for a woman. Hell, for anyone. I'd like to see them." He chuckled. "I have a stallion I'm pretty proud of. Who knows? Maybe we can get them together."

"I don't think so," I said firmly. Me and Morgan together was one thing, but his stallion and my mares was a definite not! "But, you can see them after the wedding reception tomorrow. Are you coming to the wedding?" I tried to speak calmly, as if it didn't matter one way or another.

"Yep, I'm looking forward to it. It's the kind of excitement I like," he said, smiling. Sounds of the Kentucky waltz filled the night. He held out his hand. "Will you dance with me?"

I took his hand, and we walked inside. Charlie caught my eye and winked. I just smiled.

As the evening wore on we danced the Virginia reel and then partnered up for the square dances, neither of us saying much. All I could do was feel. My body had never felt so alive. I wondered if

Morgan was experiencing the same emotions. *If he was*, I thought, *he was sure keeping them under control.*

When the music stopped, the gathering began to break up, everyone saying goodnight. Morgan asked to walk me back to the wagon. He talked about how good the cookies were and how nice and sweet the punch was. When we were at my wagon, he said, "Good night, Martha. See you tomorrow about three." He tipped his hat and strode away. I stood watching him, wondering why he hadn't tried to kiss me. *Was mama right?* I asked myself. *Was I the kind of woman a man didn't desire?* Sighing, I entered the tent and prepared for bed. The other girls were still out with their fellows. I envied them. Sleep didn't come easily. When it finally did, it was filled with images of gray eyes and full lips that seemed to hover just above mine but never touching.

CHAPTER TWENTY ONE

Over coffee the next morning everyone was in a happy mood, partly because of Bessie's wedding and partly because of last night's frolic. It was just what we needed to break up the hardship of the trail.

"Ooh, Martha, that feller you was dancin' with was mighty handsome," Becky teased.

"And nice and tall," Charlie added.

Hattie and Sara just grinned at me. Bessie was busy pressing her wedding dress.

"Yes," I agreed, unable to hide a smile. "He is handsome, isn't he? He's picking me up at three to look at my horses."

"Oh? It's the mares he's interested in, is it?" Hattie asked, raising her eyebrows.

"I don't know," I admitted. Not wanting to talk about it, I turned to Bessie. "You are going to look beautiful. Abel is going to be so proud."

She smiled shyly. "It all seems like a dream. Me gettin' married in a white folks' church. It don't seem real."

"It's real, alright, Bessie. And it couldn't happen to a more deserving couple," I told her as I refilled my coffee cup.

"Gee, Bessie, maybe you an' Abel gettin' hitched will give these other fellers some ideas," Charlie remarked with a grin.

"Do we bring duh broom?" Bessie asked.

"A broom? Why?" Becky asked the question for all of us.

"It's what dey do in the slave kwatuh's," Bessie explained. "Dey jumps ovah a broom, an' then they's married."

"You won't need a broom, Bessie," Sara said softly. "The preacher will say some words from the Bible and ask you and Abel if you take each other as man and wife. You'll both say you do, and he'll declare you married."

"You better start getting dressed," I said. "The wedding is at eleven and lunch is afterward. Let's move into the tent so we will have some privacy."

"Here, let me button your dress. Slip on this petticoat. It will make your dress stand out a little. I wish I had a tall mirror so you could see how beautiful you look." The dress was cream-colored and very full, covered with tiny delicate pink roses. It had full sleeves to the elbows and tiny buttons on the sleeves to the wrists. It fit perfectly. Sara had done a nice job on this dress.

Walking over, Bessie hugged Sara tight. "Dey no doubt about it. She is a right natural."

"That's so Sara. If you go into business as a dressmaker out west, you could make a name for yourself," said Hattie, "not to mention a good living."

"Play your cards right, and you'll have a husband like Bessie, and you can work yourself to an early grave waiting on him hand and foot," Charlie chimed in.

"Charlie, that's enough of that no account talk," Hattie barked. "Don't be spoilin' Bessie's wedding day with that kind of talk."

"Miss Hattie, ain't no one gonna spoil this day. My Abel's the kind a fella a girl wouldn't mind waitin' on han' an' foot. That's for sur'."

Charlie rolls her eyes and smiled, "Ain't love grand."

Becky walked into the tent with an armful of wildflowers. "I picked some of each kind so as to get the right ones," she said. "You look pretty, Bessie."

"Thank you, Becky." I took the flowers, laying them on the barrel.

"Let's try the veil," Sara said. "We can tuck some of these pink rosebuds in the crown."

Standing back to look at the result, she added, "There, doesn't that look nice?"

"Beautiful," we all agreed.

Sara arranged the bluebells, wild roses, and tall spikes of white lupine and tied them together with a long pink ribbon. "This is a lovely bouquet for you to throw," she told Bessie.

"Ah'z gonna throw it?" Bessie asked, looking very confused.

"Yes, that's another white folks' custom. After the ceremony, you toss the bouquet in the air, and whoever catches it will be the next bride. Let's move outside by the wagon. There's more room and more air. It's getting hot in this tent."

"Ah'z gonna need five mo' dem bouquets," Bessie stated with a chuckle. "Ah wants you all to git married."

"I better go over to Abel's wagon to see how he's doing," I said, not wanting to talk about marriage.

Abel was beside himself with excitement. He was walking back and forth beside his wagon which had been move away from the other wagon for the honeymoon. "Ah done all ah can, Miss Martha. Ah done bathed, shaved, put on my best britches an' this hyar blue shirt. Ah'z as ready as ah can be." He paused and took a deep breath. "How's my Bessie? She ain't changed her mind? Lawdy, ah does love dat woman. Duh way she moves her body jus' makes my blood start to racing." Sighing, he added "And now she gonna' be all mine."

"Abel," I said, laughing. "I think you're telling me way more than I need to know. Were you able to get a buggy to take her to the chapel?"

"Yessum, ah done burro'ed one from the fort stable."

"Good. You pick up Bessie, and the rest of us will meet you at the chapel. Now remember, wait just ten minutes and drive over to our wagon." I left him looking dazed and anxious.

The chapel's five rows of benches as well as every open space in the room were filled with well-wishers. The chaplain's wife played "Here comes the Bride" on a small pump organ. Abel held Bessie's arm as they walked down the aisle. Kneeling in front of the pulpit, they listened intently as the chaplain spoke. When he came to the part about giving the bride away, the five of us stood. "We do," we said in unison. There was a subdued trickle of laughter from the audience.

The chaplain then read verses on love from the Bible. "Love is patient. Love is kind. It does not envy. It does not boast. It is not proud. It is not self-seeking. It is not easily angered. It keeps no record of wrongs. Love does not delight in evil but rejoices with the truth. It always protects, always trusts, always hopes, and always perseveres."

I thought, *What a wonderful thing, to love that way. Was I capable of such a love? Was anyone?*

The chaplain went on to talk of God and how he made men different, but the same in His eyes. I wondered why God hadn't mentioned women. Maybe He thought it was understood. I shrugged. Obviously, men didn't understand it that way.

When the chaplain finished, Abel and Bessie exchanged rings created from horseshoe nails made by Abel. The service ended with the chaplain's wife singing, "O Promise Me."

On the chapel steps, Bessie threw her bouquet. Several women held out their arms, but Sara caught it. Cheers and laughter rang out as we all walked to the officer's mess where we danced the night before last night, this time for a potluck dinner.

On the way over, Morgan came up beside me. "Didn't see you reachin' for the flowers, Miss Martha," he commented, grinning. "Not lookin' to marry up?"

I stumbled, and he reached for my arm. A thrill surged through me. I pulled away. "No," I said firmly. "I'm not looking to get married. My plans don't include a man."

"There'll be a lot of men sorry to hear that," he said, releasing my arm.

Nothing more was said as I walked away to help with the food preparations. I decided I would stay clear of Morgan Brooks the rest of the journey. I didn't need the distraction.

The ladies at the fort had outdone themselves making a huge wedding cake with buttercream frosting. There was also a generous supply of food and punch. Soon everyone was eating and drinking and having a good time.

Around one o'clock, the men started moving back the tables so there was room to dance. Mr. Crayon got the square dancing started. I made it a point to be busy picking up dishes when Morgan approached me.

"Will you still be showin' me your horses?" he asked, after I refused his invitation to dance.

"I said I would, didn't I?" I snapped. I carried several plates to the kitchen where there were several privates cleaning up and then returned to the mess hall. I found a place to sit down.

Morgan stood by me. He looked confused as if he were wondering why I'd gotten so huffy. My behavior was not entirely due to my decision to stay clear of Morgan. I had been watching Corporal Shiloh with Becky. I was sure he was a bounder, and I worried he'd take advantage of her. My concern had made me testier than I ordinarily would have been. I hadn't had a chance to talk to her yet.

"Sorry," I apologized. "I'll be ready at three."

"Great. Well, I can see you're busy. Pick you up at three." He walked away, toward the door shaking his head.

Becky walked over to me. "You're not tossing that handsome guy off are you?"

"Speaking of handsome fellers, where's yours?"

"Oh, he'll be back. He just had to make a trip to the outhouse."

"Becky, when did you meet the corporal? He acts like he's known you forever."

"Yesterday afternoon at the remuda," She grinned. "Boy, can he talk nice." She blushed. "He tried to kiss me."

"Did you let him?" *He was a scoundrel*, I thought. *No gentleman would do that.*

"No, Martha!" she retorted. "Of course not. I slapped his face. Told him I'd let him know when I wanted to be kissed."

"Good for you, Becky," I grinned. "Doesn't seem to have scared him off."

"No, it don't, do it?" She chuckled. "Gotta go. He's back. See you later."

"Bye. Be careful." I felt a sense of relief. Becky was smarter than I had given her credit for. She could take care of herself.

Sara came up beside me. "Martha, remember we have to hire a driver for my wagon."

"Right we better go do that now." We walked down to the stable where we asked Sam about a driver.

"There's James Douglas," he told us. "He's stranded here. His horse broke its leg, and he ain't got no cash for another one. He's been doin' odd jobs. He might take the job. He was around awhile ago. I'll give him a holler." He walked to the edge of the barn and yelled. "Hey, Douglas, you out there?"

A voice answered from inside the stable, "You callin' me?" A stocky, dark-haired man with a full beard and hair tied back with a piece of rawhide came striding towards us. Piercing blue eyes stared at us, but his tone was soft. "Yes, what you need?"

Sara told him. He said he was interested. "I'll have to talk with the wagon boss first," she said. "I'm sure he'll agree to let me hire you. He'll want to meet you, of course."

"Fine. You want me to come with you now?"

"No, you go ahead and talk to Pete Morley. He's at the dance. We have to get back to our wagon to see about my child."

"I'll do that." He seemed to be a man of few words. I smiled to myself. I thought, *Men! They either talked too much or not enough.*

We walked across the field of drying grass to the wagons. Polly was sound asleep in the tent.

"She's an angel," Charlie said. Tag was lying beside the tent, and Charlie sat in one of the chairs straightening her medical supplies. "Hope any youngsters I have will be as good as her."

"Thanks for watching her," Sara said. "Yes, she is an angel. I'm lucky to have her in my life."

"I have to change," I interjected. "Morgan should be here any minute. He wants to look at my horses." I changed in the wagon so I wouldn't wake Polly, dressing hurriedly. I was excited and nervous. Why had I agreed to meet him? Oh, horse feathers!

"He's here," Charlie called.

I pulled on a vest. Head down, I stepped from the wagon, missing the bottom step. I fell head-on into Morgan, knocking him to the ground with me sprawled on top of him. I tried to get up. He tried to help. Charlie was laughing her head off. When we finally managed to get untangled, he started brushing the dust off me, but his hands kept touching the wrong places.

"Stop! I can do it," I yelled.

"Sorry, ma'am," Morgan said unable to hide a grin. "Just tryin' to help."

"Come on. Let's get this over with." I glanced at his stallion and noticed how beautiful he was.

Picking up the reins of his horse, he ran to catch up. "Sure do appreciate you showin' me your horses," Morgan said quietly. "I'm real proud of mine, too, so I can appreciate your feelings for yours." He paused. "An Indian friend gave me Raindrop, my Appaloosa. I saved his son from drowning. Wasn't anythin'. I just happened to be in the right place at the right time." He shrugged his wide shoulders. "Sure do like that horse. Plan to raise more like him."

I decided that the least I could do was be civil. It wasn't his fault I was attracted and didn't want to be. I slowed my steps.

"I was born into a horse breeding family," I said, "so I guess it's in my blood. My pa came over from Ireland and had a real knowledge of horses. He raised thoroughbreds from Kentucky and Virginia." I glanced at him, admiring his strong jaw. "You know about horseracing, don't you?"

"Yes, ma'am," he drawled. "I was around it awhile."

"My mares' bloodlines go back twenty years. Their offspring will be running in the Derby someday," I stated firmly.

"I'm sure they will. You certainly come across as a woman who knows her mind. I admire that."

"There they are," I said, pointing to the three mares busily engaged in eating. Their coats shone with a healthy glow, and their bodies looked strong. I felt as proud of them as if they were my children.

Morgan approached them slowly. They raised their heads and stared at him. When they saw me, they all three began to nicker softly. I went over to Gray Lady and stroked her neck. "This is Gray Lady. She's the oldest by a year and my favorite to ride. Moving to the chestnut, I said, "This is Boots," and stepping to the black I said, "She's the youngest—Sugar."

"She's a beauty. This gray is well over sixteen hands," Morgan said, standing beside me.

I moved away. Being too close to him, I could smell his manly scent, and it clouded my thoughts. "Yes," I agreed. "They're all three top-notch mares and will throw some fine colts."

"What would you take for them?" he asked.

The hair on the back of my neck went up, and I grew cold. "They're not for sale. Not at any price. I'm taking them to Oregon. They're my start of a horse ranch. I thought I'd made that clear."

"Yeah, that's what you said, but let's face it, Martha—you're a woman even if you are an amazing one. You can't run a ranch much less build one." He shook his head. "That's a man-sized job."

"Excuse me!" This time I looked at him and didn't see his handsome features or his charming smile. This time I saw a man who looked a lot like Abner. "That's what you think, Mr. Brooks. No man takes what belongs to me. You stay away from my mares! Stay away from me!" I turned and stomped away, so angry I could spit.

"Now what brought that on?" He yelled after me. "Lordie, lady. I can't figure you out."

I kept walking. Tears welled up, and I brushed them back. "Men! Who needs them?" I asked, determined to forget the feelings this one had aroused. I wasn't in the mood to talk to anyone, so I went for a walk along the river. I found a nice quiet spot under some cottonwoods to sit. I watched an old porcupine digging out grubs. It was around sunset when I returned to the wagon. My tears had dried, and I had made some firm decisions.

As I walked up, Hattie called to me. "Martha, come to the stable with me, okay?"

"Okay." We walked quietly across the grass. What few trees there were seemed wilted by the heat. I hoped soon there would be an evening breeze. It would have been the time to ask her what she and Morgan had talked about at the dance. Instead I made small talk.

"Wasn't the wedding beautiful? How ever did those women make such a beautiful cake on such short notice?"

"They must have stayed up all night," Hattie said. "It was right friendly of them."

At the stable the first thing I saw was Morgan currying his stallion. I stopped just inside the big dark cool barn that smelled of sweet hay and manure. I scratched a mule's ear, letting Hattie go on without me. I had nothing to say to him and didn't want him saying anything to me.

"Hello, Morgan," Hattie said. "Have you seen Private Hays? He's supposed to deliver my feed."

"He stepped out for a minute," Morgan said, putting down the brush. "Anything I can do?"

"Don't think so. I'll wait for him." She walked over and patted the stallion. "Fine horse you got here."

"Yes, he's a beauty alright," Morgan agreed, his voice ringing with pride. "Seein' as I'll be part of your escort to Fort Bridger, I could bring your feed out."

"Well, okay. Change the order to three sacks. I got a feelin' were going to need the feed."

"Would that be to Martha's wagon?"

"Yeah," Hattie turned to leave and then turned back. "Say, as long you'll be coming out, be there 'round supper and plan on eatin' with us."

"Okay with you, Martha?" he asked.

I ignored him determined not to answer.

Hattie looked from me to him, but didn't say anything except, "See you later, Morgan."

Hattie and I walked in silence for a ways. Then she asked," What is it, Martha? It's not like you to be rude."

"It's him. He played up to me and then tried to buy my mares. You know how men are. They don't think women can do anything. Hell!" I swore. "How do they think they got here?"

Hattie chuckled. "Don't think I've seen you this upset before. He really gets to you, doesn't he?"

"What do you mean? I just don't like being taken advantage of." I shook my head. "Just because he's tall and handsome, he thinks he can get anything he wants. Well, he doesn't impress me. He's just another man." *Just like Abner,* I thought.

"He didn't strike me as just any man. I put him in the same category as Pete or Guy or Abel. You consider them good guys, don't you?"

"Yes, but..."

"When he talked to me at the dance, he sounded interested in you—not your horses. He thought you were interested in Shiloh." We walk across the parade grounds of the fort and then across the field in front of the fort.

"Shiloh—that's ridiculous. Well, that's not the impression I got. He barely spoke to me when we danced. Besides, ma said I'm not the kind of girl men find attractive. She made it real clear to me that men only want women like me for one thing. They marry women like Sara. Little and sweet, blonde and blue-eyed."

"I never met your Ma, but she had a lot to learn about men. That's only true if you believe it." She chuckled. "Look at me. I'm not what anybody would call a man-catcher, and I ain't had a problem."

I laughed and shook my head. "Hattie, you're funny." We had arrived at the camp, so our discussion stopped. But, what Hattie said got me thinking. I looked around the camp, and there were all kinds of women. Short, tall, plain, attractive, skinny, and plump. None of them looked like Ma or Sara, and except for Lucinda and Arabella, all were married. Obviously, Ma was wrong. I shrugged. Why was I even thinking about it or him? Getting married was not in my plans, and I didn't intend to let any man—even one who was handsome and seemed nice—get in my way. I determined to put him out of my mind.

I busied myself with my horses, repaired tack, and returned to camp to help Bessie with supper.

Morgan arrived right on time with our feed and stowed it in the wagon. Tipping his hat, he smiled and said, "Evenin', ladies. Howdy, Abel." Rubbing his lean stomach, he added, "Sure smells good." He glanced at me, and I turned away. His easy manner wasn't going to fool me again. I fixed my plate and sat down on the wagon tongue.

"Martha," Becky called. "Ain't you gonna eat with us?"

"Come on, Martha. I don't bite," Morgan said, with a knowing grin.

I realized I'd look a bigger fool than I already felt I was if I didn't join them, so I came over and sat next to Sara.

After dinner Morgan told us stories of his early life and later adventures as an army scout. "I was sixteen when I left New York. I lived on my aunt and uncle's farm. I got tired of workin' for nothing, so I helped myself to a horse and the money out of the cookie jar." He shook his head. "I never looked back and haven't been sorry."

"Where were your parents?" I heard myself ask.

"That's a story for another time." He turned to Luke. "How about some music to liven the party up?"

Obviously, Morgan had some heartaches of his own which he didn't want to share with us. Luke took his guitar off his horse, and he and Charlie kept us entertained for the next couple of hours.

"Well, folks, if you all don' mind, me an' my new bride will be sayin' goodnight to all," Abel said, taking Bessie's hand in his. Bessie grinned shyly as

Luke broke into a lively rendition of "Camp Town Races," and we all sang overly loud and cheered.

"Guess I'll be goin', too," Morgan said, standing. "Thanks again for supper."

"Yeah, me too," Luke said, putting the guitar away and smiling at Charlie. "You're some singer, lady," he told her.

"You're not so bad yourself," she replied. "See you tomorrow."

Pete said goodnight a few minutes later after telling Sara he'd hired her driver, and he'd be starting the next morning. "I thought it would be better to have him workin' for me. He can share camp with us. He's kind of a loner. Doesn't talk much."

"Thanks, Pete. I appreciate it." She glanced at the rest of us. "I'm going for a walk with Guy. Be back pretty soon. Polly's sound asleep," she said, taking Guy's hand.

I was just ready to head for the tent when Abel came running up. Panting, he thrust a piece of paper at me. "Miss Martha, look! Bessie done asked me to lock up her free papers. But, look here. They ain't free papers. Ah can't read too good, but ah knows dis ain't no free paper. What we gonna do? What if dey come and take her away?"

Taking Abel's hand, I led him over to the lantern at the back of our wagon. "Abel, be calm," I said, looking at the document he handed me. It was a dessert recipe from Rosie O'Day, but there was no mention of Bessie or her freedom. My heart sank.

"Ah'z right, ain't ah?" Abel's eyes filled with tears. He slumped down in a chair holding his head with his hands.

"Yes, Abel, you're right." I patted his shoulder. "You go back to Bessie and don't worry. We won't let anyone take Bessie from you."

"Ah trust you, Miss Martha." He walked slowly back to his wagon. He looked like the weight of the world had just landed on his shoulders.

I recalled what Bessie had told us. She had worked as a prostitute for two years and turned over the money to Rosie. In return, the woman was supposed to give her a document of freedom. I sat down in the chair. I needed to think.

The dirty bitch, I thought. I needed help, but whose? Sara. She knew about slave papers. I waited anxiously for her to get back. She arrived a few minutes later, appearing somewhat disheveled and flushed.

"Sara, look at this!" I exclaimed, showing her the folded paper.

"It's a recipe for Shoo-Fly Pie," Sara said, looking confused. "Why are you so upset?"

"Because it's supposed to be Bessie's free papers."

"Free papers?"

"Yes. That hussy took advantage of Bessie's illiteracy. Poor Bessie—two years of workin' on her back and givin' the money to that woman, thinking she was going to be free."

"What a mean thing to do!" Sara said. "The woman should roast in hell." She paused, frowning. "Bounty hunters could cause a problem. I don't think they will come much past the Missouri border unless somebody pays them extra."

"Sara, this is awful. Is there anything we can do to protect Bessie?"

"I'll look through my papers. I may have a bill of sale for someone who fits her description. If I can't find one, we'll make one," she said, reaching out and squeezing my shoulders with both hands. "Don't worry. I was raised on a slave farm. We won't let them take Bessie."

"I guess there's no need to say anything to Bessie about this, is there?" I asked. "I mean, she thinks she bought her freedom herself. It would be a shame for to find out she had sold herself for nothing. Gosh, I hope Abel didn't say anything to her."

"I doubt that he would say anything that might hurt her. He really loves her," Sara said. "Come on, let's go to bed. We'll take care of it in the morning."

Abel had the fire going when I came out of the tent at dawn. Obviously, he hadn't slept any better than I. "It's going to be alright, Abel," I told him. "Sara will fix a paper. You haven't said anything to Bessie, have you?"

"No, ma'am. Ah don' want to upset her."

"Good. She doesn't have to know about the deception. We'll take care of it. Thanks for building the fire."

"You welcome, Miss Martha," he said, managing a grin. "Bessie be over pretty soon to fix breakfast."

I was pouring a cup of coffee when Pete rode up, dismounting. "How about a cup of coffee? Moe's tastes like yesterday's dishwater."

"Sure, help yourself. I see the army wagons are here. How long will they be with us?"

"The army will accompany us to Fort Bridger. Two wagons with six soldiers showed up a little after sunrise. Their scout, Morgan, will check the condition of the trail and report on any Indian activity."

So far, our encounters with Indians had been few and from a distance, but that could change. We were going into the territory of a different tribes of Indians.

Hattie walked out of the tent. "Mornin', Pete."

"Good morning, Hattie. You ready for a long hard day?"

"If it would get me to Oregon any sooner, I'd drive half the night."

Six Women West

Sara pulled me aside and whispered, "I haven't had a chance to look for the sales form papers. Maybe we can do it when we camp tonight."

"Fine," I agreed, thankful there was a solution to Bessie's problem. I had come to care about her as we all had. It was like we had all become sisters and would do whatever was necessary to stay a family.

Within the hour the wagons pulled out, staying on the south side of the Platte River. The sand was deep and the going was slow. When we hit solid ground, we tried to make up for the time we'd lost. We stopped every two hours to rest the stock. Still, it was a good twelve hours before Pete called for us to circle up and make camp by a small creek. The weather had turned cold, and dark clouds promised rain or snow.

Once we camped, I unhitched my mares from the back of the wagon and took them out to where they could graze. Morgan came up behind me with his stallion and the gelding, his army-issue horse that he call Bay.

"Looks like a northern might blow up tonight," he said. "Better check the ties real good. You wouldn't want them getting loose."

"I know how to take care of my horses," I snapped. "Better make sure your own are secure." I really didn't understand why I was so sharp with him. I guess I felt I had to prove myself.

"Sorry, I wasn't thinking. Of course, you don't need advice from me." He smiled. "Guess I'm so used to tellin' those green recruits what to do, I forget when to shut up. Give me another chance?"

Damn, I swore silently. *Who could resist the man's charm?* I stroked Gray Lady's neck and tried to think of something to say.

"I guess I am a bit touchy," I admitted. "I'm sorry." I held out my hand. He grasped it tightly, sending chills up my spine. I pulled away quickly.

Wanda Reed

"No problem," he said. "I understand. I'm pretty touchy myself when it comes to somebody tellin' me what to do, especially about my horses."

Well, I raised these horses from birth. Boots there lost her dam when she was only one day old. Southern raiders looted our farm and stole our horses. These were babies, and I have protected them from both armies and anyone else that tried to take them from me. They're going to Oregon with me."

"I can certainly understand that," he said. "We'll have to watch all the horses pretty close now that we're getting into Indian country. Not all of them are as friendly as the ones you've met," he frowned, "and they really appreciate good horse flesh. Especially the young bucks like a flashy war horse like your gray or my Raindrop."

Lightning flashed, and a few minutes later a loud roll of thunder sounded, startling the horses.

"Better take them back to the wagons," Morgan said, adding, "I mean, if you think so."

I grinned. He was catching on. Back at the wagon, I secured my horses between the tent and the wagon, giving them a good ration of grain. It had started to rain lightly.

Sara brought Polly and her lockbox over to the tent, and we were sorting through her papers, looking for a sales paper. Hattie had prepared a shallow pit lined with rocks for a small fire to keep the tent warm.

Morgan walked up just as the fire was burning nicely. "Well, I guess you already know how to do that," he said, pointing to the fire pit. "Here, let me open your smoke hole in the top of the tent."

"Yep," Hattie said, "learned that a long time ago when I was a muleskinner. My husband, Colton, wanted me to know as much as he did about survivin' on the trail." She grinned. "Care for coffee?"

> **Comment [CJH]:** Changed from Carl to match Hattie's story from later

"Sounds good."

"Got time for a visit?"

"Sure." He squatted, and Polly climbed up on his knee. He tottered and fell backwards on his butt. Sara and I started laughing. "Polly," Sara called, "come over here, baby."

"Aw, she's alright, ma'am," Morgan said, laughing. "Just let me get settled." He sat cross-legged on the ground and held out his arms. Polly climbed into them. She put her arms around his neck, and he responded by hugging her tightly.

"Good father material," Sara whispered, nudging me.

I ignored her. "Keep your mind on what we're doing. We have to see to Bessie."

"Here it is," she exclaimed, holding up a piece of paper. "All I have to do is fill it in."

"Wonderful," I said, sighing deeply. "How do you know how to do this?"

"I've done it many times, Martha," she confessed. "I kept the breeding book on the plantation, remember? And I learned how to forge papers."

"Why would you need to forge them?"

"That's how you made the most money." She shook her head. "It was wrong, but it was the way things were done."

Thunder rolled across the sky, and Polly screamed. She climbed out of Morgan's lap and ran to Sara. "It's alright, baby. Mama's got you."

I got up, went over by the fire, and poured myself a cup of coffee.

"I'll take some more of that if you're pourin'," Morgan said, holding up his empty cup.

I automatically bristled for a moment and then remembered that I had decided I was willing to be friends. After all, I was already up and it surely wouldn't pain me to pour him coffee.

"We were just talkin' about the mules we got," Hattie said. "Those Price kids only got two mules." She shook her head, frowning. "Can't believe I was ever that young or that ignorant. They came on this trip short on money and rations."

"Don't pay to cross the prairie short on stock," Morgan said. "Too easy to lose some along the way." He finished his coffee. "I'll speak to the troopers about helpin' them out."

He stood and stretched, his head almost touching the top of the tent. "Martha, I'm sure you've already considered wrapping your mares' legs. Since they're so fine-boned, they could easily pull a tendon or even break a leg. Rawhide's good for that." He spoke slowly, carefully, as if he were afraid of offending me.

"That's a good idea, Morgan. I know that's done when they race, but I'd never thought of it for traveling. Thank you. I'll do it right away."

Morgan looked surprised and relieved. "Well, good. If you need any help, let me know." He nodded and tipped his hat. "I'll be moseyin' off now. See you tomorrow. Stay warm."

The tent flap flew open, and Becky and Charlie burst in laughing.

"Whoa, ladies. You 'bout knocked me down, and I've already been down once tonight," Morgan told them with a grin.

"Where you girls been?" Hattie demanded.

"Oh, we just been talkin' to the troopers," Becky said.

"You girls take it easy on those boys," Morgan teased. "They aren't use to pretty girls. You're apt to make them forget what they're supposed to be doin'."

I envied the easy way other women had with Morgan. Why couldn't I just relax and be myself with him? Was it because I was attracted to him and didn't want to be? Maybe I was afraid that if I let down my guard, he'd take advantage of me?

"Will you be stoppin' by Abel's wagon?" I asked. What I really wanted to ask was, *Which of us do you think the pretty gals are?*

"I can," he said. "Somethin' you need?"

I need you, I thought but only answered, "Would you tell him everythin's fine and he doesn't need to worry?"

"Will do" he nodded. "Everythin's fine. Not to worry. Got it." He tipped his hat. "Well, good night, ladies. See y'all in the mornin'."

"Night, Morgan," we answered almost in unison as he left.

"He is the handsomest thing," Charlie whispered, loud enough for him to hear.

"Get to bed, girls. We got a long haul tomorrow," Hattie reminded us, as she banked the fire for the night.

CHAPTER TWENTY TWO

Four days out from Midway Station, Becky rode up to Pete and me. She said, "The Perkins and Rogers want to call it a day. They got some sickness in their wagons."

Shit," said Pete, always something. "Do they know what it is?"

We rode over by the wagons, and Pete yelled for them to pull out of line and stop. He yelled to Becky to ride to the front and circle the column. "Becky says your ailin'. What seems to be the matter?"

Mr. Perkins looked pale and drawn. They're all runnin' a fever except me, and I ain't feelin' too good neither. What do you suppose it is Pete?"

"Well I'm no doctor, but I'll find someone to help."

"Maybe Charlie can help, Pete," I suggested.

"Good, Martha. Go find her, and hurry. We got to get this taken care of. We can't afford to lose any more time. We're behind already. I never seen a train with so many problems." People started gathering around asking questions. He held up his hands and yelled, "Hold on, everybody."

Hattie spoke up and asked, "What's the problem?"

"Well, there's fever, and I'm waitin for Charlie since she's the closest we have to a doctor unless someone has withheld their abilities."

Charlie and Luke rode up. "What's going on?" Charlie asked.

"We got some sick people in these wagons. Do you think you can help?"

"Let me get a quick look at them and see what's going on," Charlie replied.

About ten minutes passed, and she came out on the wagon seat. "Okay," she said firmly. "I'll need two tents—one for the sick and another for the well. I'll need a tub of water and lye soap to wash all the clothes and bedclothes, some clear broth to feed them, and some help to do all this. It's measles. We don't want it to spread, so we'll stay back from the train."

Pete asked, "Any volunteers to help?" Luke and Morgan said they would help, and so did a couple of the army men.

We got busy hauling and heating water, changing clothes, and bathing the sick. We made herb tea, and the army men, Jerry and Clem, cleaned the two wagons. We sat down to rest. It was late. Charlie said she was going to talk to Pete and would be back.

"Hi, Charlie," Pet said. "How are the sick ones? Anything you need besides fourteen pair of hands?"

"No Pete, it's under control. Some of their fevers are breaking, and others will soon. The course takes about fourteen days."

"What! We can't stay here that long! We will have to leave them here to go back alone."

"No Pete, we can't do that. They can follow behind us 'til they're past contagious."

"That's a good idea. That way we won't lose any more time. When can they travel?"

"As soon as we can get them back in their wagons. They can lay there just as well as on the ground. There is one problem, though. Darrell Perkins is sick too, but it isn't the measles. He's short of breath and clammy."

"That doesn't sound good, but it looks like were goin' to roll come morning," I said. "I'll go inform the guides."

"Sure as hell hope so." Pete said, shaking his head and frowning. "Pray that it just stays in those two wagons."

"What makes you think He'll listen to me?" Hattie asked with a grin.

"Cause you're a God-fearin' woman. No man could resist," Pete said as he winked.

Sighing from relief and exhaustion, I spread two pallets on the ground close to the fire. "Come on, Charlie. You need to rest. We've done all we can for now."

"Right," she agreed, "but first we got to go bathe. Doc always told me that washing with soap and water is a nurse's best protection against sickness."

We walked to the creek, stripped down, and waded in. The water was cold. We remained only long enough to wash. Dressed in clean clothes, we returned to the wagon carrying our dirty clothes on a stick and put them in the tub. Morgan and Luke were sound asleep a few yards from the wagons. They had stacked plenty of wood near our fire where we would sleep beside the wagons for the night.

I put a couple of logs on the fire and added water to the coffeepot. "Okay, now can we rest?" I asked in a pitiful tried tone.

Charlie laughed. "Sure. Just hope that herb I put in the tea keeps everyone asleep for awhile."

"Not too long!" I exclaimed, horrified at the thought.

"Don't be silly. Of course not. I just gave them an herb Doc used to used. It'll give their bodies a rest."

"Good." I flopped down on a pallet, and she lowered herself to the other one.

"Charlie, you know a lot about takin' care of the sick. How did you come by that?" I asked.

"It's a long story. Sure you wanna hear it?"

"I'm sure I want to hear." We sat down on the bedroll near the fire, close together so we could talk real quiet.

CHAPTER TWENTY THREE

CHARLIE'S STORY

"Our family lived up in the backwoods of Taylor Mountain for as long as anyone could remember," she began, her eyes taking on an expression of sadness. "My mama, bless her soul, had fourteen young 'uns including two sets of twin boys. Me, bein' oldest of the lot, I brung the five youngest Taylors into this world."

"You delivered your ma's babies?" I exclaimed. I wasn't sure what shocked me most—the idea of giving birth to fourteen, or Charlie having to help deliver them.

"I shore did." There was a note of pride in her voice. "We almost lost the first twin boys and Mama too." She shook her head. "I was twelve at the time, but I was expected to take care of the family. You know—the washing, cleaning, cooking, takin' care of the younger ones."

"That's a lot of responsibility for a little girl." I felt a deep sadness coupled with admiration for the child, Charlie.

"Well, it weren't so bad. Rhoda May and Jenny Marie helped feed the two babies goat's milk. Ma's milk dried up. She was too sick to breastfeed them," she grinned. "They did real good for as young as they was."

Darkness was just settling in. Charlie got up and poked her head inside the Rogers' wagon and then the Perkins. "Seem to be restin' alright," she said, dropping down on the pallet.

"You're a good person, Charlie. Real caring. We're all lucky to have you around."

"Oh, so you're sayin' you're not sorry for taken' me on?"

Wanda Reed

"That's what I'm sayin'," I grinned. "Now get on with your story."

"Well, you might guess that from what I seen of Ma's life, babies and work, I decided that weren't for me. I wanted more from life. I talked Doc Brunet into teaching me what he knew. Pa didn't want me away from the house. Said I was needed. But, Ma, bless her heart, she stuck up for me." Charlie shook her head, "First time she ever went agin' him. He got real mad, and he knocked her around, but she wouldn't back down."

"She must be pretty special," I said. "Is she still alive?" I took my comb and parted off my hair to braid.

Charlie closed her eyes. "I don't know. I left about seven years ago. I ain't been back. I haven't wrote neither." Sighing, she continued, "Doc taught me reading and writin' and some nurse stuff. Then he gave me a green dress the color of the pine trees. It was only to wear it when I visited folks. I caught on real quick, and pretty soon people called me regular to attend birthing, deaths, and takin' care of their sick." She grinned wryly. "Pa didn't think it was so bad when I started bringin' home a big ham or chickens, and over the year I had stashed away a little money. I asked Ma to buy me a dress-length of fabric the next time she went to town with it."

> **Comment [CJH]:** Changed from 45 cents, which seems too little.

"Was the doctor a nice man?" I asked, hoping she would say yes.

"Yep. He was real nice. Told me I could be a real nurse an' offered to help me get a certificate. He told me people had been dying for hundreds of years without help. Said that in most cases, all they needed was somebody to hold their hand and help ease their passing."

A vision of my ma on her deathbed flashed before my eyes. I forced back the tears that were threatening to spill. Listening to Charlie talk about her family made me realize how much I missed my own.

"I worked with Doc for near a year an' a half and learned a lot," Charlie continued.

"So, you went to school and got your certificate?" I removed my boots and took a bit of a rag to clean them up some.

"No, it didn't work out like that."

"Why not?"

"Well, one night I overheard Pa tellin' Ma that he was going to marry me off. He said the feller was a widower and needed a wife to help with his young 'uns. He said this man, Jacob, would give Pa three acres of bottom land." Charlie paused and wiped away the tears sliding down her cheeks. "I listened to them talkin' about me like I was a cow for sale."

"Oh, Charlie, I'm so sorry." I wanted to cry for her. "You didn't have to marry him, did you?"

Charlie continued as though I hadn't spoken. "Ma was a sayin' she wanted me to go away to nurse school—that I deserved better than she had. That made Pa real mad. He said I'd marry up with Jacob and that was all there was to it. Said they needed that land, and we'd be better off with three acres of good black dirt. 'She needs a husband,' he said. 'She's gettin' too full of herself with all that learnin' with the doc.'"

I wanted to ask what happened, but I didn't want to interrupt her.

"Ma fussed a bit more but finally gave up. She told him he was making a mistake—that I wanted to go to school. Then Ma said I would need a new dress." She laughed bitterly. "I never had a dress that Ma didn't wear a year first. They was tight 'cause I'm just bigger all over than her. I enjoyed wearing my green dress, but I only wore it when I made calls on the sick.

"The one thing I ever coveted was when Mama got material for a new dress. Just once I wanted the new dress. A preacher I heard once said you go to hell for coveting. I figure it wasn't no worse than tradin' off a daughter for three acres of black dirt. Ma still hadn't gone to town to get my dress-length."

Shrugging, she went on, "I left the house early the next morning. Didn't want to see either one of them after hearing what I heard. It made me feel like part of the livestock to be sold when a buyer came along. I walked to the woods. I always liked it there. It was quiet and peaceful-like, and I could dream of being someone else. Anyway, I was picking berries when around the bend stepped the biggest, reddest horse I ever did see." She sat up and her eyes flashed with excitement as if it were seven years ago and she was reliving the moment.

"I'm thinkin' from the look on your face, there was a man on that horse," I ventured to say.

"Yep. He was the handsomest man I'd ever laid eyes on. The way the mornin' sun flashed off his gold-colored hair, making it look like a halo, I thought he was an angel come to save me from Jacob."

"Goodness," I murmured.

"Ha! Turned out goodness had nothin' to do with it," Charlie said, "tho' it did seem right at the time." She sighed. "I remember it like it was yesterday."

I was thinking my angel would have black hair, not gold colored.

"'Excuse me, Miss,'" Charlie's voice softened. "That's the first words he said, in a soft voice and sweeter 'n any I'd heard before." She stared at me and pressed my arm. Her eyes closed, and it was obvious she had gone back seven years to that wooded area in Tennessee where the handsome man had come to save her.

"I seem to be lost. Wonder if you could help me?" Charlie spoke in a voice unlike her own.

"Name's Jesse Saber and as, you can see, I'm a soldier."

Back in her own voice, she said, "I felt my face turnin' red, so I real quick ducked my head, wiggling my toes in the dirt."

"'I'd say I'd taken a wrong turn and ended up in Heaven, since that's the only place I know where angels live,' Jesse said softly." Charlie sighed deeply. "I'll never forget those words. Right then and there I stopped thinkin'. With that line of sweet talk, I should've realized he was the devil in disguise. He claimed he got separated from the other fellows aways back and couldn't find the trail to the main road. Asked me to tell him the way," she said, shaking her head as if appalled at what came next.

"I was dumbstruck. I hadn't said a word since first I laid eyes on him. All I done was stand there with my mouth hanging open and my face on fire. Then, finally I blurted, 'I'm Charlotte Taylor. This is the Taylor Mountain.'"

"'Well, I'll be doggoned,' he said. 'Never met a pretty gal that owned a mountain before, and a mighty pretty mountain it is with all the beautiful trees and flowers, but the most beautiful flower of all is the owner of the mountain.'"

Charlie shook her head. "Amazin' how I can remember it all so well. I managed to tell him how to get back on the trail. He thanked me but didn't seem in no hurry to get on."

She stopped and got up. Stretching, she walked over to each of the wagons and peered in. I admired her caring ways, but I was anxious to hear more of the story. "Everything okay," she confirmed. I fed the fire some small branches, thankful that Morgan had brought enough wood for our fire.

"Seems to be, but for young Darrell. He don't sound good at all."

"That's too bad," I said. "You feel like talking more, or do you want to get some sleep?" I asked, hoping she'd feel like finishing her story. The moon was real small that night.

"Might as well finish it, get it over with." She settled on the pallet. "Well, Mr. Jesse, he smiled and laughed, winked at me and said he wanted to know all about me. Where I lived, about my Ma and Pa, was I expected home soon?" She shrugged. "Stupid girl that I was, I thought he was just bein' friendly. Don't know how I could have been so stupid. It's not like I didn't know about the birds and the bees. Here I was tellin' him I was mad at my pa and not goin' home 'til dark and they didn't know where I was."

"He must have been very charming, Charlie. Probably no woman could have resisted," I said, uncomfortably relating to her reaction.

"Not many did," she admitted. "He asked if I would show him where he could water his horse. Said if it was far, we could both ride. I was thrilled at the idea of riding such a beautiful animal even behind the saddle. I'd never been on anythin' but Pa's old boney mule, and ridin' him was like ridin' a picket fence. I toed the stirrup to mount, but Jesse pulled me up in front of him. He put his arms tight around me, whisperin' in my ear that he couldn't have me fallin' off." She shivered. "I could feel the heat of his body through my thin calico dress, which was up to my thigh. I tried to pull it down, but Jesse held my arms. 'Let it be,' he said. 'That's a mighty pretty leg.'"

"My, he was rather rakish, wasn't he?" I commented.

"I'm not sure what rakish means," Charlie admitted, "but if you mean he was no gentleman, you'd be right. Anyway, his arms felt like ropes of fire through that dress right under my breast." She grimaced. "I flashed on Pa's face and I thought, 'Lord, he'd skin me alive if he knew I even spoke to a strange man let alone sat on one's lap. Oh well,' I reasoned, 'what Pa don't know can't hurt me, and he won't know. It's my secret, my afternoon to be special and to have a friend.' I stopped worryin' and enjoyed the ride to the creek."

"Might as well," I agreed, wondering if I would be able to do that if me and Morgan. I brought my attention back to Charlie.

"At the time," she said wistfully, "I thought that was the most special afternoon I'd ever had. I believed everything Jesse said. Little did I understand what a no account he was, one who would break my heart. We watered his horse, and he took off his boots and rolled up his pants to wade in that clear cold mountain creek. He called to me to come on in. We waded in the water and held hands. He fell and dragged me into the water with him. We were both drenched. We was having so much fun, I didn't think about my dress gettin' wet and stickin' to my body, 'til Jesse pulled me in his arms and kissed me, tellin' me I was more woman than he'd seen in a spell. I told him I better set in the sun and dry. With his horse munchin' grass nearby, we sat in the sun to dry off and talked. He never took his hands off me, always strokin' my hair and face, sending tingles all over my body as we gazed into each other's eyes."

She turned to look at the Perkins wagon as if she had heard something. Charlie's story had me so involved, I thought I could feel what she had felt.

"He made me feel special in a way I never had before or since."

"What's it like, Charlie? To feel that kind of special."

"It makes you feel like anythin's possible. Like you could be or do anythin' as long as this feller was by your side." She sighed. "It makes you feel more alive than you ever felt before and you'd follow him to the ends of the earth."

"Sounds wonderful, but scary, too," I said.

"Yeah, it's both alright. And it can be terrible, too, if you fall in love with a man who doesn't love the way you do. It's terrible how he can use you, and you let him because you love him." Her voice grew heavy with sorrow.

"It's alright, Charlie. You don't have to go on," I said. "I can see you're hurting."

"Martha, I'm telling you my story in hopes you'll be careful. I see the way you look at Morgan. You need to know that just because you fall in love don't mean the man does too. Not in the same way anyway. Maybe you'll see what I mean when I tell you the rest of my story."

I wanted to ask her what she meant by saying the way I looked at Morgan. Surely, my feelings didn't show on my face. Oh, no, what if he saw it, too. Oh, horse feathers!

Charlie patted my hand. "He's a nice guy, Martha. I'm just goin' by what I know. I could be wrong about him," She grinned, "but, he's so darn good lookin', he's got to have somethin' wrong."

"Oh, Charlie, I'm not interested in him," I lied. "And, he's sure not interested in me," I added, hoping I was wrong.

Charlie looked dubious but smiled a little and squeezed my hand, and she scooted a little closer to the small fire. "Okay, if you say so. Well, back to my story and the reason I'm so suspicious of those good lookin' ones. Jesse told me I was as beautiful as an angel, and then he kissed me real tender-like. Took his tongue and trailed it softly across my lips. Pretty soon his hands were rubbing all over my body. I'd never been touched in those places before. Flustered and afraid, I pulled back. He looked hurt and asked, didn't I like him kissin' me?"

"I bet you did like it, Charlie," I exclaimed. I thought it was a real sweet story and was anxious to hear the rest of it. "Go on."

Six Women West

"Course I liked it. No one had ever paid attention to me before. I liked feeling excited and warm and special," she nodded. "I told him, yes, I liked kissin' him. I just never been kissed before." She grinned. "He said I kissed real well—said I took to it natural-like."

I wondered if I kissed real good and how Morgan kissed. "Go on," I urged, eager to hear what happened next. An old owl hooted in the night.

"Jesse took my hand and said, 'Let's go for a walk.' He led me to the woods where it was dark and cool with the trees blocking out the sun. I shivered, and he put his arms around me and started kissin' me on my neck and shoulders and breathin' softly in my ear, tellin' me my skin was like velvet. He kept telling me how wonderful and beautiful I was while he was kissin' and fondlin' me. I could feel his manhood big and hard pressing against me."

"You mean?" I know my mouth dropped open.

"Yep, just what you think I mean." She nodded vigorously. "That kind of scared me. I knew what that could lead to, and I didn't want no swollen belly. I started to push away, but he held me tighter. He put his tongue in my mouth."

"His tongue?" I was getting a real education.

"Yeah, it wasn't as awful as you might think. It made me feel all hot down here. You know."

"What did you do?" I was almost afraid to ask.

"Well, my mind said, get away, but my body didn't listen. Suddenly I felt there was no one in the world but me and Jesse, and I wanted something only Jesse could give. I gave my body to him." She sighed deeply.

I sighed, too.

"Afterwards," she continued, "I lay in Jesse's arms, thinkin' there should have been more, but not knowing what 'more' was. Jesse seemed real satisfied and whispered that he loved me. I didn't know people could fall in love so fast."

"That's what love is?" I asked.

"That's what I thought at the time," she said quietly. "The best part for me was the holdin' and the kissin', receiving the special attention I craved. That other stuff just seemed like a lot of gruntin' and puffin'."

"Did it hurt?" I thought about the farm cats and the screeching they did when they were hooked together. Even the mares and cows didn't seem happy about being mounted.

"Oh, a little bit," she said. "Right at first but not enough to stop anybody from doin' it again, I reckon." She shrugged. "After awhile, we did it again. This time I knew what the more was that I'd missed the first time.

"I kept waitin' for him to say he'd talk to my pa. Instead he said, 'It's been a fun afternoon. I'd like to stay longer, little darlin', but I'd better be movin' on.'" She sighed. "He'd taken my heart and my virginity, and now he was leaving." She took a deep breath. "I was stupid and ripe for the picking."

"Oh, Charlie, I'm so sorry." My heart went out to her. "You never saw him again?"

"Way things turned out, I wish that was the case." She shook her head. "No, stupid me—thinkin' I'd found someone who loved me. Thinkin' I was in love just because he sweet-talked me and held me."

"What did you do?" The moon was now up, but it was less than a half moon.

"I talked him into taking me with him. I wasn't about to go home and marry up with old Jacob that Pa picked out for me." She shuddered. "Couldn't picture myself lettin' him do to me what Jesse did."

"How did you convince Jesse to take you?" I could see why she made the choice and thought it took a lot of courage to do so. I put another piece of wood on the fire.

"It weren't hard. Seems he kind of liked havin' sex with me. He told me to climb up behind him, and we rode off. All I had to my name was what I was wearin', but I never looked back, not once."

"You didn't say goodbye to your family?" The barking of dogs came from the wagons, and we looked over that way. Then a yipping coyote cry came across the night.

"Nope, I didn't ask, and he didn't mention it." She shrugged. "It was alright with me. I didn't want to see Ma's face, or listen to Pa tell me what a no-good daughter I was. No, I'd made my choice. It was Jesse and me from now on." I wouldn't be traded for bottom land or be married to Jacob. She yawned and glanced at me. "Heard enough yet? Aren't you sleepy?"

"Now how could I go to sleep not knowing what happened with you and Jesse?" I grinned. "I can stay awake as long as you can. Okay?"

"Okay. The first town we came to, Jesse took me to the ladies' dress shop and bought me bloomers, stockings, petticoat, shoes and a real pretty pink dress. After that, I do believe I'd have followed him anywhere. A new dress that fit me and went clear to the floor that no one else had worn! I felt like a real fancy lady in the outfit. He rented a room, and I took my first tub bath with good-smelling soap. I felt absolutely rich. He bathed, and we made love on a real bed all afternoon. Then I dressed, and we went downstairs for supper, and later he went to play cards.

It was almost daylight when he got back. He threw a big bundle of money on the bed and told me I was his lucky charm. We made love again. That afternoon he took me shopping again, and he bought me a riding outfit, carpet bag, and a little black mare with a saddle. He played cards again that night, and we left at daybreak for another town."

"Sounds as though he really cared for you, Charlie."

"Well, maybe he did in his own way. Jesse was not who I thought he was. Turned out he had deserted the army, killed a guy for a horse, and robbed the store on Taylor Mountain."

"Good heavens, Charlie. What did you do?"

"Well, I didn't know for a long time. I think I was afraid to ask. Our life was pretty good most of the time. Sure, I missed my ma, and I pined for the young ones even more, but I sure didn't miss the misery of my everyday life—Pa's trashing me, sleepin' on a pallet, working from daylight 'til dark scrubbin' clothes on a washboard . No, I didn't miss my home. I liked the pretty clothes Jesse bought me and having money, plenty to eat, things I never had on the mountain.

"It was worth it, then?"

"In a way, I guess. I got to see some of the world, even if it was hotel rooms and saloons. See, Jesse was a gambler. Sometimes we were rolling in money. Other times we left town in the middle of the night. He never said why, but I figured out later it was because he got caught cheating or had robbed somebody."

"That sounds dangerous, Charlie. Weren't you scared?"

"Guess I was too stupid to be scared. Anyway, months turned into years, and pretty soon all the towns and saloons looked alike to me. I wanted to get married and settle down. He said we needed a stake first. I was sure he truly loved me, so I didn't put any pressure on him." She shook her head as if disgusted with herself.

"I think my feelings started to change when I finally made him tell me about the army. He laughed at me and called me stupid. Said I was in as much trouble as he was. When I ask what he meant, he said I'd held the horses many times while he robbed the places."

I nearly dropped my coffee cup. "Lordie, Charlie, you mean he was using you to help steal? That dirty cur."

"Yep, lousy kind of love, huh? I lost respect for him, but I didn't know where to go, so I stayed."

"Why didn't you go home?"

"I thought about it, but I didn't want the kind of life my ma had either. Didn't want to be married to a man I didn't love, havin' one baby after another year after year." She shook her head. "No. I decided to just bide my time. A life of diggin' in the dirt for a livin' and maybe one new dress a year—that's not for me. I'd seen better things. I wanted more for myself."

I reached the coffeepot and filled our cups, handing one to Charlie, and then added a few twigs to keep a little light from the fire.

"Thanks." Big tears coursed down her cheeks.

I patted her shoulder. "I can understand why you stayed," I said, "but it must have been hard."

"It was hard. I didn't stop loving him right away. After all, he was my first fellow, my first kiss, my first taste of womanhood. The early memories are bitter and sweet, like half-ripe berries." Charlie shook her head. "The last six months were just bitter—nothin' sweet about it. Sure you want to hear the rest?" she asked me again.

"Of course, I couldn't sleep a wink without knowing what happened," I assured her. I knew it was late and we would suffer tomorrow, but I wanted to hear the rest.

"Okay, but it gets worse. As you can imagine, it grew pretty damn tiresome living out of carpetbags and owning nothin' except our clothes and our horses. I had no one to talk to 'except Jesse. The only women I knew was dance-hall girls, and Jesse didn't want me mixin' with them. One night I told

Jesse that either he married me or I was leaving. I wanted a home and family a life like real people. He laughed. Then he said, 'You left your home when you climbed aboard my horse seven years ago.'"

"So you left?"

"No, I was just bluffin', hopin' he'd do somethin'. He knew I had no place to go. Didn't stop me complaining, though. One night Jesse exploded, yelling at me to get a job at the saloon. Said I should quit whining, or he would give me something to whine about." She took a large gulp of her coffee. "I was pretty sure Jesse wouldn't hit me. He never had even when he was drunk, but when he yelled, it scared me. Made me remember Pa and the thrashin's I got from him."

"Oh, Charlie." I thought of Pa and how lucky I'd been to have him. He would never have hit me. I suddenly felt a deep sense of loss. "So, what did you do?" I asked again.

"Well, I didn't think the idea of getting' a job was so bad. 'Why I didn't think of that?' I told him. 'Thanks, I will,' I said. I'd show him, I thought. I went to the local saloon run by a man name of Harvey. The job was singin' and hustlin' drinks. I made it clear that I belonged to Jesse and wouldn't go upstairs like most of the other girls. I did good with tips. Stupid me. Jesse took my tips. Said he was savin' 'em for me. I let him think I didn't know much about money.

"One night after I'd finished my last song, he stormed over and demanded my tips. I didn't argue with him as I could see he was drunk. I gave him what I had, which wasn't very much as it had been a slow night. He yelled and called me a worthless slut in front of the whole bar."

"Oh, Charlie," I knew I was saying that too much, but I didn't know what else to say.

"Yeah, poor Charlie. Poor, stupid Charlie," her mouth twisted bitterly. "Well, I ran upstairs, and he followed, yelling at me to start makin' some real money. I told him I'd never sell myself so he could have gamblin' money."

"He wanted you to be a whore? But I thought he loved you." I couldn't understand how love could take such a turn.

"Yeah, he loved me alright. Much as he could love anybody, I guess. Anyway, I went back to our room and didn't see him until the next morning. He showed up wearing a hound-dog look and carrying a half-wilted bouquet of flowers. Said he was real sorry and things were going to be different from now on. Said he'd made a deal with Harvey for a loan. Said we'd use the money to get married and get a cabin or a homestead. Said all was needed was for me to sign the papers. I wanted to believe him."

Obviously it hadn't worked out, I thought, *or she wouldn't be here with me.*

"At the saloon," she continued, "Harvey ordered drinks and handed me a paper. They both insisted I finish my drink, which was a mistake. 'Just sign there below Jesse's name,' he told me. I didn't have a chance to read it first. I hadn't eaten, so I was feeling real dizzy. Jesse said, 'This calls for a real celebration.' Said he'd go get the wine he'd bought for the occasion. When he left, I started feeling sick. Harvey reached over and patted my hand and said, 'You'll do real good here, girl. Between singin' and whorin', we'll both make a lot of money.'"

"What did he mean?" I asked, confused at the turn the story was taking.

"He meant that that bastard sold me to him. That was the paper I signed."

"Good Heavens! What did you say?"

"I couldn't think straight. I felt drugged. I kept trying to talk, but there were no words."

"Charlie," I interrupted. "He couldn't do that. It's illegal."

"Hell, Martha, women were slaves long before they brought the blacks over. Sellin' women is nothin' new. Wait 'til you hear the rest of it."

I lay back on the pallet, exhaling a full breath, full of mixed emotions. How could a man do that to a woman he said he loved? How could you trust anybody? Morgan's face flashed before me. I rubbed my eyes. *Go away*, I whispered silently, sitting up again, leaning close to listen. Sometimes Charlie's voice was barely above a whisper.

"Anyway, shaking my head to clear my thinking, I managed to talk. I told Harvey I wouldn't whore for him. I tried to stand, and he shoved me back in the chair. You'll do what I tell you,' he said, real mean-like.

"'I won't whore, you bastard,' I screamed, but it sounded more like a whisper. He gave me a vicious slap across the face and said, 'You'll whore for me, and missy you'll do it willingly. I know how to handle whores. He doubled his fist and laid it against my chin. You'll do what and when I say,' he muttered. Said he had big plans, and that I would make him a lot of money."

"Lord, Charlie, was there no one you could ask for help?"

"Nope. The other girls were under Harvey's thumb too, and I didn't know anybody else." She shrugged her shoulders and continued. "He grabbed my arm and pulled me upstairs to a small room. I found out later it was one the whores used. Anyway, he pushed me down on the bed and told me to stay there. He brought me some kind of drink and practically forced it down me. It was drugged, I guess, 'cause I don't member nothin' that happened for the next few days. When I finally came to, I felt sore and dirty. From the smell of me, I knew somebody had used my body. God knows who or how many times. I sure as hell had no idea."

"Oh, no, Charlie," I moaned in sympathy.

"Yeah, well. Anyway, I managed to get myself off the bed and washed up some. When I was dressed, I tried the door. It was locked. I banged on it and yelled. Finally, Harvey opened it. 'Get your ass back in there and stop that screeching or I'll give you somethin' to screech about,' he said.

"He raised his fist and pushed me back on the bed. Told me I had a choice. I could cooperate and he'd treat me good, or I could choose not to and I'd be real sorry."

"Some choice," I volunteered.

"I decided to cooperate," Charlie continued. "I knew I couldn't get away locked in a room and drugged. Harvey dressed me in fancy clothes, and I still did my singing. I really didn't mind that. I liked to sing, even if the songs he chose were sexy-like. The men really liked 'em. They'd whoop and holler and throw money. When the show was over, one of the men would be waitin' in my room. Harvey ordered me to whore between shows. Most of the men were bigwigs in town and didn't want their wives to know what they were doin'."

"Men!" I sputtered. "They're no better than animals."

"Most of 'em, anyway," she agreed. "Guess there are those that aren't, but I ain't met them yet." She paused, looking thoughtful. I wondered if she was thinking of Luke.

"I'd been doin' this for a couple of months," she went on, "and Harvey was chargin' plenty for me. I figured the hundred dollars he'd given Jesse was about paid off. When I asked Harvey, he got real mad. Started tellin' me how much he'd spent on me, how much it cost in food and so on. I argued, and he slapped me real hard. I decided to just shut up, save my money, and bide my time."

"You poor thing," I said, reaching over to pat her shoulder.

"I tried a couple of times to run away. Second time was when I saw you women. Remember? At the stable?"

"Yes, I remember. I wanted to help you, but Hattie said not to get involved. That was Harvey hitting you?"

"Yeah, that was Harvey. He dragged me back and beat me bad. I was black and blue for two weeks." She laughed, but there was no humor in it. "One good thing—I didn't have to whore then. Bad thing was, Harvey didn't mind how I looked. Bastard!" She shuddered. "Never hated anyone so much in my life except Jesse."

Tears slid down her face as she relived the past. I marveled at the courage it took to tell her story. *Would I be able to reveal mine so honestly?* I wondered.

"Not much more to tell, Martha. Anytime you want me to stop, just say so."

"I want to know it all, Charlie. I need to know how you got away. I think you are one brave woman."

"Thanks. Don't know if I'm brave or stupid yet. I was with Harvey about six months. The men paid the price, and some of the men gave me extra money because I made 'em feel so good. Told me to buy myself something pretty. That's what I did. It didn't take long 'fore I had a sizable amount hidden away. I knew if I could get to a big city, I could get a job singin' and make a lot of money. Look at all Harvey was keeping that was thrown on the stage to me. He had a man sweep it up, and I didn't get it, but sometimes I would grab a double eagle when the curtain was closed.

"One day when I was supposed to be shopping, I bought herbs from an Indian woman to make a sleeping potion. One night after the last show when Harvey was real drunk, I decided to use it. This time I would make sure he wouldn't be comin' after me."

"Good for you, Charlie," I said encouragingly.

Six Women West

"Well, I acted real nice, offered to fix him a drink. Guess he figured he was going to get his ashes hauled without a fight, so he went along. I mixed the powder with the whiskey and handed it to him. I don't think he even tasted it. He just gulped it right down. I sat on his lap, playin' like I was enjoyin' myself. In a few minutes he was out cold. I took the cash out of the desk which, with what I'd saved, was a bundle. I threw a change of clothes in a bag, stole his horse, and rode like hell." She grinned. "Never learned what happened to Harvey or Jesse. Figure Jesse's either sweet-talked some other poor dope, or he's in jail. Harvey might be dead. I sure as hell gave him enough sleeping powder." She lifted her chin defiantly and added, "Hope he is."

"You did good, Charlie. I hope you never run into those two again."

"Me too, and I'm stayin' clear of those sweet-talkin' good-lookin' men." She grinned. "I've been through hell. I've been tricked, beat, and had my body sold, and once is enough. I learned a hard lesson, and I learned it well. I don't think I could ever trust or love again. Besides, what man would want a wife who's been through what I have?"

I was pretty sure she was thinking of Luke. "It will take time for your mind and body to heal," I told her. I put my arms around her while she cried. "Don't blame yourself for any of this. It wasn't your fault. I'm just glad you found us."

She drew back and stared at me. "What you said, back in the beginning, you remember? You said, 'We'll stand by you if he comes after you.' Well, you can't know how much that meant to me. I'll never forget it."

"We meant it, Charlie. We're your family now."

She hugged me tightly. "Thanks, Martha. I know you'll understand that I'm not ready for the other girls to know all this."

"Of course. You'll tell them only if you want to." I paused. "You know, we all have things in our past we're not ready to share. It takes time. I admire you so much. They say what doesn't break you makes you strong. That's you, Charlie. I'm proud to know you."

"Aw, go on with you," she joshed, nudging my shoulder. "Hey, we better check on our patients. Make sure they're still bundled up. Got to keep 'em warm if we want 'em to break out."

It was measles for sure—big red measles.

"Let's try and get some sleep."

"Good idea," I agreed and snuggled deep into my bed roll. A few minutes later, Charlie began snoring softly. It wasn't long after that I fell asleep too.

CHAPTER TWENTY FOUR

The strong aroma of coffee drifted toward us. I lay there inhaling the tang and listened to the sounds of voices.

"Junior's havin' a lot of trouble breathing," Charlie was telling Morgan and Luke. "Did you notice the blue cast on his lips and that raspy noise in his chest?"

"Yeah," Luke said. "Is it pneumonia?"

"I don't think so," Charlie said.

I got up, picked up my necessary bag, and headed for the woods.

"Coffee will be waiting when you get back," Morgan called.

I didn't respond. It embarrassed me, him knowing where I was going and why. I'd had some disturbing dreams about men in general and Morgan in particular, putting me in an unfriendly mood. Well out of sight I stopped in the bush then washed up in the creek, brushed my hair, and strolled back to the wagon.

Morgan handed me a cup of coffee. I nodded, but didn't say anything. "Bad night? You two were up real late."

"Leaning against the wagon wheel I mumbled, "Guess you could say so."

Charlie walked over by me and said," I don't think Junior's going to make it."

"Isn't there anything we can do?" I asked as I looked up at the clear blue sky watching a hawk circling above.

"I've done all I know how to do." Sighing deeply, she shook her head. "We'll just make him as comfortable as we can. It's wait and pray from here on out."

"Have any of the others broken out with the measles?"

"The young Rogers boy—Lee I think his name is—is all broke out and so are the other boys. I expect the others will break out soon." She paused thoughtfully. "I member back home one of us young 'uns would catch somethin', and a few days later another one would have it." She laughed and said, "With fourteen young 'uns you can imagine how that was."

We joined in her laughter, and I finished my coffee and went to check on the Perkins family. Darrell Senior, Gil, and Jane were busy helping the sick with their morning needs.

"Breakfast," Luke yelled from the fire, as I climbed down from the wagon. Abel and Bessie were standing at the sick line. Abel waved a kettle as Bessie held on to what I hoped was a pan of biscuits.

After we fed those who could take nourishment, Morgan, Luke, Charlie, and me sat down to eat with Gil Rogers, Jeanette, and Jane. We were all just finishing up when Darrell Senior rushed over. "Junior's mighty bad," he blabbered. I look up and he was holding his chest. He was pasty white. "I think he's dyin'." He grabbed his Jane's arm. "You best come right now."

"I'll go with you," Charlie said. A moment later we could hear the wailing from their wagon. Young Darrell, who had just turned sixteen, had gone to meet his maker. I sadly said a silent blessing, wondering how many more times I would be saying one before I got to Oregon as I hurried to the wagon to comfort the children.

"Are we gonna die, too?" Sam Perkins asked, his young face looking suddenly old.

"No," I said firmly. I put my arm around him "You all are going to be just fine. Your brother was sick, but it wasn't the measles—it was his breathing."

"I don't want to die," he cried. "I want to see Oregon. Pa says the trees there are a hundred feet tall, and there's lots of water. He said we would have a good life with lots of food."

"Sam," I interrupted, "you gotta lie down and keep quiet so your measles can go away. I'll be back in awhile, and we'll talk some more. Now lie down and rest." I patted his shoulder. I felt so sorry for these young ones. They didn't understand why Darrell died, and we didn't have an answer for them.

Later, after things calmed down, Morgan went to the sick line and yelled for Pete to inform him of the death of Darrell Perkins Junior. When he came back to us, he said that Pete said to go ahead and bury the boy here. Given the circumstances, the others wouldn't cross the sick line. Luke, Morgan, Gil Rogers, and Darrell Perkins Senior dug the grave, and Junior Perkins was buried with a short Bible reading service. No one crossed the sick line, but several did stand there and sing "The Old Rugged Cross." It was very moving.

We watched as Pete talked to Luke. Then Luke walked over to us. Charlie asked, "What did Pete want?"

"Says he's startin' up the train. Got to get movin' and we can follow, but to keep a hundred yards behind."

"Well, that's better than being left behind to catch up," I said, pleased at the thought. "All the children are broke out now except Jeanette, and she has shown no signs of sickness. It will just take time for the measles to run their course. Let's break camp and get movin'."

"Good idea," Morgan said. "Gil and Darrell can drive their wagons. You women decide which wagon you want to be in. Me and Luke will ride along and relieve the drivers."

"Sounds good to me," Luke said, and Charlie nodded her head in agreement. It didn't take long to get the tents down and the wagons ready to roll.

I sat next to Darrell Perkins, grieving with him but also glorying in the knowledge we were on our way again. Camp that night was near Gilman's Station, the pony-relay station and trader. Pete staked out a sick line. Bessie brought out a kettle of stew with pan bread for our dinner and barley broth for the sick. We talked across the line for a bit to catch up on news.

"You and Abel still honeymooning?" I teased.

"Oh, Miss Martha, you beginnin' ta sound like Miss Becky."

"How is Becky? She still seeing Shiloh?"

"Yessum, dat boy sho is a sweet talker, dat one is."

Sweet talker. I thought of Charlie and shook my head. "Tell her to be careful, Bessie. Tell her to keep her pig sticker handy." I smiled. "Give my love to Hattie and Sara, too."

"Ah'l do dat, Miss Martha. You take care now. Stay well." She turned and walked away. I started balancing the pots of food to carry back to our camp.

"You need help carryin' that food? It's too much for one person," called Morgan.

"I can get it if I can just get it started. I'll put the stew on this hand and the broth in the other and carry the pan of bread in between."

"Here, let me help you with that," Morgan said, coming up next to me. "Why didn't you give a holler? I could carry this."

"I'm not a weakling," I retorted. "Besides, I'm used to doing for myself." I guess my tone of voice was kind of sharp.

"Okay, okay. Do it yourself, then, Miss High-and-Mighty!" He stormed off without carrying anything.

Six Women West

"Well, the true Morgan Brooks finally shows up," I muttered, just loud enough for him to hear.

He turned and glared at me. "Yeah, and when is the real Martha Patterson going to show up?"

"You two sparrin' again?" Grinning widely, Luke walked over to me. He shook his head. "Sounds like a pair of lovebirds to me. Here, let me help you with those kettles, Martha. I don't want our supper spilled."

"Are you out of your mind, Morgan?" I shouted. "Why, I wouldn't..." Further words failed me. I plunked the kettle down by the fire. "Thank you Luke, you're a true gentleman."

"He's crazy," Morgan said. "He wouldn't know a pair of lovebirds from a pair of old crows."

"Right," I agreed. "Just because he's moonin' over Charlie, he thinks he knows it all."

"Yeah," Morgan said, coming over to take the bread pan out of my hands.

"Thanks." I lowered my eyes. "Sorry. I don't know what gets into me."

"I think the real Martha Patterson is fighting with the one who thinks she has to be tough." His tone was gentle and his smile sweet. "You don't have to be tough with me, Martha. I'll never hurt you."

Later after all were fed and put to bed and the camp cleaned, Morgan sat down on a box by the small fire and invited me to join him, pointing to another box. It was late, and everyone else had retired for the night. He told me about his plans for a horse ranch in Sweetwater Valley. "I plan to settle in that Wind River country and raise Appaloosa horses. Wait 'til you see the land right along the Sweetwater River. Its beautiful—grass belly deep to a horse, the river clear and cold year round with ground so fertile and game plentiful—a regular paradise."

"That's before we reach Oregon, right?" I said, both saddened and relieved. The trip would seem awfully dull without his presence. I glanced towards Bessie and Abel's wagon, and there was an amber glow from inside the wagon.

"Raindrop is the finest piece of horseflesh you're ever going to see," he said proudly.

"You mean, except for mine, don't you?" I said, only half in jest.

Morgan laughed. "Yeah, your fillies are alright. They could use a good stallion."

"Oh, is that an offer? How much will you take for him?" I teased, confident he would never consider selling Raindrop. I knew he felt as strongly about his stallion as I did about my mares.

Morgan laughed loudly and slapped his knee, causing the stallion to snort.

"Shh, you'll wake the others," I cautioned. "Now, how much did you say?"

He laughed again, softer. "The same price as your mares."

"Guess that means neither of us will be selling. We'll come around in a few years after I've gotten several thoroughbred foals. Then maybe I'll try for a good saddle horse."

"Guess so." He grinned, adding, "But, if your fillies ever need service, shall we say, Raindrop's ready, willin' and able."

As we laughed together, I knew for sure there were no more hard feelings. I could trust him, and he would be a good friend.

Towards morning, Joanna Roger's fever broke. I wipe her head with a cool cloth and gave her cool water to sip. She was on her way to recovery.

For the next week we continued to follow behind the wagon. The only real worry we had now was for Lee Rogers. The poor little guy was still suffering with a high fever and raspy lungs. No matter what we did—cool baths, elm tea—nothing seemed to help. All we could do was wait and pray.

We passed most nights sitting around the campfire listening to Luke play his guitar while he and Charlie sang duets. She sang of her home in the mountains, and he sang of the prairie. Separately, their voices were good. Together they were beautiful.

One night, before we went to sleep, she confided that she really liked Luke. "And he really likes you, too, Charlie," I told her.

"You think so?" She sounded pleased, but doubtful. "Bet he wouldn't if he knew what you know."

"First of all, he doesn't have to know every detail," I said. "Second, how do we know what kind of a past he's got? Third, he likes you for who you are now, and that's what's important. Now go to sleep."

We awoke to Joanna's screams of anguish, "Lee, no! Oh God, no! My boy's dead," she wailed.

"It's Lee. Hurry," Charlie said. "Joanna, let me check him."

"It's little Lee. He's gone," she moaned. "Oh, God, why hast thou forsaken me?"

"I'm so sorry, Joanna."

Seven-year-old Lee Rogers was buried on the vast prairie. Joanna covered her head with a black cloth and came to the gravesite with Gil, her husband, the only two family members present. Morgan said a blessing, and Luke and Charlie sang "Jesus loves me."

God, I asked silently, how many more funerals before we get to Oregon?

After a hurried breakfast, we got back on the road. We stayed one hundred yards behind as Pete had ordered. The sick ones seem to be recovering with each passing day.

After four more days, Charlie told us she felt it was safe to join up with the other wagons. "Everyone is broke out and clearing up, and no one is running any fever, so they're not contagious."

"I'll tell Pete," Morgan said, and rode off to deliver the message.

He came back smiling. "He says to join up. We'll be makin' camp a few miles down the trail. He's going to tell the other so they won't panic when we come in."

"Well let's go tell everybody here what's happening," I said.

"Joanna, we're going to join the other wagons," Charlie said.

"God bless you both," Joanna said.

"Thank you. I know how hard it was."

Jane shook her head. "Goodness, you could have gotten sick, too."

"No problem," Charlie said, adding, "Now here is what I want you to do: eat good, rest a lot, wash or bath daily, change your bedding and have it washed. Right now, me and Martha are gonna bathe before we return to our wagon. Have to make sure all those measles germs are washed off."

Scrubbed from head to toe with lye soap and hopefully free of any germs, we hurried to the wagon. There Hattie, Sara, Bessie, and Becky greeted us with smiles and hugs. "Boy, it's good to be home," I said.

"Ain't it though?" Charlie agreed. "What's that Polly's got? A new baby doll? Did mommy make you a baby? Look at her hold it out for me to see. Oh Polly, a pretty baby just like you! Sara, I sure missed playing with Polly. That's a nice doll you made."

"She is growing so fast. She needs things to keep her busy in the wagon. Guy is making her some blocks. Becky made her a button necklace on a piece of rawhide. She loves the bright buttons."

A few days later, Pete called a halt extra early. "Need to camp here for the night. Give you all time to check your stock and grease your wagons. Turn your stock out to graze. There's plenty of grass and water, and the shade from the oak trees will be a welcome relief from the sun."

We unhitched Jake and walked him and the other mules out to graze. Becky hobbled them while Hattie and I examine Jake, the lame mule. "Every time I put him in harness, he acts lame," Hattie told me. "The only thing I can figure is it's a hairline crack or he's fakin'. He had this problem awhile back."

"Mind if I take a look?" Morgan asked, riding up on his horse.

"Appreciate it," Hattie said.

He dismounted then knelt down and rubbed his hand over Jake's leg.

"What do you think?" I asked.

"I think Hattie's right. Looks like a hairline fracture." He shook his head. "Takes at least three, four months to heal, and that's if he's not working." Morgan stood. "Best to turn him loose in the remuda and then sell him at the next fort."

"Damn!" Hattie swore. "We'll have to buy another one. We still got a long way to go." She stared at Morgan with a quizzical expression. "Where were you raised, Morgan? You have a funny accent. It isn't pure Boston, and it isn't southern." She chuckled. "Bit a both, sounds like."

"Didn't know it was funny," Morgan said, grinning. "Guess it's a mixture of upstate New York and all the places I been since then."

"Is that where your folks live?" I asked. "New York?"

"No. My pa's dead. Don't know what happened to my ma." He shrugged. "An aunt and uncle raised me. They had a big farm. The family was a close community. They kept me and my cousins busy."

He laughed. "Free labor. I ran off when I turned sixteen. After that, I just moved around 'til I join the army as a scout."

Hattie smiled. "You say you don't know what happened to your Ma?" she asked.

"Well, they told me she just ran off and left me and my brother with the family. I was seven, and Heath was just six." He glanced at me. "Heath died of the measles."

Hattie had a look about her that made me curious. It was a combination of fear and anticipation. She reached over and clasped Morgan's arm. "Come by our tent tonight about an hour after supper. I need to tell you something."

"I'll be there," he said. Turning to me he said, "Guess I best get busy, or Pete will be yelling. See you tonight."

CHAPTER TWENTY FIVE

HATTIE'S STORY

Finished with supper early, we were eager to hear what Hattie was referring to when she asked Morgan to come to our tent. I asked her if she wanted us girls to disappear, and she told me no. She wanted us there. Sara put Polly down on my bedroll for the night in our tent. We picked up the camp chairs and moved them into the tent.

Hattie seemed anxious, pacing back and forth. I spotted her pouring a goodly amount of whiskey in her coffee. I wondered if it had anything to do with what she was going to tell us tonight. And why did she want Morgan here?

"Ho! You gals ready for company?" Morgan called, peering into the tent. He looked freshly shaved and bathed.

"Sh! Morgan, Polly's sleeping," Sara whispered.

"Sorry," Morgan said sheepishly. "You wanted to talk to me, Hattie? In here or do you want to go for a walk?"

It was obvious he was confused and as curious as I was about why she needed to talk with him.

"In here. I want the girls to hear this, too." She swallowed the last of the fortified coffee and motioned Morgan to sit beside her. I sat down on the other side of her. She took my hand in hers. I could feel the trembling of her hand.

"The girls have been tellin' their stories from time to time." She paused. "With what I learned today, I think it's time I told my story of how I come to be on this wagon train."

Morgan had a confused look on his face. He reached over to pet Tag who had inched his way between Morgan and Sara.

"You're part of it," she said, looking at Morgan. "A big, important part." She took a deep breath. "When you told us today how you come to be here, it was a revelation and a worry. See, I was born in Hillsboro, New York. Like you, Morgan, I worked on the family farm, doing the woman things. And, like you, I worked without pay. My ma was a sweet, God-fearin' woman, but Pa was a hard man who believed the devil found mischief for idle hands. You can figure we were kept mighty busy." She paused, glancing around the circle.

"Well, when I was around fifteen, I started noticin' the boys. One in particular caught my eye, and he seemed to notice me, too. His name was Jefferson Moore. Pa caught me and him sittin' down by the river." Hattie held my hand tightly as she stared into the flames. "He was a nice boy. He gave me my first kiss. Didn't mean no harm, but Pa caught us. Threatened Jefferson's life, drug me home by my hair, and used the buggy whip on me.

"Yelling scripture, calling me names I didn't even know the meanin' of, he yelled and cursed and said he wouldn't have a harlot in his house. I didn't even know what a harlot was. Then, he locked me up the woodshed without food or water. Terrified, I spent the night cold and hungry. I cried most the night, scared he would leave me there for a week or more, like he did Charles when he caught him in town helping a dance-hall woman across the street. The day Charles got out of the shed, he stole a mule and run off. No one seen him since."

"Oh, Hattie how awful," Sara said, "Didn't anyone help you?"

"Ma brought me a blanket, a bucket of water, and some cold biscuits the next morning. I begged her to let me out, but she said Pa ordered I was to stay in the shed." Hattie shook her head. "I guess she loved me, but she was too weak and scared to go against Pa. She told me she wasn't supposed to feed me anythin' but supper. Two days later Jed, my older brother, opened the shed door. He told me he was sorry, he wanted to help, but Pa said he would skin him with the buggy whip. Said there was water and a tub in the barn. Pa left orders I was to bathe and put on clean clothes. I thought my punishment had ended." Her mouth twisted. "Ha! That was a joke. Anyway, Ma was in the barn and helped me wash up. Told me Pa was takin' me away somewhere to work. She didn't know where, and she was sorry. I begged her to stop Pa from doing this. She cried and said she couldn't go against him. She told me, 'Work hard and go to church and God will take care of you. Remember I love you.'"

"If that's mother's love," Becky muttered. "I guess I didn't miss out, after all."

No one else said anything, waiting for Hattie to continue.

"He came to the barn. He was carrying a rope. He came over to where I was standing, and he put the rope around my waist and tightened it. He said, 'You'll not get the chance to steal and run off like Charles did,' as he helped me to climb up in the buggy and then tied me to the seat. I asked him where he was takin' me. He said, 'Sit there and be quiet, you Jezebel. We traveled all day on a well-traveled road with beautiful countryside and camped that night under a tree. The next day we continued traveling 'til early evening.

We arrived at a large farmhouse. Pa untied me. Holding tight to my arm, his finger dug into my flesh. He warned me to keep my mouth shut and do as I was told. He knocked on the door, and it was opened by a woman. We were welcomed and asked to wait in the entryway. Pa squeezed my arm again and in a hushed whisper he said, 'You do what the women say, or else you won't be going home ever.' Soon an old man greeted Pa with a handshake, and they walked into another room. Two women, Sister

Roseanne and Sister Lauren, they led me to a room off the entryway and stayed in the room with me.

They asked me to remove my bloomers. Said they had to make sure I was chaste. I felt relieved cause I thought that was what Pa wanted to know, and then he would take me home. Then Sister Lauren said to live at Shirehouse, I had to be virtuous." She paused and glanced at Morgan.

"What?" Morgan's eyes widen. "You said 'Shirehouse'?"

"Yes, Morgan. This is why I wanted you here tonight."

"Did you know Morgan's family, Hattie?" I asked, thinking what a strange coincidence.

"In a minute, Martha, I'll answer all your questions. Let me tell it my way." She patted my hand. "After that, the women left. They told me to wait there. When they returned, I asked to see Pa. Lauren told me he had made arrangements for my welfare. Roseanne told me my home was with them now. I asked, 'Am I to work here? What are my duties?' and was told I'd be gettin' married."

"Married?" Sara gasped. "To whom? That old man?"

"I got scared. Told them I didn't want to marry that old man. They laughed and said it wasn't him. Roseanne told me I was to marry Jebadiah Brookshire, a nice man, who would make me a good husband."

"You're my ma," whispered Morgan, staring at Hattie as if he couldn't believe his eyes.

"Yes, Morgan. I'm your ma." Her eyes filled with tears, and she leaned against him. "I hope you don't hate me."

"Hate you? Ah, Ma, I don't hate you. I've looked for you for years." Morgan squeezed her hand. He looked like he was on the verge of tears. "I lived there, too, remember. I know what a hell it was."

"There's more to the story, isn't there, Hattie?" Charlie asked. "What happened to make you leave?"

"Oh, yes," Hattie sighed. "I need my son..." she paused and looked at him with love in her eyes. "...my son—that sounds good—to know what happened. They fed and bathed me and locked me in a room. The next morning, I was dressed in a blue dress, put in a buggy with the two women, and we drove several miles to a large barn. That's where I first laid eyes on my husband-to-be. You look like him, Morgan. He was also tall with black hair and looked strong and healthy." She grinned. "Have to admit, gettin' married didn't seem quite so bad once I'd seen the groom. He was fifteen years older than me though."

Morgan smiled and shook his head. "Glad to hear Pa looked good to you. I don't remember much about him or you, Hattie." He grinned. "I mean, Ma. I do have memories of a nice woman, smelling good and singing to me."

"I loved you both so much," Hattie said, gazing at him intently. "The hardest thing I ever done was to leave you. But, you see, when your Pa died after four happy years, I was told I had to marry Homer."

"Uncle Homer?" Morgan asked.

"Yep, Homer, and he was no more like your Pa than a skunk is to a rose. He was as ugly and ornery as your Pa was handsome and sweet. No way was I going to marry him." She shook her head. There had been four girls brought into the family after me. The first one had to marry Homer. She delivered her fifth child in seven years. And Homer wasn't a gentle man."

"Pa slipped off the barn roof and got hurt real bad is what I was told," Morgan said.

"Yes. It was a bad fall. He died a few days later from injuries inside. Didn't know I could miss anybody much as I missed him. Didn't know how much I had come to love him." Hattie reached in her pocket and pulled out a handkerchief. She blew her nose hard and continued, "I'd been in mourning 'bout five months when Laura and Rose came to me and said I was to marry Homer at the end of the month. His wife had died in childbirth, and there was a new baby and four children who needed a mother."

"Boy, I know how that is," Charlie exclaimed. I nodded, recalling what she had shared with me. "What did you do?"

"I went to see the Elder. I tried to explain to him I wasn't going to marry Homer. Told him this time I'd would choose my own husband in my own time."

"Good for you, Ma," Morgan said. I noticed the word 'ma' came real easy for him now.

"He told me I had no choice. 'You marry where there is need. It's the way of the people,' he said." She stopped for a deep breath. "He said, 'You know the rules. Every woman has to have a man to provide for her, and each man has to have a woman to take care of his children.'"

I wiggled my fingers. Hattie had been squeezing so tight she'd cut off the circulation.

Becky got up and refilled all the coffee cups.

Hattie continued, "The custom was that a brother should take the widow, and sisters would take the widowers, but I decided I couldn't do that. I would try to escape. I'd been in the family long enough to know no one just walks away. I agonized many days and nights before I finally came to a decision. I would have to leave my boys." Tears filled her eyes. She sniffed. "I knew the Shirehouse would take care of the boys. It was the way of the people."

"Oh, Hattie, it must have been terrible for you," Sara said softly, "to leave your boys. Wasn't there some way to take them?"

"They didn't tell us why you left," Morgan said, patting her shoulder gently. "Just said you'd run away. I 'member thinkin' I'd go lookin' and find you some day."

"Bless you, son," Hattie hugged his arm. "I did plan on comin' back for you, but it didn't work out for me."

"How did you get away?" I asked.

"I had some sleeping powder left after Jebadiah died, and I put it their tea, and as soon as they were out I jumped into action." Her eyes gleamed, remembering. "I took the household money, packed a carpet bag, and dressed in Jebadiah's clothes. I kissed you boys goodbye and took off on a horse. I cried for the first hundred miles and almost turned back many times."

There was a lot of sniffing and nose blowing.

"Ma, oh Ma," Morgan whispered, taking her hand.

Her voice cracked, and a tear ran down her face, but she continued.

"I worked at cooking on farms and in hotels. I made my way to Independence. There I got hit by a freight wagon. I wasn't hurt—just shook up. The driver was real nice. Picked me up out of a muddy street. I was an awful mess. He wanted to take me home, but I explained I didn't have a home and no money to rent a room—that I would be camping somewhere. Told him I was lookin' for a job. He took me to the freight office where he worked, and they gave me a job and a place to sleep." She paused and grinned. "Colton Brown, that was the feller who was drivin' the freight wagon. Well, he started courtin' me." She looked at Morgan. "He weren't no Jeremiah, but he was real nice. When he asked me to marry him, I said yes. We got married four months after we met. I had it in my mind that we'd go and get you boys."

"What happened? Where's Colton now?" Becky asked.

"He died in a wagon wreck, Becky. We'd been together 'bout fifteen years. We had a freight line from Independence to Fort Bridger. I rode with him at first." She glanced at me. "That's where I learned to drive and know as much as I do about mules and wagons." Sighing, she went on. "During that time, I gave birth to another boy. I named him Colt after his Pa."

"You sayin' I have a brother?" Morgan's grin lit up the tent. "You know Heath died of measles, don't you, Ma?"

"Yes, I found out when I went back to the farm. The family wouldn't talk to me or answer any questions. When my name was told, they shut the door in my face. Found out about Heath and you from a stranger who watered my horse. He talked to me quietly." She turned to look at Morgan. "Colt, your brother, is running the ranch in the Willamette Valley in Oregon. I'm hoping you'll join us there." Her tone was hopeful.

"I'd like to, Ma," he hesitated. "I did have plans to settle in the Sweetwater Valley and raise Appaloosas." He glanced at me. I looked away. "But, hey, nothin's written in stone."

"Well, no matter what you decide, I'm not going to lose you again," Hattie declared. Tears flowed freely from all of us as mother and son embraced each other tightly.

"You got that right, Ma. Now how about you and me take a little stroll? We got a lot to talk about. Let these girls get their beauty sleep." He grinned at me, his dark eyes twinkling mischievously, moist with tears. I felt my face get warm. Darn. The man really stirred me. I'd like to take him in my arms and hold him close.

When they left, the rest of us talked awhile about Hattie's story and how brave she was. Then we climbed into our bedrolls. I don't know about the others, but I slept soundly, awaking for a moment when Hattie came in.

I asked, "Everything alright?"

"Couldn't be better. Life is good," she answered.

CHAPTER TWENTY SIX

Daybreak found Morgan at our wagon drinking coffee with Hattie. Shortly afterwards, Pete, Guy, Abel, Moe, and Mac arrived with much hoopla. News of Hattie and Morgan's reunion had traveled throughout the train.

"Goes to show," said Guy, "Stay in the army long enough, and you'll meet everyone you ever knew."

Laughing, Morgan replied, "I hope not. I sure met some characters. But it was worth it to find Ma."

I found myself glancing his way more than once. Several times he caught my eye and winked. I flushed and looked away. *What was wrong with me?* I wondered. Why couldn't I just take him or leave him? *You got no guts, Martha Patterson*, I told myself.

"I hate to break up the fun, but we got to get a move on. Morgan, go up to Independence Crossing and take a look-see," said Pete. "We'll keep the wagons moving."

"Sure," Morgan said. "Martha, how about riding with me? It gets kind of lonesome out there by myself."

"Go ahead, Martha. Nothin' for you to do here," Hattie encouraged.

I didn't know how to say no without seeming unfriendly. After all, Morgan was Hattie's son, I told myself. It was right that I should be friendly. "I'll just get my horse," I said and hurried over to Gray Lady and saddled up.

Morgan rode up alongside me. "Sure glad you decided to go, Martha."

"The ride is better than driving the wagon," I said. Truth be told, I wanted to be with Morgan. The first mile or so, we rode without talking. I gazed at the landscape of tall golden grass waving in the wind. Finally, I said, "I'm real happy for you and Hattie. She's a fine woman. I don't know what I would have done without her. She's been a real Godsend for us girls."

"Thanks, Martha. It seems like a miracle to have finally found her." He shook his head. "and finding out I have a brother is great. It was so hard. After the loss of Heath, I felt so alone."

"You think you'll go on to Oregon and settle with them, then?"

"I haven't made up my mind. What would you do?"

I didn't answer right away. I thought about my own dreams and Pa's plans of a horse farm. "I think I'd follow my dream," I said finally, adding, "and if you can make your dream come true with Hattie and your brother, all the better. Does it matter if you raise horses in Oregon or the Sweetwater Valley?"

"That's mighty good advice, Martha, my girl. I thank you." He pulled up and held up his hand. "Here we are. This is the Lower California crossing. Looks like a slow current. Not too deep. Shouldn't have any trouble crossing. This will make Pete happy." He looked at me and grinned. Turning his horse, he rode out into the river. "See? Not too deep. This will be an easy crossing." Riding back to the bank he said, "Let's be getting back to the wagons."

I rode over to the meadow before the river. You could see where the last wagons had camped. The grass was bare, and there were some black spots where the telltale fire rings with partially burnt branches still lay. Over to the side, there was a broken wagon wheel left to rot along with a few pieces of furniture. It was strange how people leaving furniture to rot beside the trail cover it up with canvas to protect it from the weather. The trail tapered down to a slight sandbar that led into a clear, slow-moving current. A few small

Wanda Reed

cottonwoods grew at the edge of the river mixed with cat-o-nine tails. Looking across the river, there stood a mound of large boulders. The wagons would have to veer to the right to exit the river.

"Race you back?" challenged Morgan.

I laughed. "You want to race Raindrop against Gray Lady?"

"Sure, are you scared?"

"Eat my dust!" I yelled and kicked Gray Lady into action. Morgan ate dust all the way. Laughing, I rode up to our wagon. A few seconds later, Morgan came even with Lady.

"My Appaloosa and your mare?"

"Not on your life," I countered.

"Nice race. How was the river?" Hattie asked, smiling at us. She looked downright motherly.

"Not too deep," Morgan said. "It should be an easy crossing."

"It might look that way, but the bottom's bad. Wagons bog down. Went through that several times when I was drivin' freight."

"Does Pete know?" I asked.

"I don't remember if I mentioned it or not."

"Horse feathers! I better go tell him."

"Tell me what?" Pete asked, riding up. "That Martha's mare made you eat dust?"

"I let her get a head start and held back," Morgan said.

"Horse feathers you did!" I shouted. "Anytime you want a rematch...."

"Now, you two," Hattie interrupted. "Martha, mind you mouth. You're begin to sound like a river rat. Let's stick to the matter at hand. Pete, that river looks okay, but it's got a soft sandy bottom out in the middle. I've seen wagons up to the hub."

"Damn, just what I need to hear." Pete slapped his horse and rode off, cussing. "Keep movin'," he yelled over his shoulder.

> **Comment [CJH]:** Hasn't Pete been over the Oregon Trail before? Wouldn't he know this?

Six Women West

We pulled up near the river when Pete called us to a halt, and then we waited as he directed Moe's wagon across. It made it without a problem. The supply wagon followed with no problem. The third wagon slumped on one wheel. Matt Holt cracked his whip again and again. It was no use. He was bogged down, unable to move.

The Johnson wagon waited behind. "Don't sit there, John," Pete yelled. "Go on. Take your wagon around on the left. We got to keep movin'."

Our wagon was next. Hattie held her mules and waited for Pete to signal her to across.

Holt's mules were floundering, trying to move the wagon that was sinking deeper and deeper. Prissy Holt was crying, trying to climb off the wagon. Mrs. Holt held on to her, assuring her everything would be alright.

"Hold up Hattie. Some o' you men get out there and help them mules," Pete yelled. Several riders went out, tying on to the wagon and tried to help pull the mules toward the bank. It didn't work. The wagon and the mules sank further. The mules were starting to panic, and the braying added to the confusion.

"Shit," Pete cursed. "That ain't gittin' us nowhere."

"How about we pull another wagon along side and offload into it?" Guy suggested.

"Good idea, Guy." Pete grinned. "Just what I was gonna suggest."

He motioned to Morgan. "Get over there and carry them females off the wagon." He turned to the men who had gathered. You men stop gawkin' and help unload that wagon. You there, Boyd, help Hattie unload her wagon. Billy, you ride out and hold those mules. John and Guy, get out there to offload the Holt's things into Hattie's wagon." He came up to Hattie. "Sorry to put you out, Hattie. But, it's the easiest way."

"No problem, Pete. Sorry I didn't think to tell you about this spot sooner."

"That's okay, but it's gonna cost you, lady." He laughed.

A few minutes later, our wagon was empty enough to hold the Holt's belongings. Once the plan was set into action, the mules pulled the empty wagon out of the river with the help of the riders.

"Just what they get for bringing stuff they don't need. I told them half a dozen times to leave it behind," Pete complained. "Now watch that spot. Go around it."

Once the Holt wagon was over, Hattie drove our wagon with their things across. When it was transferred, she came back and we reloaded our belongings.

When all the wagons had crossed without further incident, Becky, Charlie, and a few of the men went hunting. I helped Hattie with the fire and then rode to the river's edge to scout out a place to bathe. Prissy Holt was standing on the other side. She waved both arms frantically. "They lost me," she wailed.

"I'll come get you," I said. I urged Gray Lady into the river, and minutes later I had the little girl seated in front of me.

"I had to go to the bushes for a minute," she told me, her voice ringing with indignation. "When I got back, you all were gone." She began to sniffle.

Now that I thought about it, I realized she wasn't in the wagon when Hattie drove it across.

"I only watched the chipmunk a little while."

"Well, now you see why you must always tell someone when you go to the bushes, but I'm sure your folks will understand," I said, not at all positive that would be the case.

We rode up to the Holt wagon, and I helped Prissy slide down the saddle into her mother's waiting arms.

"Where you been, girl? Your Pa's out lookin' for you. He's going to take a switch to you soon as he gets back." It was obvious from her tone that Mrs. Holt was not only upset but angry.

"I didn't do nothin', Ma," Prissy whimpered. "Please don't let Pa switch me."

"Nothin' but worry us half to death, young lady," her mother scolded. I couldn't help but notice her tone was more consoling than angry now. Prissy was her only child, and there was no doubt she loved her.

"I guess us grownups should take some blame, Mrs. Holt. We should have noticed she wasn't on the wagon," I said.

"I suppose you're right, Martha, but I'm afraid her Pa won't see it that way. Prissy has a habit of wanderin' off. Thanks for bringing her back."

"Your welcome." Prissy had pulled away from her mother and now had her arms halfway around the neck of a big yellow dog. It was licking her face as if in sympathy. "Bye, Prissy," I called, nudging Gray Lady to move.

"Bye, Miss Martha," she whispered.

I rode back to our wagon and dismounted. Hattie was trying unsuccessfully to raise the tent. "Want to lend a hand here before it falls again? Pete says we're here for the night."

"Charlie and Becky still out?" I asked, as we managed with some difficulty to erect the tent.

"Yep," Hattie shook her head. "Those two gals are darn good hunters. Better'n most men, I'd say. We're mighty lucky they joined up with us."

We sat the rest of the poles in place to stabilize the tent. "Well, Hattie, guess we showed that tent who's the boss."

"Sure. Now you want to count the bruises the battle cost me?" she laughed.

"Where are Sara and Polly?" I asked. I knew Bessie would be at Abel's wagon, but I missed having her with us.

"They went down by the river to hunt for chickweed and greens for a salad. Maybe watercress with supper."

"A salad—that sounds good." We finished tying down the tent and putting the bedrolls inside. I added another piece of wood to the fire and then walked around and gathered up an armful of deadfall for wood while Hattie unloaded the camp chairs and a few things we would need for the night.

"Best help Abel oil up the harnesses." Hattie said. "Bein' in the water didn't do them any good."

"Glad for your hep, ladies," Abel told us when we offered. "Won't take no time now." Bessie was busy putting sourdough bread to set. She stopped a minute, "Good to see y'all. Ah gotta git this here bread made. Maybe there be enough for some sweet rolls."

As the men rode into camp, we could see their kill on the pack mules. They stopped near a large tree next to Abel's wagon. Several members of the train came over to view the kill.

"Looks like you had a good hunt," Hattie said. "You get the bison all by yourself, Luke?"

"Shore did. A nice young calf," Luke replied proudly.

"I bagged this buck. He's a six-pointer," Henry Davis said, sticking his chest out like a peacock.

"Nice work, Mr. Davis." *Anyone could see the man needed praise*, I thought. The deer was huge but too big and old to be tender.

"We got four antelope there—small ones," Becky said. "That's what me and Charlie got."

"Antelope's my favorite," I told them. Sara and Polly walked up with their aprons full of greens. Polly looked so cute imitating her ma. "Boy, antelope and salad." I licked my lips in anticipation.

Six Women West

"Looks like there's meat for ever' body." Pete said, joining us. "Good work."

Several men along with Charlie and Becky took the kill away from the camp where the animals would be skinned and butchered and then divided among the families according to need. Later that evening, the smell of roasting meat filled the air. You could hear the yelping of coyotes in the area as they smelled the scent of meat.

After supper, we had the sweet rolls Bessie had made earlier. We sat outside around the fire, stomachs full and satisfied with the work we had done that day.

"Howdy, ladies, would you all care for some entertainment this evenin'?" Luke walked up strumming his guitar.

"We sure would, Luke," answered Charlie. "Right?" She glanced at the rest of us.

We all nodded. Luke's playing and Charlie's and his singing was always a treat.

Charlie asked, "How about a sweet roll first? They have blackberry jelly on them, and a they're so good."

"Thought you'd never ask," he said. Sitting down on the wagon tongue, he leaned his guitar next to him. He smiled as he took the sweet roll Bessie handed him and wolfed it down. "Real good, Bessie. You sure you don't want to throw Abel away and marry me?"

" Oh, go on wit you Luke, a foe ah skin you alive."

After several songs, Luke put his guitar down. "You tell the folks what we're going to be up against when we leave here?" he asked, looking at Morgan.

"I was getting around to it." He glanced at us around the fire. "We'll be starting up California Hill after this. It's a little over a mile upgrade on the side of the hill with twists and turns. I went up there scouting it, and it's a rough climb."

> **Comment [CJH]:** This originally said, "Windless Hill." I did a bit of research, and what I find is Windlass (not Windless) Hill in Western Nebraska, but it goes down, not up. Also, see a few pages below where the upcoming hill is called California Hill, which is also in Nebraska but does not appear to be steep at all. It seems like it should be that they go up California Hill and then down Windlass Hill after that so I'm changing it accordingly.

"Yep," Hattie agreed, nodding her head. "It shore is a rough climb."

"How'd you go about it, Ma?" Morgan asked, reverting to her experience.

"I'd tell them to tie their belongings tight to the front of the wagons so they don't slide out the back," she answered. "They should have at least a six-up goin' up that hill."

"Best if no one's in the wagons but the drivers," Morgan said. "The extra horses can be used to help pull the wagons."

"Morgan, I don't want my horses..."

Morgan interrupted me. "No, Martha. We won't use your horses for pulling. You women can ride yours to the top." He looked at me with understanding. Also, be sure to help Cathleen Rose and little Max to get up the hill. That baby is as big as she is, he has grown so much."

"Okay." I smiled in appreciation. "Sara, you and Cathleen can ride my mares. It would be hard enough to walk two miles uphill without carrying a baby."

Just then, Pete walked up. "Evenin' all. Hate to interrupt your evenin', Abel, but we got a wagon with a cracked axle. I was hopin' we could fix it tonight. Otherwise, we'll have to lay over another day."

"Sho, Mistuh Pete." Abel smiled at Bessie. "Ah be back soon, Bessie, gal."

"Ah be waitin'," Bessie replied with a grin.

Hattie followed Pete away from the campfire. I couldn't hear what they said, but it looked as if they were doing some serious talking.

"I know, I know," I heard him say, then shaking his head he walked away.

"Gosh, I hope Abel can fix that axle. I sure don't want to lose another day," Hattie said, walking up to us. "We're already so far behind. We can't afford to lose more time. That snow's goin' to be nipping our butts going across the Rockies."

"'Well, let's all say a prayer for Abel to be able to fix it easily," Sara said. "I think I'll get ready for bed. It's been a long day." She picked up Polly where she had fallen asleep and said goodnight.

"Me, too," Becky said "Oh, how's that driver workin' out?"

"Well, like Pete said, he doesn't talk much, but he seems to know what he's doing." Sara smiled. "He tells me to sit in back with Polly, which is fine. I've been teaching her some songs. She'll be putting on a recital for you one of these days. Right now were on patty cake. Night, Bessie."

"Good night Miss Sara." Pulling her shawl about her shoulders and walking toward her wagon, Bessie said, "See y'all in da mornin."

"Thanks for the wonderful supper, Bessie." I said.

"Thankee, Miss Martha. Night all. Now ah's all in."

I woke up much later as I heard Tag growl softly. I lifted my head and listened when Tag got up and walked out of the tent. I heard Abel say, "Good boy. It's jes me. Dat old wagon fixed." I lay back, reassured we would pull out come dawn.

All wagons were hitched and ready, breakfast was finished, and the train was ready to roll. I rode out with Morgan to scout California Hill. I felt very comfortable with him now. Not sure why. Maybe knowing he was Hattie's son made him more like family. We didn't talk about anything personal—just about the hard day the wagons would have. Following the narrow trail, our eyes followed the trail of oxen bones in the ravine, bleached white by the sun, along with the debris of wrecked wagons. They reminded us how quickly disaster can happen on the trail.

> **Comment [CJH]:** See note above re. Windlass Hill.

When we got back, we reported to Pete and rode down the line with him, stopping at each wagon. "Make sure everything is tied down tight," he told them, adding, "and leave anything you don't need. Any heavy heirlooms, leave them here."

At Boyd Zinger's wagon, Jewel was in tears and turned on Pete to vent her frustrations for having to leave her sideboard beside the trail. Pete shook his head, and we rode quickly on to the next wagon.

"Can't be helped," he said to me, when I expressed sympathy for Jewel.

"Look at the furniture," I said, pointing to the china hutches and chests, and headboards, piled along the way.

"Don't look," Pete said. "I never can figure out why they hauled them in the first place."

"I think some of these people thought they were going on a Sunday drive," Morgan put in. "I don't guess most of them had any idea of the terrain or the hardships they were up against."

"Well, I had an idea, but I certainly would have been ill-prepared if it wasn't for your ma," I told Morgan. "She's been a Godsend."

"Well, from what I hear, she thinks mighty highly of you too," he said, smiling.

Gosh, he had a great smile, I thought, noting how it reached his eyes and made them twinkle.

I watched with admiration as mothers with babies on their backs, carrying something they were obviously determined to keep, started up the hill. I wasn't surprised to see Juanita's spinning wheel strapped to her back.

"She'll be spinning yarn in Oregon for sure," I said to Morgan.

"You women never cease to amaze me," he said, shaking his head. "I swear, you all got more get up and go than most of us men. Havin' babies and makin' do with whatever's on hand. Work all week and show up at a dance looking like a queen." He shook his head again. "I don't know how you women do it."

I looked at him with appreciation, and a feeling that tugged at my heart, "It's nice of you to notice, Morgan. Most men wouldn't. They seem to just take it for granted."

"Need you over here," Pete called, waving at Morgan.

"Hattie," Pete called, "Pull your wagon around front. I want you to go first."

Hattie pulled our wagon to the front hitched to our six mules as Pete had instructed earlier. "You got the most experience, Hattie girl. Take 'em up that hill."

"Happy to do so, Mr. Wagon Boss." They flirted back and forth. Truth to tell, she took a lot of pride in her ability and was real pleased that Pete noticed.

She cracked her long whip over Rowdy's ears, and the wagon lunged forward to gain speed to climb the hill. The outriders were ready to help the wagons, but Hattie had no trouble reaching the top safely and intact. When she was halfway, another wagon started up. Each time a wagon reached the top, the troopers brought back the teams to help pull the next wagon. I was surprised how quickly the job was accomplished and with no casualties.

"Good job everybody," Pete said. "We'll rest a bit and eat before we take off again. Unhitch your stock and give them a rest, too."

There were audible sighs of relief and exhaustion as each family did what needed to be done before taking a break.

Two hours later, Moe gave the signal to move out, and we all rushed to get ready. Since the road was without obstacles, we managed another four miles before dark. We made dry camp next to a grove of trees. It had been a long sixteen-hour day.

"Can't recall when I've been so tired," Hattie said, rubbing her shoulders. "Guess I'm gettin' old."

"I don't think it's a matter of age, Hattie," Sara told her. "Controlling six mules would be difficult and tiring no matter how old or young the driver was. And thanks for the loan of Rowdy and Randy to pull my wagon. James said he's a good lead mule."

"Tell James it's my pleasure to lend a hand or a mule," Hattie said, "and he ought to come to supper one night."

"Here, let me rub your shoulders," I offered. "Pa always said I had strong hands. I used to do his shoulders during the hay season."

"That'd be real nice, Martha. Thank you." She sat on a stool and I worked on her shoulders and arms for several minutes.

"My, that does feel better," she sighed.

"Why don't you lie down until supper?" I suggested.

"Now don't go treatin' me like an old woman," she said, chuckling.

I couldn't help notice how her smile was like Morgan's.

We had just finished supper when a mild wind came out of the north carrying the smell of rain. We set out buckets, but the rain only lasted long enough to wet the grass, which helped the stock. The next day began at first light. I got ready to ride with Morgan to Windlass Hill. "You and Morgan are gettin' to be a real twosome," Becky said, grinning mischievously. "He courtin' you?"

As I put a leg up around the pommel then said, "No, Becky. I just tag along when he goes scoutin'. I promised his ma I'd look out for him," I teased, looking her straight in the eyes. Thankfully, Morgan arrived and interrupted the conversation.

We rode out while everyone was getting ready to travel. A couple miles from camp, Morgan called a halt, stopping beside a grove of cedars and pointed at the cliff ahead of us.

"This is Windlass Hill. It's about three hundred feet to the bottom," he said.

"Isn't there another way to go?" I asked, thinking it would be impossible to reach bottom without somebody getting killed.

"Not that I know of. Pete told me he'd done this before. That is, gettin' the wagons down. I sure as hell wouldn't know how it's done." He pulled on his horse's reins, turning it around. "Best get back and report to the boss." He glanced at me, raising dark eyebrows. "Need a head start?"

"No," I said, meeting his eyes. "You go ahead."

He laughed loudly, throwing his head back. "You're somethin', Martha Patterson." He slapped Raindrop's flank and took off.

I held Lady back, but pride got the best of me and I let her have her way. We flew by them like they were standing still. Out of consideration for his male ego, I pulled up before I reached camp and waited for him to catch up.

"Sure takes it out of me, holding Raindrop back," he groaned, coming up beside me, rubbing his shoulders.

"I know what you mean," I replied, unable to hide a grin. We rode into camp without further conversation.

Pete and Guy were waiting for us. "Windlass Hill still there?" Pete asked.

"Still there," Morgan assured him.

"Hell, I was hopin' it would have washed away. Be easier to get to Ash Hollow."

"How do we get down that hill?" I asked, unable to imagine how it could be done.

"Well, it isn't easy, but I've done it before without losin' a wagon. Guess I can do it again." He looked at Morgan. "Trees are still there?"

Wanda Reed

"Yep. Also the remains of several wrecked wagons."

"Good. We can't get down the hill if we don't have the trees." He must have noticed the confusion on my face because he went on to explain, "We unhitch the mules, brake the wagon, tie a rope to it, tie the other end to a tree, then slow-like, and I do mean slow, lower the wagon to the bottom."

"I get it," I said, the picture forming in my mind. "And, I guess we just ride or walk the animals down."

"Just point 'em in the right direction. They'll get there, "Pete told me, grinning.

At the hill, everything went according to Pete's directions until a large rock broke loose and rolled down the hill. It crashed into Al Derosier, who was working the ropes. He fell and slid under the moving wagon.

Charlie and I were leading the mules and watching, unable to help as the rear wheel caught his leg, pulling him a couple of yards. We stared in horror as bright red blood soaked his pants leg. We dropped the reins, running and stumbling to reach him. Charlie pulled out her hunting knife and slit his pant leg.

"Lordie," I muttered, staring at the shattered bone poking through his skin. Blood spurted as if someone had turned on a spigot.

"Shit, shit," Al moaned. "Is it bad?"

"It's bad, Al," Charlie said. "An artery. Damn! We got to fix a tourniquet!"

"Here," I said, handing her my kerchief, "hold that while I get my belt off."

She wrapped it just above the knee and secured it tightly.

Several men had gathered. "Fix a litter," Pete ordered. "We'll need to get him down the hill." All but Morgan went off to prepare the litter. He knelt down beside Al. Handing him a flask, he said, "Take

> **Comment [CJH]:** This is the first mention of this character. Might this be an issue of a name that got changed? Also, were all the wagons already down? There's no mention of them getting down this terribly hard hill after this.

Six Women West

a big swig. Keep it." He patted Al's shoulder. "You're going to be okay, pal. Charlie here's a good doc. She'll take care of you."

"Mercy, Morgan. Guess I really did it this time," Al said, his voice weak and filled with pain.

"Hey, man, you didn't do it. It was done to you."

Charlie pulled me aside and whispered, "I know what has to be done. But I don't think I can do it."

"Do what?" I whispered back.

"His leg's got to be pulled out straight to line up the jagged edges. Then you wrap it real good." She frowned. "I've never even seen it done. And, if it's done wrong he'll lose his leg or be crippled."

"Oh, Cheri," Al interrupted. "Can you fix it? Will theese Frenchman dance again or will he have de peg leg?"

Charlie forced a light laugh. "You'll dance, peg leg or not. After all, you still owe me a dance."

The men came up with the litter and lifted Al on. Pete leaned over him. "We'll get you to a doc, Al. We're not that far from a fort. Just try to stay calm, okay?"

"Okay, boss," he slurred. The whiskey was obviously having an effect.

"Take him to our wagon," Charlie said. "I'll be there in a minute."

"Here, Charlie, drink this," Pete said, handing her his flask.

"Thanks, I need a drink, but I don't want the men to see me drinking."

"I'm glad you're here. Are you going to be able to fix his leg?"

Charlie shook her head. "No, Pete. It takes more knowin' then I have. He's going to need a real doctor."

"We'll put him in the supply wagon. I'll send a rider to the fort, but it'll take a few days."

> **Comment [CJH]:** What fort? All the others were named, but the next one isn't.

333

Wanda Reed

"We need to drive him to the fort. We haven't got that much time," Charlie said.

Pete handed the flask to Charlie. "You look like you could use another drink."

"Thanks," Charlie said. Her hands shook noticeably as she held the flask to her lips. "He's going to need more than this for pain. I'll give him a dose of laudanum when he gets to the wagon."

I walked off, picking up the mules we left and going on down the hill. I found Tommy and gave him Pete's orders, and he made ready to drive a wagon to the fort.

Charlie stayed at the supply wagon for the next two hours. She worked on Al's leg, sewing up the artery and cleaning the wound. I stayed close by to help. "Al wouldn't take the laudanum," she said. He said to save it for the women—said he'd rather have whiskey." She laughed.

By nightfall the supply wagon was ready to leave for the fort with Al in the back. Pete sent Billy and Tommy and Jed, an army Corporal. It was a race to save Al's leg.

Everyone worked long into the night getting them ready to roll by morning. The next day we traveled over twelve hours with just one hour-long break. At dusk we camped past Ash Hollow. After three hard days, everyone was exhausted. Even the train's children were unusually quiet.

We were awakened the next morning to Pete yelling at us. He was obviously in a foul mood and short of temper. "Let's get rollin'," he ordered. "We're already two weeks late. You want to spend the winter in the mountains?"

"Wait a minute, Pete. Hold it right there," Hattie interrupted. "You got no call to be yellin' at us. We ain't been holdin' things back."

"Sorry, Hattie," Pete apologized. "I got a bad habit of yellin' 'fore I think. You ladies been doin'

> **Comment [CJH]:** Could anyone less than a vascular surgeon do this?

just fine. I got no reason to yell at you. It's just we're so damn far behind, I'm getting worried."

Its okay, Pete," I said. "We understand. You've got a lot of responsibility, and you take it serious. We appreciate it, don't we, girls?" I glanced at the others, who nodded vigorously.

Hours later under the scorching sun, we circled for a noon break near Courthouse Rock. Hattie told us it had been estimated to have a three to four hundred foot base and was at least three hundred feet tall.

Becky, Charlie, and I rode over to read the names carved on it. We climbed as high as we could and carved our own names. We caught up with the wagons and continued on to Chimney Rock, which did look like a tall chimney sticking out of a rock.

We made camp for the night, and Becky and Charlie went hunting. Minutes later, Charlie galloped back alone, yelling that a small herd of buffalo were just over the ridge. Quickly several men mounted up. Mac followed in the supply wagon. About two hours later, they returned with three young buffalo, already cleaned, which they hung to skin.

"Where's Becky?" I asked, noticing she was nowhere to be seen.

"She was with us when we started the chase to kill the buffalo," Charlie said, frowning. "You see her?" she asked the other riders.

"No, can't say I seen her," Moe said. The others shook their heads.

"You best go look for her," Pete said. "She might be trying to get the biggest bull out there by herself."

Morgan, Luke, Charlie, and I rode out to the prairie where the buffalo were sighted. Tag managed to drag himself away from Polly to join us in the search. We had tracked for over an hour. At the edge of a burnt area from a grass fire, I spotted Fudge, Becky's horse, munching grass, his reins dragging beside him. I didn't see any sign of Becky. When I got closer, I could tell he had taken a fall and favored his left forefoot. Grabbing hold of his reins, I fired a shot to bring the others.

Fudge whinnied and pulled away from me. I called to Tag. "Find Becky. Find Becky. Go!" I ordered. "Take us to Becky." Trusting his instinct, I followed as he headed for a grove of burnt trees. The ground was burnt and parts of the trees too. Everything had the odor of fresh fire.

Sniffing the ground, he suddenly stopped, as if waiting for us to catch up. When we were close to him, he went a few more yards and began pawing a large, fallen log. I slid off Lady and walked to the other side of the log. Becky, covered with black soot, her face cut and bleeding, lay half-hidden under the burnt log.

"Becky? Becky? Can you hear me?" I knelt beside her, touching her gently. There was no movement. I heard the horses galloping, and Charlie, Morgan, and Luke arrived.

"Is she dead?" Charlie cried. "Oh, no! She can't be dead." Kneeling down, she pushed me aside and began to examine Becky. "She's got a lump on her head the size of an egg, probably a concussion, and some broken ribs, but she's breathing."

Becky moaned as Morgan and Luke carefully pulled her from under the log.

"Luke, go get a wagon," Morgan ordered. "Here's my canteen, Martha." He handed it to me along with his kerchief. "Use this. A cold rag on her face might bring her to."

Becky moaned and mumbled, "Bison charged. I fell. Got trampled. Fudge? Is he?...."

"He's fine, Becky. Don't try to talk." I wet the kerchief and wiped her forehead. She managed a small grin before she passed out. Charlie checked her for broken bones from head to toe while we waited for Luke.

"What's takin' so darn long?" Charlie muttered. I knew by her attitude she had come to care for Becky as I had. We truly were more than wagon mates. We were family. I offered up a silent prayer for Becky. *Poor kid*, I prayed. *She's had such a hard life. Please make the rest of it a happy one.*

"Here's Luke now," Morgan said.

"Hattie and others wanted to come along, but I figured we didn't need them." He raised his eyebrows. "Boy, are they mad at me."

"You were right, Luke. They'd just be in the way," Charlie said. "You brought quilts, didn't you? We need to protect her ribs."

"Yeah," Luke replied, kneeling next to Morgan, who was getting in position to move Becky. "I'll help."

She moaned softly when they slid their arms under her and began to lift. They carried her in a quilt, being careful not to bend her back.

Good," Charlie said. "Now just lay her down real easy." She pointed to the pile of quilts in the back of the wagon. "Watch her ribs."

Charlie and I got in and sat beside Becky. Luke took the reins. "Go fast, but don't hit any bumps," Charlie called out to him.

"I'll bring the horses," Morgan said.

Back at camp, Hattie and Sara had the wagon fixed to bed Becky. We moved her into the wagon. Charlie and Bessie stripped her and bathed her cuts as Becky drifted in and out of consciousness. Sara and Hattie stood outside the wagon. I could hear them talking about Becky.

"She's such a brave little thing," Sara murmured.

"Damn good hunter," Hattie said, her voice rough with emotion. "Smart as a whip."

"Yes," Sara agreed. "Poor girl. She's had a hard life. I do hope it will be better for her in Oregon."

"She has to stay awake," Charlie said, bringing my attention back inside the wagon. "I can't know if she's got a head injury lessin' she's awake. Keep talking to her, Martha. See if you can get an answer."

"What's your name? What's your pa's name? Do you know who I am?"

"Yeah, I know. Don't you?" Becky opened her eyes and grinned. "Hi, Martha. Guess I done it again, huh?" Her voice was weak and filled with pain. "Funny you askin' 'bout Pa. I was just dreamin' him and me was walkin' our trap line." She smiled. "Guess my old papa sent those bison around me so's I didn't get stomped."

"You're okay, Becky. Take more than a buffalo to hurt you," Charlie said. "You can go to sleep now that we know your head's alright."

"You gonna' be jes' fine, Miss Becky," Bessie said, lifting Becky while Charlie and I wrapped rawhide strips around her ribcage.

"It hurts to breath," Becky whispered.

"That should help some." Charlie reached for the bottle of laudanum. "This'll ease the pain and help you sleep," she said, holding a teaspoon of the liquid to Becky's lips.

"Thanks, Charlie." She closed her eyes. "Sure hope it starts helpin' real soon. I'm hurtin' like a sonofabitch. Maybe you could find a bit of red eye for me?"

"I'll get that for you, Becky," I said. "I know where there's some."

"Ah'll stay wit' her 'til she falls asleep," Bessie said, her tone suggesting that she would brook no argument.

"Good idea. Thanks, Bessie," I said. "Call us if there's a problem."

Charlie and I climbed out of the wagon to find Sara, Polly, and Hattie along with Pete and several other people waiting to hear about Becky.

"Becky had a run-in with a bison," Charlie told the group. "Don't know how the bison fared, but

Six Women West

Becky got banged up pretty good." Grinning, she added, "Main thing is her head's still on straight, so her tongue's still workin' real good."

I told them what she had said when I asked her name. Everyone laughed. I knew they were as relieved as I to know she would be alright.

"Takes awhile for ribs to heal, so we're going to have to do our huntin' without her." Charlie shook her head. "I figure we'll be eatin' a lot of beans 'til then." She grinned. "Just funnin' with you."

"Anything we can do, just let us know," one of the women called as several people walked away, but Pete stayed.

"We're all glad to hear Becky's going to be okay," Pete said.

"Is she alright? How bad is she hurt?" Shiloh yelled, riding up.

"She's going to be fine, Shiloh. Just keep your voice down and let her sleep," I said.

He slid off his horse and confronted Pete. "That girl's got no business out hunting. You got enough men to do the job." He turned to Charlie. "You sure she's okay?"

Charlie nodded.

"I want to know when she wakes up."

Charlie nodded.

"Thanks." He grabbed his horse's reins and stomped off.

We moved closer to the coffeepot and sat in the camp chairs. Now that the excitement had slowed down, we could have a cup of coffee.

"You know it wouldn't take much for me to dislike that young man," I said. "Pete, I need to talk to you. Becky would like to taste what's in that flask of your, and I told her I would get it."

"Well, young ladies that you are surely wouldn't use it for anything but a medical purpose," Pete chuckled and handed me the flask.

"Yeah, but he did seem real concerned about her," Charlie said. "He reminds me of a young rooster in a chicken yard—does a lot a crowing."

"He's a good kid. Just needs the wind knocked out of him. Still has a lot to learn about women," Pete remarked, adding, "But then, what man doesn't?" He winked at Hattie.

"Well, he's in for a big surprise if he tries to tell Becky what she can or cannot do," Hattie predicted "That girl's been fendin' for herself too long for any man to control her."

"That go for you, too, Hattie?" Pete asked, sounding as if he hoped she'd say no.

"That's for me to know. You to find out," she retorted with a grin.

"Lookin' forward to that," Pete came back.

"Bessie, I done got a buffalo hump roast for supper," Abel interrupted.

"Well, stir the fire up, an' ah'll get it cookin'." Bessie held the roast, weighing it. "Take awhile, but it should be done for supper."

"You goin' to make some o' those fine biscuits, Bessie, darlin'?" Abel patted her on the backside.

"Don' ah always?" She glared at him, but there was a give away twinkle in her eyes, as she added, "You' keep you'r hands to yo sef, mistuh."

"Yessum," he said, bowing his head. "You ladies want hep settin' up the tent?"

We took Abel up on his offer and soon were once again settled in for the night. Supper was delicious, but Becky's absence put a real dent in the conversation. Both Luke and Charlie said they didn't feel like singing, which was okay with the rest of us.

We decided to take turns sitting with Becky, and I asked for the first turn, right after supper. She looked so young and helpless, I thought. I prayed that if Shiloh was the man she'd picked to love, he would be worthy of her.

Six Women West

The sun began to set, turning the sky a blazing red and throwing long shadows on the tall rocks. I found myself wishing Morgan were seeing it with me. I'm not sure it was my guardian angel or the devil, but someone was paying attention.

"How's she doin'?" the object of my wish asked in a hushed voice as he placed some deadfall on the fire and stirred the flames.

"What'd you do? Float over? I never heard a sound, and my hearin's pretty good," I said, hoping my pleasure at his presence was not obvious.

"You learn to walk quiet when you take up scoutin'. Hope I didn't scare you." He paused. "How's Becky?" he repeated.

"Still sleeping," I said, jumping down from the wagon's tailgate. "Take a seat while I pour us some coffee." I handed him a cup and then sat down in a camp chair by him.

"Thanks. I took her horse down to Billy. Told him to clean him up and rub him down with liniment."

"That was nice of you. Has Shiloh gotten back?"

"No."

"What kind of a fellow is this Shiloh?" I asked. "He seems awful sweet on Becky, but he doesn't like the person she is—wants to change her. Did you know we wouldn't be sitting on these camp chairs if Becky hadn't made them? She just knows all sorts of things to make. She can walk into the wilderness and make any thing she needs to live. She's from the mountains and to me, he wants a parlor flower."

"No, I agree with you—Becky's not the sort he normally chases. A lady's man," Morgan replied, "and it doesn't matter if they're married. At first I thought he was serious about her, but now I believe he is trying to take advantage of her innocence."

I shook my head. "Well, I know four women who are watching him. He better tread lightly around Becky, or he'll get a load of buckshot."

"A few men around here are watching him, too," Morgan chuckled. "One woman at a time for him isn't enough. I've heard rumors that he has been flirting with several married women."

"You mean he's playing up to someone else?"

"I'm not sure. He's been seen at the Robert's wagon, making eyes at the young widow, Mary Beth. 'Course, maybe he's just being friendly." He took a long swallow from his cup. "He's been out walking with Lorraine, and then he started hanging around Sybil, but Mr. Locklander took Shiloh aside, and he's stayed shy of that wagon since."

"He strikes me as too self-centered. I can't bring myself to like him," I said.

"That's hard when your best friend could end up married to him."

"I hope she sees through him before it goes that far."

"Not to change the subject, but how are the fillies holding up?"

"They're doing okay." I guess the tone of my voice made him decide not to dwell on that subject. I don't know why I was so guarded about my horses. It wasn't that I didn't trust Morgan. *Besides*, I asked myself, *what's so bad if he did want to buy them?*

"Well, guess I'll go bed down. Hope Becky has a good night. Night, Martha." He tossed the coffee grounds out of his cup, rinsed it, and placed it with the others. "Thanks for the coffee. Don't worry too much about Shiloh. He'll be leavin' us soon."

Hattie came out of the tent as he was walking away. They spoke for a minute. Then he kissed her on the cheek and disappeared in the darkness.

"How's Becky?" Hattie asked, reaching for a cup.

"She's sleeping. She moaned a few times but hasn't really been conscious. Charlie says the more she rests, the better chance her body has to heal."

"You and Morgan have a nice chat?" Hattie sipped coffee, peering at me over the cup.

"Yeah, we talked mostly about Shiloh. Morgan says he's playing around with other women too." I tossed the remains of my coffee. "Damn men! You can't trust any of them."

"Does that include Morgan?"

"I don't know, Hattie," I replied honestly. "I'm going to bed."

"Good night, Martha. Sweet dreams," Hattie chuckled as she climbed into the wagon to sit with Becky.

I crawled into bed wondering why I was so distrustful of men. Wondering if the fact that I'd killed one had anything to do with it. Wondering if the person I didn't trust was myself. I lay there wide-eyed wondering if Morgan would leave the train at Sweetwater Range or go on to Oregon with us. I slept restlessly, my dreams anything but sweet.

The next morning, Charlie reported Becky had had a fair night. "She's hungry," Charlie said. "That's always a good sign."

A horse thundered into camp, raising a terrible dust. "She awake?" Shiloh called out as he came to a rearing halt in front of our wagon.

"Shiloh," yelled Hattie, "you enter this camp at a walk. You ride in here like that again, and I'll dust you with buckshot. You understand me?"

"Yes, ma'am. Sorry. I'm just short on time."

"No, Becky is asleep," Charlie said, answering Shiloh's question.

He stared at Charlie. "You sure she's not awake?"

"We'll let you know when she is. I figured you'll be around—if you learn to walk that horse."

"Mary Beth was asking for you," I said, lying through my teeth. I didn't know I had such a mean streak.

Shiloh looked surprised and had the grace to blush. "Well, she can just keep on lookin'. Tell Becky I been here asking about her, okay?" He directed his remarks to Charlie, avoiding my eyes.

At dawn we traveled along the North Platte, following it for many miles with no problems. The trail to Michelle Pass, made up of soft sand, was much more difficult. The wheels cut deep, slowing the wagons. The air was dry and humid, and the stench of animal dung filled my nostrils with every breath.

The combination of a hot June sun and soft sand caused the mules to move slower than molasses. From time to time, we sighted Indians. They either waved at us or came out with goods to trade. Despite talk about Indians stealing horses and women, nothing like that happened.

That night after dark, I was walking past the Macintosh wagon on my way to the bushes, when I overheard Randall talking. It sounded as if he were complaining. Curious, I paused to listen.

"Pete listens to that woman too much,"

"Yeah." I recognized Elmo Robert's voice. "Always havin' her show us how to drive like us men don't know how."

"Well, I'm gittin' mighty tired of him always askin' her how to run this train." I was surprised to hear Mac say that.

"He treats those women like they're the only ones here. You notice they don't pull guard duty." George's voice rang with indignation.

Furious, I stomped over to them. "Mac," I said calmly, though calm was not what I was feeling, "You're wrong to badmouth Pete. You got a problem? Tell it to his face, not behind his back. Hattie has driven this trail a number of times. You

Six Women West

think Pete babies our wagon? Come on over and pull some extra duties. Maybe you want to tend the sick, ride the line, or help scout. If you don't like how Pete runs this train is run, pull off and wait for the next one. As far as I'm concerned, that goes for anyone else who badmouths the wagon boss." Without waiting for their response, I spun around and headed for the bushes. I was so mad I could spit.

Back at the wagon I repeated what I had overheard to Hattie.

"Let's keep this to ourselves for now," Hattie said. "We won't tell Pete yet. Sounds like you set 'em straight, Martha. Probably took the wind out of their sails. Maybe shut 'em up."

"You know best," I agreed. "Mmm, the coffee smells good. Didn't I hear Bessie say something about peach pie?"

"Peach pie?" Pete walked up. "And fresh coffee." He winked at Hattie. "Looks like I timed it just right."

"Ah sweah, Mistuh Pete, y'all kin smell my pie no mattah wheah you ah," Bessie said, smiling with obvious pleasure.

He finished his pie and threw out the dregs of his coffee. "Best pie I ever ate," he told Bessie. Turning to Hattie, he added, "Plan on pullin' out at dawn. If we push hard and don't run into problems, we should reach the fort about the twenty fifth."

> **Comment [CJH]:** What fort? It would be good to give it a name for the sake of consistency.

"Think Al will make it to the fort?" I asked.

"I'm not sure. I hope so. Depends on how long it takes them to get him there." He inclined his head towards the wagon. "How's Becky?"

> **Comment [CJH]:** I changed this conversation. Before, the conversation showed that Al was still with them, but he was taken on the supply wagon to the next fort ahead of everyone. I'm guessing some changes were made here.

"Did somebody mention my name?" Becky called out.

"Sounds like she's alive and kickin'," Pete said. "Well, I'm off. Thanks for the pie and coffee."

"Well, girl," Hattie said. "I imagine you need to visit the bushes. Am I right?"

345

"Yes, ma'am. If I can git some help. Don't think I'm quite up to gittin' there by myself."

"I'll take her," Sara said, walking up with Polly in her arms. She handed the little girl to me.

"Hi, baby. Did you have a nice walk?" I asked, enjoying her sweet smell and soft skin.

"Baby big," she reminded me, looking indignant.

"Of course you are." I hugged her and sat her down next to Tag. "Stay here. I have to catch Pete." I took off running to catch Pete before we got out of sight of our wagon.

"Pete, who has the buffalo hides? There are three of them aren't there?"

"They're in the supply wagon. Can't get anybody to clean 'em. You want one?"

"Not me. Becky. Could I have Abel pick one up?"

"Sure, Martha. She can take 'em all if you want." He paused. "Why don't you just leave them in the wagon 'til we get to the fort?"

"Good idea. Do you think I can get someone there to clean them?"

"Yeah, the Indians."

"I'll tell her. She'll be real pleased."

"What's she plannin' on doin' with it?"

"She said something about trading it for a mule."

"Take all three. Get a good mule from the trader, Red." He waved his hand and headed for Moe's wagon.

I got back to our wagon. Charlie was indulging in pie and coffee. She looked tired.

"Becky," I said, "I asked Pete about the buffalo hides. He said you could take all three. Trade them to the Indians. They will clean them." I glanced at her.

"I plan to trade them for a mule," she replied.

"Aren't you happy with the horse?"

"Yes, but I owe Hattie. I know her horse is worth a lot more then my mule. So I want to get her another mule."

We drove twelve-hour days 'til the fort was in sight. We were happy that we would be able to rest a few days, and hopefully anyone needing a doctor could see one. Charlie wanted to restock her medical supplies.

The fort was in sight, and Charlie was excited about getting news of Al. She rode ahead the last few miles and then came back and spread the news that Al was fine—he just needs time to heal, and the doctor had saved his leg, so he wouldn't be needing a peg leg, but he would have to stay at the fort.

CHAPTER TWENTY SEVEN

Colonel Bradford sent a rider to meet Pete and invite us all to a potluck supper with a dance following. Pete accepted and spread the word, causing a stir of excitement throughout the train.

Morgan hailed me as I was riding by the army wagon. "Miss Patterson, I was wonderin'—I mean, if no one's beat me to it, well," he paused. I waited. "What I'm askin' is, can I escort you to supper and the dance?"

"Why, Mr. Brook, I'd be purely pleased to go with you," I managed to say without stammering. As I rode away, holding Lady to a canter, my heart felt like it was going to jump out of my chest. I wanted to slap her on the rump and go racing across the prairie. Morgan asked me! I'd seen Lorraine hanging around him so much, I was sure he would be taking her.

"My, what happened to you?" Sara asked, looking at me curiously when I rode up.

"Why? What do you mean?" I tried to sound as if I wasn't the happiest I'd been in a long time.

"Morgan asked you to the supper, didn't he? And the dance?"

How did you know?" I asked, surprised.

"Oh, I overheard him talking to Hattie about it," she confided. "You said yes, didn't you?"

"Yes," I admitted. "Will you help me get fixed up?"

"I'd love to." She went to the wagon and came back with a small bar of soap. "Here, take this and go wash your hair. Then, I'll roll it in rags."

"Thanks, Sara." I sniffed the soap. "Mmm, it's lilac—my favorite."

Becky and Charlie rode up. "What are you two up to?" Becky asked.

"Martha's going to the potluck with Morgan," Sara said. "She's off to wash her hair so I can roll it in rags."

"Oh, will you do mine, too?" Charlie slid off her horse. "I'll go with you, Martha. I'll wash yours and you can wash mine. Okay?"

"Alright. I'll get my honeysuckle soap. Don't want to use all of Sara's."

"Me, too," Becky said, jumping off Fudge. "Will you, Sara? Please."

"Of course. I'll ask Bessie to help. She's very good with hair." She smiled and made shooing motions. "Now, scat. We haven't got all day."

The afternoon was spent doing hair and putting on the dresses Sara had made for us. Bessie worked wonders, turning our hair into masses of ringlets, making us look much different from our usual appearance.

We oohed and aahed at each other, thanking Sara and Bessie over and over. The topic of conversation was who was going with whom to dinner. Of course, Shiloh was taking Becky. Luke and Charlie would be going together, and Pete would escort Hattie. Guy and Sara had been seeing each other, so it was understood they would go together. Bessie told us she and Abel would meet us there. Josephine Tanner, who didn't approve of dancing but loved to listen to the music, agreed to watch Polly, Prissy, and Max during the dance.

The men arrived together with their hair slicked back and smelling of rose water. Their bright shirts were obviously those they saved for special occasions. All in all, they looked real good. There were a lot of smiles and enough compliments from both sides to last a long while. We walked in pairs to the fort, enjoying the cool summer weather. I glanced at Morgan, who was wearing a bright blue shirt, thinking he was the handsomest man of all and wondering why he had chosen me.

"You are beautiful, Martha, we look like a matched set with your blue dress and my shirt," he said softly, his gray eyes staring down at me with obvious admiration.

"So are you," I murmured stupidly.

He chuckled. "Never been told that before."

"Oh, you know what I mean," I said, looking away.

It was hard to hold his gaze without becoming totally flustered. It was both a relief and a disappointment when we reached the fort.

It wasn't hard to know where the supper and dance were being held. The building was brightly lit as well as the boardwalk leading to the officers' mess. Still, several of the ladies came out to walk with us. The soldiers and their wives seemed delighted to have our company and welcomed us to the party with open arms. The tables were covered with white cloths and heavily laden with a variety of dishes. The contributions from the wagon train were added. There were baked beans, venison roast, corn fritters, black-eyed peas, biscuits, pies, cookies, and some foods I didn't recognize. No one here would go hungry this night.

Because of the tight fit of our dresses, I don't think the other girls and I ate as much as we would have liked. Or, maybe we just tried to eat like ladies instead of trail hands. The men didn't have that problem.

Later when the band, which consisted of a fiddle, a banjo, a bass fiddle, a squeeze-box, and a small piano, began to play, we all got up to dance. Across the room I saw Al propped up in a chair, one of the young women from the fort hovering over him.

He wouldn't get to dance, I thought, but he wouldn't lack for attention. "Excuse me," Charlie said. "I want to see Al for a moment. I'll be right back."

Six Women West

The first tune was the Virginia Reel, which was a lively and loud rendition of "Oh, Susanna," followed by "Camptown Races." Morgan and I whirled around the floor as if we'd been dancing together all our lives. Other partners seemed dull by comparison. I couldn't wait to get back to Morgan. By the time the bandleader declared intermission, I wasn't the only one who had a flushed face and was breathing hard.

"I could use some air. How about you?" Morgan asked, taking my arm.

"Yes, please," I agreed, leaning against him. Unseen sparks flew, and I pulled away, fighting the urge to move closer.

We stepped out on the porch and discovered we were not the only ones needing air. Becky and Shiloh were standing back in the corner, talking animatedly. She was shaking her head, and he seemed to be attempting to embrace her.

Morgan caught me staring. "It's alright, Martha. He won't do anything ungentlemanly here at the fort. There are unseen eyes on him."

"I know. She's so young and he seems so—I don't know. I worry about her."

"I'll say something if you want me to."

"No, no. You're right. Becky can take care of herself." I looked up at the sky. The moon was full, and there seemed to be more stars than usual.

"Are you enjoying yourself?" Morgan asked. "May I bring you some punch?"

"Yes, I am enjoying myself very much," I admitted, adding, "Punch would be nice, but only if you're going to have some, too."

"I'll be right back," he said. "Stay right there. You're even more beautiful in the moonlight."

As he hurried off, I took a deep breath. *Sweet Jesus*, I thought, *what is this man doing to me? What if he tries to kiss me again? Should I let him?* I groaned. *How could I not let him, when I wanted it so badly?*

"Oh Martha, out here all alone?" Lorraine asked snickering, interrupting my thoughts. I hadn't heard her approach. She was clutching the arm of a young officer to her bust. He was red in the face and looked a bit overwhelmed.

"Lorraine! Having a good time?" Morgan asked, coming up to me with our drinks. "Hello darling. Miss me?" He leaned over and brushed my cheek with a soft kiss.

Despite my surprise, I managed to return his smile and look as if I knew what was happening.

Lorraine huffed and flounced off. Giggling, I grinned at Morgan. "Now, was that nice? I do believe you've upset your lady friend."

"She's not my lady friend." He shook his head. "Not too sure she's a lady. Truth is, she's a spoilt little girl used to having her own way. I'm hoping now she'll get the message that I'm not interested, but I feel sorry for that young man."

"She does seem to be real attracted to you," I said, thinking, *who wouldn't be?* Morgan was tall, dark, and handsome in addition to being intelligent and nice. A real catch for any woman.

"Oh, it's just one of those—what do they call them?—a schoolgirl fancy. She'll get over it when someone else comes along." He shook his head. "Just hope that's soon. I'm gettin' mighty tired trying to stay out of her way."

We finished our punch just as the music started again. It was another lively tune. "Feel like more dancin'?" Morgan asked, taking my cup.

"Yes," I said. "Hope they play some slower ones."

Morgan gazed at me, a strange look in his eyes. "Slow would be nice," he said softly.

Nervously, I glanced at the corner where Becky had been. There was no one there. I was relieved when I saw them starting for the dance floor. *Good for her*, I thought. I decided not to worry about her anymore.

A young officer approached Morgan and asked permission to dance with me. Morgan gave permission and then leaned over and whispered in my ear, "The others can have the fast ones. The slow ones are mine."

And the slow ones we dance with him holding me in his arms. It was like floating on a cloud. We danced to "My Old Kentucky Home," "Aura Lea," and many more from both the North and South. There seemed to be no war on the trail.

The dance went on for several more hours with everyone obviously having a good time. The music finally ended with "Beautiful Dreamer," and people began to return to their homes or their wagons.

Morgan and I leisurely walked hand and hand, meandering behind the others. When everyone was far ahead of us, he stopped and pulled me into his arms. I had no will to resist as his lips covered mine. Unconsciously, my arms went around his neck and I pressed closer. He uttered a low groan, and his mouth moved against mine. Hungrily, I returned the kiss. I could feel his chest pressing against my breast, his hand moved softly and slowly up, enclosing my breast and sending my thoughts spinning. Suddenly afraid, I pulled away. "No," I whispered. "No."

Abruptly, he stepped back. "I'll take you home," he said hoarsely.

We walked the rest of the way in silence. I told myself I didn't care if he was mad at me or if he would choose not to be with me. I wasn't getting myself in a position of raising a woods colt. So, when he didn't make a move to kiss me goodnight, why did I feel like my heart was broken?

Inside the tent I took out my journal and wrote, "We had a wonderful party and I danced with Morgan. On the way back he kissed me. It was just a kiss—maybe a bit more. Maybe I was saying no before I was asked. Am I being prudish? I wish I knew more about courting. Ma, could you be wrong? Maybe I am someone a man could love and marry."

I lay there with my breast yearning for Morgan's touch and my heart aching for more.

"Come on, get up!" Charlie called, shaking me. "It's a beautiful morning."

"Go away," I whined. I had spent a restless night and awakened in no mood to enjoy anything.

"What's the matter? Somebody put whiskey in your punch?" she teased.

I pushed the covers back and sat up on my bedroll. "I didn't sleep good. You all got the chores figured out?"

"Yeah." She tilted her head towards Becky's pallet. "When she wakes up, she can watch over Polly so you and Sara can do the laundry. I'm going out to bring home the bacon."

"Where's Hattie?" I asked, pulling on my boots.

"She's gone to the fort for supplies. She said when she gets back, she and Becky will clean up the wagon and stow the supplies." She handed me a cup of coffee.

"Thanks, but I better wait on that 'til I get back from the bushes," I said, grabbing my necessaries bag. After taking care of Mother Nature, I stopped at the river and splashed river water on my face and swished some around in my mouth. Then I took baking soda and washed my teeth.

Back at camp, I drank coffee and ate a couple of left-over biscuits. Sara walked up with Polly on her back.

"Git-up! Go!" Polly ordered, patting Sara on the shoulder.

"No more, little lady. Mama has to do the laundry. Is Becky up?"

"I'm up," Becky called from the tent.

Six Women West

"You stay with Aunt Becky, Polly. Aunt Martha and I will be back pretty soon."

I helped Polly down. Becky came out of the tent yawning. "Want to come to the bushes with me, Polly?"

"Otay." Polly took Becky's hand, and they took off for the bushes.

Sara and I gathered up the laundry along with the tub and washboard. We were just getting ready to leave for the river when Hattie rode up on a buckboard loaded with supplies. Previously we had decided to distribute the supplies among the three wagons.

"You want us to stay and help you unload?" I asked.

"Nope, you go ahead. We get all our chores done this mornin', and we can take the afternoon off." She hopped down. "Where's Becky?"

"She's with Polly in the brush," Sara told her.

"Well, I'll wait 'til she gets here, and we'll clean the wagon and then unload it. No use doin' it twice." She poured a cup of coffee. "I got some news for Becky. Supply clerk told me at the fort 'bout an Indian fur trader. Maybe she can do some tradin' with him."

> **Comment [CJH]:** Could Becky do this with broken ribs? Also, wouldn't they unload it and then clean it, or am I missing something?

It took us nearly two hours to finish the laundry and take it back to the wagons. Hattie and Becky had finished cleaning and loading the wagons. We were free for the afternoon.

"Hey Martha, can we use the jenny mule to carry the furs on?" The jenny mule was as gentle as a puppy.

"Sure. Let me help you tie them on." We mounted our horses and left for the Indian camp.

We met a tall, handsome brave at the entrance. Becky made hand signs to him about a trade, pointing to the furs and rubbing her hands together. He didn't speak—just pointed to a large teepee with a yellow sun painted on the side. Nearby, a squaw

355

Wanda Reed

stood silently, stirring a cooking pot. She glanced at us and smiled shyly.

"What are you cooking?" I asked, not recognizing the aroma. She continued smiling and stirring without answering. I shrugged, unable to communicate with her. We walked across the village. There were several teepees and women working hides and weaving with small children playing. Camp dogs lay in the shade of the teepees. I was glad that Tag had not joined us. The campground seemed to be swept clean of any growth. We came to the teepee we thought was right, and Becky called 'hello.' A boy came out then, said something, and an old man opened the tent flap and hobbled out. He was bent over with long white hair and skin like dry leather. After examining the uncleaned hides, he spoke to the young boy, and then the young boy spoke to us. He had offered her two cleaned bison hides and a horsehair bridle.

Becky looked at me. "What do you think?"

"You know more about it than I do," I admitted.

"I'll take them," Becky said, holding out her hand. The Indian nodded several times and shook her hand vigorously.

The young brave came from the tent and led our mule away. Within a few minutes he returned with her loaded with the hides and a bridle tied to the side. We mounted our horses and rode a mile or so west to Trader Red's camp. There, Becky looked over the mules and chose a leggy buckskin mule. She got him in trade for one buffalo hide. She seemed quite pleased with him. She sold the other hide to the trader for gold coin. Back at camp we picketed him with the other mules.

"Would you go with me to the supply store? I need to buy some stuff," Becky said.

> **Comment [CJH]:** Again I find myself questioning monetary values. It would seem like a mule ($30 previously) would be worth more than a single hide.

Six Women West

"Sure. I need to go there too. Maybe they have some sweet soap," I agreed. "Okay if we walk? I need to exercise my legs."

We walked across grounds the fort used for pasture. It was dry grass and no trees. They kept it clear in case of an attack. There was nothing to hide behind. The Laramie River was a half mile from the fort. That was used for water. The fort had walls six feet thick and fifteen feet high, made out of adobe brick with sharp poles on top.

"Okay with me. Your legs didn't get enough exercise with all that dancin' you and Morgan did?" We started for the fort. She grinned at me. "He's sure sweet on you. You sweet on him?" I was glad she kept talking without waiting for an answer. "Wouldn't it be funny if we all got hitched before we got to Oregon?"

"What do you mean? Are you thinking of getting married?" *That Shiloh*, I thought. *He's leading her on with promises of marriage.*

"Well, maybe. I was thinkin' with Bessie married and Sara and Guy plannin' on it, well, Luke and Charlie might be next and…"

"How do you know Sara and Guy are planning marriage?" I interrupted, adding, "Not that I don't think it's a good idea. He seems like a real nice fellow, and he's real good with Polly."

"Uh, I overheard 'em talkin' one night."

"I suppose you know something about Luke and Charlie, too?"

"Well, I ain't heard 'em talkin' weddins', but…"

We entered the fort and Becky hurried ahead of me, apparently wanting to drop the subject. That was alright with me. I didn't want her bringing up me and Morgan again.

I looked up and noticed Sara wearing her new dress and Guy holding Polly as they came out of the chapel, smiling widely.

We ran over to the chapel. "Did we miss something?" I asked.

"You sure did," Guy said, his voice filled with pride. "I just married me a queen and got a princess in the bargain."

"Oh, Guy," Sara said. It was easy to tell the remark pleased her. She took my hand. "We didn't invite anyone. We wanted it to be just the three of us. You understand, don't you?"

"Of course. We can have a reception, can't we?"

"Well, we don't really want a reception. We both feel the party last night was enough."

"Okay. Whatever you say," I said.

"We're real happy for you both," Becky said, hugging Sara. "You're one lucky feller, Guy."

"Guess we best warn you like we warned Abel," I said sternly. "You keep her happy or you'll have some very angry women all over you. You understand?"

"Yes, ma'am. You don't have to worry," Guy assured me.

We left them after more hugs, saying we'd see them later. After arriving at the store, Becky went to the ready-made section. She held up a camel-brown linsey-woolsey dress up to her. "What d'you think?"

"The color's nice on you, but the material is really too warm for now. It's more of a winter dress. It would look nice trimmed in a bone lace. When do you plan to wear it?"

"Oh, sometime," she said vaguely. "I'll take it. Would you pick out what I need to wear with it?"

I went to the hats and gloves and collars to find matches. While I was there, Becky brought over a dark blue cotton skirt and a black skirt, a light blue cotton blouse with yellow buds, and a beige blouse. "How is this for right now?" she asked. "Would it make me look like the other women?"

"Becky, why are you buying these things?" I ask, only to be interrupted by the clerk.

"Will you need anything else?" the clerk asked.

"Yes," Becky said. "Two pair of undergarments and a nightgown."

After sizing Becky up, the clerk hurried off to find the requested items.

"Why the sudden interest in clothes, Becky? I thought you were strictly a buckskin girl."

"Shiloh said I should dress to look more like a lady. You 'member what I was sayin' before? 'Bout us all gittin' married?" She grinned impishly. "Well, Shiloh and me are gittin' hitched in Fort Bridger, and I'll be leavin' the train." Her face saddened. "I'll really hate to part from you all, but like the Bible says, I go where he goes. Since I'll be there with the other women, I should have a dress to wear."

"Oh," was all I could think of to reply at first. We walked back to the wagon as we talked.

"Oh, Becky," I whispered. "Are you sure this is what you want? I thought you were going to Oregon with us. We were going to get a place right next to each other." My voice choked, and I swallowed hard. "I mean, we're family. We all think of you as a sister."

Becky's eyes filled with tears. "I'm sorry, Martha. I'm right fond of all of you, too, but, well, what can I do? Shiloh's a soldier. He can't give that up to come to Oregon. Not now anyhow." She put her arms around me. "We'll keep in touch, and maybe one day Shiloh and me can make it to Oregon."

Arriving at the wagon, Hattie asked, "Where'd that buckskin mule come from?"

"It's yours if you still want to trade for Fudge," Becky said. "That'll make it more of an even trade."

"You don't have to do that, Becky. I'm satisfied the way it was."

"Well, you take the mule so we'll both be satisfied, okay?"

"Okay, Becky. Now I want to show you something. I traded out that lame mule for this buckskin mule." She chuckled. "Named him Zeke after an old muleskinner I once met."

We walked over to where the animals were picketed. "Which one is which?" I asked. The two new mules were identical in size and color.

"I think this is the one I got," Becky said, patting the rump of one of them. "Call it Zack. Then you got Zeke and Zack."

"Well, if you're sure, the other one must be the one I traded for. Where did you get yours?"

"I got him over at Trader Red's."

"I'll be darned. That's where I got this one. Most likely they're brothers, alright."

"Let's go over and see what the Indians have got to trade. I got lots of pelts we can use for money," Becky said, tossing me a bale of pelts. Taking a bale herself, she said, "Let's go."

"Just hold on, Becky. You think you'd better tell Hattie about your upcoming plans?"

"What's this, girl? You keepin' secrets from your ma?" Hattie teased, obviously referring to her being our wagon's mother figure.

Becky flushed and bowed her head. "I was gonna tell you. We just got to talkin' bout the mules. It's me and Shiloh. We're gittin' hitched."

"That happened pretty fast, didn't it?" Hattie asked, looking as if she didn't know whether to be glad or sad about it.

"Well, Shiloh says he don't wanna lose me. You know, me goin' on to Oregon and him here soldierin', so he says we should get married when we get to Fort Bridger."

"They got a preacher there now?" Hattie asked.

"Shiloh says they have."

"Well, girl, I wish you both all the best," Hattie said, putting her arms around Becky. "Sure gonna miss you. Hey," she stepped back and stared at

Becky, "who's gonna do the huntin' for us? Charlie can't do it all herself."

"Oh, I think Martha can do it mighty fine," Becky said, winking at me. "She won't let you go hungry. Come on. These furs are gittin' heavy."

At the Indian camp, the Indians had their trade goods out. Becky traded for a bow and arrows. Bessie traded two pies for a beaded shirt for Abel and a cooking pot for a red-fox fur wrap for herself. I got a pair of knee moccasins and a doe-skin skirt. Hattie found a buckskin riding skirt. We found a gourd rattle for Polly.

"Hey, we're gonna be all matched up," Morgan exclaimed, showing off the buckskin breeches and shirt he had traded a lariat for.

Guy and Sara walked up, looking very pleased. "We found a donkey cart to hook to the back of the schooner."

"Is that your doghouse, Guy?" Morgan joked.

"It's for the goat," Guy laughed. "And I don't plan to do anything to warrant a night in the doghouse."

"The goat can't walk and eat enough, too," Abel put in. "Got to keeps her milk flowin' 'case the cows don' produce. All dem babies on the train need milk."

"Abel's gonna help me make a canvas shade for it." Guy glanced around, apparently noticing the amount of goods to be carried back to the wagons. "Why don't we just put all your stuff in the cart, and we'll pull it back?"

"Good idea, Guy," Morgan said. "I'll push. You pull." He stared at Becky. "What's this I hear about you and Shiloh getting married? You gonna live at Fort Bridger?"

Becky spent a few minutes explaining to those who hadn't already heard. Congratulations and best wishes were offered by all—despite any mixed feelings those who cared for Becky might have.

"You better check out living conditions at Fort Bridger," Morgan said. "The last time I was there, the only women there were camp laundresses, not wives. Maybe a few Indian women too. I don't think Shiloh knows what he's asking you to do. Have him explain the living conditions, Becky."

Later at the fort, we were introduced to Walter and Ivey Henderson and their three boys and one girl. They would be joining the train. The next morning at dawn, we left the comfort and safety of the fort, refreshed and eager to be on our way.

We traveled without incident throughout the morning, covering about four miles. The terrain turned to barren prairie grasses with little to no trees. At Register Cliff, Pete called a halt and ordered everyone to meet at his wagon after we'd eaten. Anxious to get going, we ate fast and joined the others at Pete's wagon.

"Thought it would save time instead of going wagon to wagon," he began. "I need to give you all a bit of advice. You'll need to gather buffalo chips for fuel. As you've no doubt noticed, there's a shortage of trees and brush, so the chips will be 'bout the only fuel you'll have." He grinned and glanced at some of the women. "Lessen you women wanna use some of your heirlooms."

There was a vigorous shaking of heads. "Excuse me, Pete, but what are buffalo chips?" one of the women asked.

"They're dried buffalo sh…, ah, dung. They make a real hot fire—just a little smelly. It's a good job for the young ones. You ladies might want to wear gloves." He chuckled as he noted the expressions on some of the women's faces and then climbed on his horse. "Now let's get movin'."

Me and Charlie slung a canvas under the wagon to hold the chips. Hattie drove, and the three of us walked, picking up chips as we went along. The grass had been cropped close by the buffalo that had been through here, and the chips were abundant and easy to find.

Out of the blue, a chip came whizzing by my head. Ducking, I looked around for the culprit. Charlie was bent over, laughing. "Okay," I yelled, "you asked for it!" I picked up a nice, fat chip and threw it at her. She laughed and chucked one at Becky. Becky responded by pitching one at each of us. The fight was going great until a chip went astray and hit Rowdy. He bellowed and started bucking. Hattie swore and yelled at us to stop horsin' around.

"Sorry, Hattie," we called and settled back into serious chip pickin'. It was hot under the midday sun, but there was a nice breeze blowing. I got wind that someone might have scared a skunk. There was a scent in the air that was easily recognizable. The grass got taller, and we had a harder time locating chips 'til we stepped on them. After we collected a goodly amount, we rode off to scout for game. In a few hours we returned to the wagon train with four jackrabbits. They were tough and stringy, but Bessie managed to make them edible.

We covered about fifteen miles before camping at Cottonwood Creek. There were several creeks and two cottonwoods, but in any direction as far as one could see, there was only prairie. No hills. No trees. Just tall grass. The way the wind blew through the grass, it sounded like music, and the grass swaying in the wind made me think of a lake on a windy day. It was a peaceful, relaxing place to spend the night.

At supper that night Pete and Morgan join us. By now they were more like family than guests. Sara helped Bessie with the cooking, and together they served up a sumptuous meal of roasted rabbit, red beans and rice, and a large pan of cornbread.

"Guess we'll be losin' you at Fort Bridger, huh, Morgan?" Guy remarked. "I'll miss your help scoutin'."

"I plan on resigning at the fort. Don't have much to report to the commander," Morgan replied. "So far the Indians and the trail haven't been a problem."

"Does that mean you'll come along with us to Oregon?" Hattie asked, her tone hopeful.

"I'm countin' on it," He replied. He glanced at me and then turned back to Hattie. "Not going to lose you again, Ma. I'll find some land there to raise horses."

"You've changed your mind about Sweetwater Valley?" I asked, referring to our earlier conversation.

"Yep. Figure I can raise Appaloosas in Oregon." He grinned and winked. "Who knows? Might even get me a thoroughbred."

Hattie got up, and in an uncharacteristic move, she kissed Morgan on the cheek. "We got a big ranch, son—fifteen hundred acres. You can raise all the horses you want, including thoroughbreds."

I don't know why I felt both flustered and excited at Morgan's news. I began picking up the empty dishes, throwing the left over food to Tag.

"I'll help with that," Morgan offered. "Least I can do what with eatin' here so often." He shook his head. "Moe can't understand why I'd rather eat Bessie's cookin' than his."

"Well, if you're gonna help here, I'll take Hattie for a walk by the river," Pete said, reaching for her hand.

"And, I promised I'd meet Shiloh after supper." Becky thanked Morgan and left camp in the direction of the army wagon.

"I think we'd better put Polly to bed," Sara said, looking at the little girl half asleep in Guy's arms. "You don't mind?"

"No, of course not. You go too, Bessie. You cooked. We can clean up." I felt a sense of envy as both couples headed for their wagons hand in hand.

Six Women West

"I'm gonna go see what Luke's up to," Charlie said. She glanced at me with a knowing smile. I shook my head.

I filled the dishpan with hot water and shaved off some soap. "Wash or dry?" I asked.

"I'll wash." he responded. We barely said a word while we worked, but when we finished, Morgan asked, "How about a walk?" He smiled. "I promise to be good."

I felt my face redden. We hadn't spoken of the night of the kiss since it happened. "Might as well," I said, trying to ignore his comment.

We walked around the edge of camp to a small rise overlooking the creek. Pete and Hattie were skimming rocks. Suddenly, he turned her around and kissed her. She didn't appear to protest. We watched quietly as they walked to a large rock where he lifted her to sit and then knelt in front of her.

"That looks like a proposal to me," Morgan said. "Wonder if she'll say yes. Wouldn't mind havin' Pete for a pa."

"He seems like a real nice fellow," I agreed. "Little young to be your pa, though."

"Yeah, he would be more of a friend than a pa. I guess I'm a little old for a pa anyways."

"Let's go. I feel I'm intruding on a private moment," I said.

He chuckled. "I'd fancy a private moment with you. How do you feel about that? Am I out of line again?"

"Let's check on the horses."

"Looks like Becky and Shiloh are having a private moment, too," Morgan laughed, as we approached the picketed stock. There was Becky sitting with Shiloh's head in her lap. With the tall grass, you couldn't see them 'til you were right next to them.

My face started to burn, and I thought, *How can I avoid the subject when it's all around me?*

We walked back to camp without talking. I thought of what Morgan had said—about wanting a private moment. *Did he mean he wanted to propose? Should I be taking his flirting seriously?* This was all new to me. I couldn't tell if he was serious or not. I didn't want to make a fool of myself by imagining things. Besides, I always had Charlie's experience in the back of my mind along with Ma's declaration that I wasn't the type men would marry. I'd heard her tell Pa they needed to provide a good dowry or I'd never find a husband. Would Morgan consider my mares a good dowry? Maybe he'd be more interested if he knew I had a poke of gold stashed. *Well,* I told myself determinedly, *if that's what he's after, he can keep on looking.*

I barely said goodnight, not waiting to see if he would try to kiss me, but he only took my hand between his two hands and held it for a moment. I looked at the ground for fear of looking into his eyes. He walked away, shaking his head and mumbling to himself.

Becky and Charlie were still sleeping when I crawled out of my bed early the next morning. Hattie's bed was empty, and I found her clutching a cup of coffee, staring into the fire.

"Morning, Hattie," I said, heading for the other side of the wagon. "Be back in a minute."

When I returned, Hattie handed me a cup of coffee. "Martha, do you think I'm too old for startin' over?"

I thought of what Morgan and I had observed. "No, I don't." I waited.

"Last night Pete asked me to marry him. What do you think?"

"I don't think it matters what I think, Hattie. But, I do believe he's a good person. He comes across as truthful and honest." I supped my coffee. "And he's dependable. I mean, he wouldn't be in charge of a wagon train if he wasn't."

"And, he's cute, too," Becky said, joining us by the fire. "I think you should hitch up with him. You can do it with me and Shiloh at Fort Bridger."

"Have you been listening?"

"Couldn't help it," she grinned. "Mother Nature called. Pour me some coffee, okay?"

"I'll go with you," Charlie said, walking out of the tent.

"I been thinkin'," we could hear Charlie saying as they went around the wagon. "Are you sure there's a preacher at the fort?"

"Shiloh says there is," Becky replied as the two of them went off toward the bushes.

"I hope he's not just telling her that," I said to Hattie. "I'm sorry, I just don't trust him, but I do trust Becky. Hope she hasn't put her pig sticker away."

"Well, truth to tell, I don't either," Hattie said, shaking her head, "but I'm afraid Becky will have to find out for herself."

"Did you say yes to Pete?" I asked.

"Yep. I feel like a silly old fool, but I feel good too."

"You're not old, Hattie," I corrected. "Will you get married at Fort Bridger?"

"No, we'll wait 'til we reach Oregon. I want both my boys at the weddin'. Hope you can be there, too, Martha. I've gotten right fond of you." She grinned. "So has my son. How do you feel about him?"

Becky and Charlie came back, saving me from having to answer. There was a drawn look on Becky's face. She looked at me. "Luke told Charlie the same thing Morgan told you and me about Fort Bridger."

Bessie came over and started breakfast. Abel threw a couple of buffalo chips on the fire, "Ma bacon will smell like dung," she complained.

"No it won't, Missus. Gotsta have a fahr," he said.

Sara and Guy carrying Polly joined us. "Can I do anything?" Sara asked.

Bessie replied "We jes havin' bacon and cold biscuits. Ain't no trouble."

Breakfast over, we dispersed and got busy loading the wagon. It was my turn to drive the wagon, and Hattie planned to ride Boots. "I think you'd better take Sugar today," I told her. "Boots is acting a bit skittish. I have to keep an eye on her. She may be comin' into season."

"Going to mate her with an Appaloosa?" Becky teased.

"Not to anything—especially not an Appaloosa," I retorted. "She's too young, and not out here on the trail."

The day started warm and just got hotter. The sun beat down unmercifully. Sweat ran down my face, and a river of sweat gathered between my breasts. My shirt was plastered to my body like a second skin. I had already drained my canteen. At midmorning a light wind began blowing dust. By the time I thought to cover my face, I felt like a glob of mud. As the day wore on, the wind and the dirt got so thick I couldn't breathe. The animals were obviously suffering too. Pete called a halt about every five miles to wash their noses and mouths. Everyone was hot, tired, and dirty! Hour after hour the wagons rolled. We finally made camp after crossing Labante Creek around seven that night. My backside was sore and ached from sitting on the wagon seat. I decided that riding a horse was a lot more comfortable.

Labante Creek look cool and refreshing, but there were not many trees. I gathered up a blue dress and bloomers and grabbed my necessary bag, jumped on Gray Lady, and lead Boots and Sugar downstream to bathe. Dropping my boots beside the creek with my saddle, I rode Gray Lady into the water, leading Boots and Sugar so I could wash them as well as myself. After washing off the dirt and grime, they chose to graze on the tender grass beside the creek. I pulled off my trousers and shirt for a cool bath. After air drying I felt much cleaner and refreshed. I slipped into my clean clothes, smiling to myself. *What would ma would say if she knew I wasn't wearing a petticoat?* I wondered. If she'd known I'd even considered cutting off my bloomers at the knees, she'd really throw a fit. I would've been "Gott verboten!!" right into eternal damnation.

I saddled and mounted Gray Lady, riding back to camp with my hair flowing loose to dry. Putting my other clothes on the wagon tongue to dry, I walked the fillies out to a nice grassy area and picketed them.

Suddenly, I felt someone behind me. I turned and slipped right into Morgan's arms. His mouth covered mine. Surprised, I pulled back. He stared at me, his eyes filled with longing. I put my arms around his neck and returned his kiss, pressing against him, holding nothing back. I felted a familiar pressure against my belly. This time I wasn't embarrassed or afraid.

When the kiss ended, Morgan gazed at me tenderly. "Martha, I've been waiting for this response. I hope you're not mad at me—or yourself."

"I'm not mad," I admitted. "I don't know what I am. My thoughts are all confused."

"I understand. We don't have to talk about it now."

"Thanks, Morgan." I stepped away, trying to gain control, fighting the desire to kiss him again that raced through my body.

"I better tell you what I came to say," he said. "I've been cuttin' Indian signs all day."

"Have you told Pete?"

"Yes," he grinned. "Actually, the reason I came looking for you was to tell you to tie your mares to your wagon tonight. When I saw you in that blue dress with your hair loose, looking so beautiful, I forgot what I came for."

Ignoring his remarks, I asked, "Do you think there'll be trouble tonight?"

"Could be. You never know. Best to be prepared. Keep your gun handy and watch Tag. He'll hear anything before you do. If someone's there, he'll growl. He's a good watch dog."

I tried not to act worried, but it must have shone on my face.

"Pete will caution everyone to have guns handy, and there will be a double guard on the stock." He paused, and then added, "We'll have lookouts on duty all night. The wagon train will be well covered."

"That's good to know." We walked back to the wagon, a safe distance apart. Hattie was at the wagon working up a batch of sourdough biscuits.

"I'll go get your stock and bring it inside the circle," Morgan said to her, "I guess Pete's told you about the Indian signs."

"Yep," Hattie nodded. "We'll sleep in our clothes and keep our guns handy. I'm making a double batch of biscuits in case we don't have time to cook."

"Have you ever been in an Indian attack, Ma?" Morgan asked.

"Yes, Son. One or two, but I still got my hair. The only advice I can give is to stay low, aim straight, and don't panic."

Becky and Charlie rode up with a four-pointer slung across a mule. "Morgan!" Charlie yelled, "We saw at least four braves about six miles out. Don't think it was hunting party, because they're all painted up."

"Yeah, we know they're about," Morgan said. "Pete's alerted everybody. I think we're ready for 'em if they show up here." He glanced at the deer carcass. "Nice work, ladies."

"Thanks. We passed Henry Davis on the way. Told him about the Indians, and he hightailed it for camp."

"I need to go find James to help bring the stock inside the circle," said Morgan.

"Need some help?" Becky offered.

"No. Help Abel skin that deer out and start dividing it up."

Shortly after that Pete came by to tell us what Morgan had already told us. He added that Indians are usually more interested in stealing the stock and supplies than killing. "We'll be keepin' two hour watches."

"Don't think there'll be much sleepin' goin' on tonight," Hattie said.

"Charlie and me can do a watch, can't we, Charlie?" Becky said.

"Sure. When do you want us, Pete?"

"Thanks, ladies. I'll figure it out and let you know," he told them as he rode off.

A feeling of anxiety and restlessness was thick in the air. The wind still made gentle waves of the grasses, but now it had an ominous feeling as though someone was out there hiding in it. Parents called to the children more often than usual and with a strange urgency, telling them to stay close to the wagon.

"Is it me, or has Velma Johnson called to her little girls three times now?" I asked.

"Mothers are just nervous about their children. The parents are scared the Indians will steal them," Hattie said.

"Do they really do that?" I whispered.

"Not generally, but maybe once in awhile for a grieving wife who's lost her baby."

"Should we put the tent up, Hattie?" Becky asked.

"No. We'll sleep outside. It'll be easier to keep watch."

"Do you think it will get bad?" I asked.

"Never can tell with Indians. Most times they just run off with the stock, but if it's a war party, they're out to kill."

"I done fixed supper," Bessie interrupted. "Mr. Pete said to put the fire near out at dark."

"Sara, why don't you and Polly sleep in our wagon tonight?"

"Alright, Hattie. I'll get our things. I'm sure Guy will be relieved. He told me he was worried about having to leave us."

"Howdy, Pete," Hattie greeted as he dismounted, "You figured out when you want us to do the watch?"

"Well, I have enough men to stand watches on the perimeter. You four can keep watch on this section, and there'll be guards set up every third wagon."

"Put your bedrolls under the wagon," said Hattie. We'll take turns sleepin', and we'll do the watches in pairs."

"I don't think I'll be able to sleep a wink," I said.

"They don't usually attack at night, but they might try to sneak in and steal the stock. We have to be alert for that." Pete paused. "The real attack most likely would be at dawn or dusk."

"Looks like it's gonna be a coon-huntin' moon," Becky said.

"Coon-hunting moon?" I asked, unfamiliar with the term.

"That's what mountain folk call a full moon," she explained.

"A full moon's an advantage and a disadvantage both. They can see us, but we can see them too."

Six Women West

He shook his head. "Well, you gals better get some sleep. It's gonna be a long night."

We put our bedrolls under the wagon and took turns trying to sleep. It was not easy with a mind full of images of Indians in war paint brandishing tomahawks. Any sound set my heart to pounding and strained my nerves to the breaking point. Tag seemed to be aware of my fear. He stayed alert, growling deep in his throat each time I made a move.

Becky and I relieved Hattie and Charlie for the second watch. "Everythin's quiet," Hattie said, yawning.

"See y'all later," Charlie muttered and crawled into her bedroll. She looked too sleepy to worry about the threat of Indian attack.

I rested on a keg by the wagon, Tag at my feet, watching the outer area. My mind wandered back to the days of the farm in Manassas when life was simple and secure. The biggest fear I had then was Ma catching me skinny-dipping in the creek. I felt like I'd aged twenty years in these past few months. I laughed to myself. *At this rate I'll be an old granny by the time we reach Oregon*, I thought.

"You ever think you'd be in a spot like this?" Becky asked, bringing me back to the present.

"No," I said, pushing the stray hair back up under my hat. "If the war hadn't happened, I'd probably be learning how to pour tea at Miss Marbella's Finishing School."

"Honest Injun? What's a finishing school?"

"It's where you live at school and learn to be a nice lady and pour tea." I made an elaborate curtsy. We both laughed.

"Shucks, Martha, even with the dangers and hardships, I bet you'd rather be here."

"Yes, Becky. I'm not sorry." I hesitated. "Becky, are you absolutely certain you want to marry Shiloh?

Is he the one you want to spend the rest of your life with?"

"Yep," she grinned. "He makes me feel real special. I never felt like that before. You know—like there's worms in your belly, and you want to do things you know you shouldn't 'til your married?"

"You are special, Becky," I said, patting her shoulder, "and if you're happy, I'm happy for you. We all are."

Suddenly, the hair on Tag's back raised up and he began to growl. "What is it, boy?"

"It's just Arbela's cat," Becky said, pointing across the way. "She's got it on a tether so it won't get lost."

"I'll be glad when this night is over," I admitted. "It's spooky."

"Me, too, but didn't Pete say the Indians might attack come daylight?"

I shuddered. I didn't want to think about that. I'd killed one man in my life. I didn't want to think of killing another one, even if it was an Indian.

The sun was peeking over the horizon, turning the sky scarlet, when Hattie and Charlie crawled out from under the wagon.

"Go get some sleep," Hattie said. You got a couple hours before we pull out."

"Thanks, Hattie." We crawled into their warm bedrolls.

CHAPTER TWENTY EIGHT

Laying in my bedroll under the wagon, I sniffed the bouquet of coffee that engulfed the camp every morning. Suddenly remembering the Indians, I listened and didn't hear any gunfire or war whoops, so I slipped out of my bedroll and went to the far side of the wagon to relieve my bladder, drawing back the privacy blanket. There stood Becky, looking aggravated as she pulled down her britches and squatted over a bucket.

"Damn, men got it made," she swore. "All they got to do is pull it out. We gotta bare our behind. Now we gotta empty the bucket."

"Sorry Becky," I laughed. Her earthy expressions always amazed me. I hoped she would change her mind about Shiloh. I knew he would try to change her, and we loved her just the way she was. I was really going to miss her.

"Come on, girls. We ain't got all day. Got to get movin'," Hattie called. "Drink your coffee, and take your biscuits with you. We're not out of the woods yet. Pete came by. Told me we didn't lose any stock, but those red heathens are still out there. Oh, and Martha, I fed your horses, so there ready to go."

"Thanks, Hattie. I'm ready." I hurriedly checked to make sure my fillies were securely tied, gulped the last of my coffee, grabbed a couple of biscuits, and climbed onboard Gray Lady. Pete rode at the head of the column and set a brisk pace, which we maintained all morning. He had the trooper riding with the girls on the line, encouraging the driver to keep moving. We halted at noon to rest and water the stock, taking the time for a cold lunch with no coffee. We had barely got moving again when the sound of bloodcurdling screams and the thunder of hoof beats reached our ears.

"Indians! Circle up! Circle up!" Pete yelled, racing from wagon to wagon. "Get those wagons in a circle!" Panicked drivers broke column and took their wagons in every direction. Dogs barked wildly, and cries of women and children filled the air. It was complete chaos. Guy and Morgan were yelling and trying to guide the wagons into a defensive circle. The Indians charged into our midst, yelling and flailing blankets to stampede the loose stock. The animals in harness bucked, trying to get loose. Arrows flew through the air, and the sound of firing weapons rang loudly.

"Got him," Becky hollered.

Hattie pulled our wagon near a large boulder-strewn plateau. "Get off your horses and take cover," she yelled.

I slid off Lady and hunkered behind a rock. Quickly I tied my horse to the brush. I saw Harley take an arrow in the chest and slump to the ground. Twelve-year-old Gerald Perkins, the brother of Darrell who died, ran out from between the wagons, picked up the dropped rifle, and fired.

"Gerald! Get back here. You'll be killed!" Jane screamed. The boy ignored her, continuing to fire at the attackers. Becky rolled in next to me with both guns blazing. It seemed to me that a savage fell with every shot.

"Good Heavens," I thought, "how many are there and why do they keep on coming?"

They galloped by in a wild blur of vivid colors. Pete had apparently given up trying to get the wagons in a circle. Along with a few of his crew, he crouched behind the wagons and fired at the savages. Charlie came galloping up, slid to a halt, and then jumped off, quickly tying her horse to mine. Crouching beside me, she began firing her rifle.

Hattie looked up from her position in the wagon boot. "Where are Sara and Polly?" she yelled at me.

"Sara's under the wagon with James. They're okay," I called. "James is with them." I was relieved to see he had her behind a box and was hovered over her with a gun in each hand.

Turning back to the battle, I was alarmed to see Ashley Johnson running into the skirmish, screaming incoherently.

"Ashley, come back!" her grandmother shouted, chasing after her.

"Velma, go back! I'll fetch her," Hattie yelled. She jumped out of the wagon and began running after Ashley. Staying low, Hattie managed to grab the girl. Hattie kept running, bringing Ashley along and heading for cover, when an arrow hit Ashley in the thigh. The child screamed and fell to the ground. Hattie picked her up and carried her to a wagon.

I watched as Hattie ran back to Velma, who had either fainted or been wounded. Hattie reached down to pick up the fallen woman, and then I stared in horror as an arrow struck Hattie.

Both Charlie and Becky let loose with a barrage of bullets, and several Indians fell to the ground. I took off running for Hattie. Pete reached her before I did. Together, we managed to get Hattie, Velma, and Ashley to our wagon.

Then as quickly as it started, the Indians turned and rode off. Minutes passed, and nerves were strained as we waited for another charge. Pete walked out in the open, and slowly others moved from behind their cover. Things seemed fairly quiet. The Indians had stopped charging us, and there was only sporadic firing. Many of the wounded were brought to our wagon. With the help of Charlie and several other women, the wounded were taken care of.

Hattie was lucky. The arrow had entered her arm, going clear through but missed the bone. Hattie sat on a box while Charlie cut the shaft of the arrow and drove it through her arm and then poured alcohol in the wound and bandaged it. Hattie flinched with pain as the alcohol seeped into the wound.

"Lucky it ain't my shootin' arm," Hattie said, putting on a brave smile. "Ashley okay?"

"She'll be fine. It's just a flesh wound. That was the strangest thing. The arrow went through her dress, slips, bloomers and stopped in her leg, but it was just a deep scratch. That was a mighty brave thing you done, goin' after her," Charlie said.

"I couldn't believe it. What possessed that little girl to run out like that?" I asked.

"Just plumb terrified, I reckon," Hattie said "Young 'uns and animals, you never know what they'll do when they're scared."

Sara walked up, carrying Polly. Sara's face was white, streaked with dirt, and she was shaking. Polly, on the other hand, seemed to think it had been a show put on for her benefit.

"You alright?" I asked.

"I'm fine now. James helped us get under the wagon." She put Polly down. The toddler immediately started towards the dead body of a fallen Indian.

"Polly, no." Sara grabbed her and held her back. "James is taking care of our mules. Someone's wagon turned over, and I saw a mule down. I think he was dead."

"Sara, sit down," Charlie said. Reaching into the back of our wagon, she pulled out a bottle. Here, drink this," she said, handing her a cup with some whiskey to drink. "Calm down. It's over now."

"I'm going to take a look," I said, curious about the war paint. "I've never seen an Indian up close." I walked over by the dead Indian less than six feet away.

"I'm gonna get a tomahawk and a bow and arrow," said Becky.

Six Women West

Pete rode up, slid off his horse, and went straight to Hattie. "You okay, girl?"

"It's just a scratch," she told him.

Charlie handed Pete a cup. "Thanks, girl. Whiskey's just what I needed. It was a hell of a place to get hit, right out in the open with no cover and these people panicking like they did. We're lucky we didn't all get killed. I got to get these wagons ready to roll before they come back." Pete shook his head and swallowed the rest of the drink.

"We lose anybody?" asked Hattie.

"Harley. Arrow got him in the heart. He never had a chance. Alonzo is the other one. Neither one had family." Pete shook his head. They were single fellows on the way to the gold mines. I'll check their bags. See if they got people I should notify." He glanced at the rest of us. "You girls all okay?"

"Yeah, Pete, thanks for askin'," Becky said in a teasing manner. "Looked like all you cared about was Hattie."

"Girl," Pete retorted, "you got a smart mouth. Good thing you're such a fine shot." He grinned. "I'll hand it to you girls—you did as good as any man and better'n some of 'em." He got on his horse, started off, and then turned back. "Almost forgot to mention—a couple mules got hit."

"My Sugar got a powder burn on her rump, but she's alright," I told him.

The soldiers helped get the wagons upright and in a circle. "We'll keep here like this until we take care of the wounded and round up the stock," Pete said. "If we're lucky, the Indians didn't get 'em all."

He sent some of the men out looking for loose stock. Becky opted to go along. Other men moved the Indians' bodies off to the side and left them for the friends.

We buried Alonzo and Harley with a short service. Since both the Crane and Zinger families lost a mule, Pete gave them the dead men's mules.

> **Comment [CJH]:** Somewhere before this it might be good to mention that she has fully healed from her rib fractures and other injuries.

After the count, we found we'd lost six horses and several steers. I felt fortunate that I still had my fillies. Becky captured an Indian pony, which thrilled her no end.

Once everything was in order, Pete ordered us to get ready to move out. We traveled on through Red Rock Canyon to Ayres Natural Bridge. The red rock in the canyon was sandstone, and the rock formations in places were at least 300 feet tall like a great painting. The bridge was a work of art. Never had I seen a formation creating a natural crossing. We made the descent and followed the creek that had a sign—Le Prele Creek. There we made camp near the creek. Horsetail plants grew everywhere. The water was cold and clear, and there was plenty of good grass and cottonwood trees.

Pete called a meeting of all the drivers. He was very angry that the drivers didn't circle up but also understanding, telling us we weren't out of the woods yet. "They might be back," he warned. "We need to stay alert. You circle every night. Why didn't you circle up?" He frowned. "You all better learn to circle up when trouble hits, or you'll be losin' more than stock."

There was some muttering and shaking of heads, but in the end everyone agreed. Before dawn the train pulled out and headed for Ford Creek. Pete had told us it was about fifteen miles, making for a long hard day. We reached the creek near sun down. I would have been happy to camp before we crossed, but Pete said we had to cross first.

It proved a wretched crossing. The several small streams created sandbars where they joined together. Two hundred feet across total, parts of the creeks were three feet deep with large sharp rocks on the bottom and some shallow with sandbars where the water moved slowly, so the wagons sunk down and had to be unloaded and pulled across.

Six Women West

It was after dark when the last wagon was across. The stock was brought inside, and Pete posted guards. After supper folks crawled into or under their wagons and settled down for the night. Still leery of Indians, everyone kept their guns close at hand.

Towards morning, thunder shook the sky, and lightning struck again and again. I was certain we were in for a heavy downpour. I was wrong, though—it was a heat storm. We had awakened to another dreary day of dust and heat and sweat.

"It's like most fellers," Charlie laughed. "Lot of noise but no action."

For the next several days we traveled across the territory called Wyoming. You could see for miles any way you looked. There was yellow-brown grass on soft rolling hills in the distant. There were the huge mountains. There were always the antelopes, and once in awhile we would see a small buffalo herd. The sun baked our skin a dark brown. Even Sara began looking less like a lady of the manor. She still didn't do much riding, but with James' help she was turning into a good driver.

I commented to Hattie that the women on the wagons had finally accepted us. They stopped making snide remarks about us wearing britches and toting guns. "Somewhere along the trail, we earned their respect, and some of them are starting to be downright friendly."

"Shucks," Hattie said. "They saw the sense of it. Ain't you noticed some of them have gone to wearin' their husbands' britches?"

Pete rode by and announced we would spend the next couple of days at Red Buttes several miles ahead. We all needed the rest, including the stock. It wasn't a rest to lie around. While camped we would repair and clean our wagon, tend to our stocks' hoofs and shoes, mend the canvas, soak the wheels, do our wash as well as tend three families with head lice.

I was scouting up front with Morgan to locate a camp site for our rest, and we saw a family of Indians. "Let's ride up and see if they know where there's a good place to cross," Morgan suggested.

"What that they're pulling?"

"It's called a travois. They take two long poles and cover it with a hide. Then they put their belongings on it—or children. This family looks very poor."

Two small Indian children straddled the horse, while an old man and woman walked along side. They smiled shyly, indicating with hand signals they meant no harm. Morgan talked sign language with them and learned the old couple was the children's grandparents. The parents, they told him, were dead. They led us to a natural crossing at the river, and it was only three feet deep. Morgan invited them to camp with us.

Tall Man and Half Moon and the children, whose names were Sweet Grass and Red Clay, camped with us while we rested and then traveled with us several days. Half Moon made a set of buckskins in trade for Becky's Indian pony. They left the train five days later, happy with the new pony and grateful for the antelope meat and other food. I was glad for the opportunity to see for myself that Indians weren't all savages.

After a long day and roughly twelve miles, Pete called the train to a halt. "This is the start of Rock Avenue, and the next three miles is as dangerous as any trail we're gong to climb. After the climb we pass through some high narrow rocks then start down a pass a wagon can barely get through. I want everyone walking but the drivers and watch carefully. Any wagon that goes over that cliff is a goner for sure," he said. "Be careful and take it easy. Throw off those heirlooms."

Comment [CJH]: What Indian pony? Did she get one in the battle, or are we talking about Zeke that she traded to Hattie for Fudge? No pony was mentioned in the battle.

Six Women West

He wasn't exaggerating one whit! I'm sure everyone was as scared as I was. Except for the drivers and those of us on horseback, everyone walked, staying in back of the wagons as there wasn't room to walk beside them.

It was the longest three miles I ever rode. The drop-off was steep cliff and straight down at times. The view was vast—so much wilderness. The trail was so narrow, the wheels of the wagon sent pebbles and dirt over the side. Then we entered the narrow part called Rock Avenue with rocks straight up and jagged. It was hard to see the tops of them. It lasted a little over a quarter mile. Through all this, there were very little scrub brush. Finally, the last wagon finished crossing the trail safely. We left the pass. I was sure I could hear a collective sigh of relief and gratitude to Providence emanate from the train.

As we left the pass, Hattie said, "Look at that, Martha. It's the devil's backbone." She was pointing at a jagged ridge of rock formation. It was beautiful and scary at the same time. I pulled my horse to a halt and looked at it for a long time. Pete pulled up beside me and asked me to ride the line with a message—that we would keep going to Willow Springs, another twelve miles. It would be after dark when we made camp.

After finishing the ride I rode by our wagon and asked Hattie if she would like me to relieve her.

"Sure," she said. I swung aboard on the back of the wagon, tying my horse to the tailgate without stopping the wagon. I took her place on the seat, taking up the reins. Hattie stepped inside the wagon. Morgan rode up. "Okay if I ride with you awhile?"

"Sure," I said. "I'll give us twenty minutes before we start fighting."

He swung up on the wagon, and Hattie climbed out the back, untying my horse and dropping to the ground to ride my horse. I'll pick up your horse and tie him to the back," she said. "You two behave yourselves." Then she rode off to find Pete.

Morgan settled down next to me, too close for my comfort. He confused my feeling and thoughts when he got close to me.

Grinning, he said, "Well, we don't have to fight. We both know you're crazy in love with me, so you try to cover up by arguing."

I snapped the reins, resisting the urge to yell. "You, my friend, are an egotistical fool in love with yourself," I stated with controlled calmness. "If you think I'm in love with you, you're the one who's crazy." I stared off across the plains, looking at dry grass and sagebrush.

Who I am kidding? I asked myself silently. *He's right. I am crazy about him. Would I ever admit it to him? Never! It was bad enough that I admitted it to myself.*

"Martha, as much as I'd like to, I didn't come up here to talk about our courting." He looked at me, his expression serious. I didn't know if I was disappointed or relieved.

"A dispatch rider came in from Fort Laramie late last night. Said they just got the word from Fort Kearny that the army payroll had been stolen. Two men were shot. One died on the spot. The other one was far gone enough so the thief apparently figured he didn't have to waste another bullet, but this man pulled through, so he can identify the thief."

"Why warn us? Do they think he's on our train?"

"They didn't say he was. We just need to be on the lookout."

I felt my heart skip a beat. What about Sara's driver? I shook my head in denial, remembering how he had risked his life protecting Sara and Polly during the Indian attack. In my head, I silently ran through the families on the train. I couldn't put a killer's face on any of the men. "I don't suppose it could be one of the Riley boys?"

"Who are they?"

"That's right—they left the train before you joined us." It was funny, but I was finding it hard to remember Morgan hadn't always been with us. "They were a bad bunch," I continued. "I do believe any of the older ones would be capable of murder."

"You haven't seen them around have you?"

"No. You're not thinking it's one of the men?" I shook my head. "I can't believe that. I mean, they have their families to consider."

"No, I guess I can't picture any of these men robbing and killing." He reached over and patted my knee. "Martha, just keep your ears open. If you hear or see anything strange, let me or Pete know. Tell the other women to be careful."

"The only strange thing I've heard lately is what Prissy told me. Daisy is going to have puppies, and Tag is the papa."

"Congratulations. Make sure you get a couple of the pups. You'll need some mothering experience if you plan to do a good job with our young ones." He jumped off the wagon before I could hit him.

"If you think for one minute I'm going to bear you children, you better think again," I yelled, not caring who heard me.

"That's all I do think about," he murmured, just loud enough for me to hear.

Darn him, I swore silently. *He wasn't my type—too bossy. Sure, he was handsome and he did kiss nice, but...* I felt my face go all red.

"Haw! Gad-up, mules!" I yelled, cracking the reins." Dust flew, and I hoped some of it landed on Morgan. Despite my agitation, I couldn't stop thinking about him, remembering how his arms felt and how his kisses made me feel. I often thought about the incident at Labante Creek when he kissed me. *Maybe,* I decided, *a fellow like Morgan just made for good memories, but not marriage.*

We were lucky with the long days of summer that there was plenty of daylight left. It was hot and dusty coming across the trail to Willow Springs, but once we entered the valley there were cool breezes blowing, bringing the scent of moist green grass. The creek fed the underground springs and kept the valley cool and green. I could hardly wait to get camped and go for a cool swim. The water looked cool, and the brush growing near the bank made shade across the water. I just knew it would be cool. I pulled our wagon into the circle and jumped down, grabbing my necessities pack and a change of clothes. "Goin' for a swim," I called to Sara, who had stepped down from her wagon. "Be back soon." Charlie and Becky rode in as I was heading out.

"You want company?" they asked.

I waited while they grabbed their things. "You didn't bring back any meat this time out," I remarked, noting they had come back empty-handed.

"Nope, it's too hot for game to be out. Didn't see a thing except for a couple jackrabbits, an' they got away from us," Charlie said, shrugging. "Guess we'll have to settle for beans and biscuits tonight." We started to mount up.

Hattie yelled out, "You girls wait just a damn minute. You know you take care of this team first. You water and take them to pasture, and then you take care of your needs."

We stopped. "Sorry, Hattie," we said in unison. We took care of the team, knowing we were wrong to leave them hitched no matter how hot and tired we were.

Fifteen minutes later we mounted up and headed down Willow Creek, walking through the tall prairie grass. We found a nice spot with bushy green willow trees for good cover while we took turns keeping an eye out as we stripped to our bloomers. We bathed and played in the cool clear water for close to an hour. We got into a water fight and wound up dunking each other 'til we were half-drowned. It felt good to be so carefree, if only for an hour.

"Lord have mercy, this feel good!" Becky exclaimed, swimming in the cool water.

Laughing, we climbed out, dried off, and got dressed. We were halfway back to the wagon before I remembered to mention what Morgan had said. "I forgot to tell you that Morgan told me that there may be a killer on the train."

"What!" Charlie and Becky stopped dead in their tracks. "What's he mean?"

Moving in close I told them. "Well, it seems a soldier was killed bringing the army payroll into Fort Kearny. Another soldier was wounded, and they say he can identify the killer."

"Did he get the money?" Becky asked.

"I believe so."

"When did all this happen?" Charlie asked.

"Back before we got to Fort Kearny," I said.

"And Morgan says it's somebody on this train?" Becky's eyes were round with curiosity.

"Well, if the Riley boys were still with us, I'd say it was them," Charlie said, frowning. "You know, the other day when I was out huntin', I felt like somebody was watchin' me." She shuddered. "Made me real nervous."

"Maybe you should mention it to Morgan or Pete," I said.

At camp Bessie and Sara had a hindquarter turning on a spit over the campfire.

"Where'd that come from?" Becky asked.

"Mr. Pete say dis here deer jes jump right up smack dab in front a him."

"It was a good-sized mule deer, so we shared it with some of the camp. We took the Prices a large roast. That couple is hanging on by a hook and a prayer." Hattie said. "You girls all finished swimming and cooled off?" We nodded. "You can keep an eye on the camp we go wash some of the dirt off us?"

"Sure," I said. Charlie and Becky nodded. Sara gathered up Polly, and the four of them headed for the creek. "For some reason I think Hattie's displeased with us."

"Maybe it's cause we went swimming before camp was made. That wasn't fair to leave her to set up camp. It's not like when Bessie and Sara was here too."

"That's right. We better talk to her about it," I answered.

Morgan rode up. Trickles of water ran down his face. He brushed back wet hair and grinned. "Just got back from a dip in the creek. Ran into some dust a ways back." He paused and winked at me. "Mind if I join you?"

"Sure," Becky said, smiling. I glanced away, mad at myself for feeling so glad to see him.

"Say, Morgan, Martha told us about the killer on the train," Charlie said. "I was tellin' her I thought somebody was watchin' me the other day when I was huntin'. Think it could've been him?"

"Don't know," Morgan said, "but you ladies shouldn't be goin' out alone least ways 'til we find him."

"Doesn't seem likely he'd be stickin' around if he's got a bunch of money," Charlie said.

"You're right," Morgan agreed. "But until we know for sure, you girls be careful, okay?"

"Okay."

Hattie, Sara, and Polly walked up, looking clean and refreshed.

"Where's Bessie?" I asked.

Six Women West

"Oh, she went to see about Abel," Sara said. "Goodness, that water felt nice. Polly didn't want to get out." She grinned and hugged the little girl. "You're a little fish, aren't you, sweetie?"

"Fis," Polly echoed.

"How's the meat coming?" Hattie asked, probing it with a long stick.

"Should be awhile longer. About an hour, I think," I said. "Hattie, I want to say I'm sorry for running off so fast. That was wrong."

"Forget it Martha. It was a hard day, and we all forget at times."

Morgan looked at me. "In that case, would you care to walk to the top of the ridge?" He pointed to a small hill. "It's a little cooler now. We can eat after we get back."

"With you?" I asked.

"Well, that's what I had in mind."

"What else do you have in mind?" Becky teased.

"Now, Miss Becky, you're going to get me in trouble, talkin' like that. I'm having a hard enough time convincing Martha of my honorable intentions without your help."

"Go on, Martha," Hattie said. "Don't pay no never mind to either of them. The walk will do you good after sittin' so long. And thanks for takin' my turn driving today."

I wanted to say yes, and I wanted to say no. Reasoning that I would seem unfriendly saying no, I said yes.

"Good," Hattie said. "Take your time."

"Don't do anythin' I wouldn't do," Becky taunted.

"Well, I guess that gives us a lot of leeway, don't it, little missy?" Morgan told her.

Not with me, it doesn't, I retorted silently. Ignoring his outstretched hand, I shoved my hands in my pockets. He chuckled but didn't say anything.

We walked a safe distance apart. "You like this country?" he asked.

"Well, it's not as pretty as where I came from, but here at the springs it's a nice green valley and smells of damp grass along the river. I hear the summers are real hot all the way to Oregon."

"Not according to Ma. She says we'll run into real mountains and pine trees, and in Oregon it's green where her ranch is, and there are tall cedar trees, and it's not too far from the Pacific Ocean. They get plenty of rain."

"I guess you have a lot to look forward to," I said. "I mean, sharing a life with your ma and meeting a brother you didn't know you had."

"Yeah," Morgan nodded, a lock of his hair fell across his brow, and I resisted the urge to brush it back.

"Yeah, life has really taken a turn. I'd always had the hope I'd find Ma, but I'd about given up." He shook his head. "Now, I've not only got my ma but a brother as well. Why, I've just about got everything I ever wanted."

Just about, I thought. I silently wondered about a wife and babies.

"Well, if things go the way I want them to, I'll have me a horse ranch with some fine Appaloosas."

"Won't you just share the ranch with Colton?"

"In a way, but everything I ever got I had to work for. I want to build my own spread with my own hands. I'm the kind of man that has to earn what he gets. I'd always have the feeling the ranch belong to him. I would be a trespasser. A man has to earn what he gets."

We reached the top of the ridge. I felt like I could touch the sky in the late afternoon breeze, so refreshing and cool with the scattered trees and green grass. I stood staring down at the pasture below. It was a natural corral for the stock. As I looked closer, I gasped in horror. Morgan's stallion was mounting my chestnut mare! I started down the hill in a mad dash, Morgan following close behind.

"Stop that! Damn it! Morgan, make him stop!" I shouted.

"Don't be silly, Martha. There's no way we can stop him." He chuckled. "Besides she's not objecting."

"You idiot! He'll ruin my mare. She's too young. Why didn't you hobble him?"

"I'm sorry, but you've been around horses. You know there's no stopping a stallion."

Raindrop dismounted and took off triumphantly, tossing his head. "We'll take the mare to your wagon," Morgan offered. "I'll get Raindrop and tie him up."

"A little late, wouldn't you say?" I said sarcastically. "This is entirely your fault for keeping him around my mares."

"Look, Martha, it's no more my fault than yours. Remember, we agreed to keep them together because of wild animals."

Ignoring the truth of that remark, I shouted, "I'm holding you responsible if anything bad happens to her. The best I can hope for is she'll drop the foal before it's time."

Morgan grabbed my arm. "You don't mean that! He's top stock, and she's a nice mare. They'd have a great foal."

"Nice? You said nice?" I swung around, placed my hands on my hips and stuck my nose in his face. "Boots is not just nice. She's blooded stock from Kentucky. She's too good for that, that horse of yours."

"Oh, like you're too good for me?"

Morgan pushed his hat back and glared at me. "Well, for your information, Miss High-and-Mighty, Raindrop has the blood of champions from the Spanish Conquistadors. They brought the most magnificent horses from Spain to this country. He's an Appaloosa." His tone softened. It was obvious he cared as much about his horse as I did about mine.

"His foals will have the hearts of lions," Morgan continued. "And size and heart are what count in this country. Not thin spindly legs that have to be wrapped just to get where they're goin'."

I grabbed Boot's halter and began walking away. "You don't know anything about bloodlines, Morgan Brooks, just like you don't know anything about women!"

"Well, I know when a woman acts like a child, and I know why," he retorted. "When you get around to admitting you want me as much as I want you, then you're going to see lots of things different."

Raindrop had returned and was making a beeline for Boots. "Get him out of here!" I yelled. Boots tossed her head and stamped her feet. She danced around, acting as confused and agitated as I felt. I didn't want him to lure her into the wilds for their mating.

Morgan grabbed Raindrop's mane and pulled him away from Boots. He managed to get him to a tree where he double-tied him. The stallion nickered, calling to the mare.

"Come on, Boots. Come on," I urged, tugging at her halter. I returned to camp feeling angry and frustrated, not sure where my anger was directed—at Morgan, his stallion, or myself for letting his words get to me.

"How was the walk?" Hattie asked, interrupting my thoughts.

"Just lovely," I said.

"Good," Hattie said, not noticing my sarcasm. "I'm so glad you and Morgan are getting along. Where is he?"

"He's with that Appaloosa," I snapped, unable to hide my irritation. "I have to tie Boots up."

Six Women West

Hattie leaned her head towards sound coming from the demanding stallion neighing from the pasture. "Is that Raindrop?"

"I suppose." I stopped and stared at her. "Damn it, Hattie. He mounted Boots. What am I going to do? She's too young. Morgan should have kept his stallion away from her."

"Now, Martha, how was he to do that? There are no barns with stalls out here in the wilderness. Your mare's in season. Raindrop is a stallion. Nature will take its course whether you approve or not." She patted my shoulder. "You got to admit it'll be a darn good foal."

I shook my head. *Didn't they understand the importance of bloodlines and breeding?* I tied Boots to the back of the wagon. She obviously was not happy with the arrangement. Like me, she could hear the stallion's calls. She whinnied in response, stamping and tossing her head.

"I know how you feel, Boots, wanting what you can't have. Believe me, I know how you feel," I whispered reluctantly as I hugged her neck.

Morgan didn't join us for supper, and I was torn between relief and disappointment. That evening we sat around talking about the fellow who'd robbed and killed the soldiers. None of us could imagine anyone on the train doing it.

With Raindrop and Boots calling out to each other, it turned out to be a long night with little sleep. Exhausted and short-tempered, we hit the trail early the next morning without a civil word between anybody.

CHAPTER TWENTY NINE

Midmorning found us about a mile from a place called Prospect Hill. Guy and Morgan had stopped by to give us the low-down on what we faced. Morgan was riding his army gelding.

"Where's Raindrop? I asked.

"Thought I'd give him a rest. He's tied behind the army wagon at the back of the train. He smiled and winked. "I wouldn't want him getting into any more mischief."

Hattie broke in and said, "Think I'll ride up and take a look at the hill." She turned to Charlie. "Could you take over drivin' the wagon?"

"Hattie, do you mind if I ride with you?" I asked.

Arriving at the base of the hill, I stared up at the rocky climb. "Golly, that looks like a real challenge," I admitted. We rode on up to the top, and from that area of Prospect Hill there was a good view of the Sweetwater Range. "Morgan had said this was where he had plans to build a ranch. What a beautiful area!" The valley was rich in green grass that grew belly high to a horse and cool creeks, a paradise for horses—you could tell by the abundance of antelope and deer.

"We better start back. It ain't goin' to be easy, and this damnable heat won't make it any easier," Hattie said, shaking her head. "It's about four hundred feet straight up. It's near solid rock. We have to stay on the hogback, or we slide in the gulley."

"I'm sure glad you've done this before."

"Yeah, but that doesn't mean it'll be any easier. We're lucky we're ridin' with a good crew."

We returned to the wagon, and I held the horses while Hattie and Charlie traded places. When Charlie had mounted, she turned to me. "Come with me? Pete came by and told me he'd be up front, and for me to ride drag."

"Sure." We rode to the end of the train. All the wagons were moving right along, giving Charlie and me a chance to talk.

"How are you and Luke getting along?" I asked.

"Swell. He's so darn nice. I don't feel good enough for a man like him."

"Good enough?" I exclaimed. "Charlie, you're one of the best people I know. Get that not-good-enough thinking out of your head."

"Thanks, Martha." She sighed deeply. "But with my past, a man's sure to think twice about marrying me. A squeeze, yes. Not a wife."

"Look, the past is just that—the past. There's nothing you can do about that. Besides, you were just a child when you met Jessie. He hung you out to dry. Put you in a situation where you had no choice. Charlie, we all have something in our past we're ashamed of. I'm going to tell you this because I know you will never tell anyone else. I killed a man who tried to rape and blackmail me into marrying him to get control of my farm. I'm not proud of it, and I ran. I'm not going to let it spoil my life."

"I would have never guessed you could have done that. I'm sure you had no choice, and I understand how it can happen. You make what happened to me sound alright, but I'm not sure Luke or any other man would see it that way." She shook her head and slapped her horse's hindquarters. "Thanks for comin' with me, Martha. I got to go meet Luke now. See you later."

"Remember what I told you, Charlie," I called after her. "And keep an eye out for strangers." I rode back to the wagon and rode behind it as Hattie cautiously followed the wagons ahead of us. The trail was so narrow the wheels slipped over the side, and Hattie struggled to keep the mules from bolting. As each wagon carefully made the trek up the rocky

Wanda Reed

ridge, some had front riders to lead their mules. There was an overall sense of relief when the last wagon finally reached the high point.

I sat on Lady and enjoyed the vast view of the Sweetwater Mountains. It was easy to understand why Morgan would be so impressed with this country—it was beautiful. Covered with lush green trees and framed by blue sky with buttermilk clouds, it was a sight to behold. I wondered if Oregon was as pretty, but I hoped the weather was cooler in Oregon.

Becky rode up, interrupting my thoughts. "Will you ride a ways with me? Maybe we could go hunting."

"Sure, let's ride on down into the valley," I nudged Lady. Instinctively, I knew there was more to Becky's request than a need for company to go hunting. We followed a game trail leading down the hill to a creek, then climbed off the horses and settled down in the brush to watch for game. "This place smells like sage. Guess it's these bushes. Becky, what's bothering you?" I whispered.

"Martha, it's Shiloh. I don't understand him. You know what men are like."

"Has he changed his mind about marriage?" I asked hopefully. Sorry as I would be for Becky, my relief if they broke up would be greater.

"No, but, well, he said if I really loved him I wouldn't make him wait, you know? The marital rights."

I thought immediately of Charlie and Jesse. "Oh, Becky, I admit I don't know much about men, but someone once told me all men will try to taste the honey. Now it seems to me if he really loved you, he'd respect you enough to wait. Besides, we're only a couple of hundred miles from the fort. Just ten or twelve days—that's not far. Surely he can wait that long. I feel he's trying to pressure you into something you're not ready to do."

> **Comment [CJH]:** This is part of what makes me wish the end of the book were different. See note on the last page.

Six Women West

"Well, that's another problem. Shiloh says it might be a few months before the traveling chaplain gets there."

"There's not a chaplain? Let's chop this up. First: he wants to have marriage rights. Second: there was a chaplain. Three: now there not. Four: What would happen if you got with child? Five: How would Shiloh handle that? Six: Would he stand by you? Seven: Why didn't he want to get married at Fort Laramie if he knew there was only a traveling chaplain for Fort Bridger?"

"Oh, Martha, I don't know. I think I love him, but I don't know that much about love," she admitted tearfully.

"Becky, think about what we talked about, and don't make a decision for at least a week." If I'd been honest I would have told her she probably knew as much about it as I did, but she was looking to me for advice, so I kept silent about my ignorance.

Suddenly a small herd of antelope appeared on the other side of the creek. Apparently unaware of our presence, they began to drink. Becky touched my arm and pointed to the herd. The problems with Shiloh were put aside as we aimed and fired. Two antelopes fell. By the time we'd finished dressing them out and rolling the hides, I could hear the wagon train rolling into sight. Pete was leading and came over by us.

"See you girls got your dinner. Noon break," Pete yelled. The wagons came into sight and circled up in the meadow next to the creek.

Becky and I were elbow deep in cleaning the antelope when Shiloh rode up and dismounted. He ignored me, speaking directly to Becky. "Come on. Let's go for a walk. We need to talk."

"I need to wash up first." She held out her hands. "See, I'm all bloody."

"Just wash them in the creek," he said, shaking his head. "I can't figure why you hunt anyway. We got men to do that, and I've told you I want you to start dressing and acting like a lady and to talk proper."

"Huntin' is my job, and I'm good at it," Becky retorted, rinsing her hands and wiping them on her britches. "I won't be gone long," she said to me.

I could guess what Shiloh wanted, and I hoped she would take into account what we'd talked about. I didn't like the way he talked to her. As they walked away, he reached for her hand. She pulled it away. *A good sign*, I thought. I threw the dressed meat over my saddle and walked Lady and Fudge over to our wagon. Bessie and Sara had our noon meal ready. Hattie was holding Polly and doing patty cake.

"Meat for supper," I announced, feeling somewhat proud that I had made a contribution. "We'll give a hindquarter to the Prices. This looks like only half the troops. Where's everybody else?"

"Charlie came by. Said she'd be eaten' with Luke. Abel's doin' somethin' with Pete. They'll be by later."

"Boy, the sage bushes really smell the place up," I said, wrinkling my nose.

"Yassum, ah done gathered up some," Bessie said. "It do smell somepun' fierce, but it's good for cookin' with. If y'all bring me wild turkey or some prairie chickens, ah could fix up some dressing dat'd make your mouth water."

Pete and Abel rode up and dismounted, "See you brought home some meat for supper. Did you shoot both of them?"

"No, Becky was with me. She got one. This sure is muggy weather," I said, looking at Pete and Hattie.

"It sure is. If I was in Oklahoma, I'd be lookin' for a twister," said Pete.

"But not here, right?" I said.

"No, not likely," Hattie laughed. "This is just heat, and maybe a thunderstorm will come out of it. That's all."

"Dis stew won't get no doner. Y'all better get y'all's plates." Bessie said, calling us to lunch.

We had fixed our plates and were enjoying our lunch when Becky showed up without Shiloh and started dipping herself a plate of stew. She didn't say anything, and I didn't expect her to in front of everyone. I assumed she would tell me later if she wanted me to know.

"We need to wash the water barrels and rinse them with vinegar and refill them" said Hattie. "Charlie, Becky and Martha, would you take that chore?"

"Alright Hattie." After lunch we took the water barrels down to the creek with a jug of vinegar and cleaned the six barrels. It was heavy work, and sweat was dripping off us by the time we were done. Sara drove the wagon down to the creek to pick up the barrels. I looked at Sara, so small, and knew why she was never asked to do heavy work. Immediately I was sorry for such thoughts. She did her share by cooking, washing, keeping the wagons clean, and sewing. Abel helped lift the barrels back onto the wagons, and then we filled them with buckets of fresh water. We started across, being extra careful to keep the stock out and alkali deposits. The air was hot and heavy with sinister dark clouds in the distant.

With everyone rested and refreshed from our extended noon at the creek, the wagons headed for Independence Rock where we would camp. We could see the huge, turtle-shaped, granite rock looming high miles before we reached it. Hattie said it was at least a hundred feet high and over two thousand feet long. One of the many good things about Hattie was that she shared what she knew and had experienced. We learned a lot from her. I really enjoyed the times like today when we shared the driving. She talked a lot about Morgan then and how happy she was to have him back in her life.

I never said much when she talked about him. I didn't know what to say. Sharing my feelings with another woman was one thing, but with his mother? I didn't feel comfortable doing that. Still, I did enjoy listening to her.

It was now mid-July, and the wagon train was over two weeks behind. If everything had gone right, we would've been at Fort Bridger instead of out here in the middle of Wyoming territory. Not only was it in the middle of nowhere, there was nothing but scrub sage and a few outcrops of rocks that pushed up out of the earth just like Independence Rock. It was a harsh land where only the strong survived. Mostly lizards and snakes. The days had been usually hot and humid this past week, but I wasn't prepared for this searing heat. Taking a breath was like inhaling fire. Nothing moved except the heat waves shimmering in the distance.

"Let's hurry up and find some shade." Beads of sweat trickled down between my breasts, and my shirt was plastered to my skin.

"No, keep them at a walk. They're hot too. We'll be stopping for a break before long."

I shook my head to clear my vision. I was feeling dizzy and disoriented.

"Better climb inside, girl. You don't look too good," Hattie said. "Get some salt and water. You're gettin' sun sick."

"I'll be alright," I answered back as I reached for the canteen. I was lying, not wanting to seem like a weakling. I took a long drink.

Suddenly a dirt clod flew by my head. I turned, and Charlie threw another one.

"Wake up!" she yelled.

"Who's sleeping?" I yelled back.

Comment [CJH]: As a reader and knowing they're racing against winter, I really like to know when it is. What about adding at least the month to the beginning of each chapter except the personal story chapters?

"Look at those thunderheads!" She pointed upward. We watched as lightning flashed across the sky.

"Maybe we'll get some rain," I said hopefully as the lightning strikes increased and the wind started to gust. An enormous black cloud began to take shape in the sky a mile or more ahead of us.

Pete came galloping by, yelling, "Twister comin'! Find some cover!"

Hattie's face went white and took on a scared look. "Come on and help unhitch the mules," she yelled. Becky, come help. Martha, get the picket pins and rope. Hurry, girls. Becky, take them mules up behind the rocks."

Morgan raced by on the other side. "Twister comin'. Take cover up in the rocks."

Pete rode by again, yelling orders at everyone. "Unhitch the stock and get them to cover. Tie the wagons down." Pete yelled at us, "Better get up behind the rocks and lay belly down. Try to get in a crevice."

I hurried to help get ropes on the wagon, and using the picket pins we staked down the wagon. Hail the size of small stones pelted us without mercy while we finished tying the wagon down. The wind increased at an unbelievable speed. I saw several people fall trying to get to safety. Hattie and I led all the horses to the safety of the rocks. After that I lost track of everyone and just hoped they made it to safety. I watched the force of the wind lifting brush, and anything else that wasn't tied down become airborne. Wind and dirt mixed with the rain and hail covered everything in sight like a dirty blanket. The roar of the wind was deafening.

Momentarily the funnel came into view. I stood transfixed, watching the black monster move across the plains, wondering if it would suck us up never to be seen again. Had I traveled all this way to die here? Out of nowhere, Morgan appeared and pushed me down into a crevice in the rocks. Covering me with his body, he yelled, "Stay down!" I listened, terrified at the thunderous roar of the tornado as it passed over us. I was so scared I couldn't tell if it was me or the earth shaking. I clung to the ground, grateful for the protection of Morgan's body. Glancing up, I saw a wagon canvas break loose and a man chase after it. I heard screams as the man grabbed hold of the canvas and was pulled into the air. Why he didn't let go, I'll never know. He disappeared into the blackness. Morgan stroked my hair and was talking to me, and I realized it was me who was screaming. What a terrible price he paid for a bit of canvas!

Then, almost as quickly as it had come, the tornado was gone. The sound of babies crying and women calling out to their families and friends filled the stillness. Morgan climbed off me and helped me stand.

"Are you alright?" he asked. I noticed an unfamiliar tremor in his voice.

"I'm fine," I lied. "Thank you. It was foolish of me to be standing, but I was dumbstruck. I've never seen a tornado before."

"Glad I spotted you." He grinned. "Have to admit I kind of liked holding you so close." His hands still shaking, I knew it was to cover being scared.

I shook my head. "Is that all you think about? Can't you be a gentleman?" I bantered back, helping to cover the moment.

"I have no intentions of being a gentleman—just a rancher and a husband." He reached out and brushed some stray hair from my face. "If I can keep you safe."

"Ever' body okay?" Pete called loudly. "Check your families. Check your stock. Make sure they're all here."

Six Women West

I ran to Pete, "I saw some man fly away," I voiced. "He grabbed hold of a canvas and didn't let go. He just vanished. I couldn't tell who it was. It was horrible. The wind took him like a stick."

Everyone came slowly out of their hiding places and gathered around in front of the rocks. There was shock on most of the faces. After awhile everyone was accounted for but one.

"Jake Arnold's not here!" Moe yelled. "Can't find him nowhere."

Many of the family had walked back toward their wagon to see what was left. "You single men" Pete said, "form a search party to look for him. Matt Holt, you lead the search."

"We better find Ma and see if she's alright," Morgan said, taking my arm. We hurried to the wagon. She was there looking after anyone who had showed up. Everyone seemed to be gathering around our wagon. The women were dirty and scared but not hurt. "I'll go get the horses," Morgan said, "and see if I can find the mules." He was back in no time leading six horses. I tied them nose to tail so they couldn't run away, but the mules were gone. They were still in harness." I petted my horses and cried, I was so relieved they were safe. "Thank you, thank you so much Morgan. But what will we do without mules?"

"They most likely just ran off. They'll be rounded up. I got to go help now. Ma, you and Martha going to be alright for awhile?"

"Yes, son, we'll just straighten up here. Go on and tend to the others."

No wagons had been lost, but they had suffered damage. A couple of them lay on their sides with their canvasses torn off and contents blown away. Sara and Polly were both pale and shaken but not hurt. Guy, along with James, had guided them to large rocks, affording good protection. Bessie and Abel were as ashen as black people could be. Abel went with Morgan to help with the wagons. Bessie made coffee with shaking hands, inviting everyone to have a cup. The canvas was blown off Sara's wagon, and she was busy picking up her stuff, making a game of it for Polly. Some of the other women and children gathered up strewn articles and went from wagon to wagon to find the owners. The loss of food and supplies would hurt us, but we could replace as much as possible at Fort Bridger.

Charlie set up a box and took care of all the cuts and bruises. Hattie and Pete made sure everyone else was accounted for. Becky joined the search party led by Billy and Tommy to find the stock. Becky returned later, leading Charlie's horse, and our mules were still in harness. We caught them about two miles out. They were all together. Tommy and Billy brought them all in. They're plumb tuckered," she said, laughing. "Thought I was gonna have to carry 'em back."

Folks, gather around for prayer" Frank Warren said. "We thank the Lord for our safety and the hands of Providence that have delivered us this far and continue to keep us safe to Oregon or California." "Amen" was said in unison. The stock was tired as well as all the people, but we hitched up and moved another five miles and camped on the tall grass banks of the Sweetwater River across from Independence Rock.

Becky and I took a few minutes and rode down to the base of the big rock. "Look," Becky said. "A huge black granite rock settin' right in the middle of sand. Nothin' but scrub brush and a lone dwarf pine.

"Look at the names carved in the stone," I said. "Let's climb up and carve our names, so anybody that reads it will know we made it this far."

"Okay," Becky agreed, sliding off her horse. "It's sort of a spiritual feeling knowin' our names will be here long after we're gone. It'll be proof we was here."

Her words gave me goose bumps. The thought that we would be part of history was exciting. There were already several people from the wagons carving their names on the rock. With all the laughter, it was hard to believe we had just gone through a tornado. I wondered if the search party got back and if they found Jake. We finished carving our names and the date and climbed back down. We decided to walk back to camp and lead our horses across the sand and brush.

"How is it going with Shiloh and the marriage bed?" I asked.

"Oh, we've had some words and I let him know that we have to wait until we're married, and if a preacher don't show up we keep on waiting. I sure don't need a baby with the way I dress and talk. It may not work out."

"Good for you. How did he take it?" As we got nearer to the river, there was spots of grass.

"He sure as hell didn't like it. He said I didn't really love him." She took a deep breath. "I got mad, too, and tried to leave. He grabbed my arm real tight and wouldn't let go. We yelled at each other for awhile. Then we didn't talk and he cooled off." Shrugging, she added. "We kissed and made up, but I'm still not givin' in."

"Has he ever struck you, Becky?"

"Well, he's not my husband yet, but he's come close." She laughed. "Boy, being a woman is a lot of trouble. I think I was better off being a boy."

"Becky, in my family men didn't hit women, so I don't believe they have a right to. That is something you will have to talk about with Shiloh. I hope you don't believe it's alright for a man to hit a woman. As you've probably guessed, I don't know much about men, but I know that no man will hit me ever. I've learned a few things just listening," I said, choosing my words carefully. "Seems men just think of the now and don't concern themselves much with the future. It's the woman who has to worry about what happens if she gets in the family way. She's the one who has to face the humiliation and disgrace of bearing a woods colt." I shook my head. "And, even more important, the child is branded a bastard."

Becky's face took on a mask of anger. "I know how I was raised, and I don't want that for my child. Young 'uns need two parents." Her mouth twisted. "I could tell you what it's like bein' a kid without a proper home. Folks didn't think Pa should be raisin' me by himself, but he wouldn't give me up." She stopped walking and stared at me, as if willing me to understand. "He was strict, but he was fair, and my pa never hit me, and no husband of mine will either."

"Your mother died, Becky?"

"Naw, she was a saloon woman. Run off with some drifter. Never did see her again."

"Maybe you'll be like Morgan and run into her on the trail."

"Don't know that I want to. Don't remember much about her. No kid of mine will ever grow up without a Ma," she said firmly.

"Good for you, Becky. You'll make a fine mother." I smiled and patted her shoulder. "Shiloh will come around and respect you for saying no. He'll see that it's for the best. Right now he's just all stirred up."

> Comment [CJH]: Changed from "Right now he's so mad he could spit" because their last interchange was quite positive.

"How's it goin' with you and Morgan?" Becky grinned impishly. "He sure seems taken with you." Reaching down and picking up a rock, Becky threw it across the ground.

"Well, I'm not sure I fall into his idea of what a woman should be like. I guess it's hard for men to understand we have brains and can think for ourselves. That male pride is insulted when they see we don't need them to survive."

"Yeah, I've noticed that about Shiloh. He really gets upset when I go hunting. He wants me to wear a dress and talk proper. Next he'll want me to take up knittin' and pourin' tea." She climbed on Fudge. "Guess he'll just have to learn to live with me the way I am 'cause I ain't gonna change."

"Me, neither," I said, mounting Gray Lady. "Guess we better get back to camp and see if the search party found poor Jake." I shook my head. "Boy, what a stupid thing for him to do."

I could smell the aroma of coffee a few yards from camp, which inspired me to urge Lady faster. Bessie was making biscuits, and Abel was busy turning a small antelope on a spit over the campfire. We tied our horses to the wagon wheel, and I helped myself to the coffee. The sky was streaked with scarlet as the sun started to set just as the search party rode in to camp. They looked as if they rode a hundred miles and back—tired, dirty, and hungry.

Several people headed for our wagon with Pete in the lead to hear the news. The tired group of men slid off their horses. "Take care of the horses," he ordered, calling to the Henderson boys and handing the reins to the three boys. "Thanks men," Pete said. "Get some coffee and tell me how it went."

Bessie was pouring coffee, and Becky and me were passing it out to the men. "We never found Jake," Holt said, taking the mug of coffee I handed him. "We followed the trail of the twister for near fifteen miles, maybe twenty. No trace of him. Poor fellow's gone for good, I guess." He supped the coffee.

"We picked up a few things. Crane said they could've fell from the sky. Figured they might belong to somebody on the train." He took the cup of coffee I handed him and sipped it noisily.

Wanda Reed

"Mr. Pete, you should have seen the stuff out there dead. Grown cows dead," Alfred related, "just from nowhere, and an outhouse just laying there. I never seen anything like it."

"Thanks, men," Pete said, shaking his head. "We'll pull out at dawn." He turned to Bessie. "Supposin' you could feed these fellows, Bessie?"

"Yessir, Mr. Pete. There's plenty of beans and biscuits. The meat ready, Abel?" she asked, going over to the fire.

> **Comment [CJH]:** I've been thinking that Bessie and Abel might change speech patterns during the course of the book, switching from Yessir and Yessum, which sound "slavish," to more equal terms, including calling the others by their first names. It's a fairly fine point I guess.

"Ready for eatin'. Hep yo' sef, men." Abel began to cut thick slices of the roasted antelope as the men dipped up beans and picked up their biscuits.

"Let's go to the river while the men eat," Hattie suggested. "I think they need some time to get settled after that ride, and we could all use a bath while the river's nearby."

Picking up our necessary bags and towels, Becky, Charlie, Hattie, Sara, Polly, Bessie, and I went to the river for a quick bath. We didn't stay long since we hadn't eaten. "Hope they leave us something," Charlie said. "I'm starvin'."

"There be enough for us," Bessie said. "I cooked both dem animals we have."

"Too bad they didn't fine Jake," I said. "I wonder where he went and if he lived."

"He's most likely dead from the fall," Becky said, "but who knows where. There were so many dead things out there, you couldn't even follow the buzzards."

"Alright Becky," Sara groaned, "that's enough of that kind of talk. You'll have everyone sick."

Walking back to camp, we watched the men disappear to their own camps while we cleaned up ours. The talk centered on the twister. None of us had ever seen one except Hattie. Charlie built up the fire. We fixed our plates with the second antelope and biscuits. The beans were all gone, but we opened some peaches for a treat.

"It's too early to go to bed," I said. "Becky, we haven't heard your story. You feel like telling us now?"

"Yeah, come on, Becky, tell us your story," encouraged Charlie.

"Go on, Becky," Hattie teased. "I'm waitin' to hear how you got from them mountains to here."

"Well, I reckon I ought to tell y'all somethin' 'bout how I happened to hook up with Martha. I'll have to go back a ways though, so's y'all can mebbe understand a sight better."

CHAPTER THIRTY

BECKY'S STORY

Becky sat on one of the camp chairs, and we all gathered around in the others or on barrels to make a circle around the fire. It was a warm night. Sara sat with Polly in the rocking chair while Tag lay close by. Becky drank the last of her coffee and breathed deep and started.

"If I remember right, Pa told me I was about five when Ma ran off with the drifter he had hired to help with the hayin'. Pa said she was workin' in a saloon when he found her and asked her to marry up with him, and she did. He gave her a home, but after a spell she didn't cotton to being a wife. Pa said it was because she had red hair, and it was his belief all redheads are wild."

"Well, now that explains Charlie," I said, grinning. "You a wild thing, Charlie?"

"Yeah, well, now I got somethin' to blame it on," Charlie responded.

"Anyway, after Ma left, Pa said I was his git, and he'd take care of me. Said he'd do the best he could, but he had no notion on raisin' a girl. Said the least Ma could have done was to have him a boy-child."

"Didn't he know your ma had no choosing?" Hattie asked.

"Guess not."

"What did he mean you was his git?" I asked, the term being unfamiliar to me.

"Means I was his young 'un. He sired me. The town folk was all talkin' about how it was unnatural for a old man to raise a child. They was set to take me away from him, so Pa packed what we needed, put me on the back of our mule, and we took off for the high country."

"Sounds like he really held you dear," Sara said, hugging Polly to her.

"Yep, guess so." Becky nodded, and her expression became wistful, as if she were remembering. "Pa built a cabin in the Appalachian Mountains of Kentucky. It were a well-built cabin with two rooms and a fireplace in each room. Out back, there was a clear creek for drinkin' water. Pa always said we had the sweetest water this side of the Mississippi. We had us a shelter for the mule and a sizeable smokehouse. Around the clearin' there was huge trees—mostly honey maples, flowerin' dogwood, and walnut. There was lots of wild flowers. My favorites was sweet William and wild roses. If you looked real careful in the shade of the trees, you would see the pink lady slippers. I've always had a fondness fur flowers."

As Becky described her mountain home, she seemed to grow younger, and one could see the innocent girl she'd been before she learned the shady side of life.

"Sure does sound real purty," Charlie commented, and we all nodded in agreement.

"Charlie, that's pretty," Sara corrected.

"Our nearest neighbor was 'bout five miles off. Pa liked it that way since he didn't take much to other folks."

"My goodness, didn't you get lonesome?" Sara asked.

During the interruption Hattie got the coffeepot and refilled our coffee cups and then put another log on the fire before returning to her chair.

"No. Guess I didn't. You can't miss sumpin' you never did have. I didn't know what visitin' was, so I didn't miss it." She glanced at each of us. "I know now. I'd be missin' you all."

She sipped her coffee and then continued, "Pa never left me alone much in the summer. He set me on the mule, and I went along with him when he worked the cornfield. Wintertime, he took me on the trap line in a sled tied to the mule's tail piled high with fur pelts."

"You know, your pa sounds like a real good father. My pa was like that," I said. "He taught me everything he knew about raising horses and working the farm." I sighed. "I sure do miss him."

"Yep," Becky nodded. "He was a good Pa. Never struck me not once. Made sure I had new buckskin britches every year. Let me keep all sort of critters as pets. He's who taught me to hunt game. I got so's I could come within a few feet of a deer before it knowed I was there."

"And we're all mighty grateful for your hunting skills," Hattie assured her.

"Heck, you all ain't seen how good I am. Why, I can shoot the whiskers off a owl at thirty paces whilst looking into the sun," she boasted. We all burst out laughing.

"'Whew," Hattie laughed, "I was expectin' some whoppers, Becky, but that's goin' far, dontcha think?"

"Got to keep you awake," Becky laughed and continued her story. "In the winter, cooped up in the cabin, Pa taught me my numbers and how to count coin but mostly how to cure hides and pelts. By the time I was 'bout twelve, I could make a doe hide so soft it felt like the white part of the milkweed after the pod burst open.

"We had a trap line near twenty-five miles long. When we weren't out walkin' the lines, we holed up in the cabin, and Pa talked about Ma and the past. In those times I come to believe he loved her. I felt sorry for Pa and wished he would find someone else, but he was plumb down on women. He used to say once burnt, twice shy." She paused and stared at us. "Ain't you tired of listening to me?"

"Don't you dare stop now, Rebecca O'Brien," I demanded. "I want to hear how you got from there to here."

"So do we, don't we girls?" Sara asked, and the other girls agreed with a loud "yeah."

"Okay. I'll try to shorten it up. I'd say my happy times with Pa come to a sorry end when I was fifteen."

"How! what do you mean?" I asked.

"Well, we started findin' our traps empty. All we could see was a little blood scattered here and there but no varmints. Pa figured it was a poacher stealin' our take. He was right. We come across the low-life critter later on that same day. Pa yelled at him. The poacher turned, drew a bead on Pa, and shot him dead right then an' there." Becky's eyes clouded with pain at the memory. In a voice filled with hurt and anger, she continued, "I didn't even stop to think 'bout what happened. I raised my rifle and plugged that poacher straight through the heart. He fell, and my blood turned to water as cold as the creek during the wintertime."

"You poor thing," Sara murmured. "Whatever did you do?"

"Yes chile, what's did you do?" echoed Bessie.

Becky's voice faltered, but she bravely cleared her throat and continued. "It took awhile, but I fixed up a travois on the old mule so as to tote Pa home. I left the poacher where he fell, but first I stripped him of everything he had right down to his long johns an' left him for the scavengers. He had a fair bit of gold coin, a good rifle, an' a prime skinnin' knife, and there was his skinny old mule. I took it too." Becky's eyes flashed as she recounted her act of defiance toward the stranger.

"I buried Pa under the dogwood tree by the cabin, which, I'm here to tell you, weren't no easy task, the ground bein' froze an' all. I stayed the winter tendin' the trap lines and generally tryin' not to freeze to death. It had to 've been the coldest winter I ever see'd," Becky said with a shudder. "I missed Pa sumpthin' awful. It was so lonesome alone. Wintertime was when he learned me my numbers and letters. He didn't have much schoolin' hisself, but he teached me all what he knew. I kept busy checkin' the lines and workin' on the hides. That poacher's mule come in right handy. I fed him good, and he fatten up. I rode mine and used his to carry the hides. That way I could empty the trap line faster and more often."

"That's a big job for a young girl," Hattie observed. "I'm thinkin' your Pa would be mighty proud of you."

"Thanks, Hattie. I guess I didn't think about what I had to do—I just done it. One morning I woke up, and the dogwoods trees was a bloomin'. Seemed like spring was on me. It was time to leave the cabin and go out into the world. I told myself I'd just remember what Pa said: 'Don't let nary a soul know you're a woman child.' I thought on that and then took the shears and cut off my hair right on my ears. Truth is, I was skeered to death. I'd never been around anyone 'ceptin' Pa since I was five. I figgered I'd just keep my mouth shut and learn what I could by listenin'."

"That was using your head for something sides a hat rack" Charlie remarked. "I should have done that."

I patted Charlie's shoulder. "You turned out alright."

"Well, I baled my furs and loaded everthin' in the corn cart, got the poke of gold from behind the fireplace, and closed the cabin door for the last time. I went to Pa's grave and bid him goodbye. I didn't know no fancy words, so I just thanked him for bein' a good Pa. There warn't no cause for more tears. I left the mountain and headed for the nearest town. Pa had told me years ago soon as I was old 'nough to understand that the closest town of any size was near fifty miles north. I hitched Poacher the mule, as I had taken to callin' him, to the cart and rode our old rawboned mule. Had to fight him ever' step of the way. Guess he didn't want to leave the mountain no more'n I did."

"You're very brave, Becky. I'm not sure I could have managed the way you did," I said. The more I learned of the other girls' lives, the more I realized I'd had it pretty easy.

"Ah, it weren't nuthin'," she said modestly. "Anyway, on the second day, a trapper stopped by my campfire." She laughed. "He called me boy. Guess the way I was dressed and with my short hair, I did look like one. I didn't tell him no different. Figured it was safer and a lot less trouble. Guess you were the first one I told." She looked at me.

"Yes, I remember," I acknowledged smiling.

"How old was the trapper?" Charlie asked.

"Oh, I reckon he was somewhere between Hattie and my Pa. Ben kinda treated me like a younger brother. I felt like I could trust him purty well. He learned me about tradin' fur for money. Said I'd need it for eatin' and such. He didn't know I had gold coin. We decided to go to the tradin' post as a team. Figured it'd be harder to cheat two trappers workin' together," Becky laughed.

"It must have been a strange experience for you," Sara commented. "I mean, being in a town with people and all."

"You got that right," Becky exclaimed, her eyes widening. "I'd never seen such sights afore. And the sounds! We went by one place, and I could hear somethin' that sounded like icycles breakin' on rocks. I ast Ben what it was, and he told me it were a pianna. I ran over to look. There was men and women hoppin' around on the floor, laughin' and talkin'. The women was all fancied up with paint on their faces. Ben said they was dancehall girls—

saloon women. It was then I learned what my ma did."

"I seen my share of them," Charlie said, nodding.

"Well, Ben and me finished up with our tradin'. I done real good. Had me a sizeable poke. Sold Pa's rifle and the one I took from the poacher. I sold the cart and mules at the stable to a black man." She grinned. "Never saw a man 'of color before. I ask Ben what happened to him to make him black. Ben laughed and said he was born that way." She shook her head. "Never have figured out why that is." She glanced at Bessie.

"Don' look at me, child. I dun leave dat up to the Almighty."

"Ben and me parted ways then," Becky continued. "He warned me to stay away from the saloons and painted women or I'd lose my poke. I felt kind of bad lettin' him go on believin' I was a boy, but I didn't see no easy way to tell him different. I felt kinda lonesome bein' alone, with no real idea of where I was goin'."

"Lawd 'o mercy, chile, you done real good makin' it on yo' own," Bessie said softly. "You smart bein' a boy. Some man might put you to work."

"Thanks, Bessie. Well, I got myself a horse." She paused. "I'll tell you that story another time. Anyway, it didn't take long to find out all towns were alike—same ol' stables, same dirty streets, same saloons with painted ladies."

"I know what you mean," Charlie interrupted. "Funny we didn't run into each other somewhere along the way."

"Maybe we did. Just didn't know it." Becky shrugged. "I drifted from place to place. Met all kinds of people, some good some bad. I was still dressin' like a boy. I had to wear somethin' to keep these down." She touched her breasts. "I kep my hair short, wore buckskins and a slouchy hat. Guess I didn't smell too good, neither. I noticed people kinda shied away from gittin' too close."

Charlie busted out laughing, and the rest of us joined in. I was sure we were all remembering the first time we got Becky in the water to wash.

"Alright, so Pa and me weren't much for takin' baths. I'm thankful to you ladies for showin' me the need. Don't reckon Shiloh woulda took to me if I smelled the way I used to." She grinned. "I owe you all a lot more than just learnin' me to keep clean. Sara's teachin' me to read and write, and you all showed me how to be a girl. And 'til I met you all, I never dreamt I'd ever wear a purty dress." Her eyes watered, and she bent her head.

"You took to it real easy," Hattie said softly. "Ladies are born, not made."

"Well, it's gittin' late. I better wrap this up. Some months later, 'round early spring, I ended up in Charleston. I was standin' in the stable yard, waitin' for my mule to get shod when a tall, handsome woman come up to me and asked for my help. Her voice was the softest, sweetest voice I'd ever heard. I told her I didn't work there, but I'd get the smithy. I watched her close as she was throwin' the hay over the fence to her mules. After a bit she looked over to me and asked, "Say, boy, do you know how to drive a four-up?""

She paused and glanced at me. I smiled.

"Was that when you met Martha?" Sara asked.

"I thought she was a boy, and we needed a driver," I said.

"I didn't want to trick Martha, so, I 'fessed up that I was really a girl. She laughed and said I sure had her fooled. We talked 'bout a lot of stuff. I told her I didn't know how to drive, but I could learn, and anyways I could hunt and fish real good. She just listened. I finally shut up long enough to let her say yes. I had a feelin' I'd found the friend I'd been needed fur so long. And that's how I happen to be here with you all." Becky finished with a fond look at each of us.

"And we are all very happy about that, aren't we, girls?" Sara remarked and we all nodded agreement.

After awhile Hattie told us we'd better turn in as we had about three days of hard travel ahead of us.

"Don't think we have to worry anymore 'bout that killer bein' on the train," she said. "Pete thinks he's long gone from here now."

"I still think he was one of those no 'count Riley boys," Becky said.

I lay awake a long while, thinking of what she'd endured living as a boy in a man's world. I could imagine what she'd heard and seen. I was pretty sure she had run into a lot of men like Abner. I offered up a prayer for her happiness. God knows she deserved it.

CHAPTER THIRTY ONE

We traveled along the Sweetwater River where we camped at night after several days of steady moving. Today we would reach the river crossing. The river was swift, axle deep, and forty feet wide with a firm gravel bottom, so we rolled right through. About five miles down the road, we came upon a landmark called Devil's Gate—a gorge in the side of Rattlesnake Mountain that diverged from our trail.

Becky and I rode beside the wagon while Hattie drove. She gave us some idea of how deep and wide the gorge was, making us both glad we didn't have to travel that direction. The long dark shadows with the wind screaming through the rocky ravine sent shivers down my back. It sounded like haunts calling to us.

"No wonder they call it Devil's Gate," I said. "I wouldn't be too surprised if the devil himself showed up." A herd of fifteen bighorn sheep stared down at us from the top of the ridge. Morgan point up at them for us to look. Becky looked and wheeled Fudge around and took off at a gallop after them.

"She's wasting her time," said Morgan, riding up near me. "She won't get one."

"Would you like to bet on that?" I laughed.

"Sure," he said. "Easy win."

I leaned closer to Morgan and we decided on the bet. Chuckling, we shook hands. That night, thanks to Becky, the four of us indulged in hot baths, the water being provided by Morgan hauling up bucket after bucket and heating it.

Later the next day, we passed a series of crude graves. Hattie told us they were from the Mormon Handcart Party of 1856 when over one hundred people died during an early November snow. The

Wanda Reed

trail was scattered wagon parts and bleached bones of man and animal. Three miles further, the Cranes broke a wagon tongue, so we camped at Martin Cove. Pete had two men ride out to locate a large pole from an abandoned wagon.

I watched while Bessie and Abel built a spit to roast the bighorn sheep on, and we spread the word to everyone to come for supper. Fresh meat would be getting scarce the higher we climbed. At sunset Henry and Jeff joined with Luke and Charlie and entertained us all for a couple of hours. After the music ended and the fire burned low, everyone returned to their wagons, and we retired to our tent. Several of the men worked late into the night repairing the wagon.

> **Comment [CJH]:** New name

I didn't fall asleep readily. Instead, I watched a thin sliver of moon out the tent flap and wondered if I was the only one who felt the presence of ghosts. Being close to all these graves gave me goose bumps. I wondered which of us would be next. In the middle of the night I awoke to the howling of wolves. Or was it the wailing of restless spirits? Tag, curled up beside me, growled low, and the hair on his back bristled. I pulled the covers over my head and prayed for morning to come soon.

Pete had the train moving before the sun came up. Two hours out, Becky came riding fast to the front. "The Warren's wagon broke down," she reported.

"Aw, for cryin' out loud," Pete growled. I rode back with him to see what was wrong. Pete took one look, and his face turned red. "What'd I tell you folks?" he demanded, pointing to the wagon loaded to the bows with heirlooms.

"How can you people be so stupid as to be carrying that junk?" he continued angrily. "Can't you get it through your head this could cost you your lives? Haven't you seen enough graves? If you don't get rid of it, I'll leave you at the next fort," he threatened.

Nellie cried out "No. We can't leave the Grandfather clock!"

Lucinda began weeping and wringing her hands. "That was Grandpa's clock," Lucinda whined. "We can't throw that away."

"You will if you intend to stay with this train," Pete said firmly, "and anything else you don't need for survival."

"Pete, would it be alright if Lucinda keeps her spinning wheel?" asked Frank.

"Yeah, I reckon, but that and a couple of chairs is all." Pete shook his head. "No wonder your stock is worn out, man," he ranted, "You've wore out two teams since we left Fort Laramie." He turned to Abel. "Give them a hand, will you, Abel? Make sure they leave that damned clock and all them other heirlooms right here."

"Frank, where's Dora Lee?" Nellie looked around for her daughter.

"Nellie, can't you keep track of that girl?"

"She went to ride with Sara to the fort," I told her. The fifteen-year-old seemed little concerned with saving heirlooms and more with getting to the garrison. I guessed that was because she didn't want to be late for the dance that would welcome the wagon train. Abel stayed to help Frank unload and repair his wagon. I returned to my wagon with Bessie, Lucinda, and Nellie, and the train began to roll, leaving the two wagons to meet us at Split Rock Station where we would camp.

A garrison of fifty soldiers was stationed at Split Rock Station. A former Pony Express office, it was now an army outpost used to train young recruits. We arrived in the late afternoon to a thunder of welcoming cheers. It was obvious the young recruits here didn't see many people, especially young single girls. *Mary Beth would be in her glory*, I thought. She might even find a husband and a father for her child, which would please her father. One could sense his frustration at being responsible for three women and a new baby.

In anticipation of the wagon train the soldiers had cleared the mess hall for the dance. They looked freshly bathed with slicked-down hair and clean, brushed uniforms to look their best.

Everyone rushed through the potluck supper, and the men from the train with musical instruments joined with the soldiers who had instruments. The dance began with a flourish. For the next several hours, every female from four to forty danced.

I stood with Hattie and Bessie near the punch bowl and watched the belles of the ball plot their strategy to dance with the man they wanted.

Mary Beth wore a very becoming red peppermint stripe that refused to be ignored. Lorraine wore a baby-pink lawn dress, making her looking innocent and fragile. Dora Lee was dressed in sky blue which matched her eyes. The young soldiers rewarded their efforts with enthusiastic admiration. Sybil and Thelma, also of marriageable age, seemed to be enjoying the dance but were not in the competition.

Becky and Charlie got plenty of attention too, though Shiloh made it a point of letting every man know Becky was his girl. The two thirteen-year-olds, Blanche and Ruth Ann, looked quite grown up and danced every dance. I marveled that despite the limited wagon space, all the single women had somehow managed to come up with party dresses. Even the two spinsters, Lucinda in a pale green water silk, and Arabella wearing a peach water silk, were dancing every dance. Morgan, along with most of the men from the train, held back, allowing the young soldiers free rein.

Six Women West

The dance was winding down when the Warren wagon finally rolled in. I was standing nearby and heard Pete give out a roar like a buckshot bear as Frank unloaded the large grandfather clock. "I told you to leave that damn thing!"

"Just hold on Pete. We're going to leave it here at the post. They might get some use out of it. No sense just leavin' it to rot along the trail," Frank explained. "We decide to leave all our things here for the post to use."

"Well, I can see your reasonin'. Just make sure you do leave it all here. I don't want any more breakdowns from overloaded wagons."

There was talking long into the night around the campfires. The next morning, shortly after daybreak, the train pulled out. All the young men from the post were out to bid us farewell. There were a lot of tears and a discreet hug or two along with murmured promises of future encounters. I felt sorry for the girls not know where they were going and the young men training for war.

Pete trotted up to our wagon and told Hattie, "We got to make up some time. I figure to do fifteen mile today. I put another team on the Prices wagon. Grinning, he added, "You can keep up, can't you?"

"Don't worry 'bout me," she retorted, as he rode off. He pulled up his horse and looked back at me riding beside the wagon.

"You ride point with Morgan and keep your eyes open, okay?"

I nodded, feeling a twinge of excitement and anticipation at the thought.

"Good." He galloped off.

"Charlie, Becky, you two push those rear wagons," Hattie ordered. "Keep 'em movin'. We're goin' to try to move a little faster than usual." The girls headed toward the rear of the train without argument. After seeing all the graves I think Hattie's fear of being caught in the mountains in the snow had come clear to us all.

"Can't stay away from me, huh, girl?" Morgan said, as I came up even with him.

"Horse feathers! I'm here because Pete told me to," I snapped. Tossing my head, I kicked Lady in the flanks and rode ahead of him. "Damn that man," I swore under my breath. "Why do I let him bother me?" I refused to talk with Morgan. I became very interested with the surroundings—the cottonwoods along the river and the many wildflowers of pink and purple. We passed by a prairie-dog town. I stopped and watched the cute little animals.

In less than ten miles, we crossed the Sweetwater River three times. Morgan and I marked the crossing spot for the wagons with branches with a bright cloth tied to the top. Also, we passed through two high rocky ravines. Once on the flatland, we pushed the wagons as hard as we could. We were making good time until the wind began to blow. In a matter of minutes we were in the middle of a ferocious sandstorm.

"We better take cover or head back to the wagons," Morgan said. Let's try for the wagons."

I didn't argue with him. The sand was biting as well as blinding. We returned to the wagons as fast as we could. They were circling up when we reached them.

Morgan pitched in and helped Pete and Guy circle up the wagons real tight. Sand and dust was blowing hard. It took the hide off your skin, penetrating everything. We unhitched our mules, tied them with our horses to the protected side of the wagon, and covered their eyes and noses with rags. In less then ten minutes you couldn't see three feet in front of you. Everything in sight was coated with a fine dust. Everyone stayed in the shelter of their wagon for the next two hours until the storm blew itself out.

When it finally ended, we brushed the sand off the mules, hitched up, and continued on. I rejoined Morgan, and this time he kept his smart remarks to himself. I looked like I rolled in the sand and felt like it was taking the hide off my bottom. How I longed for a bath and clean clothes!

After a few hours we came to a stretch of low-rolling hills covered with sage and small pines near the Sweetwater River. Pete called a halt and ordered the wagons to camp for the night. We had only covered about twelve miles. The sandstorm had kept us from making the fifteen miles Pete had hoped for. After circling up, taking care of the stock, and cleaning the wagons, most everyone headed for the river to wash off the grime.

The night passed without incident. At dawn the next morning, Hattie and I supped hot coffee sitting outside while watching the sun rise. Becky and Charlie were still sleeping.

"Hattie, look at those mountains. Aren't they beautiful? So tall and covered with trees of all kinds—and look at the different shades of green. This land is so big. I know you told us two thousands miles, but it seems like it goes on forever," I said.

"Yes," Hattie agreed. "They're nice to look at. The ones behind them that look like pure rocks, they call them the Tetons." There's a lot of beautiful country, but the snow in the winter will kill you. We got to keep movin' to beat the snow."

"I know what you mean. I guess there's no other way to get where we're going, is there?"

"Not that I know of," Hattie said. "Up ahead, there's a real treat. It's what's called a phenomenon of nature."

"What do you mean?"

"Well, there's ice underground."

"Ice underground? Out in the middle of this heat?"

"Yep, it's a marsh that freezes in the winter and stays frozen all summer."

"You mean we can actually get some ice?!" I exclaimed.

"If we can dig it up, we can," Hattie said, with a chuckle. Becky and Charlie stumbled out of the tent and joined us.

Bessie walked up to the coffeepot and said. "Grits and biscuits for breakfast. We goin' to roll early dis mornin', I done heard Pete say. Y'all best eat quick."

Pete rode his horse up to our wagon, "Got any coffee? That Moe made ain't fit to drink." He dismounted, helping himself to the coffee. He drank while he told us we would noon at the ice marsh. "So be ready to move within the half hour. Martha just like yesterday, ride point with Morgan, and you girls push the rear wagons. I want to set a fast pace."

We kept the pace Pete set, halting every hour for ten minutes to give the stock a breather, and we reached the marsh just after noon.

"This is the marsh," Hattie said. "Look at the rich grass and beautiful flowers growing here." When the wagons finished circling, several men took out shovels and began digging.

Morgan came by with Luke. "Bring out your washtub, and we'll wash the ice before we put it into the barrels," Morgan said. "Tell Sara and Bessie to bring their tubs too."

I watched curiously as they uncovered the ice. It was about two feet below the surface, but it didn't take the men long to reach it. All of us pitched in and helped wash chunks of ice and threw them in the barrels. Sara picked up a good-sized chunk of ice, washed it off, and then wrapped it in her apron and said, "I'm going to ask Bessie to make ice tea for lunch. Be right back." She hurried off for Bessie's wagon.

During our two-hour break everyone had filled containers with ice. We were ready to get back on the trail. We traveled about four miles before we camped near Saint Mary's Station. I looked out over the wide expanse of tall grass as it waved in the breeze. We must have been climbing slowly as the air seemed cooler. We drew to a halt, and Hattie climb off the wagon.

"Charlie, you and Becky do the wash," Hattie ordered, "and me and Martha will make camp and tend to the animals."

"Alright, we'll do the wash, but don't complain if it isn't as good as when Sara did it," said Charlie.

"Don't worry. You'll do fine. It isn't like were goin' to no tea parties out here," Hattie assured her. "Martha, you unhitch the mules, and I'll unsaddle the horses. We'll take them and picket 'em over in the tall grass." It took us a good hour to tend the stock and set up the tent.

"Hattie," Abel called, "I fixed da fire so's Bessie could start supper cookin'. We goin' to have rabbit stew and dumplings."

"Thanks, Abel. I wanted to get the stock rubbed down. They had a hard day. Here come Charlie and Becky. We better string a rope to dry the clothes. Help me, please. From the back of our wagon to the front of yours should be enough line."

After the chores were finished we sat down around the fire while supper cooked, drinking a cup of coffee when Prissy ran up.

"Martha, Martha, I got news," she cried. "Daisy's had her puppies—two boys and two girls. Daddy said she had them at the marsh."

"Oh, Prissy, that's wonderful. Four puppies! My, that's a lot of babies to feed. Does Daisy have enough milk titties?"

Prissy blushed and nodded. "Yes, I counted them. You wanna come see 'em?"

"Maybe later." I walked to the back of our wagon and cut a chunk of raw antelope. "Give this to Daisy. She'll need to build up her strength."

"Thanks, Martha. I'll go give it to her right now." She took the meat and skipped off.

"That Prissy is a real cutie," I said.

"Yeah, someday you'll have one of your own," Hattie commented.

"First you have to be married," I said, shrugging.

"You will be. A pretty girl like you won't stay single long."

Pretty? Me? Did Morgan think I was pretty? I could have asked his ma what he thought, but I was too shy, or maybe just afraid of the answer. I felt I didn't want to continue the conversation. "I think I'll go see Tag's offspring," I said, motioning to Tag to join me. "Come on, Papa. Let's see what you've done." Tag waved his tail and smiled at me as if he knew what I was talking about.

"Be back in time for supper," Bessie called, "Dem dumplings ain't good cold."

At the Holt's wagon, Prissy ran out to greet me with a big smile. "You come to see the puppies?"

"Yes, and I brought their papa. Are their eyes open yet?"

"No, not yet. Daddy says pretty soon. He says we can't touch them 'til then." She took my hand and pulled me to the back of the wagon. "You can look at them now though."

I resisted the urge to pat the pups. I noticed there were three light colors of white to dark red and one black puppy. They made me think of squeaking polliwogs. Daisy smiled up at me, obviously as proud as punch of her litter.

"What's a Jezebel?" Prissy asked, looking at me with wide eyes.

Completely taken aback, I swallowed hard. "Where did you hear that word?"

"I heard Mama talking to Daddy. She said Lorraine said your wagon was a Jezebel wagon, and that's why all the men hang out there."

That little bitch! I'll show her what a Jezebel is. I swore silently. "Well, Prissy, Lorraine is wrong. The reason the men come to our wagon is for Bessie's good cooking, which is mighty fine."

"But, what's a Jezebel?" Prissy persisted.

"You best ask your mama," I said, not wanting to talk about the subject. I was saved by the appearance of Prissy's Daddy, Matt, who walked up from behind us. Boy was I glad to see him! Prissy was pushing me into a corner.

"Well, which ones will you be takin'?" Matt asked, walking up beside the wagon. He was smiling widely.

"Two?" My mouth dropped open.

"Well, isn't that what we agreed on? After all, Tag here is the pa. You can see that for yourself."

"Right," I agreed. "Of course, I intend to share the responsibility. As soon as they can be taken from their ma, I'll find homes for two of them. Meanwhile, I'll contribute to Daisy's feed. Alright, Matt?"

"That'll be fine, Martha." He grinned. "Funny lookin' little critters, ain't they? Wonder where that black one came from?"

Tag barked loudly. "I think the papa took offense to that remark," I said, laughing. "Come on, boy. We'll come back another time. See you later." I waved goodbye to Prissy, and Tag and I headed for the river. A bath would do us both good. Maybe I could wash away some of my anger at Lorraine right now. I'd like to wash her mouth out with soap—lye soap.

I was still upset when I got back to the wagon. Hattie was the only one there. Apparently Becky and Charlie were out walking.

"Guess what I heard today?" I said. "We're Jezebels."

"Where did you hear that?" she asked calmly, raising her eyebrows.

"Prissy overheard Lorraine and her ma talking. Lorraine said it." I couldn't hide my indignation.

"Jealousy. Forget it. Don't let it bother you." She poured a cup of coffee and handed it to me.

"I'll let it go for now, but if I hear anymore, I'll give that sweet young thing something to talk about."

Hattie laughed, and we let the matter drop. "Martha, don't let her get your goat. Here comes everybody. Guess they heard the dinner bell. That rabbit's ready. Doesn't it smell good?"

By first light we were up and rolling. We traveled over a deeply rutted trail across small hills and valleys, flanked by the Sweetwater River. The trail had mounds of rocks and huge boulders of large flat stones that covered the ground. In places dirt had blown away, and the rock was the trail. One of the Johnson's mules lost his footing on a slippery rock where another mule had relieved himself and went down and broke his leg. He had to be shot. Mr. Johnson was hoppin' mad and felt that Mac, the driver of the supply wagon, owed him a mule. I thought they were going to have a fist fight over the whole thing. Pete took a mule out of the remuda and gave it to Johnson's wagon. After crossing the strip of rocks, we enter a valley of tall green grass and many small shrubs. Within a mile we crossed two small creeks. Guy and Shiloh had been scouting and rode to the wagons and called a halt. Half a mile further, we came to a larger creek that was several feet wide and fairly deep but with just a trickle of water and a rickety wooden bridge. The men checked the bridge and decided it couldn't be repaired to safely cross.

We pulled the wagons into a half-circle near the creek and all gathered in the center where Pete was motioning for us to come. "We'll need to build a crossing," Pete said. "You men gather around." When they had, he continued, "Everyone get out picks and shovels and start digging. We're going to build a trail down and across and then up the bank. Some of you tear what's left of that bridge down. After we cross, we'll camp for the night."

Several work parties were formed to remove a lot of brush and small trees which made the work very hard, but the men soon had a rough trail carved through the gulch that you could drive a wagon across.

After we crossed, Pete gave the signal to circle up. Guy rode up to us and asked Becky and Charlie to spread the word of a meeting right away. "Make sure everybody shows up," he said.

I got our wagon in place and the wagon unhitched and put the stock in halters and tied them to graze near the wagon.

I walked with Hattie to Moe's wagon for the meeting. I stopped in the crowd, and Hattie went to seek out Pete. I found myself standing next to Nellie. "How's your daughter, Dora Lee?"

Nellie replied, "Oh, the poor girl's heart is broken. She met a nice young soldier at Split Rock Station. Private Leonard Hobbs somehow made quite an impression on her. She wanted to stay there. Frank near had to tie her up to make her come with us and her bawling every mile of the way." Nellie shook her head. "When you're young, everything is so emotional. Why, I remember…"

Pete's voice boomed out, interrupting her. He stood on a barrel and looked around the gathering. "We start over the South Pass tomorrow. It's a long hill that will seem to go on forever. Stay in single file, keep close, and be careful. If you have any of grandma's heirlooms left hiding in your wagons, get rid of them. Your animals are gonna' have all they can do just to pull the wagon. Be sure there's no one riding—not even a driver. At the next waterin' place, you best fill everything that'll hold water. After we cross the pass, we travel over sixty miles of dry land before we get to Fort Bridger. I can't guarantee there is water in the creeks this late in the year. That's how late we are."

There was muffled talk by some of the men and worried looks on the faces of the women. They started asking questions about South Pass. Becky nudged me and tilted her head upwards. I looked up and saw smoke in the sky. We backed out of the meetin' real slow. "Come on," Becky said, "Let's check it out."

I glanced around, saw nobody was looking our way, and followed Becky. Giggling, we mounted up and rode for about a half hour, following the direction of the smoke. In the distance there was a small knoll of a hill. At the base we could see a house, or what we took for one. It seemed not much larger than a shed. A milk cow was grazing in what was apparently the front yard. A big man with a full beard was shoeing a mule.

We rode close to the yard and stopped. "Step down and set a spell," he invited. "I'm Walter Jones. This here's my wife, Betty Lou." A young, harried-looking woman sat in a rocker on the porch. She had a breast out nursing a small baby while a toddler pulled at her skirt and two more tow-headed boys peeked out from behind the rocker.

"Howdy. Nice to meet you. I'm Martha Patterson, and this is Becky O'Brian. We're with the Oregon wagon train. You wouldn't happen to have any vegetables or maybe a hog to sell?"

"Yep," Walter said, spitting out a chaw of tobacco. "We raise a few extras for the wagons. Sit down. Got some homemade cider. You're welcome to a glass."

"Yes, that would be kind." I said.

"Betty Lou, get these gals a glass 'o cider," he ordered.

Betty Lou struggled out of the rocker with the baby still suckling. She went inside with the three little ones trailing behind her. Glancing over her shoulder, she said, "Come on in."

We stepped cautiously into the small shack. As our eyes adjusted to the light, we could see there was an open well in one corner. Surprisingly, the room extended way back into the hill, making it three times larger than it looked from the outside.

"This is amazing," I said. "Why did you build it this way?"

"Indians," Walter said, following us inside. "This way we can close off the dugout and leave through the tunnel out the other side. See here— this door has mud bricks on the outside. When it's closed, it look like a wall."

"That sure is good planning," Becky said, "Do you have much trouble with Indians?"

"Not in the past few years," Walter said, scratching his beard. "Afore that we got hit a couple of times."

"You sure have some nice pieces of furniture," Becky commented.

"We pick up what people leave on the trail," Betty Lou said, handing us each a glass filled with cider. "Sometimes Walter takes a load to town to sell for hard money."

We finished the cider, which was very good, thanked the woman, and smiled at the young 'uns. They were so bashful, hiding behind Betty Lou's skirt. Laughing, we followed Walter outside to a field of vegetables.

He handed us two gunnysacks. "Help yourself. See you back at the cabin."

We filled both sacks to the brim, oohing and aahing at the size of the vegetables. "Wonder if he'll sell us some buttermilk?" Becky said, as we made our way back to his house.

"I hope the pig is as nice as these," I said, indicating the vegetables. "Goodness, won't it be nice to have fresh fixins for dinner? Bessie will think she's died and gone to Heaven when she sees all this."

"Get all you wanted?" Walter asked, coming out to meet us. "Here, let me help you." He lifted the sacks and held them while I secured them with rope and put them across Lady's saddle. "You wantin' that hog now?"

"Oh, yes, please," I assured him.

"You wouldn't have any buttermilk to sell?" Becky asked.

"I reckon not. We need the milk for the young 'uns. We only got one cow." He grinned, showing rotten and missing teeth.

"We're mighty grateful for all you sold us," I said.

"How grateful?" Becky whispered, as we followed behind him. I punched her and gave her a dirty look. We picked out a nice-sized hog.

"Okay, ladies, the hog is yours, but it's up to you to get him on that horse," Walter laughed.

Becky started for the hog, and he ran. She ran and made a dive for him. He squealed and took off in another direction.

I said, "Here, Becky," and held out an ear of corn to him. He came close. She got a rope on his leg and pulled him down, squealing loudly. Somehow we all got on the ground wrestling the hog, but we got him tied. Walter and his family doubled over in laughter as they watched us wrestle the hog. We finally got it hoisted up on Fudge. Then we turned to each other and laughed as we brushed the dust off each other's backsides.

"Glad you enjoyed the show. How do your customers usually get the hog?" I ask laughing.

"They bring a wagon. Ain't never had one put it on a horse."

I smiled and handed Walter the money he asked for, which was considerable, but well worth it. Walter took the money and disappeared inside the house. As we were saying thanks and farewells, my eyes fell on the flock of chickens at the side of the house. "Are your chickens for sale, Missus? Betty Lou looked at me and apparently saw the hunger for fried chicken in my eyes.

"Fifty cents apiece." she answered.

"I'll take four of them," I said without hesitating. Becky looked at me as if I'd lost my mind.

"Fifty cents?" she whispered, "Your crazy girl! That's robbery without a gun."

"Bessie's fried chicken," I whispered back.

Betty Lou grabbed four good-sized young cockerels, tied their legs together with a rope, and laid them across my saddle in less than two minutes. Then she handed me up a quart tin of buttermilk. I put the three dollars in her hand and said, "Buy you a new dress."

"I surely will—a green one."

Walter walked out of the house as we turned to ride off. "Tell them at the train we got vegetables, and don't forget I got five more hogs for sale," he called as we trotted out of the yard.

Back at camp, I told Pete about the five hogs and vegetables. "I'll send some men over to pick them up. Thanks." He grinned at us. "I saw you disappear from the meeting. Think you knew all you need to know already?"

"Ah, Pete, Hattie will tell us what we need to know," I said, "over and over and over." I smiled to show him I was teasing.

I better go tell Mac and Moe to go get them hogs and vegetables. No use of everybody going. We can resell them here."

We loosed the hog and gave Abel the chickens to kill and clean.

"Lawdy lawdy," Bessie exclaimed, running her hands over the vegetables. "We's gonna have us one fine supper."

Fine was an understatement. We ate fried chicken rolled in flour, seasoned with salt, pepper and a little garlic; mashed potatoes; fresh carrots seasoned with onions; and biscuits all light and fluffy and smeared with churned butter washed down with buttermilk. We ate until our bellies hurt. We sat up late enjoying the fire and the company. Bessie was thanked several times by each of us. Bessie wouldn't take credit for the meal, saying it was thanks to me and Becky for bringing it in.

"Who's in charge of killing the hog?" Morgan asked.

"Not me," said Becky. "I just give it a ride here. Martha's the one who bought it."

"The hog isn't hurting anything," I said, glancing over at the animal lying next to Tag, who didn't seem to mind. "We can just let him follow along. He'll eat and get a little bigger before we butcher him."

"First thing you know, he'll be a pet," Morgan chuckled. "What you going to call him? Pinky?" he laughed.

I glared at him. "I just want him to get some weight on to where he's worth what I paid for him," I said defensively.

"Don't think it's wise to keep the hog, Martha," Pete said. "Better just to do the butcherin' right away."

"He's right," Hattie put in. "Abel can take care of it. Okay with you, Abel?"

"Sho'. I'll do it in the mornin when it's cool," Abel agreed, grinning widely. "Right now ah's too full of Bessie's fine cookin'."

"Well, now that you've got that settled," Morgan said, "any chance of getting a couple of carrots for my horses?"

"Why don't you take some to your horses, too, Martha?" Hattie said, grinning.

I pretended I didn't know she was setting me up with her son. We fed the carrots to the horses, not saying anything until we started back to the wagon.

"You did right fine bartering for those fresh vegetables, Miss Martha," Morgan said softly. "It's good traveling with you."

I nodded, not trusting myself to speak. *Darn him,* I thought. *He can be so nice.* I stood by Lady pulling the burs out of her tail. "They all look so un-kept. I don't know if they will ever look like they did when I started. Lady's tail touched the ground when I left Virginia. Now it's up to her knees."

"Don't worry about her looks." He said softly, "Just worry about a broken leg or snake bite, getting hurt by a wolf or something. Her hair will grow, and little scars will heal."

"Have you noticed how muscled they are now? They're much stronger than they were stabled in the barn," I expressed. "Now their chests and hindquarters are all muscle."

"No, Martha. I didn't see them when you started. How is Boots? Do you think she's carrying a foal?"

"I'm not sure about Boots. Let's go. I'll brush Lady tomorrow. Isn't that a beautiful sunset?" We walked arm in arm toward the wagon. Morgan stopped, and his lips covered mine for a brief tender kiss.

"Yes, Martha. Almost as beautiful as you," he murmured.

The sun was just rising. Pete arrived at our wagon and was having coffee and laying out the day chores. A young soldier stopped at our wagon. "I'm looking for the wagon master," he said. "I was told I might find him here," he said.

"That'd be me," Pete told him. "I stopped for a decent cup of coffee," he said.

Dismounting, he said "Leonard Hobbs is the name. I'd like to hire on and join the train."

"You resign or desert?"

"Resigned, sir." Digging in his pocket, he handed Pete several papers.

Pete looked over the papers, nodded, and held out his hand. "Welcome, young man. You can drop the sir. Just call me Pete. Go down to the remuda and ask for Tommy. He needs another horse wrangler. Tell him I sent you."

"This is the soldier Nellie told me about," I confided quietly to Hattie. "Apparently he's following Dora Lee."

"Thank you, sir. I mean, Pete." He mounted and hurried off in the direction Pete pointed him, then turned and came back. "Say, could you tell me, where's the Warren wagon?"

Pete said "It's fourteen from the front. Keep your horse at a walk inside the camp."

"Yes, sir. Thank you, sir."

"He's the one from the station who took a shine to Dora Lee," said Hattie.

"I just hired a wrangler. I don't get involved with affairs of the heart, lessin' they're mine." Pete smiled with a big wink. "Come on Hattie. I'll help you hitch up these mules so we can get rollin' over the hill."

CHAPTER THIRTY TWO

"Halfway point! Gates of the Oregon frontier," I shouted as we hitched six mules to our wagon. I took a minute to view the wide expanse of short dry grass and stunted scrub pines.

"Yep, we're here." Hattie said, "I told Abel to use our spare team 'til we're over the pass. It's a long slow climb, and most everybody will have to walk. Why don't you go ask the riders to carry some of the littler young 'uns?"

"Alright." I rode over to the Holt wagon and asked Mrs. Holt if I could carry Prissy to the top of the hill. She agreed, and I pulled Prissy up in front of me. We rode around camp. Following Hattie's suggestion, I asked several riders to carry the young ones to the top.

"Are we goin' up a mountain?" Prissy asked Hattie.

"No, it's not a mountain. It's just a big hill. When we get to the top, we'll rest. It's a long way across the top, and then we go down the hill. Up on top there's a spring that is fed by clear mountain water." She smiled at Prissy. "You'll see some of the water runs east and some runs west. It's called the Continental Divide."

"That's strange. What do you think of that, Prissy?"

"How does the water know which way to go?" Prissy asked.

"That part is called Mother Nature," Hattie chuckled.

The riders reached the top long before the first wagons. Becky, Charlie, and I stayed and rode herd on the young children as they played kick the can with an old can they found in the meadow. When the wagons reached the top, they circled up in the meadow among tall pole pines.

I took the time to ride to an overlook to see the view, removing my hat to let the breeze cool my head. Hattie had told me that from here you could look one way at a range of mountains called Oregon Bluffs or the other way at the Wind River Range. Morgan pulled Raindrop to a halt beside me.

"Great view of the mountains," he said.

"It certainly is. The sun on the snow is almost blinding. Have you crossed these mountains before?"

"Nope," he admitted. "It's going to be a real adventure for me too. I came to tell you my ma said the noon meal is ready."

Riding toward the wagon, I could smell the aroma of coffee and the roasting meat. As we got closer to the wagon, I realized how hungry I was.

"Sure smells good," Morgan said, "makes your mouth water."

"You're eating with us, aren't you?"

"Well, Ma invited me, but the food will taste even better now I know you want me there too." He smiled.

"Darn you, Morgan Brooks!" I flared. "Do you always have to…"

"I can't help myself around you, Martha. It's not just your big green eyes and beautiful hair. It's—I don't know—there's something about you. You're not like other women."

He made it sound like a compliment. I turned my head so I wouldn't have to look into his eyes. Morgan Brooks was not a man a girl could resist for very long. I was beginning to think my time for surrender was fast approaching. Replacing my hat, I nudged Lady toward the wagon wheel and dismounted.

The usual bunch was gathered around the wagon, already eating. Bessie handed me and Morgan a plate and told us to help ourselves. We filled our plates, and I went to sit away from the wagon. Morgan followed me. Sitting beside me, he asked, "You're not mad at me, Martha, for sayin' what I feel, are you?"

"No," I murmured between bites.

"Don't you feel anything for me?"

"I don't know what I feel, Morgan," I confessed. "You make me so darn mad, and yet I really like being around you."

"Well, that's a start. Tell me what I do that makes you so mad, and I'll stop doing it, okay?"

"That's the problem. I'm not sure what it is. Maybe it's just me. I mean, maybe I take offense when none is intended."

"Trust me, Martha. I would never knowingly offend you. Tease you, yes. Hurt you, no."

"Howdy, folks," Nellie Warren walked up, wearing a worried look and wiping her hands on her apron. "Not interrupting anything, am I?"

"No," Morgan and I said in unison.

"Did you want to talk to me?" I asked.

"No, I'm looking for Hattie."

"She was over by the fire," I told her. "I'll go with you." I stood, taking my cup and plate with me. I looked at Morgan who was still seated. He had the expression of being interrupted. "I'll talk to you later."

"Anytime, Miss Martha. My time is your time."

I felt a warm tug in the center of my chest when he said that. He did have a way with words. "Hattie, Mrs. Warren's here to see you," I called.

"Well, hello Nellie," Hattie said. "What brings you here?"

"I'm lookin' to you for some advice," she said, taking the cup of coffee Hattie handed her. I poured a cup of coffee and stood to the side.

"It's that soldier fellow, Leonard Hobbs. He's been over to the wagon asking Frank if he could come callin' on Dora Lee. Frank told him he could come and sit, but not to take her off alone."

"I think that's sound advice."

Nellie took a sip of her coffee. "That Bessie makes the best coffee," she commented and then continued. "That's not all. He asked Frank if he could marry her when she's sixteen. Says he aims to claim land near us in Oregon."

"Well, I don't have much experience with young people and courtin', but he sure sounds serious, and he seems like a real level-headed boy." Hattie smiled. "I think maybe I'd just let nature take its course. After all, a lot can change in a year. Leave it up to Dora Lee and keep your eyes open."

"I guess I'm just not ready to lose her yet."

"I guess there's never a good time to lose young 'uns, but you'd be gaining a son. He could be a help to Frank when you get to Oregon. Sound like he's planning to settle close by. That would keep Dora Lee close too—and future grandbabies."

"Yes, I suppose you're right. I know Frank likes him. Truth to tell, I like him too." She emptied her cup and set it down. "Thanks for listening, Hattie. Always helps to have someone to talk things out with." She hurried off to get ready for the afternoon travel.

"That was nice, Hattie," I said. "I think you made her feel better."

"Well, the secret of good advice is letting the other person talk it out. All you have to do is listen. Let's get packed up and hitch the team. It's about time to go."

Going down the hill was steep and treacherous. The men roped off the axles and kept them taut while the drivers double-braked the wagons to keep them from moving too fast. It took nearly all day, but by dark every wagon had arrived safely.

"I don't remember this marshland the last time I was across here," Hattie commented to Pete when he rode up beside our wagon.

Six Women West

"That underground river causes it. We're late crossing, and it's flooded. Damn good thing it's staying light late so we can see what we're up against. We'll follow the trail 'bout a mile then circle up for the night at Pacific Springs."

"Guy just got back from scouting. Said there was some carcasses upstream poisoning the water. They dragged them out, so maybe the water will clear. So, water your stock good tonight and in the morning. Fill your water barrels and anything else that will hold water."

"Pete, I noticed a cutoff on the map which could save us fifty miles. Why don't we take it?" I asked.

"We have to go by Fort Bridger for supplies, and that way's a lot rougher. No water—just desert. We'd lose the stock or wear them down 'til they're no good for the rest of the trip."

"Well, I think we better play it safe," Hattie put in. "If we work it right, we can get to Fort Bridger in four days."

"Sounds feasible," Pete agreed. "Got to go, but I'll be back with the boys for supper."

We all enthusiastically enjoyed the supper. There was one compliment after another for Bessie's cooking and Becky's hunting ability.

"How'd you get so lucky Abel? You got a sister, Bessie?" Luke teased. "Sure would like me a woman who can make roast duck that melts in your mouth and come up with a chocolate cake in the middle of nowhere."

"I done teached Miss Charlie. She cooks real fine," Bessie said, tilting her head at Charlie, who frowned.

"Oh? Why, that's good to know," Luke said, winking at Charlie.

Pete stood and adjusted his waistband, saying, "Thanks for the fine supper, ladies. I sure hate to bring this fine gathering to a close, but I think we better call it a night and turn in. We'll be shoving off way before daylight to get as many miles as we can while it's cool." He turned to Hattie. "Thanks for havin' us. See you in a couple hours."

After spreading around more thanks, Morgan and Luke left with Pete. Guy picked up a sleeping Polly and left with Sara. Bessie started cleaning up the dishes.

"Never mind about that," I told her. "We can do this. You and Abel go home." I patted her shoulder. "You did real good, Bessie. It was a wonderful supper."

Hattie stood up." Becky, can you and Charlie clean up so me and Martha can check on the stock?"

"Sure. We can get this cleaned up in no time."

On the way to the picket lines, Hattie said, "Martha, I think Morgan would like you and him in double harness. And I'd be real pleased to have you for a daughter. You got any feeling on that?"

"Oh Hattie," I put my arm around her waist. "I'd be proud to call you Ma, but I'm not ready to be a wife." I shrugged. "It's tempting when I look at Sara and Guy and they seem so happy. Why, all you girls have someone whose company you obviously enjoy. And, truth to tell, I do enjoy Morgan's when we get along."

"From what I've seen, I get the feeling you like him more than you think," Hattie said. "I don't know what your past experience with men has been, but it seems like you don't trust 'em much."

"I don't have any experience, Hattie. That's probably the trouble. My ma, bless her heart, convinced me I wasn't the type men marry. So, I guess I figure they just want something else— something I'm not willing to give. I'm not going to be a roll in the hay for any man."

"I don't believe that's what Morgan has in mind, Martha."

"Maybe not, but I got plans, things I want to do. I want to follow my Pa's dream of breeding horses. He taught me all about it, so I've just got to try it." I glanced at her, hoping she understood. "And I know Morgan has his own ideas for his future. An obedient wife who's willing to bake bread and tend a dozen babies. We'd probably fight all the time," I laughed. "Much as I like you and him, I think for now anyway I'll stay single." I wanted to reveal my past to Hattie, but I had to keep that my secret. No one wanted a murderess for a wife.

"I think you got Morgan wrong, Martha. He's more free thinkin' about women than most men. He wants a partner, not a maid, and I'm sure he would hire help about the sixth child." She patted my shoulder and laughed. "We still got a long way to go before we reach Oregon. Anything can happen." Grinning, she added, "Have you noticed Lucinda is meeting Oscar after supper, and Arabella has been talkin' a lot to Mr. Crayon? Those women will be married afore long. Mark my words."

We made sure the stock was secured and then returned to the wagon. Becky and Charlie were filling everything that would hold water: barrels, buckets, canteens, and cooking pots. We pitched in and helped. When we finished, there wasn't a thing left empty. We put the dried beans into a box and used the barrel for water. It was late when we finally crawled into our bedrolls, exhausted.

I don't believe my eyes got closed before Moe was beating out the wakeup call on his dishpan three hours before daylight. By the time we got hitched, Bessie had fixed coffee, bacon, and cold biscuits. With coffee in one hand and bacon and a biscuit in the other, we rolled.

The first few hours were not unpleasant, but when the sun came up, things changed quickly. The temperature rose at an unbelievable rate like Pete had warned. It was dry, and the sun seemed hot enough to boil water. There was nothing but a wide view of dry grass and sagebrush. It was hard to breathe, and each breath felt like it scorched your lungs. When Pete called for a break, we were more than ready.

"We'll need to take care of the stock," Hattie said. "Clean out their mouths and noses, but use as little water as possible. Glad we got that extra barrel."

"Can we give them some water to drink?" I asked.

"We will," Hattie said, "after they're cleaned up. They can have about a quart of water each out of the small pans. That should hold them awhile."

After chores were taken care of, I found a shady spot near a mesquite bush, laid my saddle down, and settled in for a nap in the heat of the afternoon break. I'd just barely closed my eyes when Abel walked up.

"Not asleep, are you?"

I shook my head. "Something I can do for you, Abel?"

"Well, I was jus' wonderin'—if those pups make it, might I have one?"

"They're going to make it alright. I'll see to it you get pick of the litter. I get two. Sure you don't want both?"

"No, just one. Thanks, Miss Martha. I'll tell Bessie we got a pup."

"Well, if you know of anyone else who wants one, let me know."

"Sho' will, but you won't have no trouble findin' homes for the other one. Folks is always wantin' a good dog." He waved goodbye and left.

I settled back down and dozed off in the hot afternoon heat. I woke to find Tag pawing my shoulder. I could tell he wanted me to follow him. He led me to where the horses were picketed near some tall mesquite brush. He growled low, and the

Six Women West

hair rose on his back as he sniffed at a set of boot tracks.

"What's the matter, boy? They're just boot tracks." I patted his head. "You've seen plenty of them before."

Tag stiffened and growled deep in his throat. Obviously, these tracks were not familiar to him and apparently not friendly either.

I suddenly thought of the missing robber and murderer. "Come on, Tag. Let's go find Morgan." As I hurried by the Macintosh wagon, I heard his voice. I approached the wagon. He was having coffee at the Macintosh wagon, obviously basking in Lorraine's fawning gaze. Politely refusing a cup of coffee, I managed to convey that I wanted to talk to him alone. Stifling the urge to smack her and smiling sweetly all the while, I took his arm and nearly pulled him away.

"What's so important?" Morgan asked, reaching down to pat Tag who wagged his tail in appreciation.

As we walked away, I felt the jaws of the green-eyed monster. *Lorraine may have a spiteful tongue*, I thought, *but she was young, petite, and very pretty*. Ma's words rang in my ears. *You're not the kind men marry.* Hattie must be mistaken thinking Morgan wanted me for his wife. I shook my head, putting it out of my mind.

"What is it, Martha? Got a problem?"

"No, but the train may have. I saw some tracks, and Tag growled at them."

"Show me where they're at. You didn't walk on them did you?"

"No, I know better than that. They're here in this sandy area. Yeah, here they are. Back Tag. Stay." Morgan knelt down beside them.

"Probably not anyone on this train. This may help us find the killer," he said. "Looks like he's got a chunk out of the heel in his right boot. I'll let Pete and the others know to be on the lookout."

Back at the wagon, I told the girls about the tracks. They promised to be careful and not go out alone. The day went by without incident. We watered the stock again, and then we rolled at four in the afternoon. Around suppertime we passed by several dead animals on the banks of the dry creek. The stench from the bloated bodies was terrible. You had to put a kerchief over your nose to breathe. Several large buzzards were tearing at them. It was way after nine when we made camp. It was still hot.

Pete had our riders push the loose stock past the Dry Sandy near Simpson's Hollow. A wooden sign displayed cross bones. Keeping the loose stock away from the river was a hard job. After the stock was across, Pete and the other men roped and watered each animals. Because of the heat, the going was slower here than in the high country. Everyone on the train showed signs of strain and fatigue. It was midnight when Pete made the last rounds, stopping at our wagon.

"Martha, Martha, wake up. I need to talk to you."

"What, Pete?" I asked confused, rubbing the sleep from my eyes and looking around to see what time it was. The moon was up.

"Martha, could you, Becky, and Charlie help herd the remuda to the front of the train after you hitched your wagon?"

"Sure Pete, but can I ask why?"

"Well, Martha, it's because soon as we get near the Big Sandy, they'll stampede." He shook his head. "It'd cause a hell of a mess. It's gonna be hard enough to hold the teams back."

"I never even thought of that," I admitted. "We're lucky to have you, Pete. We'll be there."

"It's my job, girl," he said, riding off. "Be there in half an hour."

Six Women West

We helped Hattie get the wagon hitched and saddled our horses. We got a quick cup of coffee and another cold biscuit with bacon. The full moon reflecting off the white sand gave us plenty of light. We joined up with the other wrangler and started the herd moving. I was thinking that I'd be hard pressed myself not to start running when I smelled the water. I couldn't remember when I had been so thirsty. We used the last of our water for the stock.

The stock stampeded when we they got a smell of the water. They plunged in up to their bellies. We drove them on across and let them graze near the river. We went upstream where the foliage was thick along the banks of the river and took a quick swim before the wagons arrived. It was midmorning when the wagons arrived at the Big Sandy. Hattie handled the mule team, keeping them from charging across the creek and then releasing them to drink. I watered my mares separately, remembering that Pa had warned me mules had more sense than horses when it came to water. He said mules knew when to stop, but horses would drink 'til they bloated. After picketing my horses, I returned to the wagon. Bessie was there, starting a fire. She looked awful tired. "Bessie," I said. "We'll make the fire and start coffee and anything else you want started. You go ahead and bathe if you want."

"Thanks, Miss Martha. Ah sho' could use a bath. Ah feel dry clean through. Ah'll be back real quick. You can cut up some bacon. Ah'll whip up a pot of stew."

"Take your time." I didn't see Hattie around so I figured she went to bathe. The three of us set up camp while we waited for Bessie to return. "Let's sleep out. The weather is nice. We don't need the tent." I got my clean clothes and necessary bag ready for my bath. The quick swim was cool, but I needed a good scrubbing. "Becky, you and Charlie want to go down to the river?"

"Not now. We'll go later," Charlie said. "We've got a couple things to do first. We'll wait 'til later tonight before bed. How about some more of that coffee?"

"Thank you, Miss Martha. That bath sho felt good. Now to get the vittles ready."

"Sounds good to me. We've been living on bacon and cold biscuits for three days." I rode near a mile downstream and found a secluded spot with tall reeds and brush. I had just stripped and was ready to get in the water when I heard groaning sounds. Holding my towel in front of me, I peered through the bushes. A man and woman were struggling on the ground. They had obviously been bathing as both naked bodies were glistening wet. The man had the woman down, thrusting his body against her again and again. She uttered a loud moan. Alarmed, I came out of my daze and yelled, "Stop! Don't hurt her."

What the hell?" The man rolled off the woman and glared at me. His blue eyes turned on me, and his face went sheet white.

The woman screeched, grabbed a shirt from the pile, and tried to cover her face, but not before I recognized her. Mary Beth! It was Mary Beth! and Shiloh!

Feeling embarrassed, stupid, and naïve, I realized they'd been coupling, not fighting. I had seen animals mating plenty of times but never humans. Shocked, I turned away without saying anything, picked up my clothes and ran further downstream.

"That dirty bastard," I swore, "and that stupid girl." *And Becky*, I thought. *How can I tell Becky?* I decided I must talk to Hattie. I had to get her alone. I dressed while running and found another place to bathe and took the longest bath in history, not wanting to return to camp. I felt everything I'd seen was written on my face for anyone to read.

Six Women West

Back at the wagon a campfire had been built, and the camp chairs were all out. It was going to be a beautiful night. The stars were so bright. Charlie, Becky, Hattie, and I filled water barrels, while Bessie and Sara got supper ready. It was so hard to keep my mind on what I was doing. I kept having flashes of what I'd seen. How was I going to tell anyone, much less Becky? Somewhere in camp, a man played the fiddle. It sounded so nice. We were all looking forward to a good meal as we'd been on jerky and biscuits for three days. Bessie had fixed venison stew and rice with cornbread. We ate 'til we were stuffed. Over one last cup of coffee, we discussed crossing Green River.

"In early days the Green was a rough crossing, but now you just ferry across," Hattie told us. "There's a good trail right to the loading dock. Before, wagons went down a half mile of steep bank. The river is shallow now, but rapid."

"At one time I heard the wagons were lowered on ropes to cross this river," Pete said. "By the way, bad news. Guy scouted ahead, and he brought back news that the ferry is out, so we cross the river the hard way."

"Well, thanks for savin' the bad news 'til after supper," Hattie said.

I bit my tongue to keep from telling everyone what I saw about Shiloh and Mary Beth. Just then, the scalawag joined us. He stared at me with an unspoken question in his eyes. "Where have you been keeping yourself?" I asked, letting him wonder if I told.

He smiled warmly, relying on my friendship with Becky that I wouldn't have told her. "I've been busy scouting. I wouldn't want anyone to get hurt." He smiled an evil smile at me.

"Well, we'll be at the fort soon," Becky said, walking up with a big smile. "That's where we'll be leaving you good folks. Pete, did you hear the ferry is out at the Green River?"

"Yeah, we were just talkin' about it. Hattie has crossed without a ferry before. I'll call a meetin' tomorrow so everybody will know what's going on."

"I imagine it's a lonely life for a soldier here in these outposts, especially for young people," I remarked quietly. "You were very fortunate to have found Becky. She'll make a wonderful wife." I stared at him. "You will be getting married at Fort Bridger, won't you? Goodness, Becky, we'll have to start thinking about your wedding day—a big wedding with all the trimmings, and a snow-white dress for purity."

Becky started to say something, but Shiloh grabbed her arm. "Come on, Becky, let's go for a walk."

After they were out of earshot, I said, "Wonder what he wants now?"

"You don't like him much, do you, Martha? You were startin' to rake him pretty good," Pete said.

"No, I don't like the bastard, and with good reason." I hesitated and then plunged ahead. "I saw that scalawag with Mary Beth down by the river. They were both naked as jaybirds. I'm afraid marriage won't change that pop-in-jay. I don't know if I should tell Becky or not. Might save her future misery."

"I wouldn't, Martha. It's sure to hurt Becky, and she might not believe you and would probably even get mad at you. Keep it to yourself awhile longer," Hattie said. "She could still see his true colors. I've noticed a change in the relationship. She has a lot of savvy for one so young."

"Do you want me to hang him by his heels and horsewhip him?" teased Morgan, as he played with a twig in the fire.

"He could use it," I said. "but I suppose we should trust Becky to do what's right for her."

"Yeah. I've got guard duty tonight," Morgan said. "Mind if I take Tag with me in case that prowler comes back?"

"Sure, go ahead and take him. Maybe I'll visit you later."

"Guess I'll be hittin' the sack," Pete said. "Comin' Morgan?"

"Yeah, I'll catch forty winks before my watch. Goodnight, Ma, Martha. Thanks for supper."

The moon was up when Becky returned. She slipped into bed, and I could hear her crying softly. I crawled over and put my arm around her. "It'll be okay, Becky. Do you want to talk about it?"

"It's just the same. Shiloh wants me to prove my love for him." She sniffled. "We can't even talk anymore. It's always about that. What's so important about that anyway?"

"Let him prove his love by waiting," I said softly, as not to awaken the others. "You don't want to end up like Mary Beth, a child and no daddy. I know they say she's a widow, but something tells me she was one who proved her love to someone who didn't love her enough to wait. Maybe he went to war and got killed, or maybe when she got pregnant, he deserted her. I admit I don't know much personally, but if you want the voice of experience, talk to Charlie. She's been around saloon women."

"Yes, Becky," said Charlie, crawling over to lie beside us. "I can tell you all about it. I didn't mean to listen, but I couldn't help but hear. If you want, I'll share what's been told to me."

"It's okay, Charlie, you don't have to. I know what he wants is wrong. I just can't do that 'til I'm married. I told him tonight I won't be stay in' at the fort because I've decided I don't want marry him. I know he's been beddin' Mary Beth. I followed him several times. She can have him. Besides, he just wants beddin', not weddin'." She turned over on her side. "I was just bawlin 'cause I'm giving up a dream of being loved."

Surprised she knew about Mary Beth, I was glad I hadn't said anything. Hattie was right. Becky was real smart. "You can dream again, Becky. There's no limits on dreams." I patted her shoulder. "Let's all get some sleep now." We all wiggled back to our bedrolls and lay in the dark. I was remembering the different stories each of the women had shared with me—how each had loved and gotten hurt, healed, and tried again. *Why was I so afraid to take a chance?*

Tag's loud barking and shouts from Morgan had us all wide-awake and complaining.

"It's still dark," Becky complained. "Do we have to get up? We're restin' today."

"Hello. You going to sleep all day?" Morgan called. "I got hot coffee waiting. "I think it's you he wants, Martha," Charlie mumbled. "Go!"

I pulled on my trousers and boots while the others snuggled deeper in their bedrolls. When I got up, Morgan handed me a mug of coffee.

"Thanks," I muttered, begrudgingly. "What's the occasion?"

"Just couldn't wait any longer to see you," he said, winking. You didn't come visit me last night. Did you forget?"

"There you go! Now, that's one of the things that offend me—that sweet talk that doesn't mean anything. Just rolls off your tongue like honey."

But, I do mean it, Martha. I don't know why you can't believe me." He smiled. "Look, let's start over. I just came by to talk to you."

"So talk."

"I'd rather not do it here. I was going to tell you last night, but you didn't come to visit me. Can't we go down by the horses?" He sounded serious.

"I need to get myself ready for the day first." I walked over to the river. "I need to wash up and tie my hair back."

"Leave it loose. Makes you look ruffled, like you just got out of bed."

I glared at him.

"Sorry," he apologized, looking contrite, picking up Raindrop's reins.

I picked up Lady's bridle. "Let's go." As we walked to the picket line, I asked, "What's so important we couldn't talk about it at the wagon?"

"Remember yesterday's boot prints?"

I nodded, breathing a sigh of relief. The grass was sparse, but close to the river it was green, and with the few scrub trees it made a good place to picket the horses. At the river I stopped and washed my face and excused myself for a nature call while Morgan bridled Lady. Thank God it was still early and no one else was around. When I returned, I sat down on a rock and started braiding my hair, and Morgan resumed his conversation.

"Martha, this is like trying to get a butterfly to stay still. Well, those boot prints belong to a marshal I knew in the army. He's been behind us since Fort Laramie."

"He was following us? I never saw him."

"He got a late start. He just caught up with us, and he told me that killer we were told about is on this train."

"On the train?" I stopped and grabbed his arm. "Who is it?"

"Jackson doesn't have a positive identification, but he's pretty sure who it is. Anyway, he made me a deputy."

"Won't that put you in danger?" I asked, feeling a twinge of fear in the pit of my stomach.

"Nothin' to worry about. Jackson thinks he'll make his move before we get to the fort. He wants to wait 'til the guy leads us to the money."

"Thanks for sharing this with me, Morgan. Sorry I snapped at you."

"That's okay. I'm sort of gettin' used to it. I know you don't mean it."

I laughed and said, "Guess I'll change and punch you instead" as I reached out and punched his arm gently, smiling. "See you at the wagon for breakfast. Hattie said bacon and buckwheat cakes with honey."

"I know I don't have to tell you not to say anything about this. Jackson doesn't want to alarm the others." He gave me a foot up on Gray Lady so I could ride back to the wagon.

"Don't worry," I assured him as I pulled the tangles from her mane.

"Great. See you later. I have to go see the army wagon. Then I'll be in for breakfast." He climbed on Raindrop and rode off.

On the way back to the wagon, I met Pete. "Mornin', Martha. I had to cancel the rest time because we'll lose time now crossing the river. We're gonna have to roll today. Tell them to be ready in two hours."

"Okay, Pete. I'll tell Hattie. Are we going all the way?"

"We'll go as far as we can, but we got to get moving."

"This will be a hard and dangerous crossing, won't it Pete?"

"Can't say. I've never had to cross that way before. I'm depending on Hattie for this one." He slapped his horse's flank. "Got to spread the word. Save me some breakfast."

Within the two-hour time limit we were rolling. We passed some old wagon skeletons. Hattie told us it was where twenty three wagons had been burned by the Mormons.

"I thought Indians were the only ones who did that," I said.

Six Women West

"It was something to do with the Mormons not wanting the wagons to reach Salt Lake. It's one of those tales where everybody's got a different story."

Several miles later we circled and camped at the base of a sun-baked hillside with a couple of scrub pines. At supper, Morgan brought his friend to meet us. "This is an old army buddy of mine," he told us.

"Any friend of Morgan's is welcome," Hattie said, handing Jackson a cup of coffee.

Jackson looked to be several years older than Morgan. He was tall and lean with dark hair and beard. He was friendly but seemed to me to be tense, and his eyes seemed to take in everything at once. *Perhaps,* I thought, *it was because of what I knew about him.*

At daybreak the train moved out, headed for the Green River. It was late afternoon when we stopped and made camp high above the river. It was a nice place to make camp with several shade trees, and the grass was green and plentiful. The trail down was narrow and made of rocky shale with a drop off on one side. It looked very treacherous. Pete called a meeting of all the drivers and asked Hattie to assist him with the instructions.

He drew a rough map in the dirt showing the trail down to the river. "It'll be a rough descent. Double-lock the wagons. Each driver will have a man to lead his team to the riverbank."

"Do we wait on the creek bank?" someone called out.

"Hattie?" Pete turned to her.

"No. Cross your wagon and take care of your team. Then come back to help someone else. This will take teamwork."

"Hattie here has crossed this before, so pay attention to her. Like she says, this is going to take teamwork. Some of you men station yourselves along the trail to help if a wagon gets in trouble. Leonard, you, Tommy, and Billy will take the loose stock across last. There's a path up river about one hundred feet. Several of you men take the women and children over there. They can climb down, but it's steep, so they'll need help. The first wagon over is to go downstream and pick up the women and children and ferry them across the river. Anyone who wants to can go look over the trail before we get started. Be ready to help, and good luck. Remember—go slow and be careful. If you feel like you're goin' to lose a wagon, jump and let the wagon go."

I walked over and stared down at the trail. It was scary.

"Hattie, let's leave the horses up here 'til we get the wagon down. After the women and children go down, I want to look at that trail. Maybe I'll take my horses down it." The trail was only about six feet wide with a steep wall of shale on one side. The other had a drop-off of at least thirty feet. It would be a difficult walk, let alone taking a wagon down.

"This is really going to be a challenge," I told the other girls. We checked our harnesses and hitched up the wagon. For added safety we put rawhide leg wraps on the mules.

We'd just finished when Pete yelled out, "Okay, lead off! Hattie, take your wagon across!"

"Martha, you drive." Hattie said, "I'll lead Rowdy." I took the reins and watched her as she walked beside the mule, talking to him as if he were human. His ears flicked, and he gave her no trouble. He slipped, fell, got up, and kept going. Following his lead, the other mules remained calm. From my seat I could see parts of wagons that hadn't made it. The tenseness I felt when I heard the murderer was on the train was nothing to what I felt now. I don't think I took a breath until we reached the bottom.

Tag limped up to me holding up a paw with blood dripping. He had a bad cut from the shale. I wrapped his paw and lifted him into the wagon and

Six Women West

ordered him to stay. There, Hattie took over the reins and went downstream to pick up the women and children. We crossed, and Hattie stayed to take care of the cuts on the mule's feet from the shale. I rode a mule back to the top to bring the horses across. As I approached the waiting wagons, I could hear Mr. Perkins yelling at his wife, who was crying.

"I need a driver!" he called out. "My woman's afraid to take the wagon down."

"I'll drive," I told him. "Jane, you and the boys go walk down that other trail."

"They'll ride. Pete's wrong this time." Perkins growled. "Anyway, what kind of a wagon boss lets a woman tell him what to do?"

"Well, Pete said ..." Jane stammered.

"Never mind. Do as I tell you. You just sit there and hold the brake."

"Mr. Perkins, I don't think..." I began and was quickly interrupted.

"Girl, this is my wagon and my family. They'll do as I say. You just drive."

I could see there was no point in arguing with him. I loose-tied Randy to the back of his wagon and climbed up on the seat. Jane sat beside me, shaking and speechless with fright. The three boys huddled in the back. I told them to sit close to the tail gate. The new baby lay in a basket behind the seat.

We were almost half way down when shale started falling. The mules spooked and reared, jerking the lead ropes out of Perkins hands. He stumbled and fell. Jane gasped and cried out. He regained his footing and, waving his hands, tried to catch the loose rope. That panicked the mules even more. Shouting obscenities, he grabbed at the rope. The lead mule reared, striking him a mighty blow to the head, knocking him over the embankment. Jane screamed and let loose of the brake. The mules bucked, jumped, and knocked into each other and then bolted. I yelled, "Jump!" The boys were yelling and crying. All I could do was hold on to the reins and pray. We were at the narrowest part of the pass, just room for a wagon. The wagon started to slide. An accident seemed unavoidable. Taking a deep breath, I yelled, "Jump! "Jump!" I shrieked as one wheel slipped over the rim. "Jump! Go!" I yelled. Jane didn't move. She was frozen, holding on to the wagon seat.

Dropping the reins, I pushed Jane and grabbed the baby from the basket and vaulted from my seat, flying through space and then hitting the ground with a thud. I lost my hold on the baby and bounced down the embankment. The wagon, separated from the mules, slid past me. I could hear Jane's shrieks mixing with the screams of the mules and the cracking of the wagon. Then, all was dark.

My head ached and throbbed. I opened my eyes and closed them quickly against the light. In the distance I heard a voice call my name. More darkness. When I woke up again, Becky and Charlie were with me. "Oh, my head," I moaned. "What happened?" There was light filtering through the canvas. I was laying down inside the wagon, "Why am I here?"

"There was an accident. You'll be okay," Charlie said softly.

I tried to lift my head without success. I was dizzy, and it hurt everywhere. "Jane? The baby? Did they make it?"

"Be still, dear. Don't try to move." Charlie put her hand on my shoulder.

"Did they make it?" I persisted.

"Jane and Gerald didn't make it. We buried them two days ago," Becky said softly.

I asked "The boys?"

They're bruised and scared, but they'll be alright. They jumped out the back."

"The baby? I had her, but..."

"I'm sorry, Martha. She was next to you on the ground. She had a broken neck. We buried her with the parents."

"Oh, God, how awful," I moaned.

"Morgan saw the wagon go over. I never saw a man move so fast in my life. He scrambled down that cliff and picked you up before anyone else got there." Charlie shook her head, as if in awe. "Hattie brought the wagon, and we got you inside and crossed over the river. After examining you, we decided to make this here hammock, so you wouldn't be bounced around on the way to the fort. You got a bruised-up foot that might take awhile to heal. Morgan wanted to take the wagon and go on ahead to get you to the doctor, but then we decided I could take care of you 'til we got there. You had us worried, girl. You've been out for a day and a half."

"I think Morgan would've killed Perkins if he wasn't already dead," Becky said, stroking my forehead.

"Morgan?" I whispered, pleased at his reaction.

"That's enough talk," Charlie said. "You rest now."

"My horses? Where are they?"

"Don't worry. Morgan's taking good care of them too. Now you rest."

"I'll tell Hattie she's awake," Becky said, climbing up front. "Hattie, Martha's awake. I'll take over if you want to say hello."

"Thanks, Becky." She crawled over the seat. "We've been waitin' for you to come to, girl. Thought you was gonna sleep for a week. How you feelin?"

"Not too good," I answered weakly. My stomach began to roll, and I felt hot, clammy, unable to breathe. "Charlie, roll up the canvas. I need some air. Hurry. I'm going to be sick."

"Hand me that bucket, Hattie," Charlie said. "And roll up the canvas, please." She held the bucket where I could reach it. "I was waiting for you to be sick. Go ahead, honey. Let it out. You'll feel better."

I rolled over on my side and threw up. "Help me to sit up," I said, when I'd finished puking. "That air feels good." I held my head. "Horse feathers, my head feels like it was hit with a rolling pin. Got a cold rag?"

"You have a good-sized lump." She placed a second pillow under my head and gave me a sip of water and put a cold rag on my head.

Pete rode up and peered in at me. "I see you're alive, girl. We've been worried about you. That was a nasty fall. You rest easy and keep your head down," Pete said.

The wagons were fanned out across the prairie. Behind him I could see several wagons pulling closer. "She okay?" someone called out. The white-canvas-covered wagons outlined against the clear blue sky came into focus.

"She's fine. Keep rollin'." He leaned in and smiled at me. "Everybody's been real concerned. We slowed the wagons so you'd have an easier ride." He turned his horse around. "Looks like Sara's havin' some trouble." He loped off in that direction.

"I got to go, Martha," Hattie said. "Somethin's goin' on at Sara's wagon."

"What is it?" I asked, trying to get to a sitting position.

"I don't know, but her wagon is sitting off the trail. I saw James ride off earlier. Pete's over there now." She climbed out the back and took off.

I grasped a wagon bow and pulled myself up enough to look out across the space. I could hear Pete calling Sara's name. She didn't answer. The

Six Women West

breeze felt cool to my face. I wiped my face with the rag.

"Becky, drive over to Sara's wagon," Charlie shouted. "There's something wrong.

We drove up just as Pete came out of the back of the wagon with Polly. She was crying hysterically. He handed her to Hattie and crawled back into the wagon. When he came out, he had Sara in his arms. She was tied and gagged.

"What happened?" he asked, removing the gag.

People crowded around the wagon. Everyone talked at once. "Who did this? What happened?"

Pete yelled, "Quiet now, folks." He began to untie Sara. "Let her talk."

"It was James," she cried. "He tied me up and stole Guy's horse."

"I saw him leave," Hattie said, rocking Polly back and forth in her arms. "Thought he was going to the brush."

"Charlie, get Morgan for me, will you?" I asked.

"I think he's ridin' drag. Why do you want him?" "I'll tell you later. Get Pete and that Jackson over here."

"What is it, Martha?" Pete said exasperated, "I got problems right now," he grumbled as he approached the wagon.

"Get Jackson. He's a federal marshal." Pete looked at me as if to ask how I would know. "Morgan told me a few days ago." I'd no sooner finished talking when Jackson rode up.

"Jackson, glad you're here. Martha tells me you're a marshal." Pete held out his hand, and the two men shook hands. "Seems this James fella tied Sara up and stole her husband's horse."

"I'm sure he's the man I've been chasin'—the one who robbed the army payroll and killed a man. I'm gonna need men to ride with me. I'd like to have the soldiers." He glanced around. "Morgan about?"

"He's riding drag. I'll send someone to get him," Shiloh said.

"I'll go," Becky volunteered, climbing down from the wagon with Tag jumping right behind her.

"Shiloh, take Jackson to the other soldiers," Pete said, "and do what he tells you." Shiloh rode off with Jackson.

"Okay, folks, we're done here," Pete shouted. "You okay to drive, Sara? Want me to send for Guy?"

"No, I'm fine. Don't bother him." She smiled bravely and held out her arms to Hattie. "I'll take Polly now, Hattie. Come on, Polly. You can sit next to me."

"Don't forget to tie her to the wagon seat," reminded Hattie.

"Yes, I will," replied Sara. "Ask Becky to come ride with me when she gets back."

"Get your wagons rollin', folks." The crowd dispersed, and within ten minutes we were on our way.

"Oh, Charlie, what a time to be laid up," I complained weakly. I lay back and closed my eyes. I was so tired.

CHAPTER THIRTY THREE

Coming out of a heat-induced sleep, I rousted up just as we pulled into Fort Bridger. "I'm goin' for the doctor," Charlie said. "If I know you, you'll be wantin' to get up and out of here. I want him to say whether it's okay." She patted me on the shoulder, "You stay put." She climbed down out of the wagon and disappeared into a crowd of soldiers who turned out to help get our wagon settled. While I waited, I could hear the hubbub outside as they unhitched our mules and led them off. Why'd they put us inside the fort? I wanted to get out of this wagon and look around.

I was still trying to untangle myself from the hammock when Charlie showed up with the doctor. He checked me over and told me to stay in bed for another day and to stay off my foot. I had a pulled tendon. Then he complimented Charlie on the care she'd given and left, saying he'd be back in a couple of days.

"Charlie," I said, "I don't care what he said. I've been laid up here until I'm cabin sick. I insist I be moved outside so I can have more air."

"Oh, Martha, you are so pigheaded. What's the use of havin' the doctor if you won't listen to him?"

"Well, he doesn't know me. I know myself better than a stranger does. I say I can at least sit outside for awhile." I looked at her in what I hoped was a beguiling manner.

"Okay. I guess there's no point in arguing. Just wait, and I'll go get Sara's rocker."

"See if there's any news about the posse," I called after her.

"You mean about Morgan, don't you?" She yelled back.

I started to protest, but she was out of earshot. *Besides,* I admitted silently, *she was right.* After what they'd told me about how he'd acted when I got hurt, I'd had a softening of the heart. Maybe I was wrong about him. Maybe he didn't just want my horses. Or a quick roll in the hay.

Charlie returned with the rocker. "Charlie, why is our wagon here inside the fort?" I asked.

"So you can be close to the doc," she replied. "The others are camped right outside the fort. Let me find someone to help get you up." Charlie returned with Sara.. They gently helped me to get out of the wagon and onto the rocker.

"What's the news?" I asked. "Did they catch the guy?"

"One of the soldiers rode ahead of the troops. Told me that they're bringing the bodies in now. They should reach the fort soon," Sara said.

"The bodies?" My heart sank. "Whose bodies?" I stammered.

"He didn't say." She apparently saw something in my eyes, because she hastened to add, "I'm sure it wasn't Morgan."

"Hell, no," Charlie agreed. "Morgan can take care of himself."

Hattie walked over from the front gate. "Glad to see you up girl. What's this about my son?" she asked, joining us.

"It's nothing, Hattie. We were just commenting on how well he handles himself," I told her.

Abel walked up, interrupting her. "How do, ladies? You lookin' real fine, Miss Martha. Be up ridin' pretty soon, I reckon."

"I surely hope so, Abel. How's Bessie?"

"She's fine. We wuz talkin' 'bout them puppies you gittin'. Might be they 'bout ready to leave their ma now." He sat down on one of the camp chairs. "This shore is a clean fort. Have y'all seen the field around da fort? Lots of grass. Nice place to camp, and here we are sittin' right inside the fort on dirt ground."

The words had no sooner left his mouth than up walked Prissy carrying a large basket filled with furry, squirming, whining puppies. "Hi, Miss Martha. I brought the puppies to visit you." She plunked the basket down in front of the rocker. "See? Aren't they cute? The captain took one. He named him Tippy because he has white on his tail."

"They certainly are," I agreed, picking one up. "Daisy's been a good mom. They all look fat and healthy."

"Daddy says you can pick your two out now and keep them."

"He does, does he? " I looked up at Abel. "Which one do you want?"

"I want the gold one with the white chest," he said, lifting it from the basket.

"Is that alright, Prissy?" I asked, not knowing whether it was one she had chosen to keep.

"That's okay. Papa said we should take turns choosing."

"Good. Abel's can be counted as one of mine. Now you choose."

Prissy had a hard time deciding which one she wanted. Finally, she picked up one of the females. "Say, Martha, a man at the post stopped me and asked about Bessie and Abel. He asked me the dumbest question. Wanted to know who they belonged to. I told him they didn't belong to nobody. They belong to themselves and if he wanted more information to ask you."

Before I could answer, the sentry called out, "Riders approaching."

"It's the posse," Abel said. "Looks like they be bringin' back some dead."

"Charlie, go see. Hurry!" I urged. "Wait. They're coming this way. Prissy, take the puppies home and stay with your mama. Go on now."

"Okay, Martha. I'll come back later. Bye."

As the riders approached across the parade grounds, I breathed a deep sigh of relief, noting that Morgan was one of them. All the men looked tired, hot, and dirty.

He nodded, looking at me with a solemn expression. Behind him plodded the horse carrying a body and then a young soldier leading another horse with a body on it also. We all stared, wondering who had been killed.

Suddenly, Becky lunged forward and screamed, "It's Shiloh! That's his ring. Oh! My God, what happened?"

Sara reached and took Becky in her arms, but Becky pulled away and stood up real straight. Jackson rode up and we turned to him for answers. "Sorry, Miss," he said. "Your man was a hero. He stood up to James and got shot. There was nothing we could do."

"James? Did you get him?" Hattie asked.

"Yes, ma'am. Leonard Hobbs shot him dead. It was a bad deal."

Becky had turned deathly white and was rocking back and forth. I reached up and pulled her down to me. She kneeled by the rocker. Putting my arms around her, I whispered, "It's alright, Becky. It's alright," I told her, knowing that it wasn't and wouldn't be for awhile. He was her first love. He wouldn't be forgotten.

Later a couple of the soldiers came and said they had orders to put up our tent. Becky had calmed down and was over with Bessie drinking a cup of coffee. I started thinking of what Prissie told me earlier. *Why was this man asking questions about Bessie and Abel? Where did he come from, and what did he want?* I asked myself. If he was one of those who hunt down slaves, I needed to put a stop to his inquires as soon as possible. Our wagon sat near the fence inside the fort, and Abel's was right behind us. We could see the entire place—the store, mess hall, cantina, hospital, men's quarters, and the office quarters.

Sara and Polly walked up. "It's so sad about Shiloh. He was so young. How's Becky doing?"

"She's pretty shook up, but she's young and strong. She'll be alright." I paused. "Sara, Becky mentioned that someone was asking about Bessie and Abel. Have you seen anyone who looks like one of those slave bounty hunters?"

"As a matter of fact, some rather scary-looking character has been asking about them. He looks mean enough to be a slave hunter. I saw him go into the saloon."

"Hand me my crutch, please. I must go talk to him."

"Martha, you can't go alone. He doesn't seem to be the type that has respect for ladies, or anyone for that matter. Get Morgan or one of the other men to go with you. Or wait for Guy. He'll be back soon."

Bessie came around the corner from the back of her wagon and hung a quilt on the wagon wheel to air. "Bessie," I called, "would you find Morgan and bring him here. I need his help."

"Sho', Miss Martha. Ah'll go right now."

"He was with the marshal at the captain's office awhile ago," Sara said. "He may still be there."

Sara and I sat by the wagon in our most unusual camp and played with Polly while we were waiting for Bessie. She returned with Morgan some ten minutes later. Apparently noticing my expression, he asked, "Is something wrong? Is it Becky?"

"No, she's upset, but she'll be alright. It's about Bessie and Abel. I've been told there's a man at the trading post asking questions about them. I suspect he's a bounty hunter. I need you to stand with me while I talk with him." I stared at Morgan. He looked truly rugged with several days' growth of beard, and trail-hardened with his gun tied down.

"Sure, Martha, but why don't you let me handle it? No need for you to go along." He shook his head. "You're not well yet."

"I'm well enough," I assured him in my no nonsense voice. "I just need a little help walking. It's not far to the saloon. He's a rough man, and I want to have a man with me."

"Boy, you are one hardheaded woman, Martha Patterson. I don't have the energy to argue with you right now, so, come on, up you go." He put his hands under my arms and pulled me out of the rocker.

"Now just lean on me. I can hold you up."

"Oh pshaw! Just hand me that crutch. I can manage fine," I insisted, and then to my humiliation, I stumbled and would have fallen if he hadn't caught me.

To his credit, he didn't make any smart remarks, just helped me regain my balance. "I'll walk alongside, alright?" he said.

"Alright," I agreed meekly.

It's not more than a hundred feet to the boardwalk. I requested that your wagon be put inside. I know it's not as nice, but that way you can make it to the store and the necessary house, and there's a bath house you ladies can use. "What's this about Bessie and Abel? Are they runaways?" Morgan asked.

"No. Bessie bought her freedom and was told she was free, but the papers she believed to be real were fakes. The woman deceived her, and Bessie couldn't read. Now she has good papers that no one could contest. I believe Abel does have papers." I frowned. "I'm not sure bounty hunters care whether or not they have papers. They're just after the reward."

A seedy character with a mean look about him leaned against the railing in front of the saloon. The bat-winged doors of the saloon were right behind him.

"I think that's him," I whispered.

"Let me talk to him first, Martha. He don't look the kind to have respect for ladies."

I nodded, unsure now of my ability to confront such a person. He reminded me of Abner and brought back bad memories.

Morgan approached the man, held out his hand and said, "Howdy. I hear you been askin' about the negroes on our train?"

"Yep, that's a fact," he replied brusquely, ignoring Morgan's hand. He spit out a stream of tobacco juice, wiped his chin on a dirty kerchief, and asked, "You know somethin?"

"Well, for one thing, they're not slaves. They have their papers, so they can't be the ones you're lookin' for."

"The female fits the description of the whore who ran away from Rosie O'Day a few months back. She's hired me to find her and bring her back. I'd like to see her papers if you don't mind." Squinting, he fingered the gun in his hip holster.

"I didn't get your name," Morgan said, stepping closer and staring into his eyes.

"Harry Jinks, and you are?" he asked, taking Morgan's measure.

"Deputy Morgan Brooks." He slid his hand near his revolver. "A word to the wise, Jinks. As a slave hunter, you're not welcome in the territory. It might be a good idea if you moved on."

Jinks stepped back, his hand hovering near his gun. "I don't want trouble, Deputy. Jes get the niggers I came for."

"You've got five minutes to be off this post, vertical or horizontal—your choice." Morgan motioned me to move away. "What's it gonna be, Jinks?" Morgan persisted.

I move quickly over to the far side of the boardwalk near the side of the cantina, out of firing range.

Jinks' face took on a scowl as if he'd like nothing better than to shoot Morgan. I held my breath as he made up his mind.

"Got some trouble here, Morgan?" Marshal Jackson stepped out of the saloon behind Jinks. Jinks turned, glanced at the star on Jackson's, and then turned back at Morgan.

"Do we, Jinks?" Morgan asked, his eyes staring into the bounty hunter's.

"I was jes leavin', Marshal. Ma'am." He tipped his hat, climbed on his horse, and rode off toward the gate.

Shaken, I leaned against the building and drew a deep breath. Leaning on my crutch, I moved back to the rail.

"You alright, Martha? You look kind of pale. Maybe we better get you back to your wagon," Morgan said, taking my arm.

"I'm fine. I just…thanks, Morgan." My head was spinning.

"No problem. Here, lean on me. You know the marshal?"

"Yes, you introduced us awhile back. Nice to see you, Marshal. It was good timing."

"Glad to be of service, ma'am." He smiled and inclined his head towards Morgan. "I have to get the report from the captain. Then I'll be on my way. Thanks for your help in nabbing James and recovering the payroll money. You did a good job. There'll be a reward for you. We need good men in this business. You interested?"

"No, Jackson. Thank you, but I'm going on to Oregon to build a horse ranch and raise a passel of young ones." He paused, then added, "That is, if I can get a certain lady to agree." He didn't look at me.

"Well, I'm glad for you and sorry for me. I hope she says yes." Jackson smiled at me.

I pulled away from his grip on my waist and held on tight to my crutch and began walking away.

"Wait, Martha. Let me help you," Morgan started towards me.

"I don't need your help," I snapped, forgetting that without it I would have fallen earlier, not to mention how he'd handled Jinks.

"Fine!" He sounded angry and disgusted. I couldn't blame him. One minute I was thanking him, and the next I was snapping at him. And I didn't know why.

I made it back to the wagon without falling and seated myself in the rocker. I was so upset I could have just spit! Gosh darn it, why did I let that man get my goat? Try as I might, I couldn't stop thinking of Morgan and the person he planned to marry. Part of me wanted to believe it was me. After the talk with Hattie, it could very well be. Still, there was that Lorraine. Young and pretty and oh so willing.

"Did you find that bounty hunter?" Sara asked, thankfully interrupting my thoughts.

"Yes, we did. Morgan made him leave the fort. I don't think we'll be hearing anymore from him. I was so scared. I thought they were going to have a gunfight."

"Good, he left." She started to leave and then obviously remembered something. "Shiloh's funeral is this afternoon. I saw Mary Beth earlier. Her eyes were all swollen. She looked awful. Poor thing. I guess she was quite smitten with Shiloh."

I thought, *Sure she was, the way she let him have his way with her.* She left, and with my foot propped up on a box I dozed until the Hattie woke me.

"You up to goin' to the funeral?" Hattie asked.

"Yes, of course. Where's Becky?"

"She took off on her horse awhile ago. Said she'd say her goodbye her own way."

"That's Becky," I answered as Hattie helped me out of the rocker and we joined up with the others of our group. The funeral was simple and nice. The post gave Shiloh a twelve-gun salute. Shiloh would have been pleased. He was buried in the fort cemetery outside the stockade. Mary Beth standing beside her mother crying openly. Her bruised and swollen cheek didn't go unnoticed. Becky's absence was noticeable.

Pete held a meeting about where the three orphaned Perkins boys would go, and a nice couple at the fort spoke up. Mr. and Mrs. Gates were heading back east. They ask for the boys. "We have a ranch in Wyoming territory. There are cattle and horses and plenty of work for all of us. You boys don't mind cowboy work, do you?"

"No, sir," Thomas replied. He looked at his brothers. They nodded. Tom held out his hand. Gates shook it, and Mrs. Gates burst into tears.

"I'm so happy, boys," she blubbered. "I got me three boys. Thank you, God." Everyone laughed and talked while congratulations passed around. Hattie hugged her close, and there were tears in everyone's eyes.

Mr. Gates had his hand on Tom's shoulder, "The captain told me he got a puppy from someone off your train. If you boys want one...."

"Want one! You bet we do. The black one!" They spoke all at once.

"On that note, let's close this meetin'."

Morgan, Hattie, and I walked back to the far side of the fort where our wagon had been placed. You could hear someone playing the harmonica from the wagons camped outside. Charlie was gone when we arrived. We guessed she had gone off with Luke. Becky hadn't returned, and I was becoming concerned.

"Suppose we should go look for Becky?" I asked.

"No need," Hattie said. "I saw her ride in as we were leavin'. She's probably in the tent restin'. She's coming to terms with Shiloh's passin'."

"I know. He was a scoundrel, but he did have charm, and Becky was truly fond of him. The Gates seemed real glad to get the boys. I surely hope they'll be happy."

"Tom said he had a big ranch with cows and horses. He'll keep them busy teaching them ridin', ropin', and brandin'. I'll have the marshal check on them from time to time," said Morgan, "and make sure they're alright. If things go wrong, I'll go get them."

I laughed, thinking of Lorraine with those three boys. I just gave him a dirty look.

What's eatin' you, Martha? You're not still worried about that bounty hunter, are you?" asked Morgan.

"No. It's nothing. I'm just tired." I went in the tent and closed the flap. I could hear Hattie and Morgan talking.

"You and Martha have a fallin' out?" Hattie asked. "She seems a bit touchy."

"Not as far as I know. She's got a burr under her saddle. Maybe her foot's botherin' her." They walked away out of my hearing.

Burr under my saddle. I'd like to put a burr under his saddle. I fell asleep, awaking a few hours later to the smell of coffee and roasting meat.

CHAPTER THIRTY FOUR

After three days at the fort, we were restocked and ready to be back on the trail. I was off the crutch. My foot was still tender, but at least I could walk. The night before, our usual group gathered around the campfire. When supper was over and the music started, several men from the fort came over to enjoy the music of Luke and Charlie. Becky was quiet but seemed to enjoy the music too. Abel and Bessie, both smiling widely, tapped their feet in rhythm.

Guy sat with his arm around Sara, her head on his shoulder. Polly was fast asleep on a blanket beside them. Morgan sat next to Hattie. Tag was curled up next to the fire sleeping. *Everyone had someone,* I thought. I had no doubt there was someone out there for Becky, but was there anyone for me? The fire burned low. Soon the others went to their respective wagons, and Becky and Charlie said their goodnights and went to bed. Only Hattie and I were left sitting by the fire.

"Martha, is something wrong between you and Morgan?"

"No, nothing wrong. Just different ways of seeing things." I didn't feel like explaining. Hattie apparently sensed it because she changed the subject.

"Bear River was easy traveling. Now we've got a hundred fifty miles of rugged mountains and wilderness between here and Fort Hall or what used to be —it's burned now. I'd like to use four-ups and change teams each day. I think it would save on the animals."

"Okay. I trust your judgment."

"I hear an artist joined the train—a young single man who wants to paint the west," Hattie smiled.

"Maybe our sweet Lorraine will leave Morgan alone and set her cap for him. Or even Mary Beth."

I laughed lightly. "Won't that break Morgan's heart?"

"The only one who can break his heart is you, girl. Sure wish you could see that."

Choosing to ignore her remark, I commented, "There are four wagons to join up with us. The Locklanders have four young ones, and Hadleys have five. They all wintered at the fort, and there's one other family. I haven't heard anything about them yet. You say there's a single man joining too. We'll have a lot of young ones. Maybe some of them are going to California.

"Only one wagon takin' the cut-off. Well, I hope they're no trouble for Pete. Guess I'll be gettin' some shut-eye. You comin'?" She walked around the wagon to the tent.

"I'll be there in a few minutes." I stood and flexed my ankle. It hardly hurt at all. I glanced across the fort parade ground near the saloon area and saw Morgan and Lorraine. She was talking, and he was shaking his head. My shoulders slumped. Who or what should I believe? Hattie's words or Morgan's actions? Pa always told me actions speak louder than words. Heartsick, I walked to our tent, and the green-eyed monster danced in my dreams of Morgan.

At breakfast we watched the morning change from an inky darkness to the dim gray of dawn as we drank coffee. Morgan and Abel brought our teams in from the pasture all harnessed and hooked them to our wagons.

"Gonna be a nice day," Hattie said. "We can pick up the other stock outside the fort."

"That's okay, Ma. I'll have them ready when you drive by. Martha, you going to ride the wagon today?"

"Yeah, I'll drive today and let my foot rest."

We were on the trail within the hour, moving single file down the barely visible trail. In the distance one could see tall pines and a jagged outcrop of rocks. Farther out, snowcapped mountains overlooked it all. The air was cooler here—almost cold.

Mile after mile we covered the faint trail as the sparse trees became thicker. After awhile the sun filtered between the trees as we moved slowly forward. Then they thin out. At noon we camped at a small clearing. You could see signs of those who had camped there before.

Morgan was riding point with Guy. I'd been doing a lot of thinking and come to the realization I'd acted stupidly and rude. I hadn't even thanked him for the way he handled that Jinks person. He could have been shot, and it would have been my fault. For one who told herself she didn't care, I certainly let the thought of him marrying someone else affect my manners and my actions. No wonder he was barely speaking to me.

I wondered what the woman he'd end up marrying would be like. Surely, I decided, it wouldn't be Lorraine. She was pretty, yes, but I couldn't see her as a partner on a ranch, helping with the horses. One minute I was telling myself I could be that person, and the next I was reminded of my own goals—the ones that didn't include a man. No man was going to hogtie me in a house, baking bread and changing diapers.

Several days passed, and I was back riding most of the time and was determined to put thoughts of Morgan, Lorraine, and marriage out of my mind. By concentrating on the daily tasks and admiring the countryside, I almost managed. It was August, but here the weather was quite cool. We climbed steadily, moving into the high mountains. They were a new experience for me. I could look down on the treetops and meadows full of colorful wildflowers. I found the wide expanses of meadow beautiful.

I had offered at noon to take over the reins so Hattie could walk or ride. I hoped having to concentrate on driving would keep my mind off Morgan. Last night's dreams had been full of him, his kisses, and his laughing eyes. How could he have kissed me like that and think of marrying someone else? A large dirt clod hit the side of the wagon, startling me. Becky yelled, "You sleepin' on the job?"

"Guess I nodded off," I admitted sheepishly, unwilling to confess I was daydreaming. I straightened up and got the mules back in line. Horse feathers! I just had to quit thinking about that man.

It was close to noon when Guy rode in. "There's a long narrow ravine ahead with a possibility of slides, so keep alert." He rode on down the line to let the others drivers know.

The terrain suddenly changed to high walls on both sides with a trail just wide enough for one wagon. I had to concentrate all my thought on the mules. They were acting skittish because of being closed in. It was all I could do to keep them under control. Hattie came back to the wagon, and seeing the struggle I was having, she took over. I stayed on the wagon in case she needed help.

We'd gone about three miles when Morgan and Pete galloped past us going down the line yelling, "Hold up the wagons, folks!" They returned riding the other way at a flat-out full run.

"Hattie, I'll be right back. I'm going to see what's going on." I got down and climbed on Lady. I caught up with Morgan and Pete nearly a quarter mile the other side of a small creek.

"Holy Cow! Look at that!" I exclaimed, as I stared at the slide at least ten feet high, completely blocking the trail. "Isn't there another way to cross?" I looked at Morgan. He glanced at me and turned away. No smile. No wink.

"This trail was carved out by earlier travelers," Morgan said. "You see the thick brush and trees all around? That's how it is for miles. We get the dirt cleaned out, and it will be an easy crossing."

"Morgan's right, Martha. It would take a lot longer and a lot more labor to clear another trail," Pete agreed.

"This is going to cost us a lot more time, isn't it?" I asked.

"Yes, afraid so!" Pete turned to me. "Go tell the others to move the wagons up by the creek, and tell 'em there will be a meeting right away."

I galloped back to the wagons, met Becky at Moe's wagon, and asked her to help spread the word. As we passed each wagon we yelled, "Camp at the creek trail. Blocked trail at the creek."

At the creek, Luke took charge of placing the wagons. He stood in front of the wagons and pointed them left or right, making a rectangle since there was no room to circle the wagons. It worked real well.

By the time Pete arrived, everyone was standing near his wagon waiting for him to give orders. He climbed on the chuck wagon and yelled, "Gather 'round. We've got a landslide ahead—a bad one." He took off his hat and wiped his brow. "We'll need skids and torches so we can work all night. Be mighty nice to have a round-the-clock kitchen with food and coffee." He looked at Bessie. "Starting now?"

"Yassir, Mr. Pete," Bessie said. Ah'll keep the coffee hot."

"We'll help," a few of the other women called out.

The group split up. Most men went ahead to look at the slide. The women started making camp. Soon poles were cut and lashed to trees to form a pen for the stock. A small footbridge was erected across the stream.

"How bad is the slide?" asked Gil Rogers.

"Pretty bad," Guy told him. "Gonna' take some real man power to get it cleaned up so we can pass."

"How much time is this going to delay us?" I asked.

"I'd guess at least four days. Depends on how much effort goes into clearing it." Guy looked at Gil as if to ask how much he'd help.

"That new guy, Harold, says he's going to draw the slide. He's always drawing the wagons or the people," Gil rambled on, ignoring Guy's silent question. Obviously he preferred talking to working.

"I got work to do. See you later." Guy walked away shaking his head. "See you later, Martha."

I walked back to our wagon where a number of women stood around choosing up shifts for cooking.

"We gonna' need some big cookin' pots and coffeepots," Bessie said. "Suppose we can get the young 'uns to tote de firewood?"

"Sure," I said, noticing that she had dropped back to her plantation speech. "It'll do them good to help."

"There are more than a hundred to be fed," Hattie informed us. "The men will be cleanin' away the slide, so it'll be up to us women to do everthin' else."

"I'll go get the children started gathering wood. Then I'll check on our stock," I said. "Be back soon."

"No need to hurry. We got plenty of help," Hattie added.

Times of crisis were about the only times we got together with the other women on the train. I suppose it was because we were all either busy or tired. The dances were an exception, giving us all a chance to gussy up and forget our cares for awhile.

Wanda Reed

After I gave instructions about teams to gather firewood to the small boys, I turned the mares out to graze. I decided to take Hattie at her word. I walked with Tag down to the creek and sat under a large pine tree while I watched a blue jay jumping from branch to branch. I was enjoying the smell of cool mountain air and the musical sound of water over rocks when a big frog jumped up on the bank, and Tag tried to catch him.

Despite my resolve, my thoughts drifted towards Morgan. I could see the dark curly hair on his chest and his muscled arms. *What would it be like,* I wondered, *to be held tightly in those arms, to be pressed against his strong chest?*

Charlie rode up, interrupting my reverie. "Are you going to loaf all day?"

I stood and stretched. "No, just daydreaming. You and Becky been hunting?"

"Yep, we got two mule deer." Suddenly a shrill scream broke the stillness. Charlie wheeled Paint and took off at a gallop towards the sound. I followed, running as fast as I could with a bad ankle.

Comment [CJH]: IMPORTANT: Something is missing after this. In the next chapter they have gone on.

CHAPTER THIRTY FIVE

At sunrise the wagons were on the trail and keeping a fast pace. I rode up alongside Pete. "How long are we going to keep this pace?" I asked.

"We'll get back to normal when we get to the California cut-off."

"How many wagons are going to California?"

"Four or five and darn near fifty of the single men. We're gonna miss them. Things could get rough without their help if there's trouble."

For awhile we rode in silence. Pete seemed tense, his gaze focused on the hills around us. "It's said there was an Indian attack right near here. Everybody was killed 'ceptin' two boys." He sighed and shook his head.

"How awful," I said, scanning the dry brown hills, hoping I didn't see anything.

"Just a ways further, they got the Adams train. That was in 1862 in this same month." He glanced at me, and apparently noticing I was upset, added, "Don't worry, Martha. We'll be okay."

Easy to say, I thought, *but hard to do*. I left him and returned to the wagon. I didn't repeat what he'd told me, figuring there was no point in worrying anyone else. I kept a sharp eye on the sun-baked hills the rest of the day.

Late in the day, the area changed from dry grass to a partial green and a scattering of trees nearby. We made camp not far from the falls. The weather-beaten sign noted they were called the American Falls. They were beautiful, cascading over the rocks with a powerful force.

Charlie, Becky, Hattie, Sara, Bessie, and I found a secluded spot and went for a swim and bathed in the cool, clear water. Charlie pulled me aside. "Mary Beth asked me if I had somethin' to start her monthly. She thinks she's with child."

Wanda Reed

The vision of Shiloh on top of the girl flashed in my mind, causing me to wonder if the baby was Shiloh's. "What did you say?" Poor Charlie, I thought. She had enough to worry about with Boris.

> **Comment [CJH]:** Who's Boris? The only other reference for that name is Josephine Tanner's husband, but I don't understand the connection here. Might this be something from the missing section?

"I gave her some slippery elm and told her it was up to her and God what she should do, but whatever she did to do it right away or it wouldn't work."

"Poor thing! How could she be so stupid to repeat the same mistake. You can't help but feel sorry for her. You know, it could have been Becky if Shiloh had had his way."

"That randy bastard," Charlie said. "Wonder how God deals with somebody like that."

> **Comment [CJH]:** I removed this phrase because it really didn't sound like something Martha would say: "God made him pay with his life here on earth," I replied, "and now his soul will be in eternal damnation."

We just stayed one night at the falls. The next day we passed Massacre Rocks. I could sense the sprits of the dead buried here. It was a big relief when we left. A few days later, we reached the California cut-off and the wagons parted, forming two circles. A meeting was held to elect a wagon boss for the California train.

Juanita came to our wagon as soon as we made camp, asking for Charlie. "She's changing clothes. I'll get her." Charlie, Mary Beth's Ma wants you."

"Let's see what she wants. Hello Mrs. Robert's. You need me?"

"Yes, Charlie. Mary Beth has a stomach problem. I think she ate something bad. Could you take a look?"

"Sure. I'll be right over. Let me get my bag. Martha come with me. You'll need to know this."

As we walked to their wagon, she said, "I know what it is. She used the slippery elm and is having a miscarriage."

We climbed in their wagon where Mary Beth lay ashen white and scared. "Hi," Charlie said. "You cramping hard? This will pass shortly. When did you take the tea?"

Six Women West

"Last night. I heard we would lay over here a couple of days." She doubled up in a cramp and shoved her fist in her mouth to stifle the cry. Then I saw the blood on the pad she lay on. Charlie raised the blanket and told her to bend her knees. Charlie pushed on her belly, and a bluish bag pass out. Charlie wrapped it in the bloody pad and put it in her bag. Then she padded Mary Beth with soft cotton material.

"You're lucky. You weren't far along. Take a teaspoon of laudanum and don't do any heavy work or lifting for a few days. It's not my business, but if you continue to have relations, you should try something to keep from getting with child. There are a couple of thing you can do. One is a condom. Try getting some at a brothel or at a drugstore. The other is having your partner pull out before he's done. Good luck. I'll tell your ma you're having female problems."

After we buried the pad we returned to our wagon and made ready for supper. "I've got somethin' to tell you," Charlie said, looking serious. "I'll be leavin' you here. I'm goin' with Luke to California."

There was a collective moan and cries of protest. "Now, ladies," Hattie said calmly, Charlie's got to do what's best for her. Much as we'll all miss her, and God knows I don't know what we'd have done without her, we can't hold her back."

"Hattie's right," I agreed, keeping back tears. "Charlie told me in the beginning she'd only be going so far with us."

"What will you do in California?" Sara asked.

"We plan on workin' as entertainers. Ranching is not what we want to do."

"You and Luke will do real fine, Miss Charlie. That Luke be a good man. He be treatin' you right," Bessie said, patting Charlie's hand.

"Thank you, Bessie," she said, hugging her tightly. "Luke is a good man. I'm a lucky woman."

"He's damn lucky, too," Becky stated firmly. "Will you be singin' in saloons?"

"We might have to in the beginning, but we want to perform on the stage. You know—buy our own establishment."

"That sounds nice," Sara said. "Who knows? Maybe you'll join up with one of those traveling shows and come to Oregon."

Charlie laughed. "Wouldn't that be somethin'? Well, nothin's for sure. That's one thing I've learned real good."

"Will you be staying with the California wagon train?" I asked.

"I don't think so. Luke didn't want to be wagon boss. We can travel faster alone."

"I'll be right back," Sara said. "I have to get something at my wagon. Polly, you stay."

"Yes, Mama," Polly said, leaning close to Tag.

Sara was back in a few minutes with a small, thin package wrapped in calico material and tied with blue yarn.

"It's not much, but I think you'll like it," Sara said, handing it to Charlie.

"Gosh, Sara, you didn't have to get me somethin'." She tried to open it without breaking the yarn, but finally gave up.

"What is it?" Becky asked.

"It's...oh, my goodness," Charlie stammered, breaking into tears. "Oh, Sara, how can I ever thank you? Look everybody!" She held up an embroidered linen cloth depicting Bessie, Hattie and Sara seated in the wagon, with Charlie, Becky, and me on our horses.

"Oh, Sara, it's beautiful. How did you do that?" I asked.

"I had Harold the artist sketch it, and I did the embroidery. I'm glad you like it, Charlie."

"Like it? I love it! A more precious gift I've never seen. Thank you, thank you," she cried, wiping at her tears. "This is so hard. You've been like sisters. It breaks my heart to leave, but like Hattie said, we have our own dreams to follow." She stared at each of us. "I'll never forget you, or crossing the Oregon Trail."

We hugged and cried, talked and reminisced 'til bedtime, and everyone returned to their wagons. "I wish them luck," Pete said. "They're good people."

"Yes," Morgan agreed. "They're lucky to have each other. It's a good partnership." He glanced at me, a question in his eyes. Not ready to answer, I looked away.

"Miss Martha," Prissy called, running up to the wagon. "Miss, Martha, Ruby Zinger wants to take one of my yellow puppies to California. Should I let her?"

"I don't know why not," I said. "Ruby seems like a responsible young lady." Smiling, I added, "You go home now. It's close to bedtime." She ran off, waving goodbye.

"Nice little girl," Morgan observed. "You're good with youngsters."

"I like children," I admitted.

A couple of the single men walked up. "Sorry to bother you, Pete, but we need your advice."

"Martha, come with me," Charlie said walking to the tent.

"Well, I'll be going too," Pete said. "Got another early mornin'. You comin', Morgan?"

"Right with you," Morgan said, rinsing his coffee cup and placing it next to the pot. "Night, Ma. See you tomorrow, ladies."

"Goodnight, son," Hattie said.

Charlie turned to me. "I'll leave you some of my medicine. I hate to pile this on you, but I want to go with Luke. I love him and he loves me. I'll keep in touch."

"I believe Luke loves you, and I'm glad for you. You're going to knock San Francisco off its feet. Charlie, too bad I didn't have a sister like you."

I was up at dawn. The early darkness slowly turned to flame-red as the sun began to appear over the horizon. I fed the fire, started coffee, and took a walk around camp. A young man leaned against a tree, staring at the sunrise. He held a large pad in front of him and would glance from it to the sky and back and make marks on the pad. I guessed he was Harold, the artist I'd been told about.

"Morning," I greeted.

"Morning, Miss," he replied in what I considered a genteel voice.

"I'm Martha Patterson." I held out my hand.

Harold Pierce." He set down the pad and shook my hand. The touch was soft but firm with his long, slender fingers.

He was attractive with a narrow face, slim build, dark wavy hair, and brown eyes.

"May I see?" I asked, indicating the sketch pad.

"It's not finished." He held it up.

"It's lovely," I said.

"Would you like to see some of my other sketches?"

"Yes, I'd like that."

"Come on," he said, and walked toward his wagon. "I'll bring them out." He went in and came back out, carrying several rolled-up papers. He held each one up for me to see.

"Why, that's me and Lady!" I exclaimed. He had drawn me leaning my head against Gray Lady. "You made me look beautiful!" I blurted.

"I just drew what I saw," he said, apparently taken aback by my reaction.

"And this is the one Sara embroidered for Charlie." The other sketches were of families doing their morning chores. Women cooking over a campfire next to a wagon. "They're all wonderful. What are you going to do with them?"

"I plan to show them to art galleries back east. There's a big demand for Western paintings. Easterners are curious about anything west of Missouri. I'm looking forward to sketching Indians, too."

"I hope you'll show me when you do."

"I'd like that," He smiled, lighting up his face.

"Well, I better get back to my wagon. It was nice meeting you. Thank you for letting me see your pictures."

"Look, why don't you take this one of you? I can do another. That is, if you don't mind." He slipped the sketch of me and Lady out from the others and handed it to me.

"Oh, are you sure you want me to have this?" I said, overwhelmed with pleasure.

"I'm sure. When I get settled I'll turn them into oil paintings."

"I don't know what to say." I shook my head. "Thank you, Mr. Pierce."

"Call me Harold. Please."

"Harold, I'm Martha." We shook hands again, holding the grasp just a bit longer.

"Martha," I turned to see Morgan approaching. "Ma's lookin' for you. Charlie and Luke are leavin'," he muttered.

"I was just leaving. Thanks again, Harold. I'll treasure it always." I looked at Morgan. "Have you two met?"

"Harold Pierce," Harold said, holding out his hand.

"Morgan Brooks." The handshake seemed to be a test of strength with Morgan winning.

Men! I thought. They acted like little children. Was Morgan jealous? Was that the reason for the frown and the show of strength? *No*, I decided. *It had nothing to do with me. He was just being a man.*

"When did you get so interested in art?" he asked sarcastically on the way back to my wagon.

"Why, I've always admired talent," I retorted, striding ahead of him. The girls along with Abel, Guy, and Pete were gathered around Charlie and Luke.

"If you get up to Oregon, ask for the Brown ranch," Hattie was saying. "I'll know where the others are."

"Thanks, Hattie. Oh, good. You found her," Charlie said as Morgan and I walked up.

"Yeah, she was looking at pictures." He poured himself a cup of coffee and stood by Hattie.

"I'm sorry. I didn't realize you'd be leaving so early." I hugged Charlie tightly, tears filling my eyes. "I'm going to miss you, girl."

"I'll miss you, too. The best thing I ever done was sign on with you," she murmured.

I hugged Luke and wished him all the best. "Now you be good to Charlie, or I'll be after you with a shotgun," I said with a grin. He assured me I didn't have to worry.

After more hugging and best wishes, they mounted their horses and rode off, leaving an empty spot in our hearts but our lives a little brighter for knowing her.

Those going to California stayed camped, waiting for the other train to catch up. We on the Oregon train followed the Snake River towards Caldron Linn. The land was dry with heat that must have been a hundred coming off the volcanic lava beds. We climbed slowly upward through outcrops of rocks, sagebrush, scrub pines, and dry buffalo grass. After fifteen miles we camped that night alongside waterfalls that fell a good forty or more feet into a large, natural pool, surrounded by pine and aspen. After chores I joined Harold and watched with admiration as he sketched. Unlike

Morgan, he did not cause strange and unwanted feelings inside me. I felt comfortable and safe.

"How did you learn to draw?" I asked.

"As a youngster, I was raised by my mother in a tenant house. My father disappeared when I was three. Mother worked in a mill and was gone ten hours a day. I wasn't allowed to go outside while she was gone. I started drawing pictures of what I could see from the window. When I got older, I sneaked out, sometimes going to the waterfront or downtown to sketch what I saw." He grinned. "Couldn't let mother see them, or she'd know I'd disobeyed her."

Once again I was reminded of how lucky I'd been as a child. Hearing his story, I wondered how come he came across as one born to the upper class.

"When I was fourteen," he continued, "I worked in a boot shop. A customer, Mr. Rutherford, saw my drawings and offered to send me to art school. In appreciation, I drove his hack and took care of his horse."

"What a nice man," I said.

"Yes, he was wonderful. Through him I sold many pen and ink drawings. I was able to help mother and would have given her all I made, but she insisted I save it for my future. That was ten years ago. When I figured I had enough to get a wagon and join a train, I told Mr. Rutherford, and he agreed it was a good idea. He felt pictures of the West would sell very well in the East. He handles the sales in New York."

Morgan rode up, leading Lady. "Pierce," he said, nodding to him, and then looked at me. "I come to see if you'd like to ride over to Shoshone Falls. It's about five miles away, but worth the ride."

I hesitated. "Can Harold come? I know he'd like to sketch it."

The look that passed between Harold and Morgan apparently affected Harold's decision. "Thanks, but I want to finish this."

"Okay. See you later then." I climbed on Lady, waved goodbye, and rode off with Morgan leading the way.

For three miles we rode without speaking, Morgan in front and me tailing behind. Fed up with his attitude, I kicked Lady in the flanks and came alongside him. "I'd really like to know why you asked me to come, or why I agreed if this is how you're going to act," I said, glaring at him.

"What do you mean? What did I do?" He reined to a stop and tried without success to look innocent.

"You know," I said, still glaring. "You're acting like a jackass. Is it because I invited Harold?"

"I don't know why you'd want that city boy along, anyway," he growled. "He got a handshake like a woman."

"Well, I know the woman's hand you've been shaking! And what do you mean, city boy? You're from New York, too."

"Not the city!" he almost yelled.

"So, why didn't you get Lorraine to come with you? She's obviously sweet on you, and you apparently think she'll make a good partner. So, why bother with me?"

"Damn it, Martha! I don't know where you get your ideas. It's you I want."

Confused and scared, I kneed Lady in the ribs and galloped off, Morgan right behind me. I didn't stop until I reached the falls. The tons of raging water seemed to echo my own emotions.

Morgan rode up beside me. "I'm sorry. I don't know what to say to you, Martha. You don't seem to want to hear the truth. Would you rather I just stay clear of you?"

"I'm sorry, too, Morgan. I don't know what my problem is. I do care for you, and I don't want you to stay clear." I shook my head, sighing. He reached over and took my hand. Lifting it to his lips, he kissed it gently. I could feel the anger slipping away.

"It's a beautiful sight, isn't it?" he said, pointing at the falls.

"It is that," I agreed, sliding off Lady. He jumped off Raindrop and stood beside me. I leaned against him.

"Oh, Martha," he moaned, wrapping his arms around my waist. I didn't object as he kissed my neck. He turned me to face him, and his mouth sought mine. As we kissed, his hands fiddled with my braid, loosening it so that my hair hung loose.

"I love your hair. You're so beautiful," he murmured, planting small, hurried kisses on my face. *How could anything that felt so good be bad?* I wondered, giving into the desire flooding my body.

I didn't resist as he gently lowered me to the grass. "So beautiful," he whispered, lying beside me. We kissed, and his hands moved over my body, turning my blood to fire. Moaning, I tried to ignore the memory of my mother's words now filling my mind. *They only want one thing from women like you, Martha. And it isn't marriage. You're too big. Men want petite women... little...small...doll like...*my mind whirled with the sound of Ma's voice.

"No," I whimpered, pushing Morgan's hands away. I turned my head from his kisses. "No, I can't." I struggled to my feet. Grabbing Lady's reins, I vaulted onto the saddle. Without looking back, I rode off, crying hysterically.

"Martha, wait!" Morgan yelled.

Breathless, I stopped at a pile of rocks and dismounted, wiping my face and trying to get control of my feelings. It was as if my mind was fighting with my body. God knows I loved his kisses, and his touch set me on fire. His words were sweet and sounded sincere, but how could I be certain they would lead to marriage? Or would I be the one drinking slippery elm and dried mushroom tea?

Morgan rode up. He didn't dismount. He just looked at me. "Martha, when will you accept the fact you're a woman?"

"I am a woman. I don't need to copulate with you to prove it. And, I won't be responsible for any woods colt. I intend to be wedded before I'm bedded."

"I didn't hear anyone ask you to be bedded before you're wedded," he said quietly, then rode off.

Tears stung my eyes. I rode back to the wagons alone. Harold, busy at his easel, waved to me. "Everything okay? I saw your fellow ride in awhile ago."

"Everythin's not okay," I admitted. "But, I'll survive. What are you drawing?"

"That group of horses grazing in the trees. I asked Gus to take me to the falls this afternoon."

"Good idea. You'll like them. See you later."

Two days later we reached Thousand Springs. It was a beautiful sight with the water bursting out of the rocks, creating a white mist. Hattie said it was called that because of the many springs flowing into the river. Each day Pete had us up before daybreak, and at night we didn't stop 'til six o'clock, putting as many miles behind us a possible. Some were complaining that Pete was pushing too hard. His only reply was, "Do you want to get to Oregon this year?"

Nearly a week later, we lined up to cross the Snake River on the ferry run by a grizzled old man who charged six dollars for each wagon. He carried a rifle as if to protect his money. He docked the ferry and nodded to Hattie and said, "Been awhile since you been around, Miss Hattie."

"Well glory be, how the hell are you, Gris? This will be my last trip, so get me across safe," said

Hattie. "How's the missus and those ten young 'uns'?"

With a loud roar of a laugh, he said, "Ten young 'uns? You been gone a long time. Now we got fourteen and another on the way." He pushed off with his fare to cross the river. You could still hear his laughter.

Once all the wagons crossed, we made camp. Sara and I walked downstream and gathered bunches of watercress, sorrel, pursuance, wild onion, and dandelions that grew in the edge of the stream emptying into the river.

"These will be good with bacon pieces, grease, and vinegar poured over them," Sara said, and the men are catching fish. What a treat—fish and salad."

"Yes, a nice change," I agreed. "I'm getting tired of meat and biscuits. Wouldn't it be good to have some garden vegetables like corn on the cob or maybe a big squash or how about...."

"Just stop it," Sara interrupted, "You're making me hungry, and we got salad tonight. I'm so glad that Becky and Bessie know the good greens to eat."

Later that day, Pete had a meeting for drivers to inform us we were just a few days' travel from the upper route. "We'll be crossin' three rivers, so make sure your wagons are water-tight." He pointed to the Indians pulling in nets. "They seem friendly. You might see about tradin' for smoked fish. They're partial to tobacco and iron pots or calico."

Sara had invited Thelma Locklander to join us for supper as she had been watching Polly today for her while Sara gathered greens. Harold was also invited for supper. He brought his drawing of the Indians. The braves had put on their ceremonial costumes and danced their native dances so he could paint them. He gave them store-bought shirts and tobacco in appreciation.

You could see that Thelma was attracted to Harold. She was only sixteen but quite lovely. I noticed she looked frail like a bird with soft curves, the planes of her cheeks long and smooth. She had large dark eyes and full lips. Her beauty couldn't be hidden even by the shapeless dark Lindsey gray-wool dress. He showed us a drawing of a squaw sitting on the blanket holding a papoose. He looked at Thelma several times.

"It's beautiful," I told him sincerely. "One can just see the love between the mother and child." He had several sketches of the Indian camp showing the squaws washing clothes at the river, the braves squatting around the fire, and the little children playing with sticks. Later while we passed around his sketchbook, he took out another, and he sketched quick pictures of us sitting around the fire. One he didn't share, putting it behind the others. I believe it was of Thelma.

There were many words of admiration and praise for his work from everyone, including Morgan. I thought Harold looked surprised. Probably he was remembering how cold and unfriendly Morgan had been when they first met. Later, Harold bid us goodnight and went to see Thelma to her wagon.

We left camp early the next morning, traveling the upper Oregon Trail. There were thirteen wagons now. From our high vantage point we could look down on the wagons going to California. They appeared as white spots amidst the green. I prayed they would have a safe journey and find what they were looking for in California.

I rode by Prissy, who was walking. "Want a lift up?" I asked, stopping alongside her. She gave me her hand, and I pulled her up and sat her in front.

"Thanks, Mize Martha. I was getting' plumb tuckered out."

I smiled, urging Lady forward.

"You got homes for your puppy yet, Miss Martha?"

"Not so far—just the one, but I'm pretty sure I know who will take it."

"My daddy said they got to go. They been chewing up his socks and going piddle in the wagon. He said to get rid of them or he would."

"How is he going to do that?" I asked, frowning.

"He said he'd dig a hole an' throw them in. You won't let him do that will you, Miss Martha?"

"No honey, we won't let anything that bad happen to the puppies."

"What are you girls up to?" Pete asked, coming along side.

"We're giving away puppies, Pete. Want one?"

Pete laughed. "Give one to Hattie and one to Becky and tell 'em they're a gift from me. If they give you any backtalk, tell 'em about the hole."

"Okay, Pete we'll do it." I hugged Prissy. "I'll take you back to your wagon and tell your daddy he doesn't have to dig a hole now. You bring the puppies to my wagon, and we'll find a home for all of them. Okay?"

She nodded.

"Prissy, you told me there were four puppies and now there are more."

"It was four each. Daddy said not to scare you. Oh, thank you." She turned in her seat and gave me a big hug. "I love you, Miss Martha."

"I love you, too, Prissy." We rode to her wagon in blissful silence. "See you later, honey," I said, lowering her to the ground.

That evening we camped at Three Island Crossing. After supper, Prissy walked into camp lugging a basket of yelping puppies that were too big for the basket. She plopped it down in front of the tent. The two pups scrambled out of the basket. We all started laughing and reaching to round them up.

Prissy took the dark gold one and handed it to Hattie. "Pete said it's a gift for you because my daddy said he was gonna dig a hole for the puppies." She looked at Becky. "You can keep that one. It's from Pete, too."

Becky laughed. "I picked this one at Fort Bridger. Pete, huh? I can pick my own puppy," she said, frowning at him. "What makes you think I want this animal?" The puppy in her arms wiggled up to her, licking her chin. "Stop that," she scolded gently. She held it up and looked underneath. "Okay, I'll keep her, just to keep her from the hole." Grinning, she added with obvious pleasure, "I'm gonna call her Charlie."

"I'll keep this one. I've had puppies before, and I know they're trouble, so that's gonna be his name. 'Trouble,'" said Hattie. The puppy licked her hand. She smiled and scratched his ears.

"This one's done spoken for," Abel declared, taking up the one with the white chest. He handed it to Bessie. She stroked the little fellow's back, whispering, "You be good, Nero. You hear?"

"What do you think, Hattie?" I asked, unwilling to take the responsibility, looking at her trying to control her pup.

"Will you come with me, Miss Martha?" Prissy asked. "I'm tryin' to find Morgan so I can offer him a puppy."

I hesitated. I didn't want Morgan to get the idea I was chasing him.

Pete arrived at the wagon and said," I think Morgan's at that artist's wagon. Saw him there earlier. Hattie, don't you think that's a nice addition to our family?"

"Please," Prissy begged. She held up the puppy for me to take. "I was gonna keep this one, but daddy said no."

"Alright," I said, yielding to her plea. "and if he doesn't mind his ma, we'll just go to all the wagons 'til we find this pup a home." Taking Prissy's hand, we walked across the grass to where Harold's wagon sat. There was a stump of a log and a small fire with a coffeepot nearby, but I didn't see Morgan or Harold around the wagon. I handed the puppy back to Prissy.

"Hello," I called. "Anyone here?"

The back canvas lifted, and Harold climbed out.

"Hello, Martha, Prissy. What have you got there?" He held out his arms, and we placed the puppy in them.

"It's for Morgan," Prissy said. "But, if he don't want her, you can have her. My daddy says we have to find homes or he'll throw her in a hole."

"Well, we can't let that happen, can we?" Harold said, rubbing the pup's head. "Not to this nice little lady." He glanced at me. "Morgan left a few minutes ago. Said he'd be right back. Said he wanted to see my oils." He handed Prissy the puppy. "I was getting them out of the wagon when I heard you call. Have a seat there on the log. Help yourself to coffee. Sorry I don't have something for you, Prissy. I'll just get the paintings."

Harold went inside the wagon, the puppy leaped out of Prissy's arms. She ran after him and ran into Morgan.

"Whoa, little lady. This critter belong to you?" he asked, swooping up the escaping pup in his arms.

"Your ma says you're to take it," Prissy told him, her tone suggesting there was no use him arguing.

"She did, did she?"

"Yep. She said you'd need a dog when you got to Oregon."

"Well, I reckon she's right about that," Morgan agreed. "But, what makes her think this one is the right one? I'm going to need one that can fight off coyotes and wolves." He held the pup up and looked it over dubiously. "This one doesn't look like it could fight off a mouse."

"It's going to grow!" Prissy assured him. "It comes from good stock, don't it, Miss Martha?"

"Yes, Prissy, it does."

"You know, Tag's the papa, and my dog Daisy's the mama. There ain't no dog braver than Tag, and Daisy is brave and strong too."

"I believe you've got yourself a dog," Harold said, smiling.

"I believe you're right," Morgan said. "Now, what am I going to call this bundle of energy?" He looked at me. "Got any suggestions?"

"Well," I paused. "She's as shiny as a copper penny. If she were mine, that's what I'd call her. Penny."

"Penny?" Morgan nodded. "Penny it is."

"Well, I better take Prissy home, or her daddy will be after me." I turned to Harold. "I'd love to stay and see your paintings, but maybe another time?"

"Anytime, Martha."

"Thanks for taking the puppy, Morgan. Mr. Holt won't have to dig that hole now," I chuckled. "Let's go, Prissy." Taking her hand, we started to leave.

"Martha," Morgan called. "Will you take the pup to Ma? I'll pick it up later. I want to look at Harold's work. I'll be along soon. If you're going to be up, could I talk to you later?"

"Alright, I'll be up for awhile. Good night, Harold."

I put the pup under the wagon where she curled up with the others. Abel's, Sara's, Becky's, Morgan's, and Hattie's puppies were all under my wagon with Tag. I smiled to myself. Somehow the pups had moved to my wagon. Somehow my two pups turned into four.

Hattie and Becky had gone to bed. I stoked the fire then sat in one of the camp chairs with a needle and thread, darning some socks and waited for Morgan. I wished I could understand the emotions he caused inside me.

"Martha?" The object of my thoughts stood beside me. "Didn't interrupt your train of thought, did I?"

Embarrassed, I shook my head. "No just darning a sock."

"Sorry, I'm so late. I had some business with Harold." He poured a cup of coffee and offered to pour one for me. I declined.

"His sketches are beautiful, aren't they?"

"Sure are. He'll have no trouble sellin' them." He supped his coffee. "I wanted to talk to you about tomorrow's crossing. I'd like to swim the mares across separate. With Boots being in foal, I figure it will be easier on her."

"That's thoughtful of you, Morgan. Thank you." I was relieved he didn't bring up Shoshone Falls. I didn't know what I would say if he did.

"If you're not driving, I'd like to ride with you tomorrow."

"I'd like that," I admitted.

"Good. See you tomorrow." He tossed the remains of cup. As he turned to leave, he winked. I went to sleep dreaming of tomorrow. I knew we were friends again.

CHAPTER THIRTY SIX

We were camped on the banks of the Snake River at Three River Crossing. Early morning found the campground covered with a ghostly white mist that came from the river. Pete had called a meeting to discuss crossing the river as the ferry had been shut down. We were gathered at Pete's wagon having coffee and waiting for it to start. When everyone arrived, he explained, "It'll take a couple of days to ford the river. We'll take ropes across and rig pulleys. Some of you men who are good on horses drive the stock over. The rest of you can cut logs to lash to the wagons so they'll float. One wagon will serve as a ferry for the women and kids. Prepare your wagon, and wrap your food supplies in oilcloth."

Morgan and Luke volunteered to swim across with the first ropes to attach the pulleys to the other side. Several other men volunteered to cut some logs.

Pete smiled. "It's good to have you all workin' as a team."

"Hey, Pete!" shouted Macintosh. "Why don't we just drive the wagons across? Let's get this over with!"

"No, this is the safest way. We can control the wagons easier," answered Pete. That water is four to five feet deep. It would be pure foolishness to take a wagon out there."

"Hell, we can do without this fuss. We're losing time. We're already behind," Macintosh scoffed. "Quit babyin' these people."

"Listen, we've got women and children in these wagons. It's too deep to be drivin' across. Sure, it'll take more time, but we'll get there safe."

"Well, I just think it's foolish!" Macintosh bellowed.

"Mac, you're free to go it alone. I won't stop you," Pete said. "Now the rest of you get to work." The men spread out in teams to do the jobs.

"The women are ready to set up communal kitchens on both sides of the river," Hattie told him. "I'll do this side, and Juanita Roberts will run one on the other side."

"Thanks, ladies. That's a big help. Mrs. Roberts, get your things together. You'll go first."

After the meeting I found Morgan at the back of the Davis wagon with three other men splicing ropes to span the river.

"It's going to take a lot of rope," he said. "Think you could scare up some?"

"Sure. I'll check with the others." I took off and came back with about two hundred feet. "This is all I could find."

"Thanks. This will help. I'll go get what Pete has on the supply wagon."

"Morgan, leave Lady when you take the horses over. Okay?"

"Right. Say, how about a walk after supper?"

"That would be fine." *Here I go again,* I thought. *Why do I do this to myself?* Back at our wagon, Hattie was feeding the campfire. Bessie was making coffee.

"Hi ladies. Looks like you have everything under control. Okay if I go upstream and take a bath?"

"Go ahead. Take your time," Hattie said.

As I started to leave, Becky rode up with Dora Lee and Thelma walking beside her horse. She had a big buck across her pack mule. The two girls carried large pans of poke salad greens.

"Here's your greens, Bessie. What do we do next?"

"Y'all girls can clean da beans and put dem to boil."

"Goodness, Becky, how did you get that big buck up there?" Sara asked, as she joined us.

Wanda Reed

"Oh, I'm stronger than I look." She looked at Bessie. "Think Abel will have time to skin it? I field dressed it already."

"Yessum, Miss Becky. He's helpin' Mr. Pete, but he be back right quick. My, dat's a fine lookin' animal."

"Nice work, Becky," I said, grabbing a towel and my necessaries bag. "I'm going for a bath. Want to come with me?"

"No thanks. There's men cutting logs all along the river. I'll drop the buck off at your wagon, Bessie. See you all later. I'm gonna see what else I can get." She rode off.

"So much for the bath. Bessie, I'm sure you need some help."

"Why sho', girl. You can make bread. 'Bout ten loaves."

"Okay. Thelma, you help me with the bread please."

All the women were kept busy with cooking and doing the chores the men usually did. Hattie and I helped some of them put up their tents. I couldn't help but feel a certain pride in my ability to do so-called men's work. My thoughts flew to Morgan. *Why couldn't he see that I would be a much better helpmate than Lorraine? Lorraine was so little and delicate. Blonde curly hair and big blue eyes with a smile of white teeth to dazzle a man.*

> **Comment [CJH]:** This really just doesn't make sense. Morgan has made it very clear that he cares about her and not Lorraine. Maybe some rewrites happened?

Becky came back into camp in the late afternoon with a smile on her face and an elk stretched across the pack mule. "Got some more work for Abel," she said. "He got that buck skinned?"

"It's skinned. He's shoeing mules at the Davis wagon," I said. "Hattie, look at this elk."

"You're one heck of a hunter, girl!" Hattie exclaimed. "Don't know what this train would do without you." She motioned to me. "Come on, let's take this over to Bessie's wagon and unload it. It

Six Women West

looks to be about three hundred pounds. " The three of us managed to get the animal off the mule and hung it from a tree where Abel could skin it and send meat over to the other camp.

"I'm gonna go see Abel," Becky said. "I came across a tree full of honey. I'd like him to come with me to get some." She took off in the direction of the Davis wagon.

"That girl," Hattie shook her head. "She's got more energy than the rest of us put together."

"Yes, she sure has," I agreed.

It was nearing supper when Abel and Becky rode in, wearing wide grins and smelling of smoke.

"Here come the happy hunters," I said, "just in time for supper."

"You all better appreciate this," said Becky, holding out a bucket of honey.

Reaching up and taking it from her hand, I asked, "How did you do it? Didn't you get stung?"

"We took cheesecloth and pulled it over our hats. Tied our pant's legs and wore gloves." Becky laughed. "Weren't no place for them buggers to sting."

"I made a smoke-torch and waved it 'round the tree to make the bees sleepy," Abel said.

"Abel robbed the tree while I put the honey in buckets. Must be at least ten pounds," Becky said proudly.

"At least," I agreed. "Sure going to go good on the bread I made."

Come supper, a bunch of very tired men and women grouped around our campfire. Dora Lee dipped plateful of beans, Bessie poured coffee, Thelma sliced bread, and Gil Rogers sliced the elk, discussing the work they'd accomplished. Even Macintosh had done his share.

The other women provided food to go along with what we had. Gil Rogers had been tending the meat on the spit and took full credit for the way it turned out. There was plenty of praise to go around.

We returned to the campfire. Pete joined Hattie, and I watched as Morgan walked up. His hair was wet, and he looked as if he'd just bathed.

"Ready for that walk?" he asked, smiling.

"I thought it over and changed my mind." I swallowed and looked down at my feet. "I don't see any good will come of it. I need the time to bathe and wash my hair."

"I'm not sure what you mean, Martha, but I truly do need to talk with you. Please come." He held out his hand.

"Well, I really don't have time. I need to heat some water to wash up."

"Please, I have some things that needs sayin'."

Sighing, unable or unwilling to resist, I took his hand. "Looks like you've been to the river. I was headed there earlier, but Becky reminded me that the men were working there."

"Well, they're not there now. If you want to bathe, I'll stand lookout for you." My expression apparently caused him to hold up his hands defensively. "Looking the other way, honest."

Torn between wanting that bath and concern for my reputation and the power of my resistance, I hesitated. Morgan's fresh, clean smell and appearance decided me.

"Alright, I'll hold you to your word. Let me get my things." I got my bag and towel, bloomers, and my blue dress. *I can't put these dirty clothes back on,* I told myself.

I hurried back, hoping no one noticed what I was carrying.

We walk away from the wagons and alongside the river, which was filled with frogs and dragonflies. The banks of the river were lined with small cottonwood trees with several smaller creeks flowing into the river. Blue jays let us know we had invaded their territory. "Now what is it you have to say to me?" I asked, as we strolled towards the river. It was a lovely evening, and a cool breeze blew gently waving the long grass.

"Let's wait until after your bath, okay?"

Suspicious, I stared at him.

"I just thought," he began, "but if you want to talk now, it's okay, too."

"I can wait, I guess. Must not be that important." The narrow creek opened into a wide creek about twelve to twenty feet wide with large brush and cottonwood trees.

"Oh, it's important alright," he assured me. "This is a good place." He pointed to an area just ahead of us with plenty of bushes for privacy and clean, clear water. "It's where I washed. I'll sit here and roll myself a smoke."

I hurried through my rituals, anxious to hear what he had to say. Listening to him as he sang a lover's ballad in a soft baritone, I felt shivers go up and down my spine. I might be just another foolish woman, but I could no longer kid myself. I was in love with Morgan Brooks. All I could do was pray he truly loved me, too. I pulled my dress back on over my head and went out to meet him.

"Here, let me do that," he offered, taking the towel from me. "Sit on this stump." I sat. He began gently but firmly ruffling my hair with the towel. Never before had I experienced such a feeling of pleasure.

"You have beautiful hair, Martha," he said softly.

"Thank you." I couldn't wait another minute. "What is it you have to say, Morgan? I want to know now."

"First of all, there is no other woman. No Lorraine. No Mary Beth. No one ever, never. No one except you. You're the one I want to spend the rest of my life with." He reached around and took my face in his hands. "I love you, Martha Patterson. I want to be with you. I have nothing to offer you now, but once I get the ranch in Oregon, I..."

"Morgan, I love you, too, but let's wait until we get to Oregon. We've a long way to go yet, and things can change." I stood and faced him. "I think it would be better if we didn't spend time alone together. It's bound to cause talk."

"I hate it, but I understand." He took my hand. "Guess we'd better get back. We got a hard day tomorrow." We walked slowly back to the wagon, and right before we left the cover of the woods and in the soft light of dusk, Morgan pulled me in his arm and we kissed, softly and deeply not wanting to stop. We pulled reluctantly from each others' arms. Walking me to my tent, he left me with the words "I love you, Martha Patterson."

Bessie, Hattie, Sara, and I were up long before daylight with hot coffee, ham, and hoecakes ready for the first men. As the men drifted in, they had breakfast. There were three other fires and several other women with breakfast and hot coffee.

The men started the first wagon with only one man aboard. It slid into the water, tilted to the side, then rocked upright. The men on the other side managed to pull it across. It took about one hour for each wagon to be floated across, which meant it would take about two days for all the wagons.

The Locklander wagon was third and was the largest of the prairie schooners to cross. As it slid into the water, it twisted, stretching the rope. Several men ran out to right it, but it was so heavy it pulled away, floundered and turned crossways. It tipped on its side. A couple of riders rode in with lassos to right it. The supplies spilled out and floated downstream.

Somebody yelled, "Shit!"

Six Women West

The Locklander children jumped up and down, crying. Mrs. Locklander screamed. "All our supplies," Hazel sobbed. "What will we do?"

"I believe some of the men are trying to save them," I told her. "You just rest. Everything will be alright. I'll call you when it's time to cross. You stay with her, Sybil."

Along with the other women and children, I watched hopefully as the men worked frantically to save the wagon. Still, its contents got soaked or swept downstream. Once across, Mr. Locklander sent word he wanted to wait until the wagon dried out before bringing his family over.

Bessie had just rung the dinner bell for the second bunch of men to eat when Sybil came running out of the tent.

"My ma's havin' the baby! Her water's broke!"

"Baby? I didn't know she was expecting." I hurried to the tent behind her. "Sybil, go get Sara. Hurry. Take them overalls off."

"Ah'll set some water to boilin," Bessie said.

In the tent, Hazel sat on the mat, rocking back and forth, holding her stomach.

"My water's broke," she said. "Get my man."

"He's across the river," I told her. "I'll send word. Let's get those overalls off." She began to tug at them, and I helped her struggle out of her clothes, praying Sara would get here soon. The only births I had seen were those of farm animals.

I gently pushed Hazel down on the pad and put a blanket over her.

"It's different this time," she moaned. "Somethin's wrong."

I lifted the cover and peered between Hazel's upraised legs. Swallowing hard, I let the blanket drop, hoping my shock didn't show. There was part of a baby's leg.

Sara entered the tent, panting hard, her face flushed. "Am I in time?"

"Thank God you're here. Look." I raised the cover.

"What is it? What's wrong?" Hazel demanded.

"The baby's trying to come out backwards," I told her.

"Oh, my God. I knew this one was different."

"I don't know anything about this kind of birth," Sara said.

"Neither do I. Maybe Bessie does. I'll go get her."

"Hurry," Sara urged.

I ran to our wagon. "Bessie! Bessie! The baby's coming out wrong. One leg's out, but I couldn't see the other one."

"Oh, Lawd. It has to be turned. She grabbed a kettle of hot water and handed me clean cloths.

At the tent she took charge, first looking under the covers. "It's gonna be alright, Miss Hazel. I done seed this before. Jus' have to reach up and turn him around. Miss Sybil, you go tell Miss Hattie to bring mo' hot water and rags."

The young girl, who had been hovering just inside the tent, took off in a hurry. "Oh Bessie, it's hurts something fierce," cried Hazel.

Bessie reached in her pocket and brought out a small bottle. "I'm gonna give you a bit of this laudanum so maybe you can relax."

"I'll borrow a nightgown from Hattie," Sara offered. "Be right back."

Bessie took a rag and washed her hands and arms with the hot water before examining Hazel. "Just be easy, Miss Hazel. Ah's gonna turn the child."

I watched in awe as Bessie reached in and pushed the baby's leg back inside of Hazel. Hazel screamed with intensity."

The fifth Locklander baby was taking his time. Hazel suffered with hard pains. Finally the baby was born, but he wasn't breathing. He was stillborn.

Six Women West

Moses sent word that he couldn't leave the job, so I stayed. At daybreak I awoke to the sound of Hazel sobbing. She was holding the baby, rocking back and forth, and tears running down her pale cheeks.

"God called him back," she told me, her voice weak and trembling.

"I'll make a coffin for him, dear. I'm sorry. We'll have to bury him here."

"Oh, Moses, out here he'll be all alone," Hazel sobbed.

"He's with God, dear. He won't be alone." He handed me the tiny bundle. "You rest. I'll go make his bed, and all the angels in Heaven will watch over him."

"Yes, it's nice, Moses. Let me lay our babe in it to sleep." Moses got up and picked the baby out of the chair and handed him to Hazel, who kissed him and wrapped him securely then placed him in his bed. Moses, I'm very tired. I think I will rest now."

He bent and kissed her. "You rest, dear. I'll take care of the buryin'."

Later, we gathered for the small service. Under the tall cottonwood tree with a beautiful sunny day with blue skies on the banks of the Snake River, we laid to rest the baby Locklander. With a service by Frank Warren and singing "Coming for to Carry Me Home," Moses helped Hazel over to say a final goodbye to her baby son. I could see both sadness and relief on the faces of the other parents.

The work went on getting the wagons across the river and repacking the wheels with grease and making sure all the food and supplies were dry. Pete came into camp for a cup of coffee. Slowly we all gathered for supper.

The train pulled out early the next morning, leaving a small grave piled high with rocks. We traveled all day, stopping at suppertime to camp the night.

> **Comment [CJH]:** Changed from "two small graves" to "a small grave." I'm assuming there was a rewrite here.

511

After supper and clean up, I left camp and walked over near a grove of small trees where we picketed our stock to graze, wanting to check on my mares and have a look to see how Boots was doing. I was picking burs out of her tail when I noticed what a beautiful night it was, boasting a breathtaking sunset that stretched across the sky from one end of the horizon to the other.

"Hi. What are you doing out here alone?" It was Sara.

"Oh, just checking on the horses," I said, adjusting Sugar's halter. "Besides, I'm not alone. I've got Tag." Tag wagged his tail, as if acknowledging the truth of my words. "And I had some thinking to do."

"Anything you want to share?" She stroked Sugar's forehead.

"I'd like to, but I don't know the words." I went over to Lady and pulled burs from her mane and patted her.

"Just start talking, Martha. The words will come." She smiled. "Besides, I know you well enough so I can read between the lines."

"I'm in love with Morgan," I blurted, admitting it out loud for the first time. "He says he wants me, but I don't know if that means marriage." I shook my head. "My ma always told me I was not the type of woman men would marry. You know what that means."

"Martha, your ma was dead wrong. A good man would only marry you for love. Of course a man, any man, would want to marry you. You're pretty, intelligent, a good worker. Any man would be lucky to have you as a partner." She sounded sincere, and I wanted very much to believe her. She patted my arm. "You and Morgan are made for each other. Open your eyes, my dear."

"Do you really think so, Sara?"

"I certainly do. You two are already friends, aren't you?"

"Yes, I guess so. Most of the time, anyway."

"I believe marriages that start with a friendship will last. Look at Guy and me."

I nodded. They did seem to be very happy.

"Now lust, well, lust cools at the first sign of trouble. Don't you worry about the wed and bed part. That will work itself out in its own time, and you'll know when the time is right."

We started back for camp. She put her hand in mine. "Morgan respects you, but all bees try to sample the honey. It doesn't mean he doesn't love you."

"Oh, Sara, I hope your right," I said, hugging her tightly.

We stood for a moment, watching the sunset. The sky looked like it could burst into flames as the sun filtered through the buttermilk clouds. "Do you think Luke and Charlie are looking at the same sunset?" Sara asked.

"I hope she finds what she is seeking in San Francisco," I responded, reaching down to pet Tag.

"She'll have to look inward to find what she is looking for," Sara said solemnly.

"What do you mean?"

"She needs to forgive herself. What happened to her was not her sin. But she is on the road to recovery."

"How did you become so understanding, my friend?"

"Life," she replied with a small grin.

"Thanks for listening, Sara. You've given me a lot to think about." I whistled for Tag, who was investigating a bush. "Let's go, boy."

The camp was quiet. Fires burned low. Everyone had apparently turned in. "Goodnight, Sara," I whispered. "Thank you."

"Goodnight, Martha. Pleasant dreams. She went to her wagon, and I crawled into the tent and in my bedroll. My dreams, which had me running from place to place in fear and confusion, were anything but pleasant.

I slept late the next morning. Outside Hattie and Becky were nowhere in sight. Bessie was stoking the fire. "Morning, Bessie. Where's everyone?"

"Oh, dey be doin' something. Dey be back soon. Dey done ate. I saved you some flapjacks. You hungry?"

"Starved," I admitted. "Just let me take a run to the bushes and wash up, okay?"

After I ate, I went to check on Hazel. She was puffy-eyed and looked as if she hadn't slept. "Are you well enough to travel?" I asked.

"Yes, I guess so. It's strange, I have four young 'uns, but the one I lost, the babe I didn't even get to know, he's sorrowful missed." Tears filled her eyes, and her chin quivered.

"I can only imagine the pain you feel. I've yet to have children, but I am truly sorry. Is there anything I can get for you?"

"No, thank you. Moses and the other men managed to save most of our supplies. I'm grateful for that."

"Alright, but if you think of anything, don't hesitate to ask, alright?"

She nodded, and I took my leave.

When I got back, Hattie and Becky had our wagon ready to roll.

"How's Hazel?" Hattie asked.

"About what you'd expect. Poor thing," I said. "Thanks for letting me sleep in."

"No problem. Weren't much to do."

"Okay if I ride up front with Pete?" I asked, mounting Lady.

"Go ahead."

Six Women West

Pete was ambling along, wearing a sour face. "Got a problem?" I asked.

"Just thinkin' of what lies ahead."

"Bad trail?"

"Well, it ain't an easy one. It's long, dry, steep, and rugged, but that's not what's botherin' me. We still have a long way to go, and if we don't get rain pretty soon, we're gonna be hurtin'. A good rain would fill up the creeks and green up the grass."

"Do you know where we'll be camping?"

"Morgan and Guy are scoutin' for a place now." He glanced at me. "I figure we'll make about ten mile a day through here. Might have to lay over so the stock can eat. You got grain for them fancy mares of yours?"

"I always keep a sack," I said. "You know, Boots is in the family way."

"Morgan's stud got anything to do with that?"

I laughed and nodded my head. "Yes, I believe so. Well, I best get back to the wagon. See you later."

"You shore gonna have a fine colt." Pete answered. Let me know if you want to sell it."

We traveled day after day through scarce grass and dry creeks. The scrub pine and junipers were brown from the sun. The cloudless sky held no hope of rain.

Ivey gathered some of the women together to form a prayer circle for rain.

"It's my fault," Josephine moaned. ["God is punishing me for what I done to my boy."]

> **Comment [CJH]:** Huh? There's no mention of her doing anything to her boy.

"Don't talk foolish," Hazel said sharply. "God doesn't punish. He is a loving, forgiving, God."

Josephine sniffled, but kept her mouth shut.

"The Indians do a dance to the rain god, asking him to send rain," Harold told us.

"We aren't savages yet," Ivey Henderson retorted.

I grinned at Harold, shrugging my shoulders. He rolled his eyes and kept his mouth shut. He sketched the women as they formed their prayer circle. The prayers to God continued without further comment, but there was no rain that day or the next.

Pete's face was drawn and anxious as the days dragged by while we moved slowly up the incline. Earlier wagon trains had left deep ruts in the trail, making it rough but easy to follow. We passed up several places to camp because the grass was scarce and the creeks were dry. Each night we loosed the stock to graze, taking turns to ride herd so they didn't wander too far off in search of food. The stock had lost weight and looked gaunt. When we did come across a creek with water, the men filled the barrels and women did the same with the containers they had.

We had been on the trail for several days when I awoke early one morning to the sound of yelling. I stepped out of the tent, and steady drops of rain splashed my face.

"The Lord done blessed us," Bessie whispered. "He done heard our prayer."

Everyone was laughing and holding out their hands. Some voiced prayers of thanks for the water. When the excitement died down, they began putting containers out to catch water.

Within the hour, the welcome rain had developed into a downpour, turning joy into alarm. The laughing stopped, and people returned to their wagons. Pete yelled for all of us to hitch up. "We got to get on the move. It's a gully washer."

We were hitched and moving in twenty minutes through the rain that was now pouring like someone had gutted a cloud. The wagon ruts were rivers of water and mud. "Whoever's praying for rain can stop now," I muttered to Lady, as we struggled through the mire.

Six Women West

It continued to rain hard all day. When the wagons begin to bog down, Pete called a halt. "Pull the wagons close together," he ordered. "Stay well back from the creek. It's already full, and it could flood. Tommy, you Billie, and Hobbs take the stock where they can graze. Keep them on high ground, and watch so they don't wander off."

Bessie, Sara, and Hattie started a large pot of beef and barley soup and a pot of coffee. Becky and I put up the tent and gathered what fuel we could find. Soon we had the tents and canopies in place. Pete came by to bring us up to date. We poured him a cup of coffee and handed him a towel.

"This rain has been a blessin' on one hand and a disaster on the other," he said, wiping his face. "Not only have we lost days here in the foothills, but we could run into snow in the mountains." He shook his head. "I'll be darned if we haven't had more than our fair share of setbacks."

"You've handled it all very well," I told him. "The train is fortunate to have you, Pete. I'm sure you'll bring us through safely."

"Thanks, Martha. That's nice of you to say."

"Got a cup of coffee for a drowned rat?" Morgan poked his head in.

"Come in and dry off, son," Hattie said, handing him a towel.

"Thanks, Ma." He rubbed his head with the towel as I poured him a cup of coffee.

"Here, this will warm you up," I said.

"Thanks, Martha." He smiled, his fingers touching mine as he cupped them around the mug. "Who's on watch tonight?" he asked, looking at Pete.

"Guy and Reed."

> **Comment [CJH]:** First time Reed's name has been mentioned. I bring this up because it seems like there are more different characters than there should be.

"Tell 'em to keep an eye on the stream. It's come up half a foot already. It could come over the bank."

"I'll tell 'em. Well, I best go check on the rest of the train. See you in the morning if we don't get washed away."

"Wait, I'll go with you," Morgan said. "Take care, ladies."

We got ready for bed, and I asked, "Hattie, do you think we'll get through the mountains before the snow?"

"No, I'm afraid not," Hattie said. "We'll be goin' a lot higher, and when it's rainin' here, it's snowin' there. No, not much of a chance now."

"What will we do? Couldn't we camp this side of the pass?"

"We'd have to spend the winter, and that wouldn't be good. We don't have enough supplies, and there's nowhere to get enough for this many people. Also, it takes time to build shelters. No, I think Pete can get us to Oregon, even if it's a month later." She patted my shoulder. "Try not to worry about it, Martha. Get some sleep."

Next morning I lay awake in my bedroll listening for the rain. Instead, there were only the usual sounds of people calling to one another, mules braying, and dogs barking. Becky and Hattie were not in the tent. I had obviously overslept again. I got dressed. Outside, the campfire was burning low. I took time for my morning routine, and when I returned I saw a pan of biscuits and ham placed close enough to the fire to keep warm. "Bless you, Bessie," I said gratefully, making a sandwich. I wandered down to Pete's wagon. He was there, along with Morgan and Guy.

"Morning," I said, taking the cup Morgan handed me. "Thanks. Will we be moving out soon?" My dreams last night had been filled with scenes of snow, making me even more anxious.

"Not until the mud dries out some," Pete said. "This time can be used to wash and dry out belongings. We'll plan on leavin' early tomorrow."

"Have you seen Hattie or Becky?" I asked.

"Think they're with Sara at our wagon," Guy said.

"Thanks. See you later." I handed the cup to Morgan and waved goodbye. I met up with Hattie and Becky as they were leaving Sara's. "Pete says we won't be leaving today—that we should take this time to dry things out."

"Yeah, I know. We were just waiting for you to get up," Becky said. "Would of woke you, but figured you needed your beauty sleep." She grinned impishly. I gave her a little push in retaliation.

"Well girls, since it's just the three of us in this pigsty we call a wagon," Hattie said, "I'm going to do you a favor. I'll take the dirty clothes and wash them, and you two take this wagon apart down to the rawhide and then clean and reload it. And after that try to keep the dogs outside."

I looked at Becky, and we said, "Uh, thanks, Hattie."

At daybreak the following morning we were on the trail. Becky and I rode to several homesteads along the way and tried to purchase vegetables with no luck. We finally talked a farmer out of an old hog. We drove him back to the wagon and gave him to Abel.

Pete kept the wagons moving at a goodly pace, and we covered twelve miles before we made camp near the Boise River. We were now halfway to Fort Boise. The terrain changed. The trees were greener, the nights cooler, and morning had a nip of frost. There was more forage for the stock, so they had begun to fill out again. Since time was now of the essence, there was no sleeping in for me or anyone else. We camped late, had supper, went to bed, and were on the trail before sunup. By nightfall we were within a few miles of where the Ward massacre took place. I was glad we camped away from it as I didn't want the haunts of those folks as company for the night. Hattie told us what she knew of the massacre.

"There was twenty wagons carryin' forty immigrants. They were all massacred, every man, woman, and child except two. The story I heard was that the Indians had trailed the wagons for several days, waiting for the rest of their tribe. When they showed up, they all attacked the wagons. Those on the train didn't have a chance. The women were raped and killed, some children taken hostage."

"Why?" I asked, sounding stupid, I guess, but I truly didn't understand. The Indians we'd met along the way were friendly and helpful.

"Well, apparently they were unhappy over the shortages of buffalo. With all the settlers moving here, taking over the Indian's hunting range, you could see why they were angry."

"Yes, I suppose so, but killing women and children!" I shook my head.

"A fellow by the name of Ward made it to old Fort Boise. Strangely enough, his brother survived, too. He was picked up by the Yantis party when they arrived, and they reported it to the army."

"Come to think of it, I think I heard somethin' about that in my travels," Becky said. "Didn't the army hang a lot of Indians and leave their bodies hanging up to let the others know what would happen?"

"Yes." Hattie nodded. "Didn't work too good, though. After that they attacked the settlers for no reason, making the trails unsafe for near a decade."

"I can see we've been very fortunate," I said.

The following day, we made it to Fort Boise. It sat right alongside the Owyhee River. We made camp at the fort, and those who were sick went over to the fort to see the fort's doctor. The next morning, taking the time to bathe and wash clothes and buy supplies, Hattie had us buy long johns. The river was high from the recent rains, making it impossible for the wagons to cross. We paid Keenan's Ferry three dollars a wagon to ferry them across. Morgan swam our teams across, and one of our mules drowned. I had paid an extra dollar to take my three mares on the ferry with my wagon. Morgan returned by ferry to buy another mule for our wagon and returned with me on the ferry. By the time the wagons were all on the other side, it was too late to start that day.

Safely on the other side, we made camp under several large oak trees. Pete said we could all relax and maybe even have some entertainment. The children, apparently feeling the relief and excitement of their parents, ran around and about the wagons, giggling and yelling. The folks didn't need any encouragement. Those who played music took out their instruments, and we all danced and laughed and had a good time. With a large bonfire and several torches that had been set up to burn for light, it was a pleasant evening. To our surprise Mr. Keenan brought several troopers who came over by ferry for the dance.

It was late after the dance. Morgan asked me to go for a walk with him. We strolled slowly along the river in the light of the moon and the torches that had been set up for the dance and talked about Oregon. "Hattie expects you to stay at the ranch until you find your land and get a cabin built," Morgan told me.

"I'd like that," I said. "Do you think I'll have any trouble finding someone to do the work?"

"No, Ma has some ranch hands. Maybe they can help. She says the winters are mild, so you may not have to wait until spring." He reached over and took my hand. I didn't resist.

"I can hardly wait to start my ranch," I confessed. "First, I'll build a barn for my mares. I can live in the barn or the wagon." I laughed. "I've gotten used to small quarters."

Wanda Reed

"I know what you mean," Morgan said, squeezing my hand.

"I suppose we should get back. It's getting late, and we have an early day tomorrow."

"I guess you're right," he grinned. "Just one thing first." He leaned forward and kissed me softly. "But, I have to admit, I don't want to get back. I like being with you, Martha."

"I like being with you, too," I admitted. "Will you be staying with Hattie in Oregon?"

"I will if my brother doesn't mind. You know, I don't even know him, but he knows I'm comin'. Ma wrote to him and told him about me."

> **Comment [CJH]:** I added this so that when they meet near the end, it makes sense that there is no surprise.

"Well, I'm sure any son of Hattie's is a pretty fine fellow."

"Any son?"

"Yes, Morgan, any son."

"Martha, will you ride point with me tomorrow?"

"I'd like that, but I'll need to check with Hattie. Make sure she doesn't have something for me to do." I couldn't believe how pleased I was he'd asked me.

"Good." He reached over and kissed me gently again. It was nice and respectful, but I missed the lusty kisses he'd given me in the past. It seemed he'd given up trying to bed me and had decided to treat me like a sister.

I thought of what Pa had often said when I used the word "wish." He'd say, "Be careful what you wish for. You might get it." If that was true, Morgan might very well change his attitude by the time we got to Oregon City.

Morning broke with the usual rustle of activity around camp. After a hasty breakfast we rolled out, happy to be on our way. A night of dancing and fun always cheered everyone up. "Oregon, here we come!" One of the men yelled.

Hattie gave me the go-ahead to ride with Morgan. Her pleasure at my request was obvious. With my new attitude towards Morgan, I was more than happy to please her.

Morgan greeted me warmly. "Glad you could make it. Nice day for a ride."

I smiled. *It was that*, I agreed silently.

"If we do a twelve-hour day, we should be at the Malheur River by nightfall," he said.

It turned out to be a long hard day. It was late evening when Pete rode up and said we'd make camp a mile down the trail. I was tired and relieved. I was deep-down tired after the many miles from Virginia. I could have settled where I sat in the Sweetwater Valley, but my dream drove me on to Oregon. "I'm looking forward to a bath. I'm dog tired," I said. "No insult to you Tag."

Morgan turned to me and said, "I hear there's a hot springs not far from the river. A soak in that should get rid of the aches and pains. Just follow the steam funnels, but be careful test the water before you get in. Some are boiling hot."

We camped on the banks of the river. The willows were thick, and the water was clear and cold. Apparently noticing I was tired, Hattie said to go ahead and soak awhile. Becky said she'd go with me. Unfortunately, we weren't the only ones wanting to use the springs. When we got there, there were already several springs full of people. We looked around and found a small but empty spring.

"It's a good thing there are so many springs," said Becky, "or we could be here all night." We tested the spring with a cup of water to make sure we wouldn't get burned. We finally lowered ourselves into the water. There was a bit of an odor of minerals. After a half an hour, I felt like a new woman.

"Do we have to get out?" Becky groaned. "I feel like I could sleep here."

"You do, and you'll wake up a prune," I told her. "Come on, now. We better get back to the wagon and get to bed. I'm sure Pete will want to do another twelve miles tomorrow."

Morning came all too fast. I felt like my head had just hit the bedroll when Hattie was saying, "It's morning, Martha. Time to get up."

After a breakfast of biscuits and gravy with gallons of strong hot coffee, we prepared to cross the river. The outriders took their places, ready for trouble. The mules pulled the wagons across where it was shallow with a nice gravel bottom. Much to everyone's relief, there were no hold ups that morning. When the last wagon cleared the bank, a cheer went up from every wagon. "Hurray!"

It was a little after noon when the Johnson's wagon broke a wheel. Pete had Abel and Morgan fall out to repair it while Velma and the three girls rode in our wagon.

It was close to suppertime when we approached Farewell Bend. Here we would leave the Snake River for the Burnt River. We camped overnight and left early next morning.

At the headwaters of Burnt River, Pete told me it was the site of another Indian massacre. "Took place in September 1860. Two people survived and walked thirty-five miles for help." I remarked on the bones lying everywhere.

"No one left to bury the dead," Pete explained. "Or they might have been buried at one time and the varmints dug them up."

"So many graves," I said. "I wonder why someone hadn't named the trail 'Cemetery Trail' as it seemed to be one long cemetery from Independence." I prayed this was the end of it.

Guy rode by, and Pete told him to have the wagons circle up and loose the stock to graze. "Tell them to gather at the supply wagon after supper. I

Six Women West

need to let the folks know what's in store for them the next few days."

A couple of hours later, everyone had come to listen to what Pete had to say. "We'll be climbing another hill, folks. Flagstaff Hill." He paused and looked at me. "No, Martha, I don't know why they call it that." A number of people chuckled. "Once we reach the summit, it'll take several days to get down it. It'll be hard work and dangerous, but you folks are used to that by now." There was a chorus of groans from the audience.

"The good news is there's a great view of Blue Mountains. Folks, we're on the last leg of our journey, so keep up the good work, and we'll be in Oregon City soon." He climbed down from the barrel. "Now get some rest."

We walked back to our wagon. I sat down in a camp chair, and Tag came up and lifted his paw to me. I took it and felt thorns in his feet and hair. On a closer look, I noticed he had some ticks. I called to Becky and the others to check their puppies for thorns and ticks and tie them up. So for the next hour I picked thorns out of Tag and got the ticks out with coal oil. I then went to check the mares and clean them. I told Hattie we needed to let Tag and the puppies ride tomorrow. "The brush is full of thorns and ticks too."

The morning air was sweet and cool, carrying the scent of pine trees laced with the familiar aroma of coffee, frying bacon, and fresh bread.

Pete rode up and asked me to look in on Mrs. Holt. "Her husband says she's complainin' of chest pains. He's worried. Sorry to bother you, but since Charlie left, I don't know who else to ask."

"I'll do it, Pete, though I don't know how much help I'll be. Charlie was the doctor, you know."

"I know. She's missed by all of us. Just glad she showed you a few things." He looked up at the sky now filled with dark clouds. "Tarnation, it's gonna rain some more. That's gonna make our job that much more difficult. Don't look like we'll move today."

He no more than galloped away when the rain came down in buckets. It was accompanied by a cold, cold wind. Shivering, I went inside the tent and began to dig a fire pit. An outside fire wouldn't last long in this weather.

When I finished, I put on my rain gear and went to check on Mrs. Holt. Matt had a fire in the pot belly and water on to heat. Prissy sat beside her mother, stroking her brow.

"My mama's sick," she said sorrowfully. "Can you make her better?"

"I'll try, Prissy. How do you feel? You're not sick, too?"

She shook her head.

"Where are you hurting, Priscilla?" I felt her forehead. She was burning up.

"It's my chest," she whispered. "When I cough, awful green stuff comes up."

I recalled what Charlie had done in a similar situation. "Do you have any eucalyptus leaves?"

"Yes, in the chest. Prissy, show Martha."

The little girl walked over and pointed to a large wooden chest, piled high with clothing and blankets. I moved the blankets and opened the chest. Inside there were several things, but I finally found a jar of leaves and crushed them. Slowly I added hot water to make a paste. Laying the soft cloth on the kettle to warm, Prissy watched intently as I rubbed it on a warm cloth and placed it on her ma's chest.

"I think this will help," I said. "Drink lots of water and stay warm. Keep a damp cloth to wipe your head if you get too warm."

"Is this rain ever going to let up?" Priscilla mumbled. This brought on a deep, hacking cough. Gasping, she spit up green mucus into the pan next to the bed. My heart went out to her, but I had done all I knew how to do. "Prissy, you stay with your mama and come tell me if she needs me." I hugged her tightly.

"Can't I come with you?"

"No dear. Your mama needs you here to take care of her."

"She loves you, Martha. She calls you her other sister," Priscilla whispered. "You'll make a good mother."

"Thank you." Touched, I hugged Prissy again, told her I'd be back later, and left after saying, "Be careful with the fire."

Bessie was in our tent. The aroma of stew and baking bread filled the air. "You reckon Mr. and Mrs. Holt and Prissy would eat some of this?" she asked.

"I think that's about all they'll get. Mrs. Holt is flat on her back," I said. "I'll take them some when it's ready." I sat down on a box and petted Tag, thinking what would happen to Prissy if her ma didn't get well. Bessie handed me a small kettle of soup and bread. I carried it to the Holts.

It was late afternoon when the rain let up. We took care of greasing the wagon wheels and getting ready to roll early the next morning.

CHAPTER THIRTY SEVEN

Early next morning we started up the mountain. It was a long, tedious climb, and the weather was dry and cold with howling gusts of wind out of the north. Cedar and pine trees dotted the hillside along with a variety of brush and undergrowth. Towards late afternoon the sky filled with big black clouds. Near sundown, just as we got to the top, Pete called a halt.

"Move those wagons in close and square them up," Pete ordered. "Get the stock in the middle. Don't set up any tents if you don't need them. Let's get a move on. When that storm hits, it's gonna be a downpour."

He was right. It was a storm right out of hell. Pelting rain, hail the size of biscuits, and tornado-force winds kept everyone with any sense inside their wagons. It took two days for the storm to blow itself out. All we could do was bemoan the time lost. Each day Morgan came to carry food to the Holts as the men checked each wagon.

On the third day we could come out of the wagons. We could see the Powder River flowing through the rich Baker Valley. It wasn't until the fourth day the ground was dry enough for Pete to declare we could now descend the hill. We emptied the wagons, removed the wheels, and mounted the wagon boxes on skids to lower them down the hill. By tying the wagons to trees, we were able to control their descent, carefully, slowly lowering them to the ground below. The women and children carried most of their belongings.

Hattie and I helped Prissy, Sara, and Polly. Mrs. Holt was too weak to walk. Becky rigged a travois behind a mule and managed to get her safely settled below. Once everyone was down the hill, Pete pushed everyone to work late into the night getting the wagons back together.

"Tomorrow we have to roll," Pete repeated over and over. "We've lost too much time already."

At dawn, desperately deprived of sleep and physically exhausted, we rolled into Baker Valley. Happily, there was good graze for the stock. The weather was surprisingly clear, enabling Becky and others to go hunting. Unfortunately, most of them, including Becky, returned with a few rabbits but no big game. Obviously with winter coming on, the big game had started moving to lower ground. Pete sent out a five-man hunting party to bring back some large game for the train. They returned with two elk.

I checked on Priscilla Holt often. Her cough had worsened, and I was afraid we would be leaving another body along the trail. Matt stayed with her as much as he could, but most of the time he was badly needed elsewhere. I asked Lucinda, Sybil, and Arabella to take shifts sitting with her, and we would take Prissy in our wagon.

"Sure appreciate you lookin' after her, Martha," Matt told me. "You've been a good friend. Prissy's right fond of you, too."

"I wish I could do more, Matt." I wanted to ask if he had relatives to help with Prissy if Priscilla didn't survive, but I decided it was not my place.

We followed the Grande Ronde River up the valley and slowly climbed the foothills and on into the mountains. The icy-cold wind blew through the narrow pass, hitting us head-on and bringing snow flurries that chilled us to the bone. We could see deep snow on the mountain above the pass. I prayed God would protect us all, reminding Him we had come too far to end up starved and frozen.

Pete had the wranglers drive the loose stock in front to break trail. Every other day we had to butcher a beef for meat, but they were bone-thin. There were no noon breaks. No time for social gatherings as we had done in the past. We had to make up for lost time. Reality was the snow was early and we were late.

An icy wind blew day and night. I was convinced I would never be warm again. Sara had knitted us all wool scarves. I wrapped mine around my head under my hat and pulled it down over my ears, tying it with a pig-string. Wearing long johns and two pair of britches, extra socks and a poncho over my coat, I was able to function.

Each night we camped in a tight circle with the stock inside. Heavy snow covered everything, so there was no graze for the stock. Rations of grain were doled out to each animal. We posted watches and built up fires. Wolves howled late into the night, hanging around the camp and keeping me awake and restless.

I didn't see much of Morgan. Like the rest of the men, he was kept busy. No one was taking time to rest or mingle. I missed him more than I ever dreamed I would. One evening, he poked his head in our wagon to tell us to keep Tag and the pups tied inside because of the wolves.

"The wolves will act like they want to play. The pups, not knowin' any better, will follow them. Tag may try to stop them, but the wolves come in a pack, and he wouldn't have a chance."

"How awful," I shuddered, pulling Tag closer to me.

"Do you have time for coffee?" I asked hopefully.

"No," he said, smiling ruefully. "Wish I did." He touched his hat to me and left. Despite the presence of Hattie and Becky, I felt very lonely.

At least one mule was lost every couple days, either from exhaustion or broken legs. Because the wolves were instantly on them, Pete had a couple of the men stand guard while the animals were shot, field dressed, and loaded on the empty supply wagon. When that was done, the pack of snarling wolves descended on what was left.

The idea of eating any mule meat was bad enough, but when it was Judy, Pa's mule, I was sure I'd have to be awful hungry. Morgan cut meat off the mules for all the dogs, so at least they had plenty. I tried not to think of the Donner party and all the stories I had heard about them eating human flesh. At last we completed the narrow pass and descended into the foothills.

Four days later at Gentry Crossing, we made camp on the banks of a swiftly flowing creek in the foothills of the Blue Mountains. The sky was filled with dark, swollen clouds, and the wind blew cold. Rain mixed with sleet soon turned to snow. I couldn't remember when I'd felt so miserable.

As we traveled day after day, the weather was terrible. On the night I had early-morning guard duty, I had turned in early. It was still dark when the sound of howling wolves brought me out of a sound sleep. They sounded closer than usual. Figuring it was about time for my shift I pulled on my boots, grabbed my rife, threw a couple of logs on the fire, lit a lantern, and made my way to the designated guard area.

I was surprised to see there was no one on guard. The old man, affectionately called Gramps because of his age, was nowhere in sight. The fire, normally kept burning high to keep away the wolves, was nearly out. At first I thought he may have gone to get more wood, but when I looked around, I could see there was plenty.

I called out, but there was no answer. I laid a couple of pine branches on the fire. Flames shot up, and I saw a pair of yellow wolf eyes shining at me from the shadows. Holding the lantern up, I scanned the snow. There were several paw prints and bright red splashes of what looked like blood. A low, guttural sound came from the bushes. My heart sank, and fear clutched at my stomach. I dropped the lantern and cocked my rifle, firing off several shots. A wolf yelped. Several seconds after I fired, I stood frozen in a trance.

"What is it?" Morgan yelled, bringing me out of a trance.

"Thank God you're here. Somethin's happened to Gramps. I think the wolves got him." I could hear the mounting hysteria in my voice.

"Are you alright?" He put his arm around me, and I leaned into him. "You're shaking. Go on back to the wagon. I'll look for him. You think you could wake up Pete and send him over?" He picked up the lantern and relit it.

"I can do that," I said. "I'm sorry to be such a ninny."

"Don't be silly. A pack of wolves would scare anyone." He hugged me tightly and kissed me softly on the cheek. "Take the lantern. I'll build up the fire." I took his lantern. Mine was out in the snow.

I woke Pete, told him what had happened, and then hurried back to the tent. Becky and Hattie stirred sleepily. "Thought I heard shots," Hattie said.

"Wolves," I murmured. "Go back to sleep. Morgan and Pete are taking care of it." I saw no need to tell them of my fears.

Morgan came around early the next morning. Over coffee he told us the sad news. "The wolves got the old man," he said "He didn't have a chance. He probably went quickly, which is some blessing to the kinfolk. We're going to bury him right away. Ma, got any breakfast left?"

"There's some ham and biscuits on the fire. Let what happened to the old man be a warning to the rest of us," Hattie commented. "We all need to stay alert and carry guns. Hungry wolves have no fear."

"That's right, Ma," Morgan said. "And we stand guard in pairs. But right now, let's get ready to roll."

"Well, in that case, I'll stand guard tonight if you'll stay with me," I offered boldly.

"Why, Martha," Morgan said, winking at me. "I thought you'd never ask."

"Now don't go teasin' her, son," Hattie cautioned, smiling.

Pete order the train to roll. We pushed on slowly making only eight miles that day. A light snow fell, and the freezing wind kept us in our wagon.

Morgan and I had the watch. We built up the fire and sat on a log we would burn later. There was no excitement that night unless I counted the feelings I got from being alone with Morgan. I felt kind of guilty, getting so much pleasure when poor old Gramps had just died.

"I'm glad you're here," I said truthfully.

He looked at me and grinned. "It's good to spend this time with you. It's more than we've had for awhile." He reached over and took my hand. My heart raced. I was afraid to move. We sat like that for a long time.

"We better make rounds," he said, "and make sure those beasts don't slip in the back door." We stood up at the same time and turned face to face. I could feel his warm breath on my face. He reached for me at the moment I reached for him. His lips covered mine in a passionate kiss, warming me down to my toes as an involuntary moan escape. *No brother ever kissed his sister like this*, I thought smugly as I gave as good as I got. I didn't want Morgan to have any doubts about the way I felt.

Breathing hard, he stepped away from me. "Easy to get emotional at a time like this," he said.

"But...."I reached out a hand to draw him back.

"We better make the rounds." He picked up his rifle and the lantern. "Come on."

Disappointed and rejected, I followed meekly. He kept his distant from me the rest of the night.

That day we moved slowly toward Emigrant Springs and camped early. Traveling in the snow was rough on the stock. Becky, Hattie, and I raked the snow off the grass for our stock to graze and doled out my mare's grain with our mules, hoping it was enough to keep them going. That night the wind blew from the north, and again it was snow mixed with rain. It came down without ceasing, turning the trail to slush and causing the wagons to bog down. After three miles of struggling to keep the wagons and animals upright, Pete called a halt. "We'll camp here and wait for the trail to clear," he told us, disappointment showing in his face.

A party went out hunting and returned empty-handed. We had only green pea soup and jerky for a noon meal and red beans and rice for supper that night and for many nights to come.

Two days later at the crossroads, Matt Holt, Gil Rogers, and Mac Macintosh decided to take the cut-off and spend the winter at the Whitman Mission. Though the weather had cleared, they didn't want to take the chance of getting stuck in the mountains. I bid a tearful goodbye to Prissy, giving her Hattie's address in Oregon. We promised to write.

"Maybe there will be a doctor or someone who knows about medicine to help get you well, Priscilla," I said to the pale, sickly woman. She nodded and smiled weakly, but the look in her eyes told me she didn't have any more faith in that happening than I did.

We parted company. Those of us deciding to go on followed the Umatilla River to the Indian Agency where we made camp in a clearing. I went with Pete to get supplies. The post consisted of one large building with washtubs and a bucket hanging on the front porch. Inside, a potbellied stove stood in the center of the room. On the back counter were jars of candy and beads. A glass case held hunting knives. The trader, a surly looking gent with oily hair

Six Women West

and a handlebar mustache leaned on the counter. He smelled of whiskey and sweat.

We placed our lists on the dirty counter. "Afternoon," Pete said. "Can you fill these?"

The man fiddled with his mustache, not looking at the lists. "You're late comin' through. I won't get supplies again for another month." He looked me up and down, making me uncomfortable. "This is an Indian agency."

"We know what it is," Pete sighed. "Maybe you could spare enough to get us to the next post." Knowing Pete as I did, I sensed he was having a hard time controlling his temper. "I've got folks short on supplies. I'm going to need eight slabs of bacon, a hundred pounds of flour, and four hundred pounds of feed for the stock just to get us through." He drew a wad of money from his pocket and placed it on the counter. I put mine next to his.

The trader stared at the money. Greed filling his eyes." No, it would run me low," he said. "I got to supply the Indians too, you know."

"Yes, I know. I'm not askin' for all your supplies—just enough to get us to the next post." There was obvious disgust and impatience in Pete's voice. I was afraid he was going to use his forty-four to persuade the man. "Good God man, I got people that need food out there."

A young Indian woman wearing a shapeless blouse and faded brown skirt walked in, and the bell rang. I look over, and she held up a small piece of calico material. Frowning, she asked, "You got?" The trader shook his head.

I leaned toward Pete and whispered, "Keep talking. I'll be right back."

In ten minutes I returned with a bag of Ruth's clothing, a bolt of red calico, and with several dresses of mine and Sara's.

The trader's eyes lit up. "Now you're talkin'. I can always use red calico. The squaws like bright calico. Got no use for money, but trade goods go a long ways."

"Okay," Pete said. "You help us. We'll help you."

"We'll need salt pork, coffee, and molasses, too," I said, thinking the trader wouldn't mind cheating the Indians if he could make a profit.

A half hour later we were loading everything we'd asked for in the supply wagon. "That was a good idea, Martha," Pete said, grinning widely. I might have had to shoot the varmint if you hadn't come up with it."

"Well, we're lucky we'd kept Ruth's clothes," I said, pleased with the compliment.

Morgan rode up, "What's keepin' you two? There are people waiting for supplies."

"Since we're not moving fast enough for you," Pete said, "you can help slice two-pound slabs of the bacon, so get a sharp knife."

Back at camp, Pete called a meeting. "Folks, bring your sacks and just take what you need. There's coffee, bacon, and flour. Hattie will dip it out for you."

Hattie stood at the back of the wagon. "Let's form a line," she called out. Baskets, sacks, and containers were filled according to family size. "Morning Cathleen Rose, how is little Max?"

"He's teething. Moe gave him a piece of rawhide to chew on."

"Rub a little paregoric on the sore place but not too much."

"Hazel, good to see you up and around. You need coffee?" Hattie asked. "There's also some barley and dried peas left in the wagon. Get what you need. Right over there, Morgan's slicing bacon. Get your share."

Chuckling, Hattie filled the offered sacks. "Nice work, Martha," she said. Glancing at Morgan, she said, "This girl got brains as well as beauty."

I felt my face turn red. Morgan winked and said, "I know that, Ma. Just tend to your job and pass out the supplies."

The rough weather and mountains had taken a toll on the stock. Besides our horses, we only had Rowdy, the two Wiggins mules, and the buckskins. All the mules had ribs showing, and some drivers were using horses along with mules to pull the wagons. We hadn't gotten to that point. Abel had only the two army mules.

The weather changed constantly from hail to rain to sleet to snow and back to hail. Starting at daylight we struggled on to Wells Spring. A few days later, we reached the Willow Creek Campground and camped overnight. The next morning we were back on the trail. I was driving, and just as we approached the John Day River, I heard a loud crack and a thump that nearly threw me off the wagon. I pulled the mules up and got down. The wagon had a broken axle.

Abel and Bessie in the wagon behind me stopped. Abel walked over, shaking his head.

"How about leaving it and putting my stuff on the supply wagon?" I suggested.

"No, Miss Martha. You will need this h'yar wagon in Oregon." He bent down and peered under the wagon. "I kin fix it. Jus' take awhile."

"Oh, Abel, what would we do without you?" He smiled shyly. "I'll unhitch the mules. Want me to unhitch yours, too?"

"That'd be fine, Miss Martha."

Taking his mules and mine, I roped off a makeshift corral around the trees so they could forge for grass. There was quite a bit here in the meadow. He got a couple of the men to help him with the wagon.

I left Abel working on the wagon and rode out with Hattie, Pete, and Morgan to check on the bridge. There we found signs of recent road work.

That was the bridge we'd be using to cross the Deschutes River. We were happy to see it was more than passable.

"Well, despite our fears, we'd made it through the Cascades. We're about a hundred miles from Oregon City," Pete said. "Shouldn't be too rough from now on. This is a well-traveled road."

"Think we'd ever make it this far, Martha?" Morgan asked.

"There were times I had doubts," I admitted, "but I'm sure glad we have." I smiled up at him, and he winked back.

When we got back, Abel had the wagon fixed. The other wagons had gone ahead under the supervision of John Johnson and were camped on the other side of the bridge. It took us a little time to cross over and join the others. They had made camp in a meadow full of trees, and there was enough grass for the stock.

The next morning we started down the Barlow Road towards the Columbia River. The trail was being worked on, but it was passable. To me, it was a Godsend. I had crossed mountains and deserts without too many qualms, but the idea of having to forge that deep, wide, powerful river had me terrified.

We moved slowly, single file down a road barely wide enough for a wagon. Tall trees of fir and cedar blocked out the sunlight except for random rays shining through the branches that glowed brightly. A variety of ferns grew around the tree trunks and among the moss-covered rocks. There was a deep-woods musty smell of rotting vegetation.

At dawn the next day, we started through Barlow Pass, ending up at Summit Meadows where we camped for the night. So many tall trees and foliage of all kinds filled the forest, and small camping areas were cut out of the forest for that purpose. The weather had improved, and spirits were up. Two days later we stopped at a small settlement called Laurel Hill. In the middle of this beautiful forest stood six buildings and a store where we bought flour and bacon. I got three pounds of corn for Boots and a half gallon of molasses, trying to keep her healthy. I asked about some hay and got three arms full. I wanted her to give birth to a strong foal, one that could carry on her bloodline. We moved out again, following the Sandy River. Pete wanted to stop for lunch a few miles outside of Oregon City. Most of us wanted to push on to Oregon City.

Pete called a meeting. Climbing on the tailgate of the supply wagon, he held up his hands. "Folks, you don't want to show up looking like the last rose of summer, do you?" There was a low murmur in the crowd and a shaking of heads.

"Well, then let's clean up first." People started to leave. "Just a minute please. I want you to know how proud I am of all of you. We ran into enough bad luck to last a lifetime, but with hard work, cooperation, and God's help, most of us made it. Sadly, we had to leave people behind, loved ones, but they won't be forgotten."

"Amen," several folks called out.

"If we're handing out praise," Frank Warren spoke up, I'd like to add our thanks to you, Pete. Your leadership brought us through when some of us would have turned back." Everyone clapped and yelled, "Hear! Hear!"

"Thanks, folks, but there's plenty of praise to go around." His gaze scanned the crowd. "There's Abel. He kept our wagons repaired and goin', and his wife, Bessie. We won't forget her biscuits and bear signs. Hattie, who was a big help since she's been on the trail before, and Martha, Charlie, and Becky who all helped." He waited for the applause to die down. "And, of course, the crew: Morgan, Guy, Moe, Billie, Tommy, and all of you who helped get us here." He waved his hand around. "All you guys. Let's get these mules curried and spruce up the wagon and go to town in style just like we had been out for a Sunday ride."

Someone yelled, "Rider comin' in". A man on a dark horse galloped across the meadow into camp and came to a dusty halt in front of Hattie. "Colton!" she screeched, turning to Morgan. "It's your brother!"

Colton jumped off his horse and grabbed her in a bear hug. He was a tall, lean man with dark hair, Hattie's smile, and eyes the same color as Morgan's.

He released Hattie and held out his hand to Morgan. "Morgan." They shook.

"Colton. Good to meet you. I've heard a lot about you."

"Same here. Some Ma we got, huh?"

Morgan nodded. "How did you figure we'd be here? We're behind schedule."

"Yeah, I know. I just had a hunch, and Ma always told me to follow my hunch." Colton hugged Hattie again. "Sure is good to see you. Anyway, Ma, I been watching the trail every day."

"It's good to see you too, son," Hattie said. "Let me introduce you around." Colton shook my hand and then Becky's. It seemed to me he held her hand just a bit longer, all the while gazing at her with obvious admiration. "You're all welcome to come to the ranch. To _our_ ranch." He stared at Morgan. "Ain't that right, brother?"

"Sounds good to me, brother," Morgan replied, smiling. "Say, let's go over by the wagon. We need to unhitch the team."

Tears ran down Hattie's face as she looked at her two sons. "God is good," she whispered. Putting her arm around each of her sons, she walked back to our wagon.

"Hattie, you, Morgan, and Colton go visit while Becky and I clean the wagon. Now Go!"

Six Women West

CHAPTER THIRTY EIGHT

LAST NIGHT

The rest of the afternoon was spent cleaning and getting the wagons spruced up and currying the horses and mules. A rumor came around that it was decided to hold a potluck and a dance in celebration of the last night we would spend together as a team.

After supper and a few hours of dancing, we pulled out all the camp chairs and anything else that could be sat on. Becky, Hattie, Bessie, and Abel along with Sara, Polly, and Guy gathered around the bonfire. Morgan, Colton, Pete, and Harold joined us, all of us aware that our journey together was coming to an end.

"Me and Bessie decided we'll stay on in Oregon City. Open a blacksmith shop. Hope they don't mind black folks."

"There's a black family on the farm not far from us," said Colton. "Nobody seems to mind what color they are."

Bessie giggled and lowered her eyes. "We got a bun in the oven. They dun said ah couldn't have chillens, but ah guess they was wrong!"

> **Comment [CJH]:** I added this to make sense of what was said during BESSIE'S STORY.

"Oh Bessie, how wonderful," I said. "I'm so happy for you both. You'll be a wonderful mother."

"So will you, Miss Martha. I see'd you with little Prissy. You'll make a fine mama."

With no conscious effort on my part, my gaze landed on Morgan. He winked.

"I'll be staying in town, too," Harold said. "Colton, I'd like to come to your ranch and do some sketches. Think I could do that?"

Colton, who hadn't taken his eyes off Becky, grinned. "Sure thing. I got some broncos I wouldn't mind havin' some pictures of."

"Harold," I said, "is it my imagination, or are you courting Thelma Locklander?"

"Well, as a matter fact, I plan on calling on her once they get settled if her pa doesn't mind."

"I think that's great. She's a nice young lady. Pretty, too. I expect you'll be painting her a lot."

"I have several of her already," he agreed, grinning widely.

"Those two aren't the only ones doin' courtin'," Becky put in. "I saw Oscar Gardner and Lucinda walkin' off together toward the trees when the dance was over."

"Goodness, Pete," Hattie remarked with a smirk. "I'm starting to think you've been boss of a honeymoon train, what with all these goins on." She glanced at me, then at Becky.

"Kind of looks that way, don't it?" Pete looked at Colton. "Did your ma tell you that we aim to be married just as soon as I can get her in front of a preacher?"

"She didn't have to tell me, Pete. Just lookin' at the two of you together says it all." He held out his hand and the older man grasped it firmly.

"Well, let's see," Hattie said. "Bessie and Sara both married off, and me next. All that's left is you and Becky, Martha."

Morgan took my hand. "Anytime. All she has to do is say yes."

"And, I'm hoping to get to know this young lady better," Colton said, grabbing Becky's hand. Like me, she didn't commit herself.

The conversation was interrupted by the rattle of a supply wagon, which stopped in front of us. The driver leaned over and said, "Lookin' for the wagon boss."

"That's me," Pete said, standing. "What's the problem?"

"You got a Martha Patterson on this train?"

"Yes, I'm her," I said. "Why?"

"I got a parcel for you, Miss," he said.

"A parcel?" I echoed.

"Well, it ain't a real parcel. It's a little tyke."

"A tyke? For Heaven's sake man, what are you talking about?" Pete demanded.

"Well, I dropped off supplies at the Whitman Mission. The Holt family missus died, and the Pa was real sick. He asked me to tell you he had the black lung. You'd understand. He told me to bring her to you. Said I'd find you on the train to Oregon City. I seen the fire and took a chance on this bein' y'all."

"Prissy. Where is she?"

"She's sleepin' in the back. Watch yourself gittin' her. That yeller dog will tear your arm off. I tried to put a blanket over her, and that dog bared its teeth, so I just tossed it in from the side."

I laughed. "That's Daisy. I'll get her. She won't hurt me. Come on, Tag, let's go get your lady friend."

"I'll get Prissy," Morgan said.

"I'll make a place in the tent." I turned to the driver. "Thank you for bringing her."

"Glad to be of help. Well, I'm gonna get some shuteye. See you folks in the mornin'."

Daisy jumped out of the wagon wagging her tail, glad to see us and Tag. Morgan carried Prissy to the tent. After a bit of conversation on the little girl's plight, everyone turned in. Morgan whispered real close to me, "Prissy needs a bath real bad."

I awakened early the next morning to find Prissy kneeling next to me, staring at my face as if willing me to wake up. I knew what Morgan meant about her needing a bath!

"Are you gonna be my mama now, Miss Martha?"

"Yes, dear," I said, pulling her down beside me. "Your mama's in Heaven, but she'll still be watching over you."

"That's good," she said, hugging me. "I'm glad I got to come to you. I didn't like that lady, Miss Thatcher. She wouldn't let Daisy in the house."

"Prissy, let's me and you heat a couple buckets of water and take a bath. And get ready to go into Oregon City."

"Ok Miss Martha...Mama."

While I had Prissy in the tub, I checked her sack of clothes and found a clean dress to put on her. Then after breakfast, Prissy and I tied ribbons to the harnesses. "This is what's called a festive occasion, Prissy," I told her. "We want everyone to see that we made it to Oregon."

Moe and Mac walked up. "Just came to say goodbye and wish you all luck."

"Thank you, and the same to you. Are you staying around Oregon City?"

"We're considerin' goin' to the Willamette Valley with the Locklanders. Have to think some more on it," Moe said.

"That's where the Warrens are going, isn't it?" I asked.

"Yep, I hear Oscar Gardner is travelin' with 'them." Mac smirked. "He's trailin' after that old-maid sister of Frank's."

I smiled, thinking of what Hattie had called the wagon train while I tied strips of rag in the mule's mane. "Our folks will be filing homesteads in the valley, probably somewhere around Hattie's ranch. Will you two be homesteading?"

"Not me," said Moe, shaking his head. "I don't want to own no land."

"Me neither." Mac scratched his chest. "We're both too old, but we'd work on a ranch for awhile, wouldn't we, partner?"

"Could do that," Moe agreed. "Maybe help you ladies, if you want. Like Mac says, for awhile. We both got itchy feet. Don't like to be tied down."

Six Women West

"'Course," Mac grinned, "if a fine lookin' woman like you came along, a wider maybe, well, I might just chase her clear to Californy."

"That'll be the day! No woman in her right mind would have an old coot like you," Moe joshed. "Well, gotta be goin'. Like I said, good luck to you and yourn."

"Goodbye, and remember you always have a job and a place to stay with any of us. Right, Becky?"

"Right. We'll be expecting you by Christmas to help start building our houses. Now don't let us down."

The two men walked away, and I sat Prissy upon the mule. "Becky, did you know we were on the trail for six months? It's hard to think about having a home again." Deep in thought, the three of us finished decorating the wagon.

Backs straight and smiles on our faces, we rolled through the streets of Oregon City to the joyful sounds of Henry Davis playing his banjo. People came out of their shops and houses to greet us. Those who were staying in town camped in a field nearby.

Along with Pete and Guy, my wagon continued on to Colton's ranch, fifteen miles north of the city. Back on well-traveled roads, we picked up time. I was amazed at the green. It was winter, and still the grass was green, and the trees looked so much like my home in Manassas.

"There it is!" Colton yelled. "Home, sweet home." It looked like a picture in a book. A large, two-story log house with a long rambling porch sprawled beneath tall pine trees with so much green. It looked so refreshing after the prairie grass!

We pulled the wagons to a halt near the big house to unhitch the mules. "We'll take care of the wagons," Colton said. "Come on, brother. Give me a hand. Ma, you take the ladies to the house."

Becky, Prissy, and I stood gazing in admiration at acres and acres of green grass and in the back a corral of horses and a pasture with cattle. "Pretty nice, ain't it?" Hattie said with obvious pride. "Let's go to the house."

"It's beautiful, Hattie," I agreed. Turning to Becky, I asked, "Think our places will ever look so good?"

"Sure they will." She took off after Colton and Morgan.

"Come on. I'll show you around," Hattie said, taking my arm. "That's the bunkhouse." She pointed to a low-slung building a few yards from the main house. "The men can sleep there. We have three bedrooms, so you and Prissy, Sara and her family, and I can each have one."

After we all got settled and had a fine supper, we sat around discussing the next move. "There's plenty of land on both sides of us," Colton said. "We can check it out tomorrow."

During the next few weeks we rode the surrounding countryside and staked homesteads. Pete took the property to the left of the ranch, Morgan took the right, and Sara and Guy staked the land next to Pete. I claimed the land next to Morgan's, and Becky's was next to mine.

Pete and Hattie had their wedding six weeks after we arrived. She wore a sky-blue gown with yards of skirt. Pete looked nice but uncomfortable in his dark suit and bow tie. The reception was held at the ranch, and everyone in town was invited. Bessie made a wedding cake with blue roses on top. She colored the frosting with blueberries. There was music and dancing 'til the wee hours. Morgan and I danced every dance. "Colton asked Becky to marry him," he whispered in my ear.

"What did she tell him?" I whispered back,

"She said yes, of course. She's a smart young lady." He drew his head back and looked at me. "When are we getting married?"

I lowered my eyes. "I'm still learning to be a ma," I stammered. Years of hearing my own ma telling me I wasn't the type men marry filled my mind, causing me to doubt Morgan and causing me to doubt myself.

"I'm a patient man, Martha. I can wait," Morgan said, twirling me around the floor. The subject of marriage didn't come up again that night.

CHAPTER THIRTY NINE

SIX MONTHS LATER IN MARTHA'S BARN

The next six months, we all were kept busy clearing land and building homes. We worked together one house at a time, with Sara's and Guy's going up first and then mine. Hattie wanted Colton to keep the big house, and she and Pete would live on Pete's new place.

Although Morgan was still sleeping at the bunkhouse, he spent most of his time at my place. We had built an especially big barn for the horses. Boots was due to foal any time, and I was keeping a close watch on her. After supper, Morgan went with me to the barn to check on Boots. I wasn't worried about her since she was now of good weight and healthy. My only real concern was the fact she was a bit young to be foaling. We found her pacing in her stall, which Morgan and I built twice as large as a regular box stall and built especially for a foaling mare.

"She's sweating."

"Yeah, I see it. It won't be long before she goes down. I sure am grateful for that load of hay you brought over."

I went inside the stall and stroked her mane, talking to her quietly. Suddenly her water broke. I urged her to the floor.

"Which end do you want?" Morgan asked, joining me.

"You sit by her head. I'll help with the birth." It seemed a long while before Boots groaned and the tiny front feet of the foal showed themselves.

"It's coming!" I exclaimed.

Morgan scooted to take a look.

"The forelegs are showing." It was exciting to watch the birthing process. The nose appeared first, followed by the rest of the head. I put a slight downward pressure on the forehead and wiped the head free. "We don't want to pull unless she has a problem," I explained.

"You're wonderful, Martha. Nothing bothers you."

You do, Morgan, You bother me a lot. I love you."

"I love you too, Martha."

Much to my relief, the small wet body slid out of Boots easily. I checked her nostrils, clearing them of mucus so she could breathe freely.

"Well, I guess this makes us in-laws or grandparents or something, doesn't it?" Morgan said, grinning widely.

We sat and watched as the newborn stumbled to her feet. "She's perfect," I said thankfully, not responding to his comment.

"So are you." Morgan pulled me close to him and kissed me gently on the lips.

I pulled away and got to my feet. "I'd better bring Boots some water and mash. What are you going to name her?"

"What would you think of Rain Spots? She better have spots like her dad," Morgan said, getting up to follow me. If he was disappointed at my reaction, it didn't show in his voice.

We carried the buckets back to the stall. "Guess we'd better leave them alone. Let them get acquainted."

"We could hang around for awhile," Morgan said. "Just in case."

"I'd like to," I said, appreciating his regard for my feelings.

Morgan spread a couple of horse blankets on the hay, and we settled down in the hay next to the stall. Morgan patted his shoulder for me to lean on. He kissed my ears, neck, and cheeks. By the time he

> **Comment [CJH]:** I took out "broke the birth sac" because her water had already broken.

reached my lips, I was yearning for more. He held me tight and I could feel the pounding of his heart.

"Oh, my darling Martha," he whispered. "I don't want to play games anymore. I love you. I have loved you almost from the day I met you. I want you for my wife. There's no one else. Will you marry me?"

"Morgan, I love you too, but, well, are you sure that's what you want? My mother always told me I was too plain and too big for a man to want for his wife—that all any man would want from me is a roll in the hay. I guess because of that, I've never fully believed that your really loved me—not that kind of love."

"Martha, your mother couldn't have been more wrong. You are beautiful! I think you're the only one who can't see it. Not only that, but you're smart, you're kind, you're great with Prissy, and you're amazing with horses," he said, grinning as he stroked my hair softly. "Martha, marry me. I want to spend the rest of my life proving my love to you."

"Yes, Morgan. Yes," I said, as our lips melted into a kiss, holding nothing back.

The wedding was one month later. The first of our little cowboys was born a year after that, and Rain Spots was the first of many famous racing horses from our ranch.

The End

Author Biography

Wanda Reed was born in Yuma AZ. and subsequently grew up in California. In her early years she was a tomboy and had a great passion for books. When she was in the third grade, she read over 100 books. The first novel that she read was "Black Stallion".

She also had a love of horses, dogs, and western movies. This interest shows up early in "Six Women West". She was still in diapers when she brought her first dog home. The dog was an Irish Wolf Hound and was taller than her.

Her early curiosity with respect to the West evolved from riding her first mule and owning her own horse. Her interest in the West and western movies grew stronger through the years. The author also became very fond of mules.

After marrying her husband Larry, the couple traveled for years across the US.

They also walked the Oregon Trail and that experience is central to "Six Women West". They visited many historical sites including plantation houses and slave quarters.

In 1999 they settled in Klamath Falls, Oregon. While her husband went back to work, Wanda joined the local writer's group. That involvement is where the idea for "Six Women West" germinated. With encouragement from fellow writers, she began writing the novel that had been running through her mind for countless months.

Other novels and novelettes based on the characters in "Six Women West" are forthcoming! The first of these will be a novel about the exciting adventures of Charlie that take place in San Francisco. This novel will be released soon as an "Indie" publication on Amazon.

Six Women West

Wanda Reed

Vedas Crane, Klamath Fall OR, Couldn't put it down, stayed up real late reading."

I just loved Charlie are you going to follow her to San Francisco? Dotte Shaffer

We started the women's movement way back then, Velma Eittin

It's a good book I enjoyed reading it Nancy Stafford

Morgan can put his boots under my wagon anytime. Renee Kerwin Olympia WA.

I was drawn into the plight of these women as I read I wanted to tell Becky what a low down no good Shiloh was. And wanted to make Martha say yes to Morgan proposal

This book tell us also tells us that even in hardships love still grows and family matters

Made in the USA
Middletown, DE
11 November 2015